AUTHOR	CLASS
HOUSTON, E.	F G

TITLE
Secrets in Prior's Ford

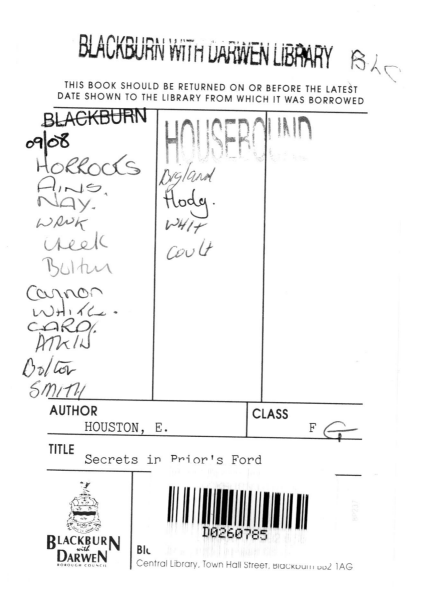

SECRETS IN PRIOR'S FORD

There's a rumble of disquiet among the villagers of pretty Scottish borders town, Prior's Ford, when a firm expresses interest in re-opening an old granite quarry. Publican Glen organises a protest group, and when Jenny Forsyth attends a protest meeting she sees a ghost from her past. Clarissa Ramsay, newly widowed, is too preoccupied to care much about the new threat facing the village ... she's just discovered her husband's secret life. While up at Linn Hall, the impoverished Ralston-Kerrs find that the quarry re-opening represents a test of loyalty to the village that regards them as its lairds.

SECRETS IN PRIOR'S FORD

For Alastair and Simon –
the best ever

SECRETS IN PRIOR'S FORD

by

Eve Houston

Magna Large Print Books
Long Preston, North Yorkshire,
BD23 4ND, England.

British Library Cataloguing in Publication Data.

Houston, Eve
    Secrets in Prior's Ford.

    A catalogue record of this book is
    available from the British Library

    ISBN   978-0-7505-2913-6

First published in Great Britain in 2008 by Sphere

Published in Large Print 2008 by arrangement with
Little, Brown Book Group Ltd.

Magna Large Print is an imprint of Library Magna Books Ltd.

Printed and bound in Great Britain by
T.J. (International) Ltd., Cornwall, PL28 8RW

Acknowledgements

This book could not have been written without the support and advice of the following people:

The Reverend Alison Burnside, Church of Scotland minister in the parishes of Glencoe: St Munda's and Duror; Janet and Duncan Beaton; Vivien Green, my agent, with thanks for her unswerving confidence in my ability to finish what I started; the curator and staff of Stewartry Museum in Kirkcudbright; Scottish National Heritage (Dumfries and Galloway); and last, but certainly not least, my husband Jim who keeps everything on an even keel and never loses faith.

Author's Note

As Naomi wisely says in this book, it is not possible to lose friends – only to lose those you mistakenly thought were friends.

So I want to take this opportunity to thank all the true friends who have stayed the course with me, and who always have been and always will be there for me, no matter what. You are pure dead brilliant, every one of you, and I will love you all, always.

Eve Houston

The Setting for the Prior's Ford Books

Dumfries and Galloway, the southernmost county in Scotland, is an area of some of the most beautiful countryside to be found in the UK. It is rich in wildlife, and its hills and valleys are scattered with farmland, attractive villages and towns of architectural beauty as well as abbeys, castles and great houses and gardens bearing witness to its long history.

It is a land of lochs, streams and rivers, and its southernmost border is the wild and magnificent Solway Firth. Dumfries and Galloway, in short, has everything.

What better place to set a book?

For more information,
visit *www.visitdumfriesandgalloway.co.uk.*

Main Characters

Glen and Libby Mason – landlord and landlady of the Neurotic Cuckoo

Ingrid MacKenzie – owns the Gift Horse gift shop and tearoom, lives on Mill Walk estate with husband **Peter** and daughters **Freya** and **Ella**

Jenny Forsyth – lives on Mill Walk estate with husband **Andrew** and son **Calum**

Helen Campbell – lives on Slaemuir housing scheme with husband Duncan and their four children **Gregor, Gemma, Lachlan** and **Irene**

Clarissa Ramsay – newcomer to the village, widow, lives in Willow Cottage

The Rev. Naomi Hennessey – Church of Scotland minister, lives in the manse with her godson **Ethan**

Alastair Marshall – artist and general jack of all trades, lives in a farm cottage on the edge of Prior's Ford

Marcy Copleton and Sam Brennan – run the

village store and post office together, live in Rowan Cottage

Hector and Fliss Ralston-Kerr – the local laird and his wife, live in dilapidated Linn Hall with their son **Lewis**

1

Saul Beckett steered the well-used and seldom-washed Land Rover along the road from Kirkcudbright, not even noticing the green lushness of the fields only to be found in Dumfries and Galloway on cold February days. Nor was he interested in the ewes, fat and woolly and resembling a small child's drawing, placidly grazing as they awaited the arrival of their lambs.

Saul was a man with a mission, a townie who had never found the countryside beguiling.

He passed the end of the lane that led up to Tarbethill Farm and only slowed down once he came to the village of Prior's Ford, cruising slowly along Main Street, past the village hall on his right and the primary school on his left, its playground busy with children enjoying their afternoon break.

He was looking out for the village inn, the Neurotic Cuckoo, but just as he reached the half-moon-shaped village green by the side of the village hall his attention was taken by three young women, each carrying a big cardboard box, waiting to cross the road. Saul braked and waved them across with a gallant flourish of one arm.

The three women smiled at him as they hurried in front of his bonnet, unaware that the polite stranger was on a mission that would soon throw their quiet little village into chaos and set neighbour against neighbour. Saul nodded in return, eyeing them idly. Two were all right, he decided: one small, with long brown hair that she kept trying to flick back with tosses of the head, while the other was taller, with fair, well-cut hair forming a neat frame for her pretty face. But the third woman was the one who captured his interest – tall, slim and an incredibly beautiful blonde.

'*You're* more than welcome, darlin',' he murmured as she smiled at him, 'any time at all!' And he let the engine idle for a moment so he could watch the gorgeous blonde and her friends walk across the village green.

It was as he followed their progress that Saul noticed the local pub, his destination, at the centre of the crescent.

He had passed the turning to the crescent without realising it, but fortunately it opened on to Main Street at the other end as well. Saul put the Land Rover into gear and moved off. As he made the turn and headed towards the pub, he saw the blonde and her friends enter a neat little shop with a sign above the door proclaiming it to be the Gift Horse. Pity that, he thought. It would have been nice if they had been making for the pub, same as he was.

'What a gentlemanly man,' Ingrid MacKenzie said to her two friends as they made their way towards the Gift Horse. 'Nice of him to stop for us.'

'For you, I think.' Helen Campbell winked at Jenny Forsyth, who grinned back at her.

'Why for me? There were three of us.'

'It's that hair – and your height. And the way

18

you carry yourself.' Helen tossed her long brown hair back from her face as best she could, with her arms full. 'He could tell you used to be a glamorous model.' Nobody could ever think that of her, she knew. Mother of four, once slim but now a little on the plump side; she could best be described as 'homely'.

'No, no, I haven't modelled for years. He saw only that I was a housewife and mother, like you and Jenny. Here...' Ingrid dumped her box on top of Jenny's. 'Hold that for a moment while I get my key.'

'I can't see!'

'There is nothing to look at,' Ingrid replied calmly as she took the key from her pocket and unlocked the door. Then, retrieving the box, 'There, now you can see again. Come in and I will make you some coffee.'

Jenny and Helen followed her in obediently. There was something about Ingrid – possibly her air of serenity – that marked her as a leader. The two of them had already been good friends when Ingrid, who had left her career and Scandinavia for love of a Scotsman, settled in Prior's Ford with her husband Peter and their daughters, Freya and Ella. Jenny and Helen had set out to make the newcomer feel at home, and when Ingrid opened her gift shop and tearoom some three years earlier, Jenny, who shared her interest in crafts, had gone into business with her. Helen helped by keeping records of the items sold in the shop, which was open during the spring and summer tourist season.

'I thought it would have been colder in here,

given how cold it is outside.' Jenny unwound the crimson scarf from around her neck and unfastened her coat, then fluffed up her fair, well-cut hair with the tips of her fingers.

'I switched the heating on this morning. We can't work in the cold.' Ingrid emptied her box of coloured cards, reels of ribbon and plastic envelopes filled with tiny pieces of coloured foam in all sort of shapes, on to one of the three small tables provided for visitors in search of light refreshments, while Jenny, hanging her coat on the back of a chair, lifted two rosy-cheeked rag dolls dressed in brightly patterned frocks from the box she had brought.

'What d'you think?' She held them aloft. 'I finished them last night.'

'Very nice; they'll be sure to sell well,' Ingrid said approvingly, while Helen, discarding the craft and exercise books she had produced from her box, reached for one of the dolls.

'They're gorgeous, Jenny.' She held the doll up, smiling into its cheerful little face. 'She makes you feel happy just looking at her.'

'What a nice thing to say!'

'It's true. She'll bring happiness to whoever buys her.' Just as Jenny herself did, Helen thought. She was a caring person who never had a bad word to say about anyone. Helen had been born and raised in Prior's Ford, as had her husband, Duncan, while Jenny and Andrew Forsyth had settled in the village a few months before the birth of their only child, Calum. Jenny never spoke about her past and Helen had never pried, though there were times when she glimpsed an inner sadness in her friend's hazel eyes and a droop to her generous, normally smiling mouth, and suspected that life had not always been as kind to Jenny as it was now.

'I wish I could make things like that,' she said as she laid the doll down gently.

'No you don't, because we need your efficient mind,' Ingrid told her. 'You're so good at making lists of all the things we have, and the things we still need.'

'Just you wait until I publish my bestseller – I'll be too busy writing the next one to do your lists for you,' Helen teased. She was taking a correspondence course on creative writing, and it was her burning ambition to become a novelist. 'Not that you need to worry about that, because it'll never happen,' she added.

'Yes it will, though you have to stop telling us and yourself that it won't,' Jenny remarked.

'What's the point in kidding myself?' The demands of a husband, a house and four children, together with the typing she did for people in order to make a little money, left her with very little time to spare for her own writing. She heaved a sigh without even realising that she was doing it, and her shoulders drooped.

Her friends glanced at each other, then Ingrid said, 'Every day and in every way, I am getting better and better. You must say that to yourself every morning, Helen.'

'Before or after making sure the children have got up and got washed and dressed and eaten breakfast and collected everything they need for school?'

'One day they'll fly the nest and you'll have more

21

time. Until then, you should learn to be more positive,' Ingrid scolded her, and then, studying Helen, her head on one side, she added, 'It must be something to do with your Scottish winters – my Peter can feel low at times, just like you, but I tell him I won't be bothered with that. When you write your bestselling book, Jenny and I will pile copies in the window and nobody will be allowed out of the shop without buying one.' Now she delved into her box and produced a bottle, 'I borrowed some of Peter's best whisky, so we can each have a tot in our coffee. That should cheer you up!'

'It'll do me well enough,' Saul Beckett said when he had followed the landlord up the narrow stairs to inspect one of the two rooms available for visitors to the Neurotic Cuckoo. 'D'you want a deposit?'

'I'll trust you,' Glen Mason told him amiably, eyeing the other's holdall, his only luggage. 'Staying long?'

'A few days, probably no more than that.'

'Holiday, is it?'

'Mmm.' The ceiling sloped, which meant Saul had to stoop to look out of the window at the village green and Main Street beyond. On the opposite side of the street he could see the local church, the village store, a butcher's shop and a greengrocer's and flower shop. A road leading off the street directly across from the pub gave him a glimpse of the river and the soft, rolling hills that the district of Dumfries and Galloway was famed for.

'Not a very big place, this.'

22

'Larger than you might think,' Glen said. 'There's a good few houses fitted in between the river and the shops across there, council housing behind the school, and a private housing estate behind the church. I always say, show a developer a few feet of ground these days and he'll manage to build a house on it.' He chuckled at his own wit.

'You're not from here, are you?'

Glen leaned back against the doorjamb, his thumbs hooked into his braces. He was in his late fifties, a tall well-built man who enjoyed talking, an asset for any pub landlord. And by his way of it, he was interested in folk though his wife, Libby, called it nosiness. 'Birmingham area. Me and the missus had a corner shop all our married life, then we got fed up with the city so we decided to look for somewhere nice and quiet. We'd always fancied running a pub, so here we are. Been here for – oh, must be comin' up for eight years now. We've never regretted makin' the move, and never will. This place is the answer to all our dreams.'

'It that so?' said the man who was about to shatter Glen Mason's dream, and the new life he had so carefully created for himself. 'Prior's Ford – where did that name come from?'

'There was a priory here hundreds of years ago – you'll see the ruins if you go out of the village in that direction.' Glen jerked his head to the right. 'It stands up on a hill, and they say the monks built it there because the river's shallow at that point – a ford. The stepping stones they used are still there. It's twenty-five pounds a night, by the way, bed and breakfast. Will you be wantin' dinner as well? It's fifteen pounds extra, but

23

worth it. She's a good cook, my Libby. Nothin' fancy and no menus. She makes it, and the guests eat it. Never had a complaint yet.' He grinned at Saul. 'It's thanks to her that I'm carryin' all this weight, but I'm not complainin' either.'

'Aye, put me down for dinner as well, why not? Do I leave the car out front?'

'There's a yard at the back with enough room to take it.'

'I'll move it now, then.' Saul Beckett went towards the door and Glen, who had been set for a chat, had no option but to let him pass.

'A walkin' holiday, is it?' he asked as they clattered back down the stairs to the small hallway. The new guest's clothes were well worn and shabbily comfortable, and his boots sturdy.

'Aye, I do a lot of that.' Saul ducked out of the front door and when he returned five minutes later Glen was waiting in the small reception area.

'Dinner at seven thirty. Here's your key, and the register – all we need's your name and address and your car registration.'

'Fine.' The guest spun the register round and swiftly scrawled the required information. 'See you later,' he said, and disappeared upstairs while Glen studied the new entry in the register, barely noticing the sound of a taxi passing by.

Clarissa Ramsay, huddled in the back seat, was scarcely aware that the taxi had reached Prior's Ford. Her mind had been a confused jumble ever since the moment, ten days earlier, when she received the phone call from her stepson to tell her that her husband, visiting his family in the Lake

District, had succumbed to a massive and totally unexpected stroke. Since then – throughout the rushed journey south, the funeral arrangements, the funeral itself, the journey back to Dumfries and Galloway – she had felt in a sort of waking trance.

When the taxi drew up outside the house on the corner of Adams Crescent and Main Street and the driver said cheerfully, 'Here we are, then – Willow Cottage,' she jerked upright and stared out at the pretty two-storey house for a few seconds before recognising it as her home. Hers and – just hers, she realised bleakly.

'Oh – thank you.' She was still fumbling with the rear door when the man opened it from the outside. 'I'll see to your luggage, love,' he said, helping her to alight. While she looked for her wallet he carried her cases up the path and placed them on the mat before the front door.

She paid him, adding a generous tip. Keith hadn't believed in tipping people. 'A fair day's work for a fair day's pay,' he always said, and when Clarissa pointed out that people such as taxi drivers and hairdressers depended on tips to make up their low wages, he had informed her that tipping them just allowed their employers to profit by keeping their wages low. But now Keith was dead, and she was free to do as she wished. And the taxi driver had been exceptionally kind.

'Want me to see you in?' he asked as he pocketed the money.

'No, I can manage, but thank you for offering.'

'You're very welcome, love,' he said, and hopped back into his cab. As he drove back to his cab rank Clarissa turned slowly to face the house that Keith had chosen for his retirement.

It looked back at her impassively, neither welcoming nor rejecting her. She walked up the flagged path between the neat borders that Keith had weeded just before leaving for the Lake District and put her key in the lock. Once inside, she put her cases down at the foot of the stairs, then sat on the second to bottom step, wondering what on earth she was going to do with the rest of her life.

When the Gift Horse was open during the tourist season, visitors were served coffee made in the small kitchen behind the shop, but when she was working there during the closed season Ingrid brought her coffee-maker from the house.

Now, as she poured coffee and added a generous tot of her husband's whisky to each mug, she took time to glance out of the window.

'Isn't that Mrs Ramsay getting out of that taxi? Poor woman,' she added as Helen joined her at the window. 'Do you think we should ask her in for a coffee?'

'She might not feel like company, when she's just back from burying her husband,' Jenny said doubtfully, joining her friends, a half-made rag doll in one hand. 'It's not as if either of them mixed much with people. They seemed to prefer their own company.'

'That might have been because they were newcomers.'

'It might also have been because they didn't care for strangers. Some people are like that.'

'Whichever it is, best leave her to get settled in,' Helen advised. 'She'll be tired after the funeral and the journey from England.'

'I wonder if she'll stay in the village?' Jenny pondered.

'I imagine she'll want to go back south now she's been widowed. Such a shame, him dying so soon after retiring. Poor woman!' Ingrid said again.

2

Inside Willow Cottage, Clarissa Ramsay sat motionless on the stairs for a good ten minutes before using the newel post to pull herself to her feet. She took off her black hat and coat and hung them both neatly on the coat stand, then looked at herself in the mirror by the door. A small, neatly built, unassuming woman with brown eyes and short brown hair looked back at her.

Keith, a keen bird watcher, had once told her affectionately that if born a bird instead of a human being, she would have been a sparrow. 'A sparrow of a woman,' he had said, smiling down at her indulgently. But today, returning from his funeral, no longer a wife but a widow, she felt more like a mouse than a sparrow.

She remembered reading out a poem by Rabbie Burns, the Ayrshire farmer poet, to one of her classes. It was about a mouse fleeing before the men who were harvesting the field where it had its nest.

Clarissa hadn't lost her home, but now she knew just how that little mouse must have felt as it scampered, panic-stricken, through the stubble, its world suddenly turned upside down.

She went into the kitchen to put the kettle on. When it had boiled she put a teabag in a mug, added water, and then sat at the kitchen table, watching the liquid in the mug turning darker and wondering what she should do. Stay here, in the village that Keith had chosen to retire to, and in the house he had opted to buy? Or return to England and the life she had lived before becoming a middle-aged bride?

'Come home soon,' her closest friend, Stella Bartholomew, had said at the funeral. 'You need to be with your friends, Clarissa.'

Clarissa had loved being a school teacher, and she had loved her flat and her quiet lifestyle. Although she had friends she had also enjoyed her own company. She liked going to museums and art galleries, seeing the occasional film, reading, attending concerts. Then she had married her headmaster, who had taken over her life. Being looked after and having decisions made for her had been quite pleasant, but now she realised that, without being aware of it, she had gradually lost the ability to be independent.

She thought, with mingled shock and guilt, that she wasn't even sure what upset her most – the fact that Keith had died, or the fact that she was going to have to get used to being on her own again.

A sudden, deep yawn took her by surprise and forced her into making her first decision – to go

28

to bed. Her new life would have to wait until tomorrow.

The doorways in the Neurotic Cuckoo were not high and Glen Mason, tall as well as burly, had learned the hard way to duck every time he went through one. Fortunately, his scalp was well padded with a layer of thick grey hair.

'Saul Beckett, from Halifax,' he reported as he entered the pub's kitchen. 'Weather-beaten sort of chap, casually dressed, and strong boots on his feet.' He poured a mug of coffee and settled his hips comfortably against the edge of the sink. 'A walker. We'll not see much of him if this weather keeps up.'

'All I'm bothered about is, will he be all right for steak and kidney pie?' Libby was chopping carrots with a speed and skill that never failed to amaze her husband. Like Glen, she was in her late fifties, and where he could be described as burly, she was comfortably plump. With her snowy-white hair, long enough to be pleated and then pinned around her head, and her gentle smile and kindly blue eyes, Libby looked like everyone's idea of the perfect granny. Sadly, in their twenty-seven years of marriage, she and Glen had never been blessed with children.

'He looks like the steak and kidney pie type. None of your vegetarian nonsense with a big man like that.'

'I've got a good sturdy broth in the freezer. Fetch it out, Glen, it's on the top shelf, well labelled. And a jam sponge and custard for afters,' Libby decided contentedly. Cooking was

29

her hobby, and she was at her happiest when guests were staying at the inn. The Scottish border country was a popular holiday venue in the summer, but she couldn't recall them having had any bookings in February before. Prior's Ford and its inhabitants were usually left to their own devices during the winter months.

She said so now, and her husband nodded agreement. 'He's a difficult man to get to know. Not keen to talk about himself. It's as if he's got a secret past.'

'Look who's talking,' Libby said. 'We don't want folk to know our business, do we? So why should you want to know his? Everyone's entitled to their secrets.'

'But they can still talk, can't they? Pass the time of day, an' that.'

'You let folk alone, Glen Mason – and if you're lucky, they'll let you alone.'

'You worry too much,' Glen said, and took himself off to the bar.

It was nice to have a visitor during the closed season, Libby thought as she scooped up a handful of diced carrots, glowing like little rubies, and tossed them into the pie dish. Nice to have someone else to cook for.

As long as Glen watched his tongue and didn't let it run away with itself, and say too much.

The Neurotic Cuckoo's one and only guest ate every crumb of his dinner and then moved from the small dining room to the bar, where he ordered a pint of beer and a whisky chaser, and settled at a small corner table with a book. When the regulars began to arrive in twos and threes he glanced up and nodded to each of them, then returned to his reading, clearly uninterested in conversation.

To Glen's disappointment, the man disappeared upstairs early, giving his host no time for conversation once the regulars had begun to head for home.

In the morning, he devoured a large breakfast, assured both Glen and Libby he had had an excellent night's sleep, and asked for a packed lunch. As soon as it was ready he set off in his Land Rover.

It took all Clarissa's courage to step out of the front door the morning after she returned from her husband's funeral.

To the best of her knowledge nobody had seen her arriving on the previous afternoon and she would have been happy to stay indoors for a day or two, giving herself some time before facing others; but unfortunately, the larder was almost bare; and needs must. There was nothing for it but to do some shopping.

As she was about to enter the village store cum post office run by her neighbours, Marcy Copleton and Sam Brennan, a young woman who was just coming out said, 'Oh, Mrs Ramsay, how are you?'

'I'm quite well, thank you...' Clarissa floundered, trying to recall the woman's name. She recognised the pretty face framed in a neat cap of fair hair, and knew she had frequently passed the time of day in the street or the shops with this girl.

31

'Jenny Forsyth – I live down by the river. I was over in the Gift Horse yesterday with my friends, Ingrid and Helen – Ingrid and I run the shop – and we saw the taxi bringing you home.'

'Oh, of course, Mrs Forsyth.' Now Clarissa placed her. She had one son, a nice wee boy who attended the local primary school.

'We thought of coming over to see how you were, but then we decided that perhaps you'd prefer to be on your own after your journey. I was – we were all so sorry to hear of your loss,' Jenny said with warm sincerity.

'Thank you, my dear.'

'Is there anything I can do to help you? Any errands at all, or if you would like company you are very welcome to drop in any time.'

'That's very kind. I'm just – trying to come to terms with what's happened at the moment.'

'Of course.' Jenny reached out and put a hand on Clarissa's arm, then said, 'I'll not keep you, but please do get in touch if you need anything at all. Our number's in the phone book.'

Clarissa thanked her again and went on into the village store, which was mercifully quiet. She worked her way round the shelves, wishing she had thought to make out a shopping list, then made her way to the counter. Normally Marcy Copleton, a down-to-earth woman in her early forties, efficient but friendly without being too in-trusive, could be found there; but today, to Clarissa's dismay, Marcy's partner Sam was at the till instead of in his usual place behind the post office grille.

Sam was clearly as embarrassed as Clarissa.

32

'You're back, Mrs Ramsay,' he said in a loud and over-cheerful voice. 'Have a good – I mean, did everything go as – as expected?'

'The funeral went well.' She concentrated her gaze on his hands, watching closely as one lifted each item from her wire basket and the other tapped busily at the till. It wasn't that she suspected him of cheating; it was just easier at the moment to look anywhere but at people's faces.

'That's good. Got your basket?'

She lifted her empty hands, then glanced down at the floor by her feet before saying helplessly, 'I must have forgotten to bring it with me today.'

'Not to worry.' Sam picked up one of the polythene bags with the shop advertised on it. 'Just as well, since it's coming on to rain. This'll keep 'em drier than in your basket.' He packed the items efficiently, remarking in an attempt to keep silence at bay, 'You're looking well.'

'I doubt that – black was never my colour.' The words were out before Clarissa could stop them. She stared at the man on the other side of the counter, her shock mirroring his, and then grabbed the bag. 'I mean – I'd better be off,' she gabbled, and shot out of the shop, almost knocking a wee boy over as they met in the doorway.

What had possessed her? she asked herself as she scurried back to the safety of Willow Cottage, where she opened the gate, closed it carefully behind her as she always did, and almost ran up the path to the green door. Once inside she paused for a moment – again, as she always did – waiting for Keith to call from his study. Then, realising that the call was never going to come

33

again, she shook her head at her own stupidity.

She carried the bag into the kitchen and un-packed it, then stood with it in her hand, at a loss as to what to do with it. Keith detested those bags; he had bought her a very nice wicker basket for her village shopping, and a large, sturdy canvas bag for Mondays, when they drove to Kirkcud-bright to do their weekly shop in a supermarket.

Finally, she folded the bag and put it carefully into the swing bin, then put the groceries away.

The doorbell had a genteel ring, a double chime as near to a discreet cough as a doorbell could get, but even so she jumped when she heard it, and peered cautiously round the door once she had opened it slightly.

'Mrs Ramsay, I've only just heard you were back in the village. I thought I would call to see how you are. Is this a bad time?' Naomi Hennessey went on as Clarissa stared at her in silence.

'Oh – Reverend Hennessey. Of course not.' Remembering her manners, Clarissa backed into the hall, opening the door properly. 'Come in, please.'

She led the way to the living room, patting her hair with a nervous hand as she went. She couldn't remember if she had combed it when she got back from the store, or the last time she had done any dusting. She cast a swift glance around the room; it was tidy, but she was sure that if the minister happened to draw a finger along a wooden surface, she would leave a clean streak.

Fortunately, Naomi Hennessey wasn't inter-ested in clean, dusted houses. She saw her mission in life as working with people rather than their surroundings. When her hostess flapped a hand at one of the armchairs in a vague invitation to sit, and said tentatively, 'Tea?' Naomi replied, 'I would love a cup, if you're making one. Why don't I come to the kitchen with you? Four hands are better than two.'

'It's – I don't think I've washed the dishes yet.'

'Oh, you should see my kitchen, Mrs Ramsay. Nothing gets washed until I have enough to fill the dishwasher, and as for Ethan – that boy never thinks of rinsing out a mug. Every time he wants a drink he uses a clean mug and then he takes it to his room, or the living room, or even the bathroom, and leaves it there. I'm for ever chasing round the house, collecting mugs. I don't think he'll ever learn,' she went on cheerfully as she followed Clarissa to the kitchen.

'The kettle...' Clarissa peered round the familiar room, as though expecting to find the kettle anywhere but in its usual place, then said with a weak laugh, 'Of course, there it is. I seem to be all at sea these days...'

'That's completely understandable. Why don't you sit down, Mrs Ramsay, and let me see to the tea?' Naomi drew out one of the chairs tucked neatly beneath the small kitchen table.

'I couldn't let you do that. You're my guest!'

'Of course you could. You look tired. Sit down,' Naomi insisted, and Clarissa, without meaning to, sank on to the chair.

'The cups are in that cupboard, and the kettle probably needs filling...'

'It does.' Naomi unplugged it and took it over to the kitchen sink. As she plugged it in again she said, 'I'm sorry if I called at a bad time. You looked so taken aback when you opened the door. Were you expecting someone else?'

'No, it was just – you're not wearing your collar – your business clothes?' Clarissa fumbled for the right word. 'I didn't recognise you for a minute.'

'Really? But that's wonderful!' Naomi Hennessey spun round, a huge white-toothed grin splitting her coffee-coloured face. 'I love it!' She leaned against the kitchen counter as laughter spilled from her, filling the room with its warm, rich sound. Delight creased her dark eyes until they disappeared from sight, and her ample body shook from head to toe.

The laughter was genuine and infectious; Clarissa felt it reach across the small kitchen to touch her, enfold her, and then enter her own body, warming a heart that had been chilled ever since the phone call telling her of Keith's death. She gave a dry, creaky chuckle, then another, and a third released the natural laughter that had started to bubble up inside her. But as the merriment in the kitchen began to slow down, her sense of propriety took over again.

'I don't know what made me say that,' she apologised. 'It just came out. It wasn't very polite.'

'It was very funny, though.' Naomi dug into the pocket of her brightly coloured flowered skirt and produced a handkerchief. Mopping her streaming eyes, she said, 'I mean, how many people with my colouring live in Prior's Ford? Now that the ice is broken, can I ask for a mug instead of a cup? People will insist on producing the best china when the minister comes to call and I much prefer mugs. I usually prefer to wear my own clothes when I visit, too – I find it helps to put people at their ease. That's why I'm not wearing my uniform. Teabags?'

'Loose tea – in that blue canister with "tea" on it.'

'Of course – all my marked canisters have the wrong thing in them. I keep thinking,' Naomi said as she took the lid off the canister, 'that I should put them right, but at the same time, there's something adventurous about opening a canister and not knowing what you'll find in it.' She lifted the open canister to her nose, and sniffed. 'Oh, Earl Grey – how wonderful.'

She continued to talk as she took two mugs from the hooks Keith had put beneath one of the cupboards, and made the tea. She was a large woman – tall and well proportioned rather than fat, but even if she had been small and thin, Clarissa was convinced she would still have filled the house with her presence.

Keith had always done that, too, but his presence had been austere – once a headmaster, always a headmaster, Clarissa's friend Stella had once remarked.

Naomi, on the other hand, filled the air around her with something that Clarissa could only describe as joy. Not the spiritual, God-loving joy one might expect from a minister, but the joy of being alive and being with whomever she happened to be with at that moment. It sparkled in her eyes, and in the smile that showed a flash of strong white teeth, and it fuelled the laughter which, like her voice, was filled with the warmth of the Jamaican sun.

'Shall we have our tea in here, or in your front room?' she asked now.

'The living room would be more comfortable. I don't take sugar, but we – I do have some. And would you like a biscuit?'

'Neither for me. I've just come from a visit, and the lady of the house happens to be an excellent baker. No wonder I'm big,' Naomi said as she put mugs, teapot and milk jug onto a tray then moved out of the kitchen, swaying gracefully along the hall before Clarissa, her skirt swinging from side to side like a bell. 'My kind parishioners seem to think that because I don't have a wife to look after me as most ministers do, I need feeding up.'

3

'So,' Naomi said once the two of them were settled in the living room, 'how are you, Mrs Ramsay?'

'I'm – coping. It's kind of you to call. It's not as if we're – I'm – a member of your congregation.'

'You're one of my parishioners, and if there's anything I can do to help you, I hope you'll tell me.'

'There's nothing, really. It's just going to take some time to get used to being on my own again.'

'How long were you married?'

'Only seven years. We met when I taught in the school where Keith was head teacher. I left when we married. He'd been divorced – he has two

38

grown children – but it was my first marriage. My only marriage,' Clarissa added. 'And now – well, I don't quite know what I'm going to do next.'

'As you say, you need time to think about it.'

'Do I stay or do I go?' Clarissa shrugged helplessly. 'I don't know. Keith was the one who wanted to retire to Scotland.'

'Do you have family back in England?'

'Nobody close, just some cousins I never saw much.'

'And your stepchildren.'

'Oh, they're grown, with their own lives. We've never been close – they still have their own mother.'

'I'm sure you had friends, though.'

'Some good friends.' Clarissa suddenly realised that she would give anything to have Stella close at hand at a time like this.

'Well, Prior's Ford's a friendly place, should you decide to stay. I'm certainly glad I found my way here.' Naomi finished her tea. 'Would you mind if I had another cup?'

'Of course not.' Before Clarissa could struggle out of her chair, Naomi had lifted the pot and come across the room to top up her hostess's mug before refilling her own.

'I love tea,' she said contentedly as she sat down again, her warm voice giving the word such meaning that it sounded as though she really was in love with the drink. 'I drink gallons of it every day, but even so, I do love it!' Watching the way she cradled the mug in her two brown hands, Clarissa decided that this woman possessed the rare gift of appreciating even the smallest things in her life.

'My mother would be horrified if she saw me sitting here,' she admitted, 'letting a guest serve me in my own house.'

Naomi's laugh filled the room once again. 'And my mother would have told yours that life is too short and too full of things to do, to trouble with etiquette. We were born to serve each other, she always said.'

'Were you born in...?' Clarissa hesitated.

'Leicester. My father was an English sailor and my mother a Jamaican woman. He fell in love with her at first sight, and managed to persuade her to leave her country and go with him to his. She didn't take much persuasion – it was love at first sight for her, too. I pick up accents easily,' Naomi explained. 'From my mother I got the Jamaican way of speaking and her looks and colour, and from my father, the English way of speaking. Then I got a place at Dundee University to read modern literature, so I picked up some Scottish words.' She smiled over the rim of her mug. 'So you see, Mrs Ramsay, I am all of those cultures in one body large enough to house them. And in answer to your next question, I gave up modern literature and my plan to teach, when I met a young Church of Scotland minister. He changed my life.'

'You married him?'

Naomi shook her head. 'Oh no, he already had a very nice wife. I've never been married.'

'But you have a son–' Clarissa began, and then, horrified by her own tactlessness, she clapped a hand to her lips and said through her fingers, 'I'm so sorry, it's none of my business!'

'I don't blame you for being confused,' Naomi

said blithely. 'Ethan's my godson. He's my cousin's boy and he's pure Jamaican. She has a big family, more than she and her husband can feed and clothe, so I brought Ethan to Britain a few years ago. He's a clever boy when he puts his mind to it, and we all want him to have a chance to do something with his life. The man I mentioned before – the minister I met in Dundee – presented me with a very special gift: he helped me find my true path through life. Now, I hope, I'm helping others, including Ethan, to find the paths that are right for them.'

'He must have found it difficult when he first came to Britain.'

'Yes, he did, and at times he still does. But problems are two-sided, Mrs Ramsay. They can crush us if we let them, or they can be turned around and used to strengthen our belief in ourselves and the world we live in.' Naomi finished her tea, and set the mug down. 'If you ever want to talk to me, you know where the manse is. And if you ever decide to attend one of our services you'll be very welcome. But that must be your decision.'

At the door she turned to take Clarissa's hand in both of hers. 'Take your time,' she said, 'don't make any hurried decisions. You need to be kind to yourself. May God bless you, Mrs Ramsay – and I know that He does, for He's very understanding.'

Then, her white-toothed grin flashing out again, she added, 'Which I find comforting, given that He's a he and not a she.'

Saul Beckett didn't return to the Neurotic Cuckoo until seven that evening. Again, he demolished the large dinner Libby had prepared for him.

'Walkin's given you an appetite, eh?' Glen said as he cleared the main course away.

'Aye.'

'Prior's Ford's in a bonny part of the world.'

'Aye.'

'Been in this area before?'

'Not for a good while.'

'I'll fetch your pudding.' Glen went into the kitchen, where he said, 'It's like tryin' to get blood from a stone.'

'Give over, Glen, not everyone's got your gift of the gab. The man's on holiday – maybe he spends his days in an office with folk talking at him all the time, and he just wants some peace and quiet now. For all you know,' Libby observed, 'he might work in one of those terrible call centres, with a phone at his ear all day, five or six days a week.'

'He doesn't look like an indoors man – he's weather-beaten. More like a gardener or maybe even a ghillie.'

'Then he might not be used to talking,' Libby pointed out. 'He might prefer his own company to anyone else's.'

Saul Beckett went through the same routine on the following day, and again on the day after that. 'I'll be off tomorrow morning,' he said that evening when Glen brought his soup – a large bowl of cock-a-leekie with a crisp warm roll on the side – to the dining room, 'right after breakfast. Can you have my bill ready?'

'I can.' Glen set the plate down carefully. 'I hope you've enjoyed your stay?'

'Very satisfactory,' said Sam, picking up his spoon.

He came into the bar later, book in hand, but this time he only stayed for half an hour before going upstairs.

'I thought he'd be with us for a wee while longer,' Glen said as he and Libby got ready for bed. 'D'you think he's leaving because he's not enjoyed himself?'

'He certainly seemed to enjoy the food. And if he'd a complaint I expect he would have told us quick enough. Maybe he's travelling around.'

'Maybe.' The bed creaked as Glen got into it. 'But if you ask me, there's somethin' secretive about that one. It's not natural for a man to be so quiet.'

'You and your imagination,' his wife said fondly as she picked up her hairbrush and settled herself before the dressing-table mirror. 'They're not all talkers like you, you know. And you shouldn't pry into other folks' lives too deeply, for they might start prying into ours, and we don't want that, do we?'

Jenny Forsyth's son Calum had bitten too hard on a mint humbug and broken a tooth. After an uncomfortable night, he tried hard in the morning to pretend that the toothache was almost gone. But mothers aren't easily fooled, and so Jenny telephoned Ingrid in the morning to tell her she would not be available to help in the gift shop and then bore her son off, protesting loudly, to the dental surgery in Kirkcudbright, Prior's Ford's nearest town.

'I'll not expect you to go to school this afternoon,' she assured him as she used her body to wedge him into an inside seat on the bus, just in case he had any thought of escaping.

'But I *want* to go to school! I want to go to school right *now!*'

'Calum, neither of us could put up with another night like last night. You're going to the dentist.'

'I think it's definitely getting better,' Calum said later as they neared the door with the polished brass plaque screwed to the wall beside it. 'Yes, it's absolutely definitely getting better. It's not hurting a bit now. And I'm too old to be holding hands.'

Jenny clung on. 'It's called sod's law, dear. Toothache always starts to go away when you get within range of a dentist. But just think it'll be gone for good in just a wee while. It's only a first tooth – it'll come out easily. And I meant it about having the afternoon off school.'

Calum doubted as they went up the steps that the reward was worth the misery before him, but as he skipped back down those same steps less than an hour later, the aching tooth gone and his mouth interestingly numb, the afternoon off school began to look good; especially when, back home, he discovered that a numb mouth made it impossible to take soup tidily. Drooling was fun, and so was drinking fruit juice through a straw.

When the numbness had worn off and the ache in his gum been subdued by junior aspirin he claimed the right to go out to play, and skipped off happily, along Main Street, across the humpback bridge only wide enough for a single vehicle at a time, and out past the ruins of the fourteenth-century priory that gave the village its name.

The priory had been an imposing building before being abandoned by its monks to the ravages of storm and time. As the walls slowly collapsed over the ensuing centuries people from the growing village seized on its fallen stones, which could still be seen in rockeries, or playing their part in garden walls. One of its graceful, carved pillars stood in the rose garden of Linn Hall, the largest dwelling in the village.

Now, in 2003, all that remained of the priory was a tower standing solidly enough on its grassy mound, the lower walls still managing to defy time's passage. But as the eye moved up to where the roof had once been, the stone, worn down by wind and rain, took on a fragile, almost lacy appearance, broken here and there by gaping windows, elegantly long and slender. Even in decay, the priory seemed to be reaching up in homage to the heavens above, an impression given substance by the way the ground dropped away before it, sloping in a series of terraces once tilled and planted by the monks to the road that in the priory's day had been a cart track running along the bank of the River Dee. At this stretch the Dee was shallow, and the large stepping stones set down by the monks so that they and their visitors might cross the river dry-shod were still in place.

To Calum the priory was nothing more than an old building, scarcely worth a glance as he hurried towards his goal – the abandoned granite quarry. Over the years since the last quarryman had gone, winds had carried soil and seeds into crannies in the great man-made gash on the hillside.

Encouraged by the rain and sun, grasses and bushes had struggled into being; the bushes were used as handholds by older children testing their rock-climbing skills, though few ever managed to get more than a few feet up the man-made cliffs.

Most of the village children were content to make use of the large flat quarry floor; it was an ideal place for games, and the old bothy, once used as a store by the quarrymen, had become a gang hut.

Calum had almost reached the quarry when he spotted the Land Rover parked at the foot of the cliff. He froze, and then slid with the skill and silence of an Australian bush tracker (a skill he had been practising for some time) behind a nearby clump of bushes. Parting the thick leafless twigs he peered out cautiously and saw a man taking photographs of the area.

Calum watched for some time, puzzled as to who would want to do such a thing, and then glanced up into the sky as he heard a long, screeching call. One of the big birds he had seen around the quarry before circled high above, its great wings wide as it rode the air currents, its short fan-shaped tail spread. The man glanced up too, then returned to his work.

After a while, as the photographer showed no intention of leaving, Calum moved quietly away and, once out of sight, went to throw stones in the river.

'I saw a man taking photographs of the quarry today,' he remarked when he and his parents were having their dinner that evening.

'What sort of man? Did he speak to you? What

46

did he say?' The mother-on-child-protection-duty part of Jenny's brain kicked into action immediately.

'He didn't even see me. I hid behind the bushes.'

'What sort of pictures?'

'Just pictures, with a camera on a stand. And he had a Land Rover.'

Jenny and Andrew were eating gammon steak, but Calum, because his mouth was still tender, had been given macaroni cheese, his favourite food. He took another forkful, swallowed, then said, 'I think he might be a spy because he was writing things down as well.'

'Probably an amateur photographer,' Andrew said casually.

'But why the old quarry? There's nothing of interest there.'

'That's what I thought,' Calum agreed with his mother.

'Photographers can get good shots out of anything – it's all to do with the angle of vision,' Andrew said. 'Nice gammon, Jenny.' Then he changed the subject, much to his son's annoyance.

'I think he was a spy,' Calum reported to his pals in the school playground in the morning.

'Did he go into our hut?' someone asked.

'I didn't see him near it, but he might have done.'

'We've got some good comics in there,' one of the boys said. 'He might have stolen them. We'd better go there after school to make sure everything's safe.'

The school bell rang and they hurried to line

47

up at the door. An hour later, while they were all hard at work in their classroom, the Land Rover rattled past on its way out of Prior's Ford, leaving the villagers oblivious to the problems its driver had brought into their midst.

4

A few hours after the Land Rover left the village, Clarissa's stepdaughter phoned to arrange for her and her brother to help pack their father's possessions.

'Unfortunately, we're both busy this weekend, but the following weekend suits. We could be with you by noon on the Saturday. We'll have to leave just after lunch on the Sunday, but that gives us a good twenty-four hours. We can get a lot done in twenty-four hours.'

'You don't have to trouble yourselves, Alexandra,' Clarissa protested into the receiver. 'I can manage.'

'It's no trouble, and we both feel that it's our way of helping Pops.' Alexandra's voice was so strong and firm that it seemed to leach what little energy Clarissa had from her very bones. 'I've made sure that my weekend's clear, and Steven's assistant manager is very capable, so he can be left to run the office on his own for half a day. Don't worry too much about lunch – sandwiches will do. And some soup would be nice after the journey – you always make good soup, Clarissa, much better than Mother's. The sooner Pops' belongings are dealt with the better, and the three of us should be able to clear most of them by noon on Sunday. We'll come up together, in my car. See you Saturday lunchtime.'

The handset in Kendal was replaced with a decisive click, leaving Clarissa listening to the contented-cat purr of a disconnected line. Suddenly the receiver she held felt very heavy; her thin wrist bent beneath its weight, and then her exhausted fingers drooped open, letting the receiver fall to the hall table with a loud, solid 'clunk'.

She glanced around guiltily, half expecting to hear Keith call, 'What have you done *now*, Clarissa?' before snatching it up and checking to make sure she hadn't broken it. When it purred forgivingly at her she breathed a sigh of relief and laid it carefully on its cradle.

Steven and Alexandra were very like their father – clever, confident and ambitious. Alexandra had followed Keith into education, and was head of business studies in a girls' school, while Steven was manager of an estate agents'.

The very thought of having the two of them in the house for twenty-four hours, stifling her with their efficiency, terrified Clarissa. She hadn't as yet summoned up the energy to start sorting through Keith's belongings, but suddenly more pressing matters were crowding in on her – getting the house ready for visitors, making up beds in the two spare rooms, buying in food – proper food, and not just the tins she had been living on since being widowed.

She rose from the telephone seat in a panic and

fluttered into the living room, her head already buzzing with things to be done before the invasion.

A silver tray stood on the sideboard with a decanter of whisky and a bottle of sherry on it, together with suitable glasses. Keith had always enjoyed a dram before bedtime, and they both took a small sherry before dinner and, once a week, wine with the meal.

Clarissa had not touched the tray since being widowed, but now, on a sudden impulse, she poured out a small glassful of whisky and drank it quickly. Once the choking had ceased, it made her feel a bit stronger. She eyed the decanter again, and then, deciding that using alcohol as a prop would not be the right thing to do, she took the empty glass to the kitchen, where she washed, dried and polished it before returning it to the tray.

Feeling a little more fortified, she went upstairs to her double bedroom, opened Keith's wardrobe, looked at the suits and shirts hanging neatly inside – and then decided that even with the whisky's help she couldn't possibly bring herself to start packing everything away.

So she lay down on the bed, soothed by the whisky, and fell asleep as soon as her head touched the pillow.

Jenny was in the kitchen, chopping vegetables and listening to Calum struggle his way through the multiplication table when her husband arrived home from work.

'Calum – that day last week when you had to go

to the dentist...' he said as soon as he had dropped a kiss on his wife's cheek and ruffled his son's hair.

'For goodness' sake, Andrew, can't you see we're busy? This is the only way he can learn his tables!'

'He can get back to them in a minute, but this is important. Calum, the day you had your tooth out and then went to play at the old quarry, didn't you say something to us afterwards about seeing a man there?'

'Uh-huh.'

'Tell me what he was doing.'

'I already told you all about him, but you weren't interested *then*.'

'Don't be cheeky,' Jenny said automatically, while Andrew told his son, 'Well, I'm interested now so spit it out.'

'He was just taking pictures.'

'What sort of camera did he have?'

'How would I know that?' Calum protested, and then when his father fixed him with a steady stare, said, 'It was one of those cameras with long legs, and he kept moving it about to take more pictures.'

'Did he write things down?'

'Yes, I told you that as well. Why?'

'That wasn't a camera, Jenny, it was a theodolite. The man Calum saw at the old quarry was taking measurements. Didn't you say he had a Land Rover, Calum?'

Calum nodded, adding, 'It needed a good wash. When I told the boys at school we thought the man might be after our comic collection, but it was all right, he hadn't gone into the hut.'

Andrew waved the final sentence aside. 'Now then, Jenny, why would this man be so interested in an old abandoned quarry?'

Jenny used the edge of her knife to organise a fistful of chopped parsnip into a neat pile before starting on an onion. 'You said he was an amateur photographer looking for unusual shots.'

'That was before I realised he was working with a theodolite, not a camera. But why was he in a quarry that hasn't been worked for God knows how long?' Andrew said emphatically. And then, as Calum merely gazed at him in mild confusion and Jenny concentrated on her chopping board, 'A quarry,' he said, raising his voice slightly, 'that could soon start working again.'

'What?' Jenny stopped work and gave him her full attention. Calum took advantage of the opportunity to scoop up a handful of chopped carrots and then wandered out of the kitchen, chewing.

'That old quarry starting up again? Surely not!'

'They were talking about it in the office this afternoon.' Andrew, an architect, worked for a firm in Kirkcudbright. 'From what I heard today, a man from an English company was surveying the quarry a couple of weeks ago. I'm willing to bet he was the man who stayed at the Neurotic Cuckoo – the quiet one who sat in a corner and didn't speak to anyone. He probably didn't want any of us to ask what he was doing here.'

'I heard that Glen Mason reckoned he was a walker.'

'A walking holiday in February?'

'It's possible.'

'But unlikely. Just think, Jenny – the noise and

the dust, and lorries coming and going...'

'I don't like the idea at all,' she admitted.

'Nor do I. I think I'll go along to the Neurotic Cuckoo for a pint after dinner – to find out if anyone else has heard about this.'

'I don't fancy the idea of lorries thundering through Prior's Ford.' Jenny returned to the vegetables, her knife demolishing what remained of the onion with renewed vigour. 'Right, Calum,' she said, and then, as there was no reply, she glanced round to find her son had disappeared. 'Calum? Get back in here, we've not finished the multiplication tables yet.'

'I think,' Calum said hopefully from the doorway, 'we'd reached the nines.'

'We were halfway through the sixes. Start at six ones again.'

'Oh, *Mum,* I *hate* the sevens! I can never remember them.'

'Repetition's the best way. Come on,' Jenny said mercilessly.

As Andrew went upstairs to change into jeans and a T-shirt, Calum's monotonous chant, 'Six ones are six, six twos are twelve, six threes are eighteen, six fours are...' followed him, growing fainter as he climbed.

'Evenin', Andy – the usual?' Glen Mason said cheerfully.

'I do believe I'll make it a double whisky tonight.'

'Bad day at the office? Or is every day a bad day for an architect? I expect you get bored with nothing to do but draw pictures.' Glen was fond of trotting out the same old jokes over and over again, and this was one of them. 'I'd as soon pull pints than have your job.' He set Andrew's glass before him.

'That's good, because you're going to have plenty of exercise once the workmen start coming in.'

'What workmen?' Libby asked sharply.

'Haven't you heard? Someone's planning to get the old quarry going again.' It was still early and there weren't many in the pub as yet. Andrew deliberately raised his voice on the second sentence, and immediately the background conversation ceased.

'The granite quarry? Never!' Glen scoffed. 'That place is as dead as a dodo.'

'That's not what I heard in the office today. I even know the name of the company – Redmond Brown and Son, based in Manchester. They work several quarries throughout the UK. Apparently there's still granite here, and they want it.'

'But that quarry's been idle for years and years. Isn't that right, Bert?' Glen asked the oldest man in the bar.

'Twenty year at least, maybe longer.' Bert Mc-Nair was in his mid-seventies, and struggling, along with his wife Jess and their two sons, to keep Tarbethill, the family farm, going. The ravages of BSE and, only a few years before, foot and mouth disease, had made their task almost impossible.

'Hang on a minute,' someone else said, 'I think I heard a rumour like that a while back, but I didn't take it seriously Who'd want to go to the bother of startin' up that old place? It's all overgrown.'

54

'That can soon be put right,' Andrew pointed out, and was surprised when Glen snapped, 'Over my dead body!'

'If that's what it takes,' another customer called out, 'so be it. Once a big company decides on somethin' there's not much that ordinary folk like you and me can do about it. And at least it would bring work to the area. You can't say that's a bad thing.'

'I would,' Lachie Wilkins said from one end of the bar. 'That quarry was being worked all the time I was growing up and it was a right noisy business. My parents had our house before me, and my ma was nearly driven mad by the dust. She said she could never keep the place clean, God rest her. My young brother – our Tom who lives in Australia now – nearly got run down by one of their lorries on Main Street when he was little. He could have been killed or maimed for life. We're going to have to watch out for the kids if lorries start to rumble along Main Street again.'

'What about the tourists?' someone else asked. 'The folk that come to look at the old priory and take pictures of the scenery hereabouts. They're not going to want to be around a workin' quarry, are they?'

'We don't get all that much in the way of tourists here, so what difference would that make?' asked the man who had mentioned the quarry bringing work to the area. 'We need jobs, not tourism.'

'I thought you'd be pleased, Glen,' Andrew commented. 'Quarrying's thirsty work. Think of all the extra customers you'll get.'

'He's right,' another drinker spoke up. 'With all

55

that dust flyin' around they'll be lookin' for pints to wet their throats.'

'That's all very well, but it'll mean an end to the peace and quiet of this place, and that's what Libby and me were looking for when we moved here – peace and quiet. Isn't that right, Libby?'

'It is, though I get little enough of it with you about the place.'

Glen shot his wife an exasperated look and then said, 'But it's probably just a rumour. I mean, nobody's been seen nosing around the old quarry, have they?'

Andrew took a sip from his glass and then prepared to break the news. 'Now that's where you're wrong. As it happens, our Calum was off school the other week, getting a tooth out, and he went to play at the quarry afterwards. He came home with some story about seeing a man there, taking pictures with a camera on a tripod. I didn't pay any attention at the time, but when I heard about this company today it struck me that the man was probably a surveyor using a theodolite. Calum said he had a dusty four-by-four.' He took another drink, then said casually, 'Didn't that fellow who stayed here the other week drive a dirty old four-by-four?'

'My God – Saul Beckett!' Glen's eyes bulged and colour swept into his face. 'He was out all day for the three days he stayed here.'

'There you are, then,' Bert said, winking at his drinking companions. 'You've been givin' hospitality to the wrong man, Glen. Fraternisin' with the enemy, that used to be called.'

'But he said he liked walkin'!'

'He'd not have been likely to tell us the truth, would he?' Libby asked. 'Imagine the reception he'd have got if he'd said he was surveying the quarry for folk who want to open it up again.'

Glen crashed his large fist down on the counter, making Andrew's glass rattle against the polished wood. 'If he ever shows his face in here again he'll be told to sleep in his damned car, for he'll not be welcome in one of our rooms!'

'If he comes back he'll be treated like the paying guest he is, and none of your nonsense. There's nothing we can do about the quarry, so no sense in getting yourself all upset.' Libby patted her husband's hand, and he pulled it away and glared at her.

'Nothin' we can do? Of course there is! We can put a stop to it before it starts – can't we?' he appealed to the people lining the bar.

'And how do we do that?' Bert McNair asked.

'Well, we'll – what d'you think, Andy?'

'The first thing would be to find out if the local newspaper knows anything about it. They'll look into the story for you, though I expect they already have the details.'

'Aye, that's it. I'll phone them tomorrow.'

'We should set up a committee,' suggested Robert Kavanagh, an elderly man who had retired to the village from Carlisle some four years earlier. 'Me and the missus came here because we were after a nice quiet life. We live in Main Street, and I don't fancy having quarry vehicles roaring past my windows day and night. I'll go on a committee if you want to set it up, Glen.'

'He doesn't,' Libby said swiftly, but the light of

57

battle was in Glen's eyes.

'No point in moanin' about things if you're not prepared to do somethin' about them,' he argued. 'I'll go on the committee too. Anyone else?'

'Not me,' Sam Brennan said. 'The village store can always do with more customers, and I think you'll find the other shopkeepers in the village'll agree with me.'

'I'd go on the committee,' Lachie Wilkins said. 'I'm village born and bred and my youngest's got a bad chest. Dust from the quarry wouldn't help her at all.'

'It looks as if you're beginning to put your committee together already, Glen,' Andrew said.

'So what's next?' Glen asked eagerly, avoiding Libby's hard gaze.

'Posters,' a voice said, while another suggested, 'A petition?'

'A petition – that's a good idea. If they want a fight,' Glen said, 'they can have one!'

There was a general murmur of agreement from most of the people at the bar, and Sam Brennan took his pint glass to a quiet corner table – the very table that the surveyor in walker's clothing had used during his brief stay

Sam's brain was already adding up the pounds and pence the reopened quarry could bring to his business.

5

On Saturday a brisk toot from a car horn summoned Clarissa to the front window just as the small carriage clock on the mantelpiece sent out the first of twelve melodious chimes.

By the time she reached the door, Alexandra and her brother Steven were emerging from a grey Rover. They surged in, Alexandra first, dropping a swift, cool kiss on her stepmother's cheek as she passed.

'How are you, Clarissa? We had a very good journey, didn't we, Steven? We brought a good supply of bin bags and some cardboard boxes,' she went on as the other two followed her into the sitting room.

'I've got bin bags, and Mr Brennan at the village shop gave me some strong cardboard boxes. Hello, Steven, how are you?'

'Fine thanks, Clarissa. I did tell her – didn't I say, Alex, that Clarissa would probably have everything organised?'

'You can't have too many bin bags and boxes.' Alexandra – only her brother ever called her Alex – stripped off her driving gloves and began to unbutton her jacket. 'Remember the time Mother moved house? We couldn't believe the amount of stuff she'd amassed.'

'Lord yes, she even had our old toys. It took ages to persuade her to part with them. So – how are you, Clarissa? Bearing up?'

'Yes, I suppose I am.'

'She did very well to hold on to those old toys,' Alex told her brother sharply. 'That auction netted her a small fortune.'

'I doubt if Clarissa and Pops have much to clear, since they moved here less than a year ago.' Steven had taken both Clarissa's hands in his when he came into the room; he still held on to them, his grey eyes, like his father's but warmer and kinder, studying her closely. 'You look tired. It must have been the most dreadful shock for you, Pops going the way he did. Such a terrible waste of a life.'

'Yes, it was.' Clarissa heard her voice wobble.

'Let's all have a glass of sherry,' he suggested. 'I'm ready for it after that journey, and you could do with a bit of topping up yourself, probably.' He released her hands. 'I'll see to it, shall I? Sherry, Alex?'

'Why not.' Alex's eyes, blue like her mother's, but as sharp as her father's, were already travelling about the room, taking an inventory of the ornaments and the pictures.

'How is your mother?'

'Well enough. In a bit of shock, still. I know they've been divorced for a long time, but even so – a marriage is a marriage, isn't it?'

'How would you know?' Steven asked. 'You're a loner.'

'And why do you *think* I'm a loner?' his sister countered sharply 'From what I've seen of marriage, I don't want it for myself.'

'Pay no heed to her, Clarissa,' Steven advised her cheerfully, handing his stepmother a glass of sherry. 'She's one of life's cynics.'

Alex gave a sarcastic snort, while Clarissa, knowing full well that they had probably been sniping at each other all the way north, tried to change the subject. 'How's Chris?'

'Very well, and very busy, thanks for asking. Sends his regards.' It had hit Keith hard when his only son set up house with another man, a vet, but he had sensibly decided he would rather stay in contact with Steven than cut him out of his life. Clarissa liked Chris, and found Steven more approachable than his elder sister, though she was well aware that he, like Alexandra, considered his stepmother to be a bit of a dry old stick.

As soon as lunch was over the two of them packed her off to the kitchen to wash the dishes while they advanced upstairs. By the time she joined them, Keith's wardrobe was almost empty and the bed covered with neatly folded clothes.

'You could start packing them into boxes,' Alexandra suggested when she saw Clarissa hovering in the doorway. 'I don't suppose you want to keep any of them, do you?'

'I thought they could go to a charity shop in Kirkcudbright.'

'D'you think so? Pops always bought really good clothes – some of these shirts aren't even out of their packaging. There are shops that buy good second-hand clothing – they could pay you quite well for them.'

'Easier to donate them to charity,' Steven argued. 'Why should Clarissa trek round looking for a shop that might buy? Unless you need the money – do you, Clarissa? Because I'm sure we

61

could share out what Pops left.'

'Steven!' Alexandra protested swiftly while Clarissa, reddening, said, 'I'm comfortably off – honestly. No need to worry about me!'

'That's all right, then,' Alexandra said, relief in her voice, and the three of them got on with the business of packing Keith's clothes.

The last thing Clarissa wanted from her stepchildren was charity. She had always had a talent for saving and investing wisely, and she had a good pension. When he and Clarissa married, Keith had altered his will so that his share in the marital home would revert to Clarissa in the event of his death, while any money he left would be divided between his two children. It was an arrangement that suited her well.

The three of them enjoyed a good dinner in the Neurotic Cuckoo's dining room that evening before going into the bar for a brandy. The bar was buzzing with tension.

'What's this quarry they're all talking about?' Steven asked as he brought their drinks to the table.

'I believe someone is thinking of reopening the old granite quarry outside the village,' Clarissa said vaguely. Since Keith's death she had switched off from what was happening around her.

'That would be shame, wouldn't it? It's a nice village, this.'

'Hang on, Steven,' Alexandra said sharply, 'this might change things. Wouldn't reopening the local quarry have a bad effect on local house prices?'

'It could, of course. On the other hand, if the quarry brings workers to the area, it could help house prices.'

'But you can't be sure of that. The sooner you sell the house, Clarissa, the better.'

'Sell the house?'

'You'll be moving back to England soon, surely?'

'I – I don't know. I hadn't thought about it.'

'Why would you want to stay here on your own? Better to get back to Cumbria, where you have friends. And us, of course.'

'You should go as soon as possible to the building society Pops used when he bought the house,' Steven advised. 'First thing on Monday morning. It's a nice little property, in good condition and with a well-stocked garden. You shouldn't have too much trouble finding a buyer.'

'Don't let the grass grow under your feet. You'll feel a lot better once you get settled back in England,' Alexandra encouraged. 'There's the car, too; that'll bring in a good amount. Pops always looked after his cars. You'll have to sell that, since you can't drive.'

'I thought that you might want the car, Steven.'

He shook his head. 'I'm happy with what I've got, thanks. I don't go for expensive cars; they're more likely to be stolen than any other sort. What about you, Alex?'

'I like the car I have. Sell it, Clarissa,' Alexandra urged. 'Have it valued by a responsible garage first, or the AA. Pops was a member, so they'll do it for you.'

Clarissa nodded, thinking that the car had become yet another responsibility to be dealt with, once she managed to summon up the energy to tackle it.

By the time Alexandra and Steven left early on the following afternoon, one of the two spare rooms was stacked with neatly packed, labelled and sealed boxes of clothing and Clarissa had promised to telephone a Kirkcudbright charity shop to make arrangements to have them collected. Alex and Steven had checked their father's small study, and made sure all the papers Clarissa needed were easily accessible, in the top drawer of the writing bureau. They had each selected a number of personal items to take away with them.

Steven rolled down the passenger window as Alexandra switched on the engine. 'Phone me if you want any advice,' he said kindly. 'You've got my office number as well as the home number, haven't you?'

'Yes, they're in the phone book on the hall table.'

'It's a very nice little property. You should do quite well from the sale.'

'Steven, we've got to go! Let us know if you need any other help, Clarissa,' Alexandra added as she put the car into gear. 'We're still family, you know. Pops would want us to keep an eye on you.'

Then they drove away, leaving Clarissa alone at the gate.

'Let's go to the pub for a drink,' Sam Brennan suggested to his partner that evening.

'I'm tired – it's been a busy week. Tell you what,' Marcy Copleton said, 'you go – it'll do you good – and then I can spend a lazy evening pampering myself.'

'If you're sure...'

'I am, really. And if I change my mind I know where to find you.'

After Sam left she spent the best part of an hour in a hot, fragrant bath, then washed her hair and blow-dried it. Wrapped in a cosy terry-towelling robe she went downstairs and put an easy listening CD on the music centre before settling down to give herself a manicure and apply pale pink nail varnish to her toenails as well as her fingernails. Finally, she smoothed in some expensive face and hand cream before pouring herself a glass of wine and settling down with a novel.

She was in a pleasantly mellow mood when Sam returned home.

'Glen's still going on about this bloke who stayed at the pub while he was surveying the quarry,' he said cheerfully as he dropped into an armchair. 'To listen to him you'd think he'd played host to Satan himself.'

Marcy put the bookmark in place and closed the book.

'Is there any more news on that?'

'Apparently the rumour's true – this English company really is interested in working the quarry. And I hope they do.'

'I don't.'

He stared at her, surprised, then said, 'What are you talking about? It would bring more customers to the shop.'

'We don't need more customers; we're fine as we are. We can pay the bills and the mortgage, can't we? And pay for meals out and visits to the pub.'

'But there's more to life than work. If we get

more customers we can make improvements to the shop, perhaps afford to get more staff in so we can take some time off. We could retire earlier. I don't know why Glen's making such a fuss; he stands to gain as well, probably more than we will. Fancy a cuppa?'

Without waiting for a reply Sam went into the kitchen, where Marcy heard him whistling as he filled the kettle.

Her relaxed mood began to evaporate like snow on a warm day. *By the pricking of my thumbs – something wicked this way comes.* For some weird reason, the words she had learned for a school production of *Macbeth* came into her head. A feeling of apprehension she thought she had managed to eradicate long ago made her spine tingle. She shivered, and drew the terry-towelling robe more closely about her throat.

Although he knew something of her past, even Sam didn't realise that Marcy's relaxed, confident manner had been carefully created with the help of a good counsellor, and that it was worn like a coat of armour to protect the vulnerable woman within. Born to parents dismayed by the sudden arrival of an unwanted child at a late stage in life – her mother had been forty-two at the time, the age Marcy was now – she had had an unhappy and lonely childhood and had grown up convinced of her own lack of worth. Despite that, she had managed to work her way through teacher training college and taught for a year before rushing into marriage as a way of escaping her parents.

Too late, she discovered that her husband was an addicted gambler who lost all his earnings as well as every penny he could coax from – or on many occasions, steal from – his wife. Marcy, exhausted by teaching in a school in a deprived area of Glasgow and struggling to cope with a growing mountain of debt, had finally given up and walked out of the house and the job one day with little but the clothes on her back.

Counselling had helped put her past behind her, but, unable to settle down or return to teaching, she had travelled from place to place, taking any job she could get, ending up as a barmaid in the Neurotic Cuckoo. She had met Sam, who fell in love with her almost at once, but it had taken him a long time to persuade her to put her trust in another relationship. Finally, she moved in with him, and went to work in the village store.

For the past ten years she had been happier than she had ever dreamed possible, but deep in the recesses of her mind lurked the constant fear that one day she might lose her hard-won security. And now, she could feel that fear stirring uneasily.

When Sam returned, bearing a tray of mugs and the biscuit tin, she said, 'The village won't be the same if the quarry starts up again.'

'It's just what this place needs. It'll benefit from a local industry, and so will we. This place has been a backwater for too long.'

'But I like living in a backwater. Once the quarry starts working we'll hear it all over the village!'

'I doubt that. It's quite a distance from here.'

'My parents had a quarry quite a distance from their house, and we could hear it all the time – and see the lorries coming and going. My mother was never done dusting and sweeping the floors, and when I was a little girl the warning siren and the bang that followed when they set an explosion frightened me every time.'

'It was probably a different kind of quarry, and in any case, everything's modernised now. Concentrate on the money we'll make.'

'Money isn't everything!' She almost shouted the words at him and he looked at her in surprise. Then his face softened.

'You're thinking about that man you were married to, aren't you? The gambler. I'm not like him, Marcy, you must know that by now. It's time you put the past behind you and looked to the future. Wouldn't you like to retire early and enjoy the rest of your life in some sunny spot, with your own swimming pool? That's what I'm aiming for.'

'You mean, retire abroad?'

'Yes, it would be great,' Sam said, and went on to discuss the merits of Spain and Portugal, while Marcy sipped at her cooling tea and tried to rid herself of the feeling that the past could have a way of repeating itself.

6

Marcy wasn't the only person to be affected by the latest news on the quarry. Helen Campbell and her husband Duncan lived with their four children in Slaemuir, the small council housing scheme tucked between the primary school and the river.

Helen's dream was to go up in the world, starting with a move to the nearby, and more select, Mill Walk private housing estate, where her best friends, Jenny Forsyth and Ingrid MacKenzie, lived, but to her secret frustration, Duncan was quite content with his present home and with his job as the head gardener – in truth, the only gardener – at Linn Hall, the big house on the hill behind the village.

When she finally realised that any advancement in their lifestyle would have to come from her, Helen had decided to turn her dream of becoming a published writer into reality. She scraped up enough money to buy a secondhand computer and pay for an evening-class computer course in Kirkcudbright, and now she was earning a little money by typing papers for students and lecturers at the college where Ingrid's husband Peter worked.

While Marcy Copleton cosseted herself in Rowan Cottage and Duncan, like Sam, was in the Neurotic Cuckoo, Helen got all four children to bed and gave the small living room a speedy tidy-up consisting of cramming books into the already overfilled bookcase, tossing toys into the box kept behind the couch and banging the shape back into cushions that had been used as medieval weapons, bucking broncos, and anything else her imaginative brood could make of them.

At least, she thought as she hurried upstairs to the computer in her bedroom, her four *had* imagination. So many youngsters these days needed to be told what to play at, but her kids could keep themselves happy for hours with mundane things like cushions and empty cornflakes packets.

She wondered if this meant that all four had inherited her creative imagination, and felt quite cheered for a moment before realising that the more likely answer was that as she and Duncan had no money to spend on computer games and expensive toys, their offspring had had to learn to make do with whatever came to hand. At least they did it without complaint. And one day, she hoped, she would be able to give them all the better life they deserved.

This was her favourite time of day – with the children in bed and Duncan either reading his newspaper or at the Neurotic Cuckoo, it was the moment when she finally got the chance to please herself. Sighing with contentment, she settled down on the old kitchen chair and switched on the computer, which sat on a desk made from a large piece of wood resting on two small chests of drawers. It was an old machine, and she had to wait patiently as, with much grinding and sighing and internal struggling, it booted itself up. 'There now,' she said softly, giving it a pat. She loved it dearly, and felt it appreciated her affection and repaid it by struggling on. Tonight she was working on a short story for her writing course. She brought up the work she had done on it so far, tucked her wispy brown hair back behind both ears, pushed her glasses further up her nose and set to work.

She had been keying happily for ten minutes when Duncan arrived home. Helen kept on working, unwilling to break her concentration, but it wasn't long before he walked into the bedroom.

'Tapping away as usual.' He bent to give her a

kiss that tasted and smelled of beer. 'Kids in bed?'

'Mmm. Have a nice time?' she mumbled, her fingers still working busily and her focus on the words appearing on the screen.

'Could have been a lot better.' He sat down on the bed. 'Glen was banging on about this dratted quarry.'

'I heard folk talking about it in the butcher's this morning.'

'You go to the pub to have a nice quiet drink and a game of darts in peace,' Duncan grumbled. 'It's a bit much when the blooming publican nags at you while you're having it. Oh, and he says could you write a letter of protest about it, so he can do copies for everyone to send to the council?'

'What?' Helen stopped work and turned to stare at him with anguished hazel eyes. 'Why does he want *me* to do it?'

'He knows you've got that computer.'

'But he's got one as well, hasn't he? Why can't he do it?'

'He says you know more about writing things down than he does. And you do, don't you? You do typing for all sorts of people – and you're a writer, too.'

'But I don't do letters. Duncan, I'm trying to get on with this story!'

'He didn't mean you had to do the letter right now. You don't *have* to do it at all, if you don't want to.'

She had just pushed her glasses back into place, and now she peered through them suspiciously. 'Have you said that I will?'

'I didn't say anything,' protested Duncan. 'He

71

said he'd have a word with you himself and I said that was best.'

'Haven't I got enough on my plate already?'

'I did *say* you were busy.'

'I *am* busy. I've to get this finished and polished and posted off by next Wednesday, and there's a thesis I'm doing for a college student. But Glen will be ringing the doorbell tomorrow morning – just you wait and see. Oh blast it!'

'You've got a tongue in your head, haven't you? Just tell him no, if you don't want to do it. It's your decision, not mine.'

Like everything else, Helen thought resentfully. Duncan hated having to make decisions. He could never even tell her what he fancied to his dinner. Now he yawned, ran his hands through his brown curly hair, then asked hopefully, 'When'll supper be ready?'

Helen sighed, but only inside. 'Go downstairs and put the kettle on while I try to finish this scene. I won't be long.'

'Okay.' He came to stand behind her. 'How's it going?'

'I don't know, to be honest.'

He went off downstairs, moving quietly so as not to wake the children, while Helen stared at the screen before her. 'I'll tell you what,' one of her characters had been saying when Duncan came into the room. Unfortunately, the interruption meant that she hadn't the faintest idea what he had been going to tell.

'Oh sugar!' she said, tears of sheer frustration thickening her voice. 'Thanks a bunch, Duncan!'

72

Once or twice a week Ingrid, Helen and Jenny met for coffee. Today it was to be at Ingrid's, so as soon as Helen had seen the three oldest children, ten-year-old Gregor, eight-year-old Gemma, and Lachlan, who was six, in to school, and settled four-year-old Irene at the nursery attached to the primary school, she hurried back down River Lane.

She loved going to Ingrid's house because unlike her own, it was spacious and always as neat as a new pin. Ingrid's daughters, fourteen-year-old Freya and Ella, who was ten, had their own play-room as well as separate bedrooms, and so Ingrid's living room was an immaculate child-free zone.

She was turning to the right towards the Mill Walk estate instead of left to the council house scheme where she herself lived when she heard Glen Mason call her name.

She muttered a curse and ducked her head in the way small children do when they want to make themselves invisible, but it was no use.

'Helen!' His loud voice rang out as he caught up with her. 'I was just on my way to see you. Come to the pub and I'll make you a coffee.'

'I can't, Glen. I'm having coffee with Ingrid and Jenny.'

'The coven meets again, eh?' His dark eyes creased at the corners with appreciation at his own joke, which had stopped being funny some time ago. 'Bubble, bubble, toil and–'

'I'm late, actually. Must dash!'

'Hang on a minute – did Duncan tell you we need a letter of protest about this quarry business?'

'Who's we?'

'The folk who don't want the noise and dirt of a working quarry on their doorstep. Do you want it?'

'No, I don't,' she admitted.

'There you are then. Could you draft a letter for us to send to the council?'

'I wouldn't know what to say.'

'But everyone knows you're good at writing; it comes easy to you.'

'I type essays and things for students and lecturers and I'm trying to learn to write fiction, but it's not the same. I wouldn't know what to say,' Helen protested again.

'We're setting up a committee of local people who are against the quarry being reopened – I've got some names already. We'll all get together and work something out, and then you can put it down the right way for us. In fact,' Glen said enthusiastically, 'you could be the committee secretary. You know, do the minutes and that?'

'What? Glen, I'm really busy at the moment as it happens. I'm typing a thesis just now, and working on a short story for my correspondence–'

'It wouldn't take up much of your time. I'd see to the photocopying and distribution, of course. As for the committee, it'll just be a few of us meeting on the occasional evening in our living room. Drinks on the house.'

'I really–'

'I knew I could rely on you.' Glen beamed. Then, as she took a firmer grip on her bag and opened her mouth to tell him that unfortunately, she simply could not find the time to help him, 'Don't let me keep you. I'll be in touch.' And giving her a cheerful wink, he hurried back up River Lane.

'Glen's organising some sort of protest about reopening the quarry, and he wants me to draft a letter!' Helen moaned as she sank into a chair in Ingrid's stylish living room. 'He's talking about me being the secretary.'

'You have enough to do.' Ingrid poured coffee and handed round some little sugar biscuits. 'You have a novel to write.'

'It isn't easy to refuse Glen once he's made his mind up.'

'Just say no – you are too busy.'

'Or have you already agreed?' Jenny asked.

'No – but I think that he thinks I did!'

'Glen Mason is a man who likes to have his own way, always,' Ingrid said.

'I hate it when he gets hold of a joke and refuses to let it go,' Jenny added, 'like calling the three of us a coven. Though I suppose we should be glad that at least he's stopped chanting "Bubble, bubble, toil and trouble" every time he meets us.'

'He hasn't stopped. He said it to me this morning,' Helen remarked, and Jenny rolled her eyes and groaned.

'His head is empty. The best way to deal with such people is to ignore them. When I was a tiny girl I learned from my grandmother that worrying about something just gives it power over us. Ignore it and it will go away.' Ingrid sipped her coffee. 'Never bother bother until bother bothers you – is that not one of your sayings?'

'Never trouble trouble until trouble troubles

you,' Helen corrected her automatically.

'It is the same thing.'

'But what do you do when trouble *does* trouble you?'

The doorbell rang, and Ingrid put her cup down. 'Then you kick it out of the door and tell it not to come back,' she said over her shoulder as she went into the hall.

'It must be lovely to be Ingrid – nothing ever bothers her,' Jenny said wistfully.

'You've not got problems, have you?' Helen was surprised. She often envied both her friends, living in lovely houses and married to men who earned far more than Duncan did.

'No, of course not,' Jenny said swiftly – too swiftly

'You know you could always talk to me or to Ingrid if you were worried about something. It would never go any further.'

'I know – but everything's fine,' Jenny was insisting when Ingrid returned with Marcy.

'A quick coffee would be lovely,' the newcomer said, sinking into a comfortable armchair. 'Old Mrs McCormack left her purse in the shop so I grabbed the chance to escape for a few minutes and return it. I thought I'd find all of you here. Helen, I met Glen Mason when I was coming down River Lane and he's asked me to go on to this protest committee he's organising. He needs more women, apparently, so I said yes.'

'You said yes? But Sam's all for the quarry, isn't he?'

'We're partners, Jenny, not Siamese twins. We're entitled to have our own opinions and I'm against the idea of bringing industry to the village. I've reached the age where I hate change. Thanks, Ingrid.' Marcy took the proffered cup and sipped at it.

'Is that your only reason for joining this committee?' Ingrid asked. 'Isn't there something else?'

'What else could there be?' Marcy asked innocently, widening her eyes.

'I think you're playing a game with poor Sam. I believe that nowadays they call it, rattling his cage.'

'You're a sharp one, Ingrid!'

'And you,' Ingrid said, 'need to be careful. Don't push him too far.'

'Oh, it'll be all right,' Marcy said confidently. 'And it might be fun to sit on a committee. I haven't done anything like that for years.'

7

Felicity Ralston-Kerr dipped the brush into the paint pot and leaned over precariously, one hand on the side of the wooden ladder, the other arm stretching over towards the windowsill. She managed to draw a wide white ribbon across the sill's cracked wood before returning to the comparative safety of the ladder, and then balanced the brush across the top of the tin so she could use her sweatered forearm to wipe a drip from the end of her nose.

It was quite a pleasant day, but Linn Hall, on

the hill above the village, tended to be open to the wind and today was no exception. Felicity – or Fliss as she was usually called – wore a thick paint-smeared sweater under one of her late father-in-law's old tweed waistcoats, and her thin legs were encased in corduroy trousers stuffed into wellington boots. A woollen scarf covered her untidy hair and protected her ears from the wind, but even so she was feeling quite chilly.

She dipped the brush into the paint pot again and got back to work, thinking longingly of housewives in the village below, women who, with hair tended regularly by hairdressers, would be cooking lunch in their warm modern kitchens. They might even have luxuries such as dishwashers and blenders. It would be nice, now and again, to be like them instead of having to cook in a huge old-fashioned kitchen meant to be staffed by an army of trained servants; nice to use a modern stove instead of the big difficult range.

Then she gave herself a good shake – mentally, since it wasn't safe at the moment to do it physically – and told herself to dismiss the self-pity and get on with the job in hand. 'Sooner started, sooner finished,' she chanted softly over and over again as she worked.

She could, if she had wanted, have been one of those housewives. She could have married a man who lived in a snug little bungalow or a semi-detached or terraced house and had a job that brought in a monthly salary, modest but adequate. But from the moment she set eyes on Hector Ralston-Kerr, the penniless heir to slowly rotting Linn Hall, she had wanted to be his wife.

They had been university students at the time, and although she had felt a slight pang of apprehension and dismay when she first set eyes on his noble but crumbling home, she was too deeply in love with him to change her mind. She had married him gladly, knowing full well that the rest of her life would be spent trying to keep the Hall going, despite never having enough money.

She sloshed more paint onto the sill and told herself with determination that she was a very lucky woman to have a husband like Hector and a son like Lewis, and a whole village full of good, caring friends who looked on Hector as their laird, even though the title meant nothing nowadays.

'Fliss?' The wind carried his call around the corner of the house.

'I'm here, Hector, painting the library windows.'

She glanced down as her husband arrived and clutched at the ladder, staring up at her in horror. 'My dear girl, what on earth do you think you're doing?'

'I told you, painting the library windows.'

'But you should have asked me to do it, or Lewis, or Duncan. Come down, for goodness' sake!'

'Lewis and Duncan are busy in the grounds somewhere, and we both know you don't have a head for heights.' Fliss had gone stiff with cold and she clambered down the ladder like an old woman, glad of Hector's supporting arm as she stepped onto the terrace's uneven paving stones.

'You shouldn't be doing that – it's not right,' he fretted.

'I'm absolutely fine!' Every time Fliss looked up

into his blue eyes, a little faded now, but still his best feature, she knew that her long-ago decision to forgo the comforts of a kitchen with all mod cons had been worthwhile. She reached up and rescued some strands of his grey hair from the wind, smoothing them neatly back across his balding pate. 'You should be wearing a cap and a jacket. You don't want to get your chest starting up again.'

'Oh.' He clapped a hand to his head and then looked down with mild surprise at his home-knitted cardigan. 'I didn't think. It's this letter that's just arrived – you need to read it, Fliss.'

He thrust it into her hand and she pulled her woollen gloves off and turned her back on the stiff breeze to save the sheet of paper from being blown away. 'My goodness – they're thinking of starting up the quarry? Our old quarry?'

'Apparently.'

Fuss looked at the letter again. As the owner of the land the quarry was on, Hector was being offered a handsome sum of money to lease the area to an English company.

Her first reaction was one of delight. Used wisely, this monthly sum could make quite a difference to their meagre income. Then she read the letter again.

'Oh dear, Hector. What do you think the villagers will think about this business?'

'Exactly,' he agreed glumly. 'Duncan and Lewis are in the kitchen now, having a cup of tea, so I asked Duncan if he knew anything about it. Apparently there's quite a lot of feeling – for and against.'

'I can imagine.' The thing about being a laird, even in name only, was that there were always others to consider. Much as they needed the money that leasing the quarry land would bring, the decision could not be theirs alone.

'What on earth are we going to do, Fliss?' he asked now

She folded the letter carefully and pushed it into her waistcoat pocket before tucking a hand, now almost blue with cold, into the crook of his elbow.

'First of all, she said, 'we're going to the kitchen to make two mugs of hot chocolate. And then we'll have to start working out what's best for Prior's Ford.'

8

For several days after Alexandra and Steven's visit Clarissa did nothing at all, other than walk along to the village shop each day to collect necessities such as milk and bread. She didn't buy a news-paper, because she wasn't interested in the outside world; she just felt numb and unreal.

'Let me worry about that,' Keith had said so often, smiling down at her and patting her hand or her shoulder. 'I'll see to it.'

After years of combining a demanding job with caring for her elderly parents until they were laid to rest in the local cemetery, her father not long after her mother, Clarissa had enjoyed being looked after. She had protested mildly when

Keith suggested just before their marriage that she should give up her job and become a housewife, but his argument had been sensible enough.

'It's not really on, is it, both of us at the same school, and me the principal? How can the others talk about me in the staff room with my wife sitting there? And in any case, why should you work when I earn enough to keep the two of us comfortably?'

'Perhaps I could move to another school?'

'What's the point of looking for another position at this late stage in your career? To tell the truth,' Keith said, 'it was Marion's insistence on returning to work when the children went into secondary school that ended my first marriage. Call me old fashioned, but two people putting more emphasis on their careers than their marriage is a recipe for disaster. And we want this marriage to last, don't we?'

Much as she loved teaching, the prospect of being able to get out and about during the day, and spend her evenings reading and doing crosswords rather than marking piles of homework, appealed to Clarissa, so she agreed. She left work at the start of the summer holidays, the envious comments of exhausted colleagues ringing in her ears, and married Keith two weeks later.

She had settled into her new life quite happily, and the next five years passed pleasantly enough. Then Keith retired, and suddenly decided that he wanted to move to Scotland.

'But your children both live near here – you surely don't want to move away from them,' Clarissa protested.

'They have cars and so do I. I thought a comfortable house in a nice rural area near the borders would suit me. We'd only be an hour or two away from Alexandra and Steven.'

'But my friends are here! My book group, and the sewing bee.'

'My dear, the Scots aren't all wild clansmen, you know.' Keith patted her arm soothingly. 'Bonnie Prince Charlie doesn't live there any more. They have book groups and sewing bees and libraries just the same as we have here. You'll enjoy Scotland.'

Then followed a year of travelling back and forth across the border, viewing house after house, with each being rejected by Keith for one reason or another. Clarissa was rarely consulted, just as she was rarely consulted over anything – what they ate, what radio programmes they listened to, what television programmes they viewed, or even what direction they headed in when setting out for their daily walks.

When Keith settled on Willow Cottage, a pretty detached house overlooking the village green in Prior's Ford, Clarissa, along with everything else that he owned, was moved from the area she had lived in all her life to a different country – not that there seemed to be much of a difference, since there were as many English accents in Prior's Ford as there were Scots.

Keith's assurance that she would soon find things to join came to nothing, for they ended up spending every day together. They gardened – or, rather, Keith gardened while Clarissa fetched and carried – and they walked every day, as before, and they used the car to explore further afield. They visited museums and bookshops, but although they did some shopping in the village store – the bulk of the household items were bought from a supermarket in Kirkcudbright – and used its post office facilities, they didn't go to the Neurotic Cuckoo, or to any of the events held in the village hall.

This meant that Clarissa had not managed to get to know anyone in the village. People smiled at her when they met her in the local shops, and asked after her health. They assured her that she only needed to ask if she required help in any way but, like Keith, Clarissa drew the line at expecting favours from total strangers.

Alexandra was right, she decided, staring out of the window at the village green. She should sell the house and move back to the Lake District, where she still had friends. She must find a small flat and take up her hobbies again. The thought of having to deal with selling and buying property was exhausting, but it had to be done, and the first task before calling in an estate agent was to rid herself of any unnecessary clutter.

It had started to rain, which made it a perfect day for indoor duties. As soon as Clarissa had made her decision she brewed a cup of strong coffee to act as a stimulant, and carried it into Keith's small study.

The walls were lined with his books, all of which would have to go. She would be sure to find a buyer in Wigtown, the nearby book town. Pulling out a few drawers in the writing desk she found they were empty. Keith had always been neat and methodical, and Steven had taken away all the business papers, assuring Clarissa they would be kept safe until she required them.

The corner cupboard held neatly labelled box files relating to Keith's years as a head teacher – the contents would all have to be run through the shredder sitting in a corner of the room, since they were no longer of use to anyone.

Clarissa began to empty the files and shred their contents after a cursory glance at each sheet of paper to make sure it could be safely disposed of. She had no wish to read them; Keith was gone for ever, and she had to learn, slowly and painfully, to look to the future – her future.

To her surprise, a box that had once held chocolates had been put at the bottom of the second box file. Taking the lid off, she discovered a small photograph album. A quick flip through the first half showed that it held pictures of Keith, Marion and their two children through the years. That would go to Alexandra and Steven – or they might pass them to their mother. Somehow, Clarissa doubted if the brisk, competent woman she had met on a few occasions when Marion was still her headmaster's wife, and more recently at the funeral, was the type to cherish photographs of a failed marriage and children now grown, but she could be wrong.

The second part of the album held school photographs, some of which included Clarissa. She thought she would probably keep them. At the back was a wedding portrait of her in a cream suit, with a small cluster of deep red roses pinned to her lapel, arm in arm with Keith, tall and broad and confident. Jarvis Peters, his best man, and Stella Bartholomew, Clarissa's maid of honour, flanked them.

Beneath the album lay a bundle of letters neatly secured by an elastic band, which she removed carefully. Keith had always date-stamped incoming mail, and the envelopes, all bearing typed address labels, were in chronological order, and all received after their move to Dumfries and Galloway.

They looked like business correspondence; presumably Steven and Alexandra had only glanced into the file, and had not burrowed beneath the album. Clarissa withdrew the first letter from its envelope and unfolded it.

Almost immediately, she found herself wishing she had heeded her first impulse and shredded the entire bundle unopened.

'Alastair, you're a darling!' Ingrid said warmly.

'I don't know about that. It's just a few shelves – nothing to it,' Alastair Marshall said diffidently.

'Just a few shelves? Here we are, three married women, and not one with a husband capable of putting shelves up – am I not right?' Ingrid appealed to Jenny and Helen. They were, as was usual on weekday mornings at this time of the year, working in the Gift Horse. Alastair, who had gone along to deliver some of his paintings, had found them trying to put up the shelving and taken over the job.

'She's right, Alastair,' Helen agreed, tucking her hair behind one ear. 'Duncan could have done it, but he's always too busy up at Linn Hall during the week, and at weekends he's caught up in his dratted darts practice.'

'My Peter is a very clever man, but with his head, not his hands,' Ingrid said fondly. 'He would probably manage to nail himself to the wall, the poor darling. You'll have a glass of red wine, Alastair?'

'Thanks, that would be nice.'

'Andrew's not much of a DIY man either,' Jenny said. 'He'd rather pay someone to do that sort of thing than risk making a mess of it.'

'I'm not a DIY man myself,' Alastair admitted as Ingrid handed the glass to him. 'I've just had to learn to do a bit of this and a bit of that, helping out in the pub and at Linn Hall, and on the farms when I'm needed. Jack of all trades, master of none. Cheers!'

'But you are a master of your own trade – you are a very good painter. One day,' Ingrid prophesied, 'everyone will want to buy your pictures and you will have no more need to make ends meet.'

'I'll drink to that.' Alastair propped his tall, gangly body on the edge of a table. His dark brown hair, worn slightly longer than was the fashion, framed a rather solemn face with a straight, strong nose, calm hazel eyes and a wide mouth.

'We drink to that too, and,' Ingrid added, 'to you as well, Helen. One day you will be a famous writer.'

'I wish!'

'Yes, you will, if you want it hard enough.'

'One day,' Jenny smiled at Helen and Alastair, 'there will be plaques on the walls of your houses saying that Helen Campbell, famous writer, and Alastair Marshall, famous artist, lived here.'

'I like the sound of that.' Alastair grinned.

'It could happen for you, Alastair.' Helen was sifting through the work he had brought. 'I do like your paintings.'

'Thanks, I appreciate that.' He finished his wine. 'I'd best be getting back.'

'The rain's worse now,' Jenny glanced out of the window, where fat raindrops raced each other down the glass. 'Maybe you should wait until it eases off a bit.'

'I don't think it will.' He fastened his anorak and pulled a baseball cap over his head before covering it with the anorak hood. 'I might as well get wet now than later.'

The rain was coming down hard outside, and Main Street was almost empty apart from a few people half hidden under umbrellas as he set off for his home, a tiny farm cottage on the outskirts of Prior's Ford.

A Scot by birth, Alastair was used to wet weather, and he liked the way his surroundings could change in an instant from light to dark, from welcoming to menacing, even from summer to winter. An American tourist had once told him, 'You Scots don't have weather, you have samples,' a comment which, to Alastair, summed up his native country's climate perfectly.

He left the village and crossed the river by the old stone bridge, heading into the countryside, enjoying the taste of rain on the tip of his tongue, the sound of it pattering on leaves and the sight of it dimpling the puddles in the rutted lanes.

On days such as this most people preferred to stay indoors unless they absolutely had to go out;

so he was surprised, as he crossed the final field on his way back to his cottage, to see through the downpour the figure of a woman sitting on the stile he had to climb in order to reach home.

He was even more surprised as he drew near to see that the light coat she wore over her dress was unbuttoned, and that her bowed head was uncovered and her hair soaked. She crouched on the stile, as still as a statue, not even looking up as he approached, his sturdy walking boots swishing through the long grass.

'Good afternoon – refreshing weather, isn't it?' he remarked cheerfully, but she continued to stare down at the ground – or perhaps at her wet, gloveless hands, linked in her lap. Alastair came to a standstill before her, a puzzled frown beginning to stitch itself between his eyebrows.

'Are you all right?' Clearly she wasn't, but he couldn't think of anything else to say. He put a hand on her arm, then took a step back as she suddenly flinched and brought her head up, staring at him with startled brown eyes.

'I'm sorry, I didn't mean to give you a fright. I just wondered,' he said carefully as she stared in a bewildered way at the field and the nearby thicket of trees, 'if you were all right. You're very wet.'

She turned her attention to the stile, reaching out with one hand to touch the wood as though wondering if it were real or a figment of her imagination. Then she glanced up at him from beneath wet eyelashes. Her lips moved but nothing came out, so she cleared her throat before trying again.

'I don't know,' she said. 'I don't know anything.' And again she looked around before adding, 'Where am I?'

'Prior's Ford – in a field just outside the village. Are you lost?'

She nodded as though at last he had said something she understood. 'Oh yes,' she said, 'yes, I'm very lost.' She had an English accent.

'Can I telephone someone for you?' Alastair asked, then as she shook her head, scattering raindrops, he realised that since he had never cared to join the craze for mobile phones, the nearest telephone was in his cottage, which wasn't far away.

'Look, why don't you come to my place and have something hot to drink? I've got a towel, too. You look as though you could do with one.' Tentatively, he touched her arm again and this time she didn't flinch.

'Let's get out of this rain,' he said encouragingly, and to his relief she nodded and allowed him to help her to stand and then climb over the stile. Once he had joined her on the other side he took her arm, and was further relieved when she walked obediently by his side.

'Where do you live?'

'Nowhere, any more,' she said, and his heart sank. She must have lost her memory, or perhaps she was an Alzheimer's sufferer who had wandered away from whoever was supposed to be caring for her. He would have to telephone the police in Kirkcudbright, since Prior's Ford no longer had its own police presence.

9

Fortunately Alastair's cottage was only a matter of seven minutes' walk from the stile. The woman waited patiently while he unlocked the door, her head lowered and her shoulders slumped, then allowed him to usher her inside. The door opened straight into the living room, which doubled as his studio.

'It's not very tidy, I'm afraid. I live on my own and I like it the way it is.' Alastair glanced at the telephone, and then decided that getting her dry was more important than calling for help. 'Wait here while I fetch a towel.'

By luck more than custom, he had a large clean towel in the bathroom. He went up the narrow stairs two at a time, concerned in case she took it into her confused head to go back out into the rain while he was away, but to his relief she was still there when he returned to the living room.

'So do I,' she said when he reappeared.

'Excuse me?'

'I like it the way it is.' She gestured to the cluttered room, then to the easel by the window. 'You're a painter.'

'Yes, I am. Look, we should get you out of those wet clothes,' he suggested. She looked at him, surprised, then glanced down at herself and said in a firmer voice than she had used before, 'My goodness, look at me! What was I thinking of, coming out on a wet day dressed like this?'

Alastair felt quite weak with relief at the first signs of sanity.

'The bathroom's upstairs, first door. If you want to go up and get out of those wet things and give yourself a good rub with the towel, I'll leave some clothes of mine outside the door. Not very suitable, I know, but we need to get you into something dry before you catch a chill.'

'Thank you.' She took the towel and headed for the open wooden staircase set against one wall. He watched as she mounted the treads, and when he heard the bathroom door close he followed her up and went into his bedroom, where he found a sweater and jeans, both clean apart from paint splashes, and a belt to thread through the jeans, which would be too large for her. He added thick socks and a pair of trainers that were a bit tight for him and then, after a bit of thought, finished off with a pair of clean Y-fronts.

His laundry basket consisted of a bin bag; he tipped the dirty clothes from it, leaving them in a pile on the floor, and put it, together with the clothes he had gathered for her, outside the bathroom door.

'All right?' he called.

'Yes, thank you.'

'There's hot water, and I've left clothes out here for you, and a bag to put your wet things in. I'll make tea,' Alastair said, and hurried downstairs, where he glanced at the telephone again before going to the kitchen to put the kettle on. Once she was dry and warm she might give him a number to call. Best to keep the police out of it if possible.

When the woman came downstairs she moved at once towards the front door and for a moment Alastair thought she was going to lift the latch and plunge back into the rain. Instead, she placed the bin bag holding her wet clothes beside the door, and then turned to look at him.

'Thank you, you've been very kind.'

'Sorry about the clothes, but I live on my own, so I don't have anything more suitable.'

She glanced down at the jeans, folded several times just above the large trainers, and the sweater, which fell almost to her knees. A lock of damp hair fell over her face and she pushed it back as she smiled up at him.

'They're dry and warm and that's all that matters.'

'I have a comb – it's clean,' he added hurriedly. While waiting for her to come down, he had scrubbed and rinsed it in the kitchen sink.

'Thank you. I must look an absolute fright,' she apologised as she sat down and started to work the comb through her tangled hair.

'You look better than you did when I first saw you.' Alastair moved a small table to her side, and placed a steaming mug on it carefully. 'The table's a bit rickety but if you treat it kindly, it's all right.'

'A bit like myself.'

'Milk?' He handed her the bottle, and when she had poured milk into the mug and handed the bottle back, he said, 'Sugar? I think you should,' when she began to shake her head, 'it's supposed to be good for shock.'

'You believe I'm in shock?'

'I don't know for sure, but I think you might be,' he said, and she put a spoonful of sugar into the mug and stirred it carefully before lifting it in both hands and holding it so the steam bathed her face.

'Perhaps I am. Have you ever been in shock?'

'I probably was, the first time someone actually bought one of my paintings, but I'm not sure what being in shock feels like, so I can't advise you. Is there someone I can phone? Someone who can fetch you and take you home?'

'I'm perfectly capable of going home by myself. I might be middle-aged but I'm not senile,' she said sharply.

Alastair felt colour rise into his face. 'Sorry – but when I found you, you said you were lost. You said you didn't know where you lived.'

'Oh Lord, I did, didn't I? I'm the one who should apologise; I didn't mean to snap at you like that. I do know who I am and where I live, of course I do. It's just that – oh, it's all too complicated and embarrassing! My name is Clarissa Ramsay, Mrs Clarissa Ramsay, and I live in Willow Cottage, in the village,' she said, and then, as he gave a long sigh of relief, 'I've caused you such a lot of bother. You must have thought that I was a mad old biddy who'd given her carers the slip and gone wandering the moors like Jane Eyre – or more like the first Mrs Rochester.'

The description so suited the sodden, blank-faced woman he had first met at the stile that he burst out laughing, and after a moment, so did she.

'How do you do, Mrs Ramsay? I'm Alastair Marshall.'

'A very kind young man, and an artist too,' she said as they shook hands.

'A struggling artist. I do a bit of everything else to keep the wolf from the door – helping in the gardens up at the big house in summer, and working for the farmers when they're taking in the harvests in the autumn. I work in the pub sometimes and I do the occasional art class in the local primary school too.'

'Good for you.' Clarissa Ramsay drank thirstily from the mug and then set it down carefully on the table. 'That was enjoyable. Thank you. And now, I must go home.'

'I don't have a car, and it's still raining. Is there someone I could phone? Your husband, perhaps?'

For the second time since they met she flinched, then sat up straight-backed in the chair and said firmly, 'My husband died – recently.'

'I'm so sorry.'

'So was I, at the time,' she said, and then, while he was still puzzling over the last three words, added, 'It must be good to be needed to help out with the farm and the pub and the other things you mentioned.'

'We're all needed at times.'

'I don't think I am, any more. I used to be a teacher, but I'm retired now. I'm not a daughter or a mother – or a wife, now.' Again he heard the sudden bite that came to her voice with the final words. Then, turning a hand palm up in a hopeless gesture, she said, 'I'm nothing.'

'That's not true. You're somebody, but just a different somebody from the one you were before. You'll have to reshape yourself.'

'I don't think I can be bothered.'

'You will be, once you get over your loss,' Alastair said awkwardly, cursing himself for sounding like some terrible pseudo couch psychiatrist. He couldn't think of anything else to say. Fortunately his visitor seemed more interested in watching the rain running down the window than listening to him.

'Do you have a raincoat or an umbrella I could borrow?'

'I'll find something.'

While he was in the kitchen Clarissa hauled her wet coat from the bin bag and had just retrieved her house key from the pocket and pushed the coat back into the bag when he returned with a light waterproof jacket in one hand.

'I'm afraid this is all I have.' He helped her into the jacket then said vaguely, 'There's an umbrella somewhere...'

'I'll be fine, my hair's wet anyway. And you don't have to come with me,' she added as he began to put on his anorak. 'You've done enough already.'

'I'm going to see you home.' He plunged into the depths of a wall cupboard and reappeared brandishing a large black umbrella. 'Here it is – someone left it once and never came back for it.'

The rain was sheeting down now, and he opened the umbrella as soon as they were outside, only to discover that the material was ripped at one side. 'No wonder the legal owner didn't bother retrieving it,' he said ruefully. 'Take my arm.' He revolved the umbrella so that Clarissa Ramsay got the side without the rip.

When they arrived at Willow Cottage, Alastair waited until Clarissa had put her key into the lock, then said, 'Well, goodbye. You'll be all right now, will you?'

'Yes, thank you. Won't you come in? It's my turn to lend you a towel,' she added, noticing for the first time that rainwater coming in through the rip in the umbrella had plastered his long brown hair to his skull, and was now dripping from his chin and finding its way below the collar of his anorak. 'I can even lend you a decent umbrella for your journey home.'

She unlocked the door and led him into her neat sitting room. 'There's a towel in the kitchen; take your jacket off.'

When she had delivered the towel she switched on the gas fire before hurrying upstairs to give her own hair another towelling and a comb through. It was beginning to dry, curling round her face in a style she had never seen before, since this was the first time it had ever been left to dry on its own. She ran her fingers through the curls, fluffing them up slightly. The cold rain had brought some colour into her face.

Downstairs, Alastair finished drying his hair and looked about the room. A framed photograph on the mantelpiece showed a middle-aged couple in a garden, the woman vaguely familiar, neat haired and with a tentative smile. She was holding a plant pot and the man taller, broader and handsome in a confident way, leaned on a hoe.

Hearing footsteps on the stairs, he moved hastily to the window, and was looking out at the village green when Clarissa arrived. 'I've always been fascinated by views from windows,' he said, 'they tend to be so different from the outside view.'

'I've noticed that myself. Would you like a coffee? Or could I give you a meal?' Clarissa asked, astonished by her daring.

'I'd better be getting back. I don't want to be a nuisance...'

'I'm the one who's been the nuisance.'

'You haven't, really.'

'Please stay and eat with me,' Clarissa said. 'I haven't had much company since Keith died – well, his son and daughter came recently to help me sort his things out, but they're not what I'd call company. I'd like to cook for two again.'

'Well, in that case, I'd be happy to stay,' he said, smiling down at her. 'As long as I can help with the cooking.'

10

Keith had always considered the kitchen to be Clarissa's domain and never encroached on it, so she was unused to someone sharing the small space with her; but Alastair Marshall had such a relaxed manner that she found it easy to allow him to help her.

Since she had scarcely eaten since Keith's death there was little food in the house, but the carton of soup she found in the freezer was easily thawed in the microwave, as was the carton of cooked mince. When she looked in the vegetable basket she saw the potatoes had started to sprout, but Alastair immediately announced that if there was one thing he could cook, it was spaghetti Bolognese. Fortunately, she had spaghetti in the store cupboard.

While they ate, he told her about his childhood in Dundee with his parents, sister and brother, his time at art school and the family holidays in Dumfries and Galloway that had resulted in his decision to settle, at least for a while, in Prior's Ford.

'I always liked this area – the light, the people, the very atmosphere in this part of Scotland.'

'I like it too, but I don't think I'll be staying, not now Keith's gone.'

'Take time to think about it,' he advised her, helping himself to more bread. 'This soup, by the way, is delicious. It's great to have home-made soup again instead of out of packets. My mum makes soup all the time – I was raised on it.'

'My stepchildren say that I should contact an estate agent soon and get the house valued.'

'Do you need the money?'

'No.'

'Then take your time. Don't rush into anything. Listen to me,' he said, 'poking my nose in and giving you advice.'

'It's good to talk to someone.'

'You're easy to talk to. I don't normally talk so much. You must be a good listener.'

She smiled across the table at him. 'I'll take some time to clear the house in any case, and then I would have to look for somewhere to live in Cumbria – if I decide to go back,' she added, suddenly recalling why she had snatched up the nearest coat and rushed out into the rain without an umbrella.

'That's true. You might decide to move to an entirely new place, or travel the world. Your future's in your own hands.'

'That's a frightening thought.'

'No, it's an exciting thought; you'll realise that when you've had time to get used to the idea of being your own person again.' Alastair pushed back a strand of his long dark brown hair. 'And you have all the time in the world.'

'I've never really held my own future in my hands,' Clarissa said slowly. She had been raised in a loving but disciplined home, and then school, university, and teacher training college had followed each other with orderly, pre-planned precision. Then it had been back to the classroom, this time as a teacher, and, finally, marriage.

Now she felt as though she were in free-fall, with no support; she was just starting to panic at the thought when Alastair said easily, 'Then you're in for a treat. It's a good feeling, knowing you can do whatever you want without having to consider anyone else.'

'Do you really think so?'

'Of course. That's why I've never married or moved in with anyone. I like being free. You'll like it too, once you get used to the idea.' Alastair rose from the table. 'I'll fetch the spag bol.'

Clarissa had always hated to hear words abbreviated, but tonight, she didn't mind it a bit.

While Clarissa and Alastair were enjoying their supper, Glen Mason was chairing the first meeting of the quarry protest committee. The committee consisted of six people – Glen had been

100

voted in as chairman, much to Libby's annoyance, Helen was the reluctant secretary and there were four ordinary members: Marcy Copleton, village-born Lachie Wilkins, Robert Kavanagh and Pete McDermott, a fairly new resident.

The letter Helen had drafted, opposing the quarry reopening, was swiftly approved. 'I'll get it photocopied, and I think we should give two copies to everyone willing to sign it – one going to the quarry people and the other to our local councillor,' Glen suggested. 'We'll have them delivered to every household – any volunteers?'

'My two lads will take some round, and perhaps some of the other kids in the village will help out,' Lachie offered. 'After all, it's their village too. Do 'em good to get involved. Mind you, not everyone'll sign the letters. I'd say that the village is more or less split in half over this business at the moment.'

'At least we'll get to the folk who are of the same mind as we are. Any other ideas?'

'We need petitions in all the shops,' Marcy said, while Pete McDermott chipped in with, 'And we should think about setting up a meeting with the quarry company and the council.'

'This is all going to cost money. What about fund raising?' Lachie wanted to know.

'Let's wait until we find out just how serious these people are before we start anything like that,' Robert Kavanagh advised, and Glen nodded.

'For the moment, I'm willing to carry the cost of the letters. Helen, could you phone the local paper and tell them that we've set up a protest committee?'

'Me? I – I don't know...'

'Nothing to it, love,' Glen said breezily. 'Ask for the editorial department and get talking to one of their reporters. Tell whoever it is that you'll keep them in touch with events. Anything else before we draw our first meeting to a close?'

'I've got a question.' At the start of the meeting, Robert Kavanagh, to Helen's consternation, had taken a pipe from his pocket. Fortunately, after a bit of thought, he had decided to put it in his mouth without lighting it, so they were spared clouds of tobacco smoke. Now he took it from his mouth, studied it thoughtfully for a moment, then put it back and said round the stem, 'Who owns the land the quarry's on?'

'I don't know,' Glen admitted. 'I never thought of that.'

'Seems to me that someone must own that land, and this quarry company would surely need to rent it or at least get permission from the owner to work it. You want to look into that.'

'Linn Quarry – Linn Hall,' Marcy said. 'Could it be the Ralston-Kerrs?'

'It could,' Glen acknowledged. 'I'll ask Hector Ralston-Kerr about that.'

'I've heard they're only just managing to keep that place together,' Pete McDermott volunteered. 'If they own the quarry they might be glad of a bit of income from it. If I were you, Glen, I'd go and see this Ralston-Kerr chap as soon as you can.'

'First thing tomorrow morning. And you'll phone the newspaper tomorrow, Helen?'

'I suppose so.'

'Good,' Glen said heartily, ignoring her lack of

102

enthusiasm. 'Well now, let's have a drink to mark the end of the first meeting of the quarry protest committee!'

After they had eaten, Clarissa and Alastair settled by the fire with coffee and some of Keith's good brandy while Alastair reminisced about his days as a student.

'Much more interesting than mine,' Clarissa said ruefully.

'Didn't you ever kick over the traces?'

'I don't believe I did.'

'We all have to do that some time or another,' he said, and then, grinning his wide grin, 'perhaps your turn's still to come.'

'I doubt that, at my age.' She raised a hand to muffle a sudden yawn.

'Never say never. You're tired, and it's time I was on my way.'

'You don't have to rush off.'

'Time I went anyway.' He raised an eyebrow as they heard a spatter of rain hit the curtained window. 'The mad March weather's not let up yet.'

'At least let me lend you a decent umbrella. There's a big one in the hall stand. And I'll wash the clothes you loaned me and return them.'

'No hurry.' As they went into the hall he zipped his anorak up and took the umbrella from her. 'Thanks for this and for supper – I enjoyed it.'

'Thank you for rescuing me – and cooking.'

'My pleasure.' He opened the door and a surge of rain-wet wind immediately swirled into the hall.

'Better get going. Good night,' he said, and then opened the umbrella and stepped into the blustery darkness.

Clarissa sang under her breath as she cleared the table and washed the dishes. For the first time since Keith's death, the house had a lived-in feeling.

For the first time ever, she realised, it felt like her home.

She returned to the living room and switched on the television set, but found her eyes closing as she watched the news. While the cheerful weather girl was in the middle of promising her that the rain was going to move away overnight, Clarissa switched her off and went upstairs.

In the bedroom, she caught sight of herself in the bedroom mirror, and laughed. She had forgotten that she was still wearing the oversized, paint-splashed sweater and jeans and Alastair's trainers. She looked like a female Worzel Gummidge.

Hauling the sweater over her head she caught a mixed smell of wool and fresh outdoors air. For a moment she buried her face in its warmth before putting on her nightdress and going to bed, where she fell asleep swiftly, lulled by the sound of rain on the windows.

11

In the nineteenth century, three-storeyed Linn Hall had been a very handsome building, set like a jewel in grounds tended by an army of gardeners. But now, in the twenty-first century there was no staff to keep the carpets clean and the woodwork polished. The entrance hall's wooden floor was scuffed, covered here and there by shabby rugs that had once glowed with soft pastel shades. The huge fireplace lay empty and the carpeting on the wide staircase leading up to a broad half-landing with a magnificent stained-glass window was almost threadbare.

The front door was rarely locked and all the local people knew that the bell hadn't worked for years. Even if it had, there was nobody around to answer it. Glen Mason pushed the door open, strode into the entrance hall and made for the door at the back, once used only by servants. On its other side, a short corridor led to the kitchen, where Felicity Ralston-Kerr was rolling out pastry on the wooden table while Jinty McDonald, a local woman who helped out at Linn Hall when needed, peeled potatoes at the large sink.

'Morning, Mrs Ralston-Kerr – morning, Jinty.'

Fliss, glad of the chance to stop work for a moment, straightened her back and smiled at the visitor.

'Good morning, Mr Mason. How are you?'

'Very well, thanks. Mr Ralston-Kerr around?'

'In the pantry.' Fliss nodded at a door leading off the kitchen. 'It's warmer there than in the study. Would you like a cup of tea?'

'Thanks, that'd be grand. All right if I just go on in?'

'Of course,' Fliss said, while Jinty dried her hands and went to the ancient stove, where a massive kettle plumed steam into the air.

The Linn Hall pantry resembled a broad

corridor with a door at one end and a window at the other. The two long walls held tiers of shelves once stocked with enough food to keep the large household, plus visitors, well supplied with nourishment; now the room, furnished with an ordinary table, three straight-backed chairs and an electric heater, served as Hector's study and the family room.

When Glen knocked at the door and went in, Hector Ralston-Kerr was scribbling busily in a ledger with his right hand while his left hand tapped figures into a calculator. He glanced over his spectacles at the newcomer.

'Good morning, Mr Mason.'

'Morning. I wondered if I could have a word, if it's not inconvenient?'

If he was being interrupted at a delicate time, Hector was too well mannered to show it. 'Of course, of course. Take a seat – just put those things on that shelf,' he said as Glen looked at the precarious pile of papers on the nearest chair. And then, when the papers had been transferred carefully, 'Has anyone offered you tea?'

'Yes, thanks. I wanted to see you about–'

The door opened and Jinty came in bearing a tray. She balanced it on one hip while she used her free arm to clear a space on the table, then dumped the tray down. It held two steaming mugs, a tin of sugar with a spoon in it, a large milk jug and a plate of digestive biscuits.

'That do you?'

'Thank you, Jinty,' Hector said.

'No problem,' she assured him cheerfully, and left.

'What can I do for you, Mr Mason?'

'It's this quarry business. I take it you've heard about it.'

'Ah – yes.' Hector cleared his throat, then asked, 'Sugar and milk?'

'A good dash of milk and two sugars, please.' Glen waited impatiently as his host spooned sugar into his mug, added milk and then stirred carefully.

'Biscuit?'

'Not for me, thanks. About the qu–' Glen tried again, then subsided once more as Hector went through the business of attending to his own tea, each movement precise and careful – like a blooming Japanese tea-making ceremony, Glen thought to himself.

'You don't mind if I take a biscuit?'

'You help yourself – they're your biscuits. About the quarry,' Glen forged ahead, 'you know they're thinking of reopening it?'

Hector concentrated hard on stirring his tea, but finally had to admit to knowing about the plan.

'The thing is, we've set up a protest committee, and it had its first meeting last night. Someone suggested you might own the land, Mr Ralston-Kerr.'

'Ah.' Hector's shoulders, already rounded with the worries of keeping his ancestral home going, seemed to sag a little further.

'You do, don't you? Have you been approached?'

'As a matter of fact, we have.'

'With an offer to buy the land?'

'To lease it, as before.'

'But you're not going to agree to that.' Glen

deliberately made it a statement rather than a question.

Hector's grey eyebrows came together in a worried frown. 'I don't know yet. There's quite a lot to consider, Mr Mason. For instance, reopening the quarry could bring employment to the area.'

'There's plenty folk in the village who hate the thought of the noise and the dirt.'

'Yes, we're aware of that, too. It really depends on the general mood of the people who live in Prior's Ford. Have you done a survey among the villagers?'

'Not yet, but we're going to ask for an open meeting with the council and representatives of the company involved.'

'I think that's a good idea. Obviously, my wife and son and I have discussed this offer at some length, and we all feel that the final decision is a matter for the village rather than for us.'

'With respect, Mr Ralston-Kerr, I believe it's a matter for you more than anyone else. The folk who live in Prior's Ford look up to you. They could want a lead from you.'

'That,' Hector pointed out, 'is what makes things so difficult for us.'

'Nobody can start extracting the granite again without your say-so. You hold the casting vote, so to speak.'

'And I wish I didn't, Mr Mason.'

'Is it all that difficult?' Glen held out his two hands, palms up and fingers cupped, as though each hand held something. 'On the one hand, the villagers, and on the other, this company that wants to reopen the quarry.' He rocked both

108

hands up and down, turning them into scales. 'For you, it's a fairly simple matter of deciding where your loyalties lie. Prior's Ford's a tranquil village, a jewel set in beautiful countryside. A haven for holiday makers and tourists, a chance to get away from the hustle and bustle of everyday life and relax. That's why me and the missus moved here. We love this place, Mr Ralston-Kerr. And then there's the thought of this bonny village of ours being turned into an industrial site with noise and dust and the whole place upset.'

'I doubt if it would be as bad as that.'

'You might not be aware of it, living up here as you do, but reopening that quarry could make life noisy for us folk down at the foot of the hill.'

'It could mean work for some of the villagers too.'

'It'd be a hefty price to pay. We live in a mercenary world,' Glen said sorrowfully. 'Some people think money can buy anything, even integrity. But you're not like that, are you? You're descended from real gentry, and the likes of you can't be bought.'

Hector took a mouthful of tea, retaining the mug in his hands as though relishing its warmth. 'The fact is that my wife and I find ourselves in a very difficult situation here. The upkeep of Linn Hall is moving beyond our means – you can see for yourself how much needs to be done just to hold the place together. If it wasn't for the sale of flowers and vegetables to shops in the area we would be in serious financial trouble. Leasing some of our land could be of great benefit to us.'

'You're not telling me you've decided to do it?'

Hector drew himself up, straightening his shoulders. 'I'm telling you we're still weighing the pros and cons. The important thing is that we don't let the villagers down.'

'Ah yes, the old squire thing. A bit middle ages, isn't it?'

'In Scotland they're called lairds, and I agree with you that the idea of the people in the big house lording it over the villagers is outdated. But much as I wish the whole system had been forgotten generations ago, it still survives to some extent. My family have always cared about the well-being of the people who live in Prior's Ford, and Fliss and I still care,' Hector said, and then, raising his eyebrows at his visitor, 'And to be honest, Mr Mason, I can't understand why you yourself are opposed to the project. It would surely bring you increased custom.'

'Money isn't everything, Mr Ralston-Kerr.'

'It is if you don't have enough,' Hector said wistfully.

'Me and Libby are from ordinary hard-working stock. We ran a corner shop all our married lives until we retired. Then we sold up and moved here for two reasons – because it was always our ambition to run a pub and because we wanted a better quality of life. And that's what Prior's Ford has – quality. We do enough business to keep the brewery happy and that's all we want to do.'

Glen let his final words hang in the air for a moment, then heaved a gusty sigh and got to his feet. 'Well, I've had my say on behalf of my committee. I'll go now and let you get on with your work.'

He held out his hand, and Hector got up and shook it.

'Thank you for coming, Mr Mason. I can promise you that my wife and son and I will think over your comments very carefully.'

'I can't ask for anything more than that,' Glen said, and left.

Helen had never had occasion to contact a newspaper before, and it took some time before she summoned the courage to pick up the telephone and dial the number of the *Dumfries News*. But as things turned out, there was nothing to it – in less than a minute she found herself talking to someone in the editorial department.

'Yes, we know about the old quarry – how do the local people feel about it going into production again?'

'Most of us are against it. A protest committee's been formed and we had our first meeting last night.'

'And you're on this committee?'

'I'm the secretary. Mrs Helen Campbell.'

'Okay, Helen,' the man on the other end of the phone said breezily, 'give me the names of your fellow committee members.'

Fifteen minutes later Helen put the phone back on its cradle. She had a contact name – Bob Green – and had promised to keep him in touch with events. They had become quite chatty, and when she admitted that she had been steamrollered into becoming secretary for the protest committee, Bob said that he admired her for taking it on and for doing something for her community.

Enveloped in a self-satisfied glow, Helen switched on her computer and treated herself to half an hour working on the short story she was due to submit to her tutor.

'Hi, Clarissa, it's me,' Steven said breezily down the phone line. 'Just wondered how things are going and if you've put the house on the market yet.'

'I'm still thinking about it,' Clarissa admitted guiltily.

'But I thought we'd decided you were going to see an estate agent the day after we left.'

'I've been busy – you know how it is.'

'The thing is, a flat's just come on the market, not far from where you and Pops lived before. Two bedrooms – you wouldn't need anything larger than that, would you? – and a good spacious living room with a dining alcove. Well-fitted kitchen too, and a good-sized bathroom. There's an en-suite in the master bedroom and the asking price is reasonable; in fact, I think you could make quite a good profit for yourself. Why don't you come south for a few days to have a look at it? You can stay with me and Chris.'

'I don't know if I can get away at the moment.'

'Why? What's happening that's so important?'

'Well, there's...' Her eye fell on the envelope that had come through her letterbox the day before. 'There's quite a bit of concern about this quarry business. We've all been given two letters of protest to sign and send to the local council and to the quarry company. And there's going to be petitions, and a meeting to discuss it all, apparently.'

'But that won't affect you one way or the other, since you're moving.'

'I haven't made a definite decision. I need a bit of time to get used to losing Keith.'

A faint note of anxiety softened his voice. 'Are you all right, Clarissa? Alexandra and I both think you're being absolutely marvellous about everything, but if you need someone to talk to, I could try to get up there for a day or two. Pops wouldn't want you to feel that you've no one to lean on.'

'You mustn't think of coming back so soon,' Clarissa said hurriedly, and then wondered if she had been too swift. 'I mean – the people here are kind, and I don't feel lonely I just need to take a little longer to consider my future.'

'The flat won't be on the market for long. It's a desirable property in a nice area, and it's just right for you.'

'If I do decide to leave Prior's Ford and if the flat's gone by that time, it means it wasn't meant for me. You're being very kind, Steven, and I do appreciate it, but I don't want you to worry about me. I shall be perfectly all right, and I'll make a decision one way or the other soon, I promise you.'

Clarissa ended the call with a sigh of relief. She had lied, of course; she didn't feel up to making a sensible decision as yet, for her thoughts were still floating about in some sort of limbo.

Steven was right; she would have to start making decisions. But first, she needed to lay some demons to rest.

12

On the morning after Steven's phone call Clarissa woke to a clear and sunny day with wisps of soft white cloud bowled across the sky by a stiff breeze. It was a good day for a walk, she decided, collecting the clothes that Alastair Marshall had loaned her.

The last time she had gone walking it had been pouring with rain and she had been in no mood to pay attention to her surroundings, but today she took her time as she struck out into the country-side, tasting the fresh air and appreciating the roll-ing green hills scattered with copses, bushes and, here and there in the distance, neat whitewashed farms with their attendant byres and barns.

There were a few ruins, too, long-abandoned farmhouses and farm workers' cottages, roofs gone now they were no longer needed, glassless windows gaping like empty eye sockets and thick walls that had once sheltered families tumbling down to reveal big stone fireplaces where logs had blazed on winter nights. By one ruin, she could just make out the borders of a garden. There was something sad about a home that had once protected entire families and was then abandoned to the elements, no longer wanted. She shivered at the thought and then, realising that melancholy was threatening to creep back, she pushed it away firmly and marched on.

The lambing season had begun and some of the sturdy ewes in the fields had their lambs close by – small white bundles, some of them already grazing in imitation of their mothers. Clarissa took in a deep breath, fancying that as well as the clear country air she could taste salt from the Solway Firth, little more than a mile away but hidden by hills as rounded and comforting as a nursing mother's breast. No wonder they called it Mother Earth. She had read somewhere that a number of farmers from the north of England had moved across the border to buy farms in this area because the soil was so fertile.

Reaching the stile where she and Alastair had met, she paused for a moment. Two fields away, a man was repairing a drystone wall while a flock of sheep watched with interest from a polite distance. Clarissa laughed at the sight, and was about to climb the stile when she saw that there were cows in the field she was to cross. She hesitated, then realising that they were definitely cows, and her only access to Alastair's small cottage was through their field, she clambered over and set off. One or two of the animals looked up at her with large brown eyes, but most continued to graze on the rich green grass that never died off entirely in that part of Scotland, even in the winter months.

She crossed the field without any problems and headed to where a wisp of smoke rising from a chimney among the trees marked the cottage she sought.

When Alastair Marshall opened the door his face had an intent, closed-in look about it, and for a few seconds he stared at her as though she were a complete stranger. Clarissa's heart sank. He had forgotten her.

'Clarissa Ramsay – I brought back the clothes you loaned me when mine got soaked. I'm sorry to have taken so long...' She was about to thrust the bag at him and then hurry away, but suddenly recollection warmed his hazel eyes and his wide mouth curved in a smile.

'Of course. Come on in.' He stepped back, opening the door wide.

'Are you sure I'm not intruding? You're working, aren't you?' It didn't take a Sherlock Holmes or even a Doctor Watson to deduce that, for his shirt and jeans were daubed with paint. A long green streak ran from one cheekbone almost to the point of his chin and a brush dripping yellow colour was poised in his right hand.

'No – I mean, I *am* working, but I was thinking of taking a break. Please come in and I'll make some coffee. It's only instant,' he apologised as she stepped past him and into the cluttered cottage.

'Instant's fine. Here you are.' She handed the bag over. 'I laundered them.'

'That's kind of you.' He reached out to take the bag, realised that he still held a brush, put it down on the table by his easel, then took the clothes from her and deposited them on the third step of the staircase to the upper floor. 'Won't be a minute,' he said, and disappeared through the kitchen door, calling back over his shoulder, 'Have a seat – that one by the fire's the most comfortable.'

'Thanks,' Clarissa called after him, but instead of sitting down she wandered about the room, peering out through the small deep-set windows, which gave a breath-taking view right down the valley, and then turning her attention to the easel close by. The canvas was almost completed – a watercolour of the priory ruins that gave the village its name.

Several other paintings were propped against the whitewashed stone walls, many of them fairly small. Some were of the priory viewed from different angles, and there was one of the single-arch stone bridge over the river that ran through the village. There were views of the village street, too, with the hills beyond glimpsed over the roofs, and one of the old quarry with greenery softening the gashes where men had once sliced into the grey rock, which particularly held her attention.

'I like that one,' she said without turning round as she heard Alastair come into the room.

'It's a fascinating place. I admire the way nature's managed to reclaim its own. It only needs enough wind to blow a handful of earth and a few seeds into a crevice and before we know it, there's a tree or a clump of flowers. Even mosses add their own beauty. It's humbling – makes me realise we might think we rule the earth, but we don't and never will. Sugar?'

'Just some milk, thanks. This is lovely,' Clarissa said with genuine pleasure. She had found a painting of a country road with trees on either side curving overhead to meet and form a perfect arch. Sun shining through the trees dappled the road below. 'It looks as though the picture stretches on into the distance. I feel as though I could almost walk into it.'

'Really?' She wasn't looking at him, but she

could almost feel his voice glow with pleasure. 'That's good, because it's the way I wanted it to be. It's amazing – I was walking along that road last summer, and I thought it was a stone archway ahead, perhaps part of a viaduct. Then as I got nearer I realised it wasn't stone at all, but trees. And as I got nearer still, the single arch began to break up into an avenue of leafy arches. Fascinating.' He appeared by her side. 'Here's your coffee.'

'Thanks. You've been busy – are all your paintings watercolours?'

'No, I do oils as well. These' – he indicated the paintings by the wall – 'are for Ingrid MacKenzie – the woman who runs the Gift Horse.'

'The craft shop and tearoom in the village? She sells your work?'

'Amazingly, yes – some of it, at least. She'll be opening the shop at Easter, so she's looking for some new paintings from me. These subjects are popular – the priory and the village street and so on.' Alastair leaned one shoulder against the banister of the staircase. 'She usually sells a few every summer. The trees arching over the road are a new idea. We'll have to wait and see how the public like them – or *if* they like them.'

Clarissa settled in the chair by the fire, both hands curled about the large mug of coffee. 'I spent all afternoon yesterday drinking coffee and looking at pictures of me and Keith – my husband. Mainly our wedding photographs. They were so stilted – so posed.'

'That's special occasions for you. People can't relax when they're conscious of the fact that they're recording themselves for posterity.'

'I think that's exactly what we were both thinking about. That, or wondering whether we were doing the right thing. I didn't recognise us. We weren't who I thought we were going to be.' Then, as he said nothing, she went on, 'And when I'd looked my fill I finished the last of the coffee and poured out a large brandy and burned them. All of them. And some...' she hesitated, years of hiding her innermost thoughts and emotions cautioning her to say no more; then, deciding that the young man looking down at her was probably a better friend already than anyone had ever been, she plunged on, 'some other papers that he should never have left behind for me to read.'

'How did you feel after you'd burned them?'

'Different, in a healthy way. I made a plate of egg and chips and beans and ate the lot, then I went to bed early and slept all night.'

'No regrets in the morning, then?'

She smiled at him. 'Not a one.'

'Then you did the correct thing.'

She had been right to trust him; he understood where others might not. She nodded, and for a while they drank their coffee in a companionable silence. Finally, her mug empty, Clarissa said, 'I must go.'

'You don't have to.'

'I do, really. Perhaps we'll meet again.' She eased herself out of the soft, sagging chair and he took the mug from her.

'I'm sure we will. You know where I am if you ever need to talk.'

'And you know where I am if you ever feel like sharing a home-cooked meal,' Clarissa said.

'Oh – your umbrella,' he remembered suddenly as they got to the door. 'The one you loaned me that night – it's here somewhere...' He glanced at the clutter of items piled beneath the staircase.

'Keep it.'

'Are you sure?'

'Absolutely – it's not mine anyway, it belonged to my husband. I have my own.'

'Thanks, it'll come in useful.' He opened the door and she moved forward and then hesitated, turning back to look up at him. She offered her hand, and as he took it in his she said, 'Thank you.'

'For what?'

'Just – thank you,' Clarissa said.

The next edition of the *Dumfries News* carried an account of the possible quarry reopening on the front page, causing quite a stir in the village. Rumour was one thing, but to see the story in black and white was quite another.

As the village store sold newspapers as well as almost everything else, Sam Brennan, who usually glanced through the paper as he and Marcy laid out the copies on the counter, was one of the first to see the story.

'Here we go – now this quarry business is going to be expanded out of all proportion,' he grumbled.

'Let me see.' Marcy peered round his arm at the paper. 'Oh – good for Helen, she said there might be something in this week.' She took the paper from Sam and ran her eyes over the story. 'Look, we're all named – the others will be pleased.'

'I'm not – I don't like your name appearing in a newspaper.'

'It's none of your business where my name appears,' Marcy told him sharply. 'We're a protest committee – where's the sense in huddling round a table in the pub, muttering to each other? We have to have our voice heard. And talking of having voices heard, I know you tore up those letters that came through the door the other day.'

'What letters?' Sam blustered, turning red.

'The protest letters that have been put through all the doors. You don't have to sign and post them if you don't want to, but you're not the only person who lives in Rowan Cottage. You might have handed them over to me; though as it happens, I'd already got my own copies and they've been signed and posted.'

'Marcy, starting up the quarry again will bring in more business. We need the money – can't you see that?'

'We do all right.'

'We work hard and we work long hours. "All right" isn't good enough.'

'Then why did you set up shop in a village in the first place? If all you want is profit, you should have gone to Dumfries or Glasgow or Carlisle – somewhere with a lot of people.'

'I happen to like it here.'

'And so do I. I like village life and I don't want things to change.'

'I'm coming up to fifty-five now and I'm beginning to think about retirement. I don't want to work until I drop. We're partners, aren't we? What one wants, the other should want. So why are you bent on making a fool of me by going on to this committee? If making more money makes me happy then you should be happy about it too.'

Marcy gave him a long, hard look, hands fisted on her hips, then she said slowly, 'I've never heard such arrogance in my life. Look at your argument from my point of view – if doing something for the village by joining a committee makes me happy, as it does, then knowing that I'm happy should make you happy. Right?'

'Women–' Sam started, then the bell hanging over the door signalled the arrival of a customer, and the argument ended before it became a full-blown quarrel.

13

'Ralston-Kerr's been asked to lease the land to that quarry company in England,' Glen reported to the next committee meeting. 'He's tempted–'

'Who wouldn't be?' Pete McDermott put in, and was ignored.

'But he's not said aye or no to them because he reckons he wants to do what's best for the village. The trouble with that man is that he's too damned nice. Too unwilling to offend anyone by making a decision. And yet when it comes down to it, he's the one with the casting vote over this business. He's the man the villagers will listen to.'

'He's an honourable man – a gentleman,' Helen said. 'He's always wanted what's best for the village, but he doesn't know what really is best – employment, or peace and quiet.'

'If the quarry does start up again, he and his family won't be badly affected. His great-great-grandfather or whoever it was that built the hall wasn't daft – it's far enough away to avoid any dust the work'll cause. And the noise won't be so bad either – not as bad as it'll be for the rest of us. Selfish, I call it.'

'But he hasn't agreed yet to rent the land to the company, has he? Even though they've probably offered him a good financial deal. The Ralston-Kerrs' lives would be easier if they agreed to rent out the quarry land, but they haven't done that because they don't want to upset the villagers.'

'Whose side are you on, Helen?' Marcy Copleton wanted to know, and Helen flushed and tucked her hair behind her ears.

'I don't want the quarry any more than you do – that's why I'm here, taking notes, when I'd as soon be home with my family I'm just pointing out that Mr Ralston-Kerr's not just thinking of his own comfort.'

'Sitting on the fence, more like,' one of the other committee members grumbled. 'For all we know he might be holding out for more money.'

'That's not fair!' Helen snapped.

'No sense in us going at each other's throats.' Glen got to his feet, anxious to avert a feud within the committee. 'Same again? I'll get them in while the rest of you try to come up with some idea on what we should do next.'

As he opened the door the faint sound of voices from the bar was heard, then the sound was cut off sharply and the remaining committee members seated round the table stared down at their hands, trying hard to think of a good idea.

'What about your Duncan, Helen?' Lachie asked. 'He works for the Ralston-Kerrs – couldn't he have a word with them? They'd listen to him, surely.'

'Duncan doesn't want to be involved in this business. He wasn't best pleased about me being on this committee.'

'Oh. Right.'

Silence fell. Helen doodled on her notepad and wondered if Duncan had remembered to video *Coronation Street* for her. Perhaps he was too busy making sure the children were doing their homework. Or had he forgotten that, as well? She began to feel anxious. Duncan tended to leave all the domestic chores like making the children do their homework to her. He even left the gardening to her, saying it was enough to have to look after the Linn Hall grounds without gardening in his free time. And he wasn't good at remembering things.

She tried to push domestic concerns to one side in favour of rummaging about in the untidy broom cupboard she always felt her mind to be, but could come up with nothing worth suggesting to Glen when he returned. Instead, she started to note down some ideas for the novel she planned to write one day.

At last Glen returned, the door opening to admit another brief burst of cheerful noise as he brought in a tray filled with glasses.

'Petitions,' he said, dumping the tray on the table. 'That's the next thing, isn't it? Let's map one out and then you can tidy it up for us, Helen, and print it out. I'll photocopy it and we'll flood the place with 'em!'

Since the social hub of Prior's Ford tended to be the local pub, most of the arguments for and against the quarry took place there. It was getting to the stage, as Andrew Forsyth grumbled one night, where a man couldn't enjoy a quiet pint among friends any more.

'I get enough talk in the office about politics and the state the world's in today, without having to listen to more of it once I get home.'

'So which side are you on, then, Andy?' Glen spread his hands on the counter.

'Do I have to be on anyone's side? Whatever's decided, we can't do much to change things.'

'But that's where you're wrong. We're the very folk that should put our tuppence in, since we live here. We're taxpayers, aren't we – income tax, council tax and every other damned stealth tax this government can think of into the bargain. We've got more right to speak out than any of the councillors, cos we're the public.'

'Ah, but what do we elect councillors for?' one of the other customers chimed in. 'It's to make decisions for us, isn't it?'

'And sometimes they need to be told what decisions we want them to make,' Glen was saying, when a man marched into the public bar and dumped a handful of screwed-up paper in front of him.

'I don't like unasked-for junk mail and I've got a lad coming out of school next year lookin' for a job,' he said loudly. 'And if he can get one in Linn Quarry that's fine by me. And now I'll have a half pint of beer and a whisky chaser.'

'Fair enough, Jock,' Glen said amicably, and served him.

'Had much of that?' Andrew asked, grinning, when the customer had moved to a table with his drinks.

'A fair amount,' Libby told him.

'Some, but not much,' Glen countered, dropping the unwanted letters into a waste bin behind the counter. 'As long as Jock and others like him go on drinkin' here I'm all for 'em havin' the right to their opinions, same as I've a right to mine. It's a free country. I hope you and Jenny have signed the letters and posted them, Andy.'

'Ah now, that would be telling,' Andrew said enigmatically. 'As you say, it's a free country.'

Sam Brennan's reluctance to have a petition in the village store exasperated Marcy.

'No matter how we might feel about village activities, it's our duty to give folk access to information.' She slapped the petition onto the counter and scrawled her name in determined black swirls and loops along the first line of the first page. 'There now – I formally declare this petition open. May it and all the others save Prior's Ford from noise, dust and lorries.'

'I'm not signing it,' Sam told her, 'and I don't think you should have either.'

'Just because we live together, it doesn't mean I have to agree with you on everything. I like Prior's Ford just as it is – peaceful.'

'So you don't care if business is slow.'

'Who needs a fortune? As I said, I like things as they are,' Marcy retorted, and went off to restock shelves.'

It was the end of March, and Clarissa had been widowed for almost two months, yet still she could not make a decision as to whether or not she should sell the house and move back south.

She was browsing along the shelves in the village store, not even able to make up her mind about what she wanted to have for her lunch, when she met Alastair Marshall.

'How are you?' His face split into its easy grin.

'Very well, thank you. Isn't it a pleasant morning?'

'Not bad for the time of year.'

'Can I offer you a cup of coffee?' Clarissa heard herself say before she realised she was going to say it.

'Now? I mean, this morning?'

'Yes, if you've got the time.'

'I do. Thanks, I'd like that. I've just got a couple of other things to get,' he said, and hurried off. She stood looking after him, a smile on her face.

They arrived at the checkout at the same time, and Alastair stepped back. 'After you, Mrs Ramsay.'

'I hope you've both signed the petition against the quarry,' Marcy Copleton said as she started to lift items from Clarissa's basket.

'I have.' Alastair nodded.

'I haven't, yet,' Clarissa admitted.

'It's right there – complete with pen. The more

the merrier.'

'You leave Mrs Ramsay alone, Marcy – no sense in folk signing something if they don't believe in it,' Sam snapped from behind the post office grille.

'We all have to stand up and be counted. We're all in this together.'

'That's my problem – I might be moving back to England,' Clarissa explained, 'so I don't think I'm entitled to have an opinion.'

'Oh, you're not going to leave us, are you? You've got a lovely house here, and it's such a nice part of the world. A nice *peaceful* part of the world,' Marcy emphasised, glaring at Sam, who glared back.

'Yes, I do like it here, but I'm still trying to work out what's best.'

'Well, I hope you stay. That's six pounds twenty-seven pence.' Marcy put Clarissa's ten pound note into the till and scooped change out with practised speed.

Clarissa put the coins in her pocket and then, on impulse, picked up the pen and signed the petition. Marcy smiled and thanked her, while Sam scowled.

'Look here, Marcy,' Clarissa heard him say as she left the shop, 'you shouldn't bludgeon folk into signing your petition when they're not sure what they think...'

She missed Marcy's reply, but as she began to walk slowly along the pavement, waiting for Alastair to catch up with her, she could hear the sharp note in the woman's voice.

'If people aren't careful,' Alastair said thoughtfully, reaching her side and taking her basket, 'this quarry business is going to split the village.'

'You're not talking about Marcy and Mr Brennan, are you? They seem such a close couple.' Right from the first, Clarissa had envied the way the two of them worked together, good business partners as well as life partners.

'Probably not, in their case. They both have minds of their own, but arguing's never damaged their relationship before, so I doubt if it will now. Though one of them's going to have to lose and I hope it isn't Marcy – partly because I like her and partly because I know how much she loves this place. I was really talking about the community as a whole – neighbour disagreeing with neighbour. Feelings are beginning to run high in the Neurotic Cuckoo in the evenings. It must have been like this when the quarry closed in the first place – everyone railing against it and wondering how life could go on without the work it had brought to the village. Have you noticed that most folk hate change?'

'I used to be like that myself,' Clarissa said, and felt, rather than saw, his sidelong glance at her.

'But not now?'

'Sometimes it's forced on you and you can't do anything but accept it and make the most of it.'

'Good for you. Some people just crumble or opt out.'

'That,' Clarissa said, 'is not an option for me. Or so I've come to realise.'

'Even better for you!' he said as they reached Willow Cottage.

14

'Do you know how to drive?' Clarissa asked when she and Alastair had settled at the kitchen table with mugs of coffee and the biscuit box within easy reach.

'My father bought me a provisional licence for my seventeenth birthday and taught me himself. He was very proud of the fact that I passed the test first time, but the truth was that I was so scared of annoying him I couldn't allow myself to fail. Not that I've ever been able to afford a car.'

'Would you teach me? I've got a car,' Clarissa said as he stared at her, a chocolate-wafer biscuit halfway to his mouth, 'though it's not mine, it's Keith's. Well, I suppose it *is* mine now.'

'Wouldn't you be better going to a proper driving school?'

'If I must, but I'd rather be taught by someone I know; someone I feel comfortable with.'

'We've only just met,' he pointed out gently.

'I know, but–' To her horror, Clarissa felt her face growing hot. She looked down at the table as she struggled on, 'But somehow, you've helped me to feel more confident about myself. Keith started giving me lessons when we were first married, but he tended to get impatient – and when I failed my test, that was that.'

'Well – I suppose we could give it a go – see how we both feel about it. But we'd have to be honest with each other,' Alastair said. 'If you felt uncomfortable with my teaching methods you'd have to say so, and I'd do the same if I felt it wasn't working.'

'Agreed. I'll pay you, of course. Yes, I will,' she insisted as he began to shake his head.

'The occasional coffee would be fine, and perhaps an invitation to a meal now and again.'

'You'll get those anyway. I'll find out what the going rate is and pay you.'

'Are you sure you can afford it?'

'Quite sure. And if you don't mind me saying so, you could probably do with the money. After all, I'll be taking you away from your painting and any other work you might be doing. Do we have a deal?'

Alastair chewed on his lower lip for a moment. It didn't seem right to take money from someone who was turning out to be a friend, but on the other hand, she was quite right when she guessed he could do with the extra income.

'We have a deal,' he said, and when Clarissa stretched her hand across the table, he shook it.

'Good. When we've finished our coffee we'll go and inspect the car.'

When the garage's automatic door rolled up to reveal a large grey car it seemed to Alastair that its headlamps were looking him up and down scornfully – as well they might...

'It's a Jaguar,' he said huskily.

'Yes, it is. Keith loved Jaguars. He got a new one every two years.'

'This isn't a car for learners.'

'Isn't it? I'll get something more suitable, then,' Clarissa said briskly. 'I can't afford to be sentimental. In any case, I would probably be worrying all the time in case it got scratched or dented. Keith wouldn't rest in his grave if he knew I was learning to drive in his beloved car. When he tried to teach me, it was in a much cheaper car than this one, bought specially. It was going to be my little runabout, but when I failed my test he sold it.'

'You could have tried again.'

'There didn't seem to be much sense in that. In any case, Keith liked to do all the driving – he always liked to be in control,' Clarissa said, and immediately wished she hadn't let that remark pop out. It made her feel disloyal. 'He was a very good driver, everyone said so,' she hurried on, 'and we both agreed it wasn't worthwhile me having another shot at my licence.'

In actual fact, it was Keith who hadn't thought it worthwhile. He had no time for failure, though he had tried to be nice about her being unable to pass her test first time.

'Never mind, dear,' he said as he drove her away from the test centre, 'some people are natural drivers and some aren't. And it's not as though you need to be able to drive, is it? You've got me as your chauffeur, and several of your friends can drive. We'll sell the car tomorrow and you can bank the money as a consolation prize.'

'Is it true that you're either a natural driver or you'll never be a driver?' she asked now, eyeing the Jaguar's opulent curves. The very sight of the car that had been Keith's had begun to sap her enthusiasm for driving lessons. Perhaps he had been right and she was best to stick to public transport.

'No, it's rubbish. Learning to drive is like learning to ride a bike, or to read and write. Some people might need to have several goes at it, but there's no reason why they shouldn't succeed eventually,' Alastair said, and Clarissa immediately began to feel her confidence returning.

Alastair had never in his life seen such a well-ordered garage. Everything was hung up, or placed carefully on shelves. The interior was a veritable jewel box, with the Jaguar in pride of place like a fabulous diamond in a flawless setting. And – the very thought made the hairs on the back of his neck tingle – the car seemed to be aware of its own perfection.

He touched the bonnet very gently with the tips of his fingers, and then jerked his hand back as Clarissa said from the doorway, 'Would you like to try it out?'

'I couldn't!' Alastair's father and brother loved cars, though neither of them had ever owned anything as magnificent as a Jaguar, but to him, cars were like buses – a useful way of getting from one place to another, and a very handy way of transporting items. This one, however, was more like a mobile Peacock Throne than a useful vehicle.

'Of course you could. You've got your driving licence, haven't you? And it hasn't been driven since – for ages. Steven – my stepson – didn't have time to take it out when he visited, though he did run the engine for several minutes. It probably needs an outing. I'll fetch the keys,' Clarissa said, and hurried into the house. When she returned, she had her coat on.

'Come on, then.' She tossed the keys to Alastair, seized by a sudden sense of adventure. 'Let's go!'

It was like floating on a soft, luxurious cloud. The car handled like a dream, and once Alastair had overcome his initial terror at being in charge of such a magnificent beast he began to relax and enjoy himself. As he drove the Jaguar through the village and towards the open countryside he revelled in the expressions on the faces of the people they passed.

Once out in the country he was able to increase speed and the car responded immediately, as though it had been waiting for such an event. Several miles further on it soared with ease up a fairly steep hill, and at the top he drew it into a parking space and turned off the almost silent engine. The two of them got out and leaned on a gate to look at the fields, resembling the differently shaped pieces of cloth in a patchwork quilt, stretching below them.

'Look!' Clarissa pointed to a group of lambs scampering about together, butting and chasing and thoroughly enjoying themselves. 'Aren't they beautiful?'

The breeze carried the shrill, anxious cries of a solitary lamb seeking its mother, and the deeper, reassuring baa-ing from the ewe. They watched as mother and child were reunited and the little one nuzzled into its mother's body.

'How could anyone eat lamb?' Clarissa wanted to know. Alastair, who was very partial to a plate of well-cooked lamb, especially local lamb fed on the best grass, said nothing.

'It's a beautiful part of the world, isn't it?'

'If you like it so much, why not stay?'

'I don't know yet if I belong here.'

'People can belong anywhere if they put their minds to it.'

While Clarissa was turning the thought over in her mind a cloud covered the sun. The shadow it caused began to rush across the fields towards where they stood, turning the emerald-green grass to a deeper, darker green as it came. She shivered and turned back to the car.

'Let's drive back to Prior's Ford,' she said.

'I'm going to sell this car and buy something easier to drive,' Clarissa said as Alastair eased the Jaguar into the garage, 'and then have another shot at getting my licence – if you're still willing to teach me.'

'Didn't you say your husband had grown children? Surely they should have the car.'

'I suggested that to them, but Alexandra already has a lovely car, and Steven says a machine like this would only attract thieves. So – I shall sell this one and use the money to buy something more suitable. And I'll still have enough left over to pay you for driving lessons. That way, we'll both benefit.'

'You should find out what it's worth, first – and not from the people you hope to sell to. They'll want to pay you as little as they can.'

'That's a good idea.' Clarissa pressed the remote control and the garage door began to rumble down. 'Let's go inside and have another coffee to celebrate. Or something stronger – I think we could safely say that the sun's gone over the yardarm by now, whatever that means.'

When they went into the house her eye fell on the protest letters, still lying on the hall table. Once Alastair had left, she signed them, slipped them into their envelopes, and hurried across the green to post them in the pillar box outside the village store.

She had made two decisions that day, and it felt good. There was still another to be made and, as it was the most difficult one, it would have wait until she felt able to face it.

'We're on our way,' Glen Mason told his wife gleefully as he placed writing pads on their living-room table in readiness for the forthcoming meeting of the protest committee. 'The petitions are all over the village and it looks as though all the folk opposed to the quarry being started up again have sent off their protest letters. The next thing to do is organise a meeting in the village hall.'

'You're getting too involved in this business, Glen. I thought we came here for a quiet life, away from – all that hassle we hated. Why can't you leave it to the villagers themselves to run this committee?'

'We're the pub landlord and landlady – it's part of our job to become involved in local interests.'

'Involved, yes, but you're out in front, leading the band. The local paper's already interested, and who knows what that might stir up?'

'Don't you fret, I know what I'm doing. Everything's under control. I even remembered to arrange for Alastair to come in tonight to help you behind the bar. Where did I put those biros I bought?' Glen wondered. 'Ah yes, in the kitchen drawer.' He bustled out, giving his wife's bottom a friendly pat as he went by

Libby sighed. Glen had always loved being in the thick of things. Back home, when they were running the corner shop together, he had been the coordinator of the local neighbourhood watch scheme, and she had lost count of the number of other causes he had fought. He had been well known for his determination to make life better for everyone in the neighbourhood, which was one of the reasons why, when their lives suddenly and unexpectedly changed, they had to move to a place where nobody knew them.

They had been content here, running the Neurotic Cuckoo and being part of a small community, before the dratted quarry business flared up, reigniting Glen's love of organisation. She knew it was born of a desire to be important and looked up to. That was just the way Glen was, and she still loved him, warts and all.

But she wished he could settle for what they had now – and if he didn't, she feared they might both come to regret it.

'We'll invite representatives from the council and the quarry company to speak to the meeting,' Glen said two hours later. 'Helen, we'll need letters of invitation to both lots, which means we must have a date to give them.'

Robert Kavanagh raised his eyebrows. 'Isn't setting a date before sending out the invitations like putting the cart before the horse?'

'We could invite them to a meeting at a date to be arranged – giving them advance warning,' Marcy suggested, while Helen wanted to know, 'What exactly do I say in these letters?'

'Oh – the usual.' Glen gave an airy sweep of one hand. 'The local community would like to know more about the quarry plans and how they'll affect our everyday lives. Keep it polite, though. Could you do them tomorrow? Then bring them to the pub so that we can go over them together. The sooner the better, love.'

Helen's heart sank. At this rate, she was going to take ages to complete her writing course and get started on her novel. She wished she could turn the clock back and find a way of wiping all thoughts of the old quarry from the English company's minds.

15

There was something about Alastair Marshall that made Clarissa feel good. She didn't know what it was, or why he had that effect on her, but when she was with him, her problems always seemed to be solvable.

The day after he agreed to teach her to drive on condition that she find a smaller car, she woke up filled with an inner sense of purpose she had not known since the day Keith put the wedding ring on her finger and took control of her life.

Since she had returned to the village as a widow,

breakfast had consisted of half a slice of toast and a cup of tea, but today she made a bowl of porridge and enjoyed every mouthful. She finished off with two cups of tea and a full slice of toast with marmalade, then collected her shopping basket and went out into the spring sunshine.

Instead of going directly to the village store she bypassed it and walked down River Lane, between the council houses on one side and the private housing estate on the other to where the local garage stood at the end of the lane and beside the river. An overalled man working beneath the bonnet of a car straightened as she approached and came to meet her, wiping his hands on a cloth that looked more likely to add oil to the skin than to remove it.

'Can I help you, madam?'

'I hope so. My husband died a few months ago and I want to sell his car. I've been advised to find out what a fair price would be.'

'Mrs ... Ramsay, isn't it? A Jaguar?'

'How did you know?'

He grinned at her. 'My mum used to say that if someone saw you pick a feather up from the gutter outside the post office, by the time you got home it'd be all round the village that you'd stolen a hen. You want me to have a look at the car, is that it?'

'That's right, but I can't drive so I can't bring it here.'

He nodded. 'I could look in after work – about seven tonight do you?'

Another decision made, Clarissa thought as she returned home. And at last she felt strong enough

139

to cope with her most serious problem – something that had been hanging over her head or, to be honest, dragging around after her like a weight chained to her ankle – ever since the day she had decided to finish clearing out Keith's study.

After lunch she poured herself a generous glass of wine and carried it into the living room where she put on a CD of soothing, easy listening music – the sort of music that Keith, a classical man, couldn't stand. Then she settled into an armchair and picked up the telephone.

Stella Bartholomew, her closest friend ever since the two of them met at teacher training college, was at home. 'Clarissa! How lovely to hear from you – how are you?'

'I'm very well, Stella.'

'My dear, I didn't know whether to phone you or leave you alone. I know that when Richard died there was so much to do; then I went through a period of needing to be left alone, d'you remember?'

'Yes, I do.'

'I've been thinking about you so much. When are you moving back south?'

'I haven't decided yet.'

'But what's the point in staying up in Scotland? Your friends are here, the book group and the card club – and me. I miss you, Clarissa. D'you want me to come to you for a few days? Sometimes it helps to talk things over with someone you can trust.'

Someone she could trust? Clarissa took a sip of wine and closed her eyes for a second, then opened them and said, 'No, don't do that. There's something else that I want you to do for me, though. Something I really, really want you to do, Stella.'

'Anything – just name it!'

'I want you to get out of my life, and stay out of it,' Clarissa said pleasantly, and took another sip from her glass.

She heard Stella's sharp intake of breath, and felt she could see her former friend's face – her dark eyes wide with shock and her full lips parted. One beautifully manicured hand had probably flown to Stella's throat, or to her short, ever-immaculate black hair. Clarissa took another sip of wine and waited.

'What did you say?' Stella's voice, when it finally came, trembled with shock.

'You heard me, and you're not a fool – not you. I was the fool, wasn't I? I found your letters. Keith didn't even have the sense to destroy them. Not that he'd any reason to,' Clarissa went on in a conversational voice. 'He probably enjoyed reading them over and over again. You said such flattering things about him, and my husband always enjoyed flattery. I'm sure your letters massaged his ego.'

Just as Stella's slim, capable hands probably massaged – don't even begin to think those sort of thoughts, Clarissa told herself sharply, and managed to keep her own voice under control as she went on, 'You know what men are like. In fact, you probably know more about men than I do. How could you do that to me, Stella?' she said in a sudden burst of hurt anger. 'We've been best friends ever since college – how *could* you have an affair with my husband behind my back?'

'It wasn't – I didn't mean to.' Stella's voice, normally confident, was tearful. 'You know how hard it was for me when Richard had his stroke – holding down a full-time job and trying to give the children as normal a family life as I could.'

'I admired you for it – at the time.' When Richard Bartholomew, a college lecturer, became an invalid, the two younger of Stella's three children were university students, still living at home. Stella had kept on with her job, brought in carers to look after Richard and been both mother and father to her offspring until they finished their education.

'It was so hard, Clarissa. I don't know how I would have managed without your support, and Keith's.'

Keith's support. Keith, who had grumbled about the time Clarissa devoted to Stella.

'When did it start, Stella – your affair with my husband?'

'You make it sound sordid and it wasn't. Please, Clarissa, try to–'

'When did it start?'

'When he helped me to sort out Richard's funeral, and then went through all his papers and advised me.'

'But that was six years ago,' Clarissa said in disbelief, and then, her voice rising, 'Keith and I had been married for *less than a year* when Richard died!'

'I was worn out by all the responsibility.' The tears were thickening Stella's voice now. Clarissa could almost see them welling up and rolling down her cheeks, carrying with them the mascara Stella always wore. 'Keith was so kind – I couldn't help myself.'

'But we were in the first year of our marriage!'

'I couldn't *help* myself,' Stella wailed in return. 'I was so *vulnerable* at the time!'

'You – you bitch!'

Stella was sobbing noisily. 'Clarissa, how could you say such a terrible thing to me?'

'Just be glad that I'm not close enough to scratch your eyes out.'

'I told you – Keith offered me a shoulder to cry on, that's all.'

'And were you still crying on his shoulder right up until he died? The last letter you sent was just before he went to visit Alexandra and Steven. And, I now realise, you.'

'You read them all? But they were private – personal!'

'What do you mean, personal? They were in official envelopes, Stella, with typed labels. How was I to know they were personal?'

'That was Keith's idea. I collected return envelopes from all the junk mail I got and put labels on them with his typed address so you wouldn't suspect–'

'This gets worse!'

'It's not as bad as you're making it out to be. Keith loved you – he would never have left you.'

'I'll bet you tried to persuade him, though.'

'I – of course not. I knew how much he respected you. We both did. And there's something you've forgotten, Clarissa,' Stella rushed on, her voice getting stronger, 'I loved Keith too. I'm mourning him too. We should be comforting each other, not quarrelling. Keith wouldn't have wanted us to fall out over him.'

'This conversation,' Clarissa said, 'is becoming bizarre. Good night, Stella.'

'Wait! What about my letters?'

'What about them?'

'Can I have them back, please?'

'Oh, I don't know about that,' Clarissa said thoughtfully. 'I suppose I could return them care of Roger or Anna or perhaps Penelope.' Stella's three children were all in their twenties now, and had all done well. Anna and Penelope were married, and Anna was soon to make Stella a grandmother. Clarissa doubted if she, or her siblings, would care to know about their mother's underhand affair with her best friend's husband.

'Clarissa, you *wouldn't!* You *couldn't!*'

'Of course I wouldn't. That's the difference between you and me, Stella. I'm honourable, and you're not. Nor, I now know, was Keith. I burned the letters, and now I'm going to end this call because it's becoming very tedious. Goodbye.'

Clarissa hung up, ignoring the sudden babble of sound from the receiver, and finished her wine. Then she poured herself another glass. She was going to enjoy getting rid of Keith's car – his pride and joy.

'It's like driving pure silk or floating on a magic carpet,' Alastair said as he drove the Jaguar along the road to Kirkcudbright. 'Are you absolutely sure you want to sell it?'

'Of course – you said yourself it isn't the sort of car a learner should use.'

'Once you get your licence you might wish you

still had this beauty You could always get something cheaper for lessons, and keep the Jag for later – if you can afford to do that.'

'I don't think a Jaguar is my kind of car,' Clarissa said blithely. Mr Harper had given her the name of a car sales company in the town, and now she directed Alastair to it.

'I'm not very good with sales people,' he said anxiously as he eased the car into the forecourt. 'I can't bargain.'

'Don't worry, I'll see to it. I know what Keith paid for the car, and Mr Harper's an honest man. I don't intend to accept a penny less than the amount he named.' Clarissa gave his knee a swift, comforting pat before getting out of the car.

The Jaguar had been spotted immediately, and as soon as they entered the showroom a salesman approached. 'Good morning, madam – sir. What can I do for you?'

'I want to learn to drive, and my instructor,' Clarissa indicated Alastair with a wave of one hand, 'tells me that my late husband's Jaguar isn't the right car for a beginner. So I've decided to trade it in for something smaller.'

It was interesting, she thought, that whenever men spotted the Jaguar, their eyes suddenly flared. 'Of course, madam.' The salesman had to struggle to bring his eyes under control. 'Our new models are here, under cover.'

'I'm looking for a small, second-hand car. I'll probably be a bit rough on it at the beginning, and I certainly don't want something brand new. That can come later,' Clarissa said sweetly.

'Any particular colour?' he enquired as he

ushered them outside to where used cars waited in ranks, each with a huge price sticker on its windscreen. 'We find that ladies tend to choose their cars by colour rather than make.'

'Good heavens no,' Clarissa said airily. 'As long as it's efficient, reliable and easy to drive I don't much care what it looks like.'

Keith had always taken weeks if not months to choose a new car, but Clarissa was amazed at how bored she became as they moved from one row to the other, with Alastair and the salesman talking about horsepower, miles per gallon and reliability. It was a relief when Alastair settled on one particular model, a neat, dark blue car.

'You'll want to test drive it, of course.'

'Of course. In fact,' Clarissa told the salesman, 'I'd like to ask my local garage owner to have a look at it, if you don't mind letting us take the car for an hour or perhaps two?'

'Our pleasure, madam. And if you could give me the keys, we can have a look at your Jaguar while you're away.'

'It's nice of them to trust us with their car for so long,' Clarissa said as she and Alastair headed back to Prior's Ford.

'I don't think they'll worry about this car when they've got your Jaguar as their hostage. Nice little mover, this one.'

'It feels quite comfortable. Would you buy it?'

'Oh yes, if I had the asking price – which isn't bad, by the way You're getting power steering, airbags, a radio' – he switched it on – 'and cassette player and central locking. And it's five door, too.'

Clarissa twisted around in her seat, checking

146

each door, then said, 'I can only find four.'

'The fifth is the boot. This is a hatchback.'

'Really?' She had no idea what a hatchback was, but she was happy to take his word for it. 'The colour's quite nice, isn't it?'

'Nothing wrong with it at all.'

'That's what I think. What kind of car is it?'

'A Vauxhall Astra.'

'Sounds good,' said Clarissa, already basking in the glow of ownership.

16

When Clarissa and Alastair returned to the car salesroom the man who had dealt with them earlier insisted on giving them coffee before settling them down at a small table.

'So – you like the Astra?'

'It's just what I'm looking for,' Clarissa told him.

'And you're happy with our asking price?'

'Absolutely'

'Good. Now, about the Jaguar…'

This was the part that Alastair had been dreading. He glanced over at Clarissa, perched on the edge of her chair, the coffee mug clasped in both hands and a trusting smile on her face, and his heart sank. He gnawed at his lower lip wondering if he should try to argue for a thousand pounds, or perhaps two thousand, above the salesman's offer. Whatever it was, it was surely not going to be as much as it should be.

But no sum was mentioned. Instead, the man scribbled something on a sheet of paper and pushed it over to Clarissa, who read it and then, still with the smile curving her lips, said gently, 'Oh dear, I think it's worth more than that, don't you? Especially when I'm buying the – what is it, Alastair?'

'Astra.'

'Oh yes,' Clarissa said, 'such a pretty name. Astra. It sounds like a flower – an aster. Or a star in the heavens. Come to think of it' – she beamed at the two men – 'Astra is an anagram of "a star". I wonder if the makers realised that?'

'I really wouldn't know. The thing is, Mrs Ramsay, we have to overhaul your car, and get it into a saleable condition.'

'Isn't it already in a saleable condition? My husband always treated his cars with love and consideration. I'm sure you could eat your dinner off the engine if you had to, without coming to any harm.'

'Well...' The man made a show of deliberating, and then, shaking his head, he took back the paper and wrote something else on it. 'There, madam, will that suit you?'

Clarissa studied the paper and then held out her hand. 'May I?'

The salesman handed over his pen and watched, his jaw dropping, as she drew a swift, firm line through his latest offer and then, just as decisively and swiftly, wrote something under it.

'Less, of course, the trade-in,' she murmured, and wrote something else then drew a line and finished with a total. 'There.'

The salesman looked at her latest figure and swallowed hard. 'Mrs Ramsay, I doubt if we could–'

Clarissa's smile vanished and a crisp snap came into her voice. 'Young man, I spent my entire working life as a teacher, which means I know when I'm being taken advantage of. And if you were to speak to any of my former pupils, I think you would find they still remember the day they were foolish enough to try to pull the wool over my eyes.' She gathered up her bag and got to her feet. 'I'm sure there are other cars in other showrooms that will suit me just as well as the Astra. Thank you for your time.'

'Wait! I'll just have a word with the manager.' The man bounced to his feet. 'More coffee?'

'No thank you, we really should be on our way, shouldn't we, Alastair? We've taken up more than enough of your time.'

'One moment, that's all it will take – honestly!' The man hurried off.

'Clarissa Ramsay, I didn't realise you were such a hard-headed businesswoman!'

'I'm not, but as I said to that young man, a school teacher quickly learns to tell when he or she is being taken for a ride. Mr Harper told me how much they could pay me and still make a reasonable profit on the car, and that's what I'm holding them to. Nothing more – and nothing less.'

'I think you lulled him into a false sense of security with that discussion about the anagram of Astra,' Alastair said, and to his astonishment, Clarissa winked at him.

149

'That,' she said sweetly, 'was the intention.'

He gave a shout of laughter, then warned her, 'You may have to try a few more showrooms before you get the result you're looking for.'

'I think you could be wrong,' Clarissa was saying when the salesman returned, wreathed in anxious smiles. 'And how I wish,' she said as they returned to the Jaguar, 'that I was a betting woman. I could have won five pounds from you there.'

'And deserved every penny of it. Remind me not to play cards for money with you.' He opened the passenger door and ushered her into the seat.

'Thank you for your assistance,' Clarissa said as they drove back to Prior's Ford.

'It was a pleasure. And I'll be happy to drive you back next Wednesday to hand this beauty over and collect your new car.'

'Thank you again. I have a casserole in the freezer, and I bought a bottle of wine in the village store this morning, in anticipation. Please come for dinner tonight.'

'I look forward to it,' Alastair said warmly.

'So do I,' Clarissa said.

The council and the quarry firm agreed to a meeting and set a date, and Glen lost no time in booking the village hall. The next task was to appoint a chairman for the occasion.

'We need someone who hasn't shown themselves for or against the quarry. What about Hector Ralston-Kerr?'

'I doubt if he'd be willing to get dragged into it, given what he said when you spoke to him,' Robert argued. 'And that offer to lease the land means he's got a financial interest in the quarry restarting. What about the minister?'

'Does anyone know if she signed and posted the protest letters that were put through her letterbox?' Glen asked his committee.

'She refrained from signing the petition in the shop because she felt she couldn't be seen to be taking sides,' Marcy said, 'and she hasn't mentioned it in her sermons – other than praying that the villagers can find a way to settle any problems they may be experiencing. I doubt if she's sent the letters out.'

'Then I'll go and see her tomorrow,' Glen said.

On the following afternoon he was about to knock on the manse door when someone called, 'Hey, man,' from the street and he turned to see Ethan on his way home from school.

'Looking for Naomi?' he asked as he jogged through the gate and up the path.

'D'you know if she's home?'

'Will be. This is the day she writes her sermon – I warn you, she's like a bear with a sore head when she's writing her sermons.' The boy, almost as tall as Glen himself, grinned at him as he fished a key from his pocket. 'Is your journey really necessary, is what you have to ask yourself.' He had Naomi's lilting way of speaking.

'It's important, yes.'

'Okay, man, on your own head be it.' Ethan twirled the key in the lock and opened the door. 'Best go into the living room and I'll tell her you're here. Mr Mason, isn't it?'

'That's right.' The narrow hall was crowded. A

bike leaned against one wall, and a skateboard was tucked beneath a row of pegs crowded with coats, jackets, anoraks and scarves. Ethan dropped his bulging school bag at the bottom of the stairs and indicated the room to the left with a nod of a neatly shaped head covered with tight black curls.

The living room was as crowded as the hall. Books filled three bookcases and were piled on the floor as well. An overflowing knitting bag took up an armchair by the fireplace and a jacket had been tossed over the back of the opposite chair. Glen started to sit down on the couch, then jumped upright again with a barely subdued yelp as a marmalade cat, all but invisible against the brightly patterned couch cover, shot out from beneath his backside. As it darted through the door Naomi came in and narrowly avoided tripping over the animal.

'Casper, watch where you're going,' she scolded him. 'We're going to break each other's legs one of these days!' Then, bathing Glen in her wide, warm smile, 'Mr Mason, what can I do for you? Did Ethan offer you some tea? I'll switch on the fire, it's a little chilly in here, don't you think?'

While she talked she seemed to flow about the room, gathering up the knitting bag and the jacket from the back of the couch, secreting them with that smooth sleight of hand ease that women seemed to be born with, and switching on the electric fire.

'Er – no tea, thank you. I won't take up much of your time; I understand you're busy with your sermon.'

'Ethan's been talking, has he? Take as long as

you want, Mr Mason, I'm glad of the chance to leave the sermon on its own for a while. Please, sit down.'

She indicated the couch, and when he had lowered himself on to it, giving it a swift glance first to make sure the cat hadn't returned, she settled down on one of the armchairs. She was in civilian clothes today – a long wraparound skirt and a loose-fitting pale grey sweater.

'I'm here as the chairman of the quarry protest committee. You may have heard we've managed to secure a meeting with representatives of both the council and the firm that wants to start working the quarry again. It's to be in the village hall two weeks tomorrow – in the evening, of course.'

'You've done well to get a meeting agreed so quickly. In my experience it usually takes months.'

'Yes, we are fortunate.'

'Two weeks tomorrow in the village hall. Isn't that...?'

'The line dancers have kindly agreed to give up their regular evening booking so we can get the meeting over and done with as soon as possible. We don't want it to drag on for any longer than it must.'

'You know,' Naomi said thoughtfully, 'I really fancy the idea of line dancing. It looks like fun – but I never seem to find the time to join things just for fun.'

Glen eyed her ample figure and tried to imagine the minister line dancing in a Stetson and fringed jacket; then, aware that she was watching him with some amusement, as though reading his thoughts, he dragged himself back to the

153

business in hand.

'The thing is, we'd like you to chair the meeting.'

'Oh.' The smile disappeared from her generous mouth and she sat upright. 'I don't know about that, Mr Mason. As minister of this parish I should remain neutral when it comes to matters like the quarry. As you must be aware, it's beginning to cause a lot of discussion even to the point where families are disagreeing among themselves.'

'Your neutrality is the very reason why we need you in the chair. You haven't made a single comment in public on the matter, which means that nobody could accuse you of trying to sway the village one way or the other. You know what folk are like,' Glen rushed on as she continued to look doubtful, 'without someone they respect in the chair, they'll just turn it into a talking shop – start arguing with each other and that sort of thing. We don't want our invited guests to think we can't conduct a public meeting properly. You're the perfect choice to chair it.'

'Well, since you put it like that – as long as I'm not expected to put forward views of my own – because I haven't got any, not where this quarry business is concerned.'

'Thank you! Now then, the meeting's starting at seven, and our guests are arriving an hour earlier. Can I tell them to gather here for refreshments first, so they can walk to the hall with you? We'll provide the refreshments,' Glen hurried on as the minister shot him a startled look. 'Libby will see to the food, and I'll provide tea and coffee, and perhaps a bottle of wine or sherry – both might be best.'

154

'I've only got mugs and some of them are chipped – Ethan's just beginning to think of washing the occasional mug after use, but he hasn't worked out yet how to remove it from under the tap without chipping the rim off the mug.'

'I'll provide everything – cups, saucers, plates, cutlery, glasses and napkins.' Glen got to his feet and shook her hand warmly 'Thank you again!'

'I can't guarantee this place will look much tidier than it is today,' Naomi said as she followed him along the hall to the front door. 'But I'll have a good shot at it. Perhaps I can get some kind soul to adopt Ethan for the evening – or even the week.'

17

As Glen reached the Neurotic Cuckoo on his way back from visiting the minister, a young woman warmly dressed in an anorak, corduroy trousers and sturdy walking boots came towards him, moving with a lithe, easy gait. A brown knitted hat was pulled down over her forehead; two thick, bright red plaits bounced against her chest as she walked and a bulging rucksack was slung over her shoulders.

'Hello, there,' she called as he was about to open the pub door. 'Can you tell me how to get to Linn Hall?'

'Looking for Mr Ralston-Kerr, are you?'

'Mrs Ralston-Kerr. I've heard the estate uses casual labour.'

Glen nodded. 'They always need help during the summer. They'll probably be starting to look for temporary staff round about now.'

'That's handy, because I can't live on thin air, can I?' She grinned at him as though they had known each other for ages.

'You go up Kilmartin Road, at the side of the pub. Ten minutes' walk'll take you to the gates of the Hall, and then you've got another five minutes along the drive to the house. Go round to the back,' Glen advised her. 'Mrs Ralston-Kerr's usually to be found in the kitchen.'

'Thanks.' Her green eyes ran over him in a swift appraising glance. 'Live round here, do you?'

He indicated the public house with a jerk of one thumb. 'Right here, in the Neurotic Cuckoo. I'm the landlord.'

'If I get lucky, I'll become one of your regulars.'

'I look forward to it. You're welcome to come in for a drink now, before you go to the hall.'

'Thanks, but I'd best get on,' the girl said. 'Though if I don't find work I might drown my sorrows in your bar before I head off into the great blue yonder. Cheers.' Dimples showed in both rounded cheeks as she smiled up at him, her eyes sparkling like emeralds, and then she hoisted her rucksack into a more comfortable position on her back and went on her way.

Glen watched her go. A grand lass, he thought, and just the thing to brighten up the pub. If he was ten – well, maybe twenty years – younger, he mused, and if he wasn't happily married to his Libby, he could really fancy a girl like that.

As he opened the pub door and went inside he

had a broad grin on his face.

'What's got you so happy?' demanded Libby, who was polishing the bar.

'Oh – Naomi Hennessey's agreed to chair the meeting,' Glen told her. 'So that's one thing less to worry about.'

'I wish you'd never got involved in this committee, let alone agreeing to be the chairman.' Libby, who wasn't easily troubled, looked unhappy.

'You don't want a noisy quarry less than a mile away, do you?'

'No, but I don't want you making an exhibition of yourself either. We said when we found this place that all we were going to do was keep our heads down and enjoy life. But you couldn't resist getting involved, could you?'

Her husband patted her shoulder reassuringly. 'It'll be fine, you'll see. Fancy a brew?' he said.

Linn Hall's handsome wrought-iron gates had been taken down during World War Two and never replaced. The sign that read 'Linn Hall' was completely hidden now by the ivy that covered the stone gateposts, but Molly Ewing guessed from the two little gatehouses, one on either side of the entrance, that she had reached her destination. She paused for a moment, studying the drive that badly needed weeding, then murmuring to herself, 'Molly, girl – let the fun commence!' she started up towards the Hall.

She had just come within sight of the building when the sound of machinery caught her attention. Pushing her way into the overgrown shrubbery flanking the drive she saw a brown-haired young man on the far side of the large lawn, pruning bushes with an electric trimmer.

'Hmmm,' Molly murmured, surveying him thoughtfully.

Then she stepped back to the driveway, brushed herself down to remove any leaves or twigs she might have collected, and continued on her way.

Now they could no longer afford a staff of permanent gardeners, Hector and Fliss Ralston-Kerr relied on Duncan Campbell and on Lewis, who had done a college course on horticulture, to keep the gardens and vegetable beds going. During the summer season they enlisted the help of young people backpacking around the country and looking for temporary work to keep them solvent. They weren't paid much, but they were fed in the Hall kitchen, and the two gatehouses, one originally built for the head gardener and the other for the chauffeur, were pressed into use as dormitories.

When Molly knocked on the back door, Fliss and Jinty McDonald were at the big kitchen table, sorting out bedding for the gatehouses.

'It's open,' Fliss called, and Molly pushed the door wider and came in, staring in awe at the size of the kitchen.

'Blimey, this is big, isn't it? You could get lost in a place like this. I'm looking for Mrs Ralston-Kerr.'

'That's me.'

'Really? I mean, how do you do.' Molly, who had assumed that both women were servants, struggled to hide her surprise. 'I'm looking for work and the man who runs the pub in the village said you might be hiring people.'

'We employ temporary summer staff to work in the gardens and here in the kitchen.'

'I don't mind which,' Molly said.

'In that case, she could be kitchen staff,' Jinty suggested. 'First come, first grabbed.'

'I don't see why not. A few of the people who worked here last summer have written to say they want to come back, but they were all outdoor staff,' Fliss explained to Molly, who had lowered her rucksack to the ground and was stretching her arms to ease stiff muscles. 'We haven't got anyone for the kitchen yet. The kitchen staff keep the others fed – it's a full-time job and it's yours if you want it.'

'Don't you want references or anything like that?'

'We've never needed them before,' Fliss said. 'I find that if you trust people, they generally prove they're worth trusting. When do you want to start?'

'Right now, if it's all right with you,' Molly said cheerfully.

'We're expecting the first lot of people at the weekend, but until then you'd be on your own down in one of the gatehouses – that's where the summer staff sleep, the girls in one and the boys in the other. Would you mind being alone for a few nights?'

'Not a bit.'

'We've aired the cottages,' Jinty said briskly, 'and cleaned them out, and now we're just about to make up the beds.'

'I've come at the right time, then. What d'you

want me to carry?'

Each of the gatehouse cottages had two bedrooms containing two beds, allowing accommodation for four females in one cottage and four males in the other.

Molly fell in love with her new accommodation at once, and shrugged off Fliss's concern at her being the only tenant.

'It's lovely here – like living in the little gingerbread cottage in that fairy tale.'

'Didn't a witch live in that one?' Jinty reminded her, and Molly giggled.

'This one has a nice feel to it – no witches at all. Let me do that, Mrs Ralston-Kerr,' she added as Fliss shook out a sheet and began to tuck it over the mattress. 'You do the pillowcases. Can I have this bed by the window?'

'Of course. I sometimes wonder,' Fliss said, 'if the gatehouses are comfortable enough.'

'You should see some of the hostels I've slept in.'

'Perhaps we should try to get more pillows instead of just one each.'

'One pillow each is fine, really.' Molly straightened up and glanced round the small room, then beamed at Fliss. 'I'm looking forward to spending the summer here!'

Sometimes, Fliss thought as the three of them went over to the other cottage, she envied young people. Nothing seemed to bother them.

The sound of the electric trimmer could be heard as the three women returned to the hall. Molly glanced round, then, nodding in the direction of the gardener, she asked Jinty, 'Is that another of the summer workers?'

'No, he lives here. That's Lewis Ralston-Kerr.'

'Oh – nice,' Molly said.

Back in the kitchen, she set to work with an enthusiasm that impressed Fliss and Jinty. When Jinty announced that she was going to pick some herbs, Molly promptly offered to do it for her.

'Just point me in the right direction and tell me what you want.'

'The herbs are in the kitchen garden – over to the right when you go outside, and through the gate in the wall. Do you know what rosemary looks like?'

'Oh yes. Won't be long,' Molly said blithely. Once outside, she glanced back at the door to make sure that neither of the women could see her, and then, ignoring the gateway leading to the kitchen garden, she hurried round the side of the house and made her way purposefully across the lawn towards her quarry.

Lewis had managed to cut back a fair length of shrubbery; now he was gathering the cuttings up and stacking them in a wheelbarrow.

He dumped another armful of greenery into the barrow and then took a moment to stretch his back and run an arm across his sweating face. It was a sunny day, with just enough of a breeze to cool him as he rolled his shoulders forwards then back.

He was working in an area just beyond the terraced lawns to the side of the hall. A photograph album kept in the rarely used drawing room held pictures of his grandparents playing croquet with guests on the lawns, probably close to the very spot where he stood. In those days, the lawns had been kept in perfect condition, but now the grass was cut only when Lewis, his father or Duncan could find the time. Since the sale of as much produce as they could grow was essential to the family income, the flower and vegetable beds, greenhouses and the small orchard took priority.

It was Lewis's hope that one day they would be able to open the gardens to visitors, but at the moment they were in a Catch-22 situation. The grounds had been attractive in their heyday and could be again, but they had been so badly neglected that a great deal of work was required before the public could be asked to pay entrance fees.

He circled his shoulders again, lifting his gaze from the lawns to the house. Today, with sunlight making the best of its honey-coloured stone and large, handsome windows, it looked good, but he knew that behind the brave façade lay dust and decay. It was a pity, he thought, that he was an only child; if his parents had only had a large family there would be more Ralston-Kerrs to help with the upkeep of the place. On the other hand, brothers and sisters might have had their own ideas as to their futures.

Lewis loved the house and the estate and always had. He enjoyed working in the gardens and liked being part of the village life. He had good friends of his own age among the local people and had never felt any desire to live elsewhere.

He shook his arms vigorously and was about to

gather up one last armful of shrubbery when a voice said, 'Hi there, I'm looking for rosemary.'

Startled, he whipped round to see a redheaded girl advancing across the lawn towards him, an earthenware dish in her hands.

'Where did you come from?'

'The kitchen. I've just been taken on.' Her cheeks dimpled as she smiled at him, repeating, 'I'm looking for rosemary.'

'Rosemary?' he repeated, confused. 'Is she new to the place?'

She stared, and then began to laugh. 'Not Rosemary a person – rosemary the herb.'

'Oh.' Lewis felt his recently cooled face bursting with heat again.

'Sorry, I'm not laughing at you – it was my fault in any case. I didn't think. I've only just started and Mrs McDonald told me to get some rosemary for tonight's dinner. You don't happen to know where the herb garden is, do you?'

She was almost as tall as he was, with a long, slim body. She wore a man's checked shirt, the sleeves folded back to just above her elbows, and well-worn jeans. Her eyes, Lewis noticed, were an incredible sea green.

'It's round the back of the house, close to the kitchen for convenience.'

She screwed up her face. 'Now why didn't I think that one out for myself? You must think I'm a right idiot.'

'Not at all. I'll show you.'

'Are you sure? I'm not taking you away from essential work, or getting you into trouble?'

'Of course not.' He gripped the handles of the

163

wheelbarrow. 'I'm going in that direction myself to get rid of this lot. This way.'

They walked side by side towards the house, the girl keeping up with him effortlessly as he man-handled the barrow along the lower lawn and then ran it up a grassy slope to the upper lawn. A second slope took them to the flagged terrace, where she grabbed the front of the barrow and helped lift it on to the paving stones, then ran over to cup her hands around her face so she could peer through one of the tall windows.

'Isn't this a beautiful house?'

'Not as beautiful as it once was. It takes a lot of money to keep a place like this in good repair.'

'I can imagine! But it'll be lovely, spending the summer here. The kitchen's enormous, isn't it? You could almost fit our house inside it.' She giggled. 'Our kitchen at home in Inverness is like one of the cupboards here.'

'This way. You're planning on staying all summer, then?'

'If all goes well. I've been doing this for a few years now,' she said. 'After school, I did a secre-tarial and bookkeeping course, and now I'm with an agency. That means I can stay with my parents during the autumn and winter and do office work in Inverness, then in the spring and summer I backpack. Last year I was in Canada – I've an aunt in Toronto. Have you ever been to Canada?'

'No.'

'It's beautiful. I saw Niagara Falls,' she said proudly. 'I love travelling around, taking on work where I can find it. This year I decided it was time I saw more of Scotland.' She glanced up at him. 'Have you been here long?'

'A while.'

'What are the Ralston-Kerrs like to work for?'

'They're okay,' Lewis said, amused.

'That's good to know. I've worked for some real horrors in my time – never stayed long in these places. Mrs Ralston-Kerr's a lovely lady, isn't she? A real lady. I've not met her husband, though I saw him walking through the kitchen. He looks nice, too. And the gatehouse where we're living is really sweet. Do you live there too?'

'I live locally.' Lewis let go of the wheelbarrow and opened a squeaky gate leading into a large walled area. 'This is the kitchen garden where you'll find onions and leeks and so on for the house. The apple orchard is through that gate at the far end, and the herb garden's here, against the south wall. And there,' he pointed, 'is the rosemary.'

'So it is. Thank you.' Her green eyes sparkled up at him and she held out her free hand. 'I'm Molly, by the way.'

'Lewis.' He shook hands. 'Happy to meet you, Molly.'

'Well, I'd better get on with my work and let you get on with yours. I'll see you around?'

'You can bank on it,' Lewis said, and started to whistle as he trundled the barrow across to the rubbish dump behind the stable block.

Molly Ewing watched him go then began to gather rosemary, well pleased with the way her plans were shaping up.

18

Several young backpackers had arrived at Linn Hall and were hard at work with Duncan and Lewis in the grounds. The temporary staff ate in the kitchen, but the Ralston-Kerrs usually ate as a family in the pantry that Hector used as a study and where he spent most of his time trying without much success to balance the books.

The three of them were discussing the day's plans over breakfast when Jinty McDonald, who always came in early when they had staff to feed, beat a swift tattoo on the door with her knuckles before barging in.

'Mornin' all, post's arrived.' She dropped a handful of envelopes and several plastic-wrapped booklets on the table. 'Want any more hot water? The kettle's just boiled.'

'We're fine, thanks, Jinty,' Fliss said, while Hector rummaged around in search of the silver letter-opener – one of the few things his father had been able to leave him. 'I'll be out in five minutes to help with the dishes.'

'No hurry, m'dear, they're all on second cups – they'll be a good ten minutes yet.' Jinty and her husband Tom lived in Slaemuir, the council house area by the river. She was the mother of eight children, their ages ranging from sixteen to six years old. As well as helping Fliss during the summer and at other times if needed, she did some cleaning work at the Neurotic Cuckoo. Even so, she always managed to be cheerful and unflappable.

Voices and laughter could be heard through the partly opened door. Lewis would have preferred to eat at the big kitchen table along with the others, especially the red-haired girl he had spoken to on her first day at Linn Hall, but he knew his parents liked to spend what little spare time they had as a family.

'One for you, Lewis,' his father said as Jinty went out, closing the door behind her and shutting out the sound of voices from the kitchen.

'For me?' That didn't happen often, since Lewis's friends all tended to be local. He took the letter and saw it was from someone he had known in college.

'One for the Ralston-Kerrs – looks official,' Hector said gloomily. Official letters were always bills. 'And another one for me.' He felt the envelope with his fingers. 'Stiff paper – expensive. It'll be official too.' He sighed, and pushed the slippery plastic packages towards Fliss, who cast a glance at them and saw they were from companies specialising in clothing and furniture, items she couldn't afford. Something else to fill the dustbin.

Hector was staring down at his envelope, clearly reluctant to open it. Over the past few years, as money became tighter, he had begun to develop paranoia about opening official-looking post; knowing this, his wife took the letter-opener and the envelope from his limp hands and sliced with one decisive movement through the top of the flap.

Hector was right – the envelope was made of strong, expensive paper, and so was the single sheet of paper within. Since it was addressed only to him, she handed the envelope back with the letter still inside it, and opened the other envelope, the one addressed to the family.

'They've agreed a date for the meeting about the quarry. It's to be next Thursday in the village hall, and representatives from the quarry firm and the council will be there.'

Hector looked up at her, panic in his eyes. 'Do we have to go to it?'

'I think we should, dear.'

'Oh, God, I wish I could just go to bed and stay there until the whole thing's been decided one way or another.' He rubbed both hands over his face. 'We haven't even answered the quarry people's letter yet. I don't know what to do for the best!'

'Wait until the meeting,' Lewis suggested. 'Find out then what the general feeling is in the village. If most of them are for the quarry you can agree to lease the land, and if they're against, you can refuse.'

'We could do with the money,' Fliss said wistfully. 'We're reaching the stage where it could mean the difference between the house standing or falling down.'

'There's little point in taking the money and saving the house if most of the villagers hate us for it,' her husband pointed out.

'Why don't you leave the decision until after the meeting?' Lewis said again. 'And if you want, I'll represent you there and report back afterwards. Okay, Dad?'

'I suppose so – thank you, Lewis.' Hector heaved another sigh, this time one that seemed to come from the soles of his shabby boots, and Fliss reached across the table to put a hand on his.

'In the meantime, dear, have another cup of tea and put this quarry business out of your mind. I don't want you making yourself ill over it.'

'Come and work in the grounds today, Dad. The weather's set fair and an hour or two's digging would help to clear your mind.'

'Yes, Hector, out you go. It'll do you good.'

Hector looked from one face to the other, then smiled. 'D'you know, I think I might. Work the muscles, rest the mind, eh?' Then he picked up the second envelope. 'I might as well get this blighter over and done with before I go out.' He unfolded the single sheet of paper. 'It's got an official heading.' It was his experience that the worst kind of letters always had official headings.

Fliss got to her feet and began to gather the dishes together. 'Finished your tea, Hector?'

'Almost.' He snatched his mug up and poured the last of the cooling tea into his mouth before scanning the letter. Then his lean body jerked from the chair, propelled by a spasm shooting through him from head to toe.

'Gggahhh!' Half of the tea he had just taken went down his windpipe while the other half exited through his mouth and nose. Plates and papers were sent spinning as he lurched over the table, clawed fingers grasping at the edge for support.

'Hector? Oh my God, Lewis, he's having a seizure! Hector, speak to me!' Fliss tried to catch

169

at her husband's flailing arm and was almost knocked off her feet as it hit her. His face began to flush, the colour deepening swiftly from red to purple.

'Hector! Lewis, help him!'

'He's choking!' Lewis wrapped a long arm about his father's chest and banged Hector's back with his free hand. The horrible gargling sounds being torn from Hector's throat changed to wrenching coughs, then to whooping noises as he started to drag air into his embattled lungs.

'Hector? What happened?' Fliss was shaking uncontrollably.

As her husband's breathing changed from whooping to whistling, his face returned to its usual colour. He mopped himself with a napkin and then subsided into his chair again. 'The letter...' he gasped, flapping a hand at it.

Lewis picked it up and read it, then blinked several times before reading it again.

'What is it? Lewis?' Fliss began to panic.

'It's all right, Mum. At least, it seems to be. Perhaps it's someone's idea of a sick joke?' Lewis asked his father, who shook his head feebly and tried to pour tea with trembling hands.

'Give it to me.' Fliss took the battered old teapot from him, splashed tea and milk into his cup, and added a heaped spoonful of sugar.

'It's from some legal firm in England,' Lewis stared down at the letter as though expecting it to turn into a snake in his hands, 'on behalf of some client of theirs. They're offering to donate two hundred thousand pounds towards the upkeep of Linn Hall if Dad'll say no to leasing the land to the quarry people.'

On the following morning Hector and Fliss Ralston-Kerr, dressed in their rather shabby best clothes, drove in their old Ford car to Dumfries where they had arranged an appointment with the family lawyer.

They watched anxiously as he read the letter, perusing it twice before laying it down on his desk and remarking, 'Well, well, you seem to have a generous benefactor.'

'But an anonymous one,' Fliss pointed out. She had lain awake for most of the night, worrying about this mysterious person who suddenly wanted to give them a great deal of money for no good reason.

'Is the letter genuine?' Hector wanted to know. 'Who is this client the letter mentions, and why would he or she want to give us money? Are there conditions attached that we know nothing about? We can't take money from someone we don't know!'

'According to this, you get the money if you write to this lawyer agreeing with his client's request that you do not lease land to some English company. What's the story behind that?'

'There's talk of the quarry being worked again and as the land it's on belongs to the estate, they would need to lease it from us first. Fliss, did you remember to bring that letter too?' Hector asked, and his wife rummaged in the depths of her large handbag before locating it and handing it over.

The lawyer read it, too, twice. 'It would seem that either way, you stand to benefit financially.'

171

'Not,' Fliss said, 'if the quarry doesn't go ahead.'

'If it doesn't go ahead because you refuse to lease the land, then you stand to get two hundred thousand pounds from this unknown person.' The lawyer tapped the first letter they had given him.

'I meant, if they don't get planning permission. Are you sure,' Fliss went on anxiously, 'that it isn't one of those terrible things one reads about in the newspapers? Those – what do they call them? Sounds like cold meat in a tin.'

The lawyer thought for a puzzled moment before offering, 'Scams?'

'That's the word – reminds me of spam.'

'I've always had a weakness for spam,' Hector said. 'I don't know why people look down on it. Very tasty.'

'Yes, dear.' Fliss patted his hand. 'But about this offer, Mr Heatherington?'

'I believe I've heard of the legal firm that sent it. Give me a moment,' the lawyer said, and carried the letter from the room.

'And tell them that we need to know who this person is,' Hector called after him. 'We will not take money from a stranger!'

'You make us sound like well-warned children,' his wife said.

'You know what I mean!'

'Yes dear, I do, and I agree.' She patted his hand again.

'Even if the offer *is* genuine, it doesn't make our problem any easier,' Hector said after a strained silence. 'If we lease the land we'll displease some of the villagers, and if we refuse to lease it and take this new offer – if it's proved to be genuine –

we'll displease other villagers.'

'It's very difficult,' Fliss agreed.

'And if we keep this new offer quiet, and refuse, then get money to refurbish the manor, people will wonder where we got it from, won't they? We'll be accused of selling out.'

'I never thought of that. Oh, Hector, why did this dratted company have to set their sights on our little quarry? There's probably not all that much granite left in it!' Fliss began to wish she could return to the old days, when all she had to worry about was being able to afford food for her family and whoever happened to be working for them at the time. They lived mainly on home-grown vegetables, fruit from the orchard when it was in season, and the occasional piece of meat. Their diet was plain and quite monotonous, and it was fortunate for them that Jinty was a good cook who knew how to make a little food go far. Fliss had made up a book of Jinty's recipes to follow in the winter months, when the family was on its own.

'Spam *is* quite tasty isn't it?' she said now.

Hector nodded, then they lapsed back into silence, each wrestling with their own thoughts, until the lawyer breezed back into the office, his face wreathed in smiles.

'Well now, you'll be pleased to know that the offer you've received is perfectly legitimate and safe. I've had a word on the phone with the legal firm, and although they refused to give me their client's name, they assured me that he is extremely wealthy and his offer has been made in good faith. It seems to me you stand to do quite well one way or the other – by taking this offer, or leasing the quarry. So – good news all round, eh?'

'We really do need to know who it is. We cannot accept the money if we don't know who our benefactor is,' Hector insisted.

'I'm afraid there's no way of finding out who it is. But it is genuine, not a scam.'

'Who can it be?' Fliss wondered as they left the office and stepped back on to the pavement.

'Someone who grew up in the village and then left to make his or her fortune? Someone who still has family in Prior's Ford who keeps them informed of what's going on?'

'I can't think of anyone. There's Jinty's sister – you won't remember her, but she was a pretty little thing. Became a legal secretary and then married and went off to Australia,' Fliss said thoughtfully. 'Jinty reads me bits of her letters sometimes. Her husband has his own building company and they live in a nice house with a swimming pool. But that's apparently quite normal in Australia. And they have five children. I don't think she could afford to offer us two hundred thousand pounds. Even if she could, it would go to Jinty, not us.'

She took her husband's arm as they walked to where they had parked the car. 'There's one thing for sure, though, Hector – we'll have to get money from one place or the other. That visit to the lawyer will have cost us more than we have in the bank right now.'

19

The Gift Horse opened its summer season with a cheese and wine party on a beautiful Saturday in April. The three tables used for visitors in search of refreshments were set up outside the shop, which had been lavishly decorated with streamers and balloons. Teenagers congregated around the handsome old Mercat Cross, bottles of soft drinks in their hands, while the younger children ran about the grass, each with a Gift Horse balloon.

Clarissa bought one of Alastair Marshall's paintings, the one she had admired in his cottage, of trees forming a natural arch over a sun-dappled country road. She also bought some of Ingrid's hand-made cards, and was introduced to her hostess's family. Peter MacKenzie, a pleasant, studious-looking man, was clearly immensely proud of his wife, who looked striking in white trousers and a white sleeveless sweater under a filmy black jacket with a pattern of large white flowers splashed over it. Her hair, today, hung down her back in a long plait. Her elder daughter Freya was a Nordic beauty like her mother, while Ella, the younger girl, took after her dark-haired father.

'Wine?' Peter MacKenzie offered, but Clarissa opted for coffee. Ingrid announced she was ready for a cup herself and ushered Clarissa outside to one of the tables.

'So now you have seen my little shop – our little

shop, I should say, since Jenny runs it with me. I am hoping to find more people willing to make things we can sell; it would be good to develop the business.'

The coffee arrived, and turned out to be very good. Clarissa lingered on, even when Ingrid was called away, enjoying the feeling of being part of a community.

Notices advertising the forthcoming meeting to discuss the proposed quarry reopening lay on the tables and, when she finally left, she took one with her.

Fifteen minutes before the meeting was due to open the village hall was filled with people, most occupying the chairs laid out in rows while others roamed around from group to group to mull, and in some cases, argue, over the pros and cons of the quarry reopening.

Clarissa, hesitating in the doorway, might have retreated if she hadn't caught sight of Alastair in a far corner. He waved to her, and she was about to pick her way towards him when she heard someone call, 'Mrs Ramsay, there's a seat here, beside us,' and turned to see Ingrid and her friends waving at her from their seats a few rows from the front.

Clarissa glanced over at Alastair, who smiled, shrugged a shoulder and motioned to her to take the seat.

'Thank you.' She settled beside Jenny Forsyth, unbuttoning her coat. 'To tell the truth, I'm not sure that I should be here.'

'Why ever not?' Ingrid leaned past Helen to

ask. This evening her hair, almost the exact shade of a field of corn in sunlight, was caught back in a ponytail and tied with a ribbon that, together with the colour of her knitted sweater, was a perfect match for her clear blue eyes.

'We – I haven't lived here for long, and I don't have any opinions on this quarry business. I don't know whether it's a good thing or a bad thing for Prior's Ford.'

'I'm not from these parts, nor is Jenny, but we're here,' Ingrid pointed out while Helen said warmly, 'Of course you're entitled to attend the meeting, and as to whether it's a good thing or a bad thing, none of us can decide on that. Take the craft shop – the quarry being reopened won't benefit it, and might chase the tourists away.'

'I can't see workmen being interested in our little shop,' Ingrid agreed in her attractive sing-song accent.

'I don't know which way to turn,' Jenny admitted. 'Local employment can only be good; we don't want our young people moving away, do we? But at the same time, I love Prior's Ford just as it is. Then I wonder – is that selfish of me? Should I be looking at the other side of the coin?'

'Jenny, stop fretting,' Ingrid chided her. 'That is exactly why we are all here this evening – to find out the pros and cons of the matter, although we know that the final decision will be made by those in power, not by mere mortals like us.' Then, leaning over to touch Clarissa's hand lightly, 'It is very nice to see you again, Mrs Ramsay. How are you?'

'Keeping quite busy, clearing things up. You know how it is,' Clarissa said, and then, as the three younger women looked back at her politely, 'but of course you don't. I mean – are your husbands here as well?' she hurried on in an attempt to cover her confusion.

'My Peter is at home marking papers. He's a lecturer in Dumfries, and not as interested in village business as I am because the village is not part of his work. So I told him to stay home, do his marking, and look after our two daughters. And he was quite happy to do that.'

'The same goes for Andrew – he's home with Calum,' Jenny said, while Helen nodded and said, 'My husband too. Have you noticed that it tends to be the women who attend meetings and school evenings rather than the men?'

'They feel they have done a hard day's work and deserve to put their feet up in the evening – or perhaps go to the pub for a drink. So they send us out so we can report back to them. They do this because they know that being women, we have been lazing around all day and need some mental exercise,' Ingrid said, and the three young women laughed together at what was clearly a popular joke between them.

Clarissa thought of Stella, her closest friend – now her former closest friend – and envied the easy bond her companions shared. For a moment she was in danger of feeling sorry for herself.

Ingrid waved at Sam Brennan, who was leaning against a side wall, arms folded. 'I don't see Marcy with him – isn't she coming tonight?'

'I saw her when I came in,' Clarissa volunteered. 'She's sitting near the back, on this side.'

'Oh dear, that sounds as though they're not

talking to each other.' Jenny sighed. 'They've been at loggerheads over that petition she insists on getting people to sign.'

'They'll get over it, they always do. Marcy and Sam have been together for years now,' Helen explained to Clarissa. 'We all think they're perfect for each other, but they're both strong-willed and so they have their fair share of dis-agreements. Sometimes you could cut the air in the village store with a knife. But they always make up again.' Then a sudden hush swept over the audience and she settled back in her chair as Naomi Hennessey led in the platform party.

Naomi had avoided discussing the quarry with anyone, though for her sermon on the previous Sunday she had chosen to speak of the importance of loving thy neighbours and respecting their views while her dark eyes swept the congregation seated below her, lingering for a few seconds on each and every upturned face. Now she rapped firmly on the table with her gavel and waited until the mutterings and shuffling died away.

'Good evening, ladies and gentlemen.' Her rich, warm voice had no difficulty in reaching the back of the hall as she introduced the people who had seated themselves to either side of her – two representatives from the local council, and two from the firm interested in reopening the quarry.

Clarissa was trying to take in their names when Jenny Forsyth suddenly gave a strangled gasp. Her entire body seemed to twitch, while one of her hands reached out and caught at Clarissa's arm.

'My dear, are you all right?' she whispered, alarmed, and Jenny pulled her hand away as though the fabric of Clarissa's coat had scorched it.

'I'm absolutely fine – sorry – a sudden cramp in my leg.' The younger woman rubbed her thigh vigorously.

'Decisions as to whether or not the quarry should be or will reopen will *not* be made tonight. This meeting has been called in order to give everyone a chance to hear what representatives of the company have to say, and to hear the local council's thoughts on the matter. And I know that our guests for this evening' – with a graceful sweep of the arm she indicated the platform party – 'are interested in hearing your views, too.'

'No they're not,' a man called from the back of the hall. 'They've already made their minds up – the lot of 'em. This meeting's just an attempt to con us into believing that our views'll be listened to.'

'I can assure you, sir, that no decisions have been made,' one of the quarry representatives rapped back as a rumble of agreement was heard throughout the hall.

'We've made *our* decision – the folk who live here!' Marcy Copleton shouted out. 'We like our village the way it is.'

'Don't run away with idea that you're speaking for me,' a man responded from halfway along the hall. 'I've got two teenage boys – what chance of work is there for them around here? More local industry's just what they need.'

'Hear hear,' Sam Brennan roared, and Marcy jumped to her feet and turned to face him.

'We don't want dust all over the place, and

180

lorries rumbling through our streets day and night,' she stormed, 'and folk afraid to let their children cross Main Street on their own in case they get knocked down.'

'That's nonsense!' he shot back at her. 'Lots of places have local industries, and the people cope very well. You can't speak for the entire village!'

'And what makes you think *you* can?' she yelled. Heads turned and people began to murmur to each other. Sam took a step towards her and opened his mouth to retaliate, but Naomi Hennessey interceded, banging the gavel hard against the table.

'That's enough! I didn't give up an evening to listen to you arguing among yourselves, and I'm sure our visitors didn't, either. Now then,' she went on as the audience subsided, shifting guiltily in their chairs, 'we're going to do this like adults. First of all, I will invite the representatives from Redmond Brown and Son to explain just what they intend to do if – *if*,' she repeated, fixing a stern eye on a man who was waving one arm in the air, 'they get planning permission. And then I'm going to ask the gentlemen from the council to say a few words. After we've heard from them, the meeting will be thrown open so you can ask questions and air your own views.'

Respect for the local minister, who could switch from her normally sparkling dark eyes and wide smile to a stony glare when she had to, caused the villagers to hold their tongues and listen in silence while one of the men from the quarry company got up to have his say. As he painted a glowing picture of the benefits that his

181

company could bring to the area, Helen nudged Jenny's arm.

'That man's staring at you.'

'What man?'

'The other quarry man. I think he fancies you.'

'Don't be daft!' Jenny snapped as a woman seated just in front of her said loudly, 'More dust than industry if you ask me. My gran had a terrible time trying to keep the house clean when that quarry was operating.'

'Industry has moved on from those days, madam,' the speaker told her. 'Today's quarrying is cleaner and quieter than it used to be.'

He sat down, giving way to the local councillor, who emphasised that no decision had been taken as yet on planning permission. 'We've got quite a way to go before we get to that stage, and I can promise you that every aspect of this possible venture will be very carefully considered. We will also listen to local opinions at all times.'

'That's what every politician says,' Clarissa heard Glen Mason mutter to the person next to him. 'But every one of 'em's got cloth ears, you mark my words.'

When the meeting was thrown open to questions, things got quite heated and Naomi's gavel pounded the table so often that Clarissa would not have been surprised if the wooden surface had burst into flames. The quarry company's employees began to look uneasy, while the councillor and the official from the planning department murmured together and started to glance frequently at their watches. Finally one of them whispered something to Naomi, who nodded and then announced that there was time for one more quick question before the meeting came to a close.

Marcy Copleton's hand went up. 'Can we get a definite guarantee that planning permission has not yet been granted?'

'Madam, you have my word on that,' the representative from the council's planning department told her. 'Before planning permission can be granted, or even discussed, Redmond Brown and Son have to obtain permission to lease the land where the quarry stands. We don't own it.'

'Who does, then?' someone called out.

'We do,' a new voice cut in and every head swivelled towards a young man leaning against the left-hand wall. 'At least, my family own it.'

'Lewis Ralston-Kerr,' Helen murmured to Clarissa. 'From the big house.'

'So what's your dad goin' to do, Lewis?' someone called from the back, 'and why isn't he at this meetin' along with the rest of us?'

Lewis moved to stand before the platform, so that everyone could see him. 'You all know my father – he's a shy man and he's not good at meetings. He's been approached by the quarry company, and the truth is that he doesn't know what to do for the best.' He held up a hand to quell the rising murmur and said loudly and clearly, 'You all know that my parents only want to do what's best for Prior's Ford. That's why they're waiting to find out more about what *you* want, and what the quarry people intend to do. And that's all I can tell you at the moment.'

'Ladies and gentlemen!' Naomi's gavel pounded the table once again. 'You've heard what Lewis has to say; now, please, let our councillor have the last word before we close the meeting!'

'Thank you, Madam Chairwoman. As we all said at the start of this meeting, several formalities have to be observed before any decision can be made, and I can assure you that you will be kept informed of events.' The councillor glanced at his watch again, then began to gather up his papers. 'Madam Chairman, I have another event to attend...'

As soon as the platform party began to leave the stage Jenny shot to her feet, buttoning her coat. 'I'm off.'

Helen caught at her friend's arm as Jenny began to squeeze past her.

'Aren't you coming to the pub? It should be interesting.'

'I've got a bit of a headache with all this shouting. See you tomorrow.'

20

'You're home early,' Andrew said in surprise as Jenny went into the living room. And then, as she glanced at Calum, curled up in an armchair watching television, 'He was just going to bed – weren't you, old son?'

'Mmm.' Calum, in his pyjamas, didn't take his eyes from the screen, where a lion was stalking a herd of zebras. 'When this finishes.'

'Now.' Jenny snapped the picture off just as the

lion was crouching to spring.

'Mu-um!'

'You should have been in bed thirty minutes ago, and that's not what you want to watch before you go to sleep. It'll give you nightmares.'

'Mum, it's only nature! It won't give me nightmares.'

'But it'll give them to me. Go on. Now!' Jenny snapped.

'You could have allowed him another ten minutes,' Andrew said when their son, mumbling under his breath, had trailed upstairs.

'Don't let's argue, I'm not in the mood.' Jenny slumped into the chair Calum had just vacated.

'Rotten meeting?'

'Noisy meeting; it gave me a headache.'

'I thought you would have gone to the pub with Ingrid and Helen afterwards, to mull everything over.'

'Which is why you allowed Calum to stay up later than usual,' Jenny said, and he shot her an embarrassed grin. 'I didn't feel like it. I'd rather have a cup of tea than a gin and tonic.'

'I'll make it.' Andrew got up, stretching and yawning. 'So what did they decide to do about this old quarry, then?'

'Nothing. It turns out that the land belongs to the Ralston-Kerrs, so the first thing the quarry people have to do is lease it, apparently.'

'Really? That's a bit awkward for poor old Hector Ralston-Kerr. He could do with the money coming in, from what I hear in the pub, but at the same time he's up against strong feelings in the village. Damned if he does lease, and damned if he doesn't.'

'And even if he agrees, they'd have to get planning permission. It was all a lot of noise about nothing, really.'

'A cup of strong tea, then.'

As soon as Andrew had disappeared into the kitchen, Jenny got out of her chair and went to the window. It was dark, and there was nothing to be seen but lights from the houses opposite. She glanced up and down the road, but it was empty.

All was quiet, peaceful and unthreatening. But even so, she felt uneasy. She had glimpsed her past that evening, and now she didn't feel safe.

Most of the people who had attended the meeting gathered in the Neurotic Cuckoo afterwards to discuss it. The place was full, and as soon as Glen arrived he was summoned to help Libby, already trying to deal with orders from all directions.

'Which way d'you reckon the Ralston-Kerrs'll jump?' one of the men standing at the bar asked his companions.

'I've already spoken to Hector Ralston-Kerr,' Glen told them, 'and he's not made his mind up yet. A pint and a brandy, was it?'

'Aye. If it was me I'd take the money,' the first speaker announced. 'A few pounds in the wallet's worth more than nothing at all.'

'But there's plenty of folk round here wouldn't want him to do that. It'd be like selling us down the river,' said another man.

'If they found granite or oil or gold under my back garden and offered me rent money to let 'em dig the place up,' someone else chimed in, 'I'd say come in and welcome, lads, and be damned to the wife's precious conservatory.'

Glen, handing over a filled glass, noticed Lewis at a table by the window. 'I think I'll have a word with young Ralston-Kerr.'

'You'll stay put, Glen Mason, and get on with serving folk,' his wife said sharply. 'That meeting seems to have given them all a thirst and I can't cope on my own!'

'Alastair, you wouldn't mind helping Libby for a while would you?' Glen coaxed.

'Well – I only came in for the one pint. I've got work waiting at home.'

'Another pint on the house – and the usual money rounded up to the nearest hour if you'll come behind the bar till closing time,' Glen pledged, ignoring his wife's glare. Alastair immediately moved round the end of the bar, leaving Glen free to wend his way to Lewis's table.

'Is it true your father's not decided yet about leasing that old quarry?'

'Not so far.'

'Can't you convince him it'd be a bad thing for the village?'

'Hang on there,' a burly young man at the opposite side of the table protested. 'If the quarry opens it might be to the advantage of kids like my brother, coming out of school soon and not likely to make it to college or university. Don't you go putting the wrong idea into your dad's head, Lewis. Better to work the quarry if there's still granite in it than have it lying there idle.'

'I don't fancy having big dirty lorries rumbling

187

through the village day and night,' a girl protested.

'See my dad's problem?' Lewis appealed to Glen. 'There's no way he can please everyone. I'm keeping right out of it.' He drained his glass. 'Same again all round? One for yourself, Glen?'

'No thanks – and I'll fetch your order. I should be getting back to work anyway. But tell your dad I was asking, okay?'

As Glen turned away the door opened and Lewis glanced up in the hope that it might be the red-headed girl he had met in the garden. He had glimpsed her once or twice since then, but always when there were other people around. Although she seemed to be friendly with everyone, each time Lewis caught her eye she immediately glanced away as though she hadn't noticed him. He was disappointed, and puzzled. She had seemed to like him at their first and only meeting, and he could not understand why she had changed towards him. If only he could get a chance to talk to her...

But his hopes were dashed again, for the new-comer was a middle-aged man, a stranger. He hesitated just inside the door for a moment, looking around as though in search of someone, and then crossed to one of the tables at the other side of the room.

'I hope you and Sam aren't going to fall out over this quarry business,' Ingrid was saying to Marcy Copleton. 'It's not worth that.'

Marcy sighed, gazing down into the depths of her shandy. 'He's being so pig-headed – sometimes I wonder why I bother.'

'You don't mean that,' Helen protested.

'Of course she doesn't. You and Sam are the perfect couple,' Ingrid told Marcy 'Like – Posh and Becks.'

'More like Mutt and Jeff if you ask me.'

'Not at all. I can see him from here.' Ingrid shot a glance over Marcy's shoulder to where Sam sat with a group of local men. 'He keeps looking over at you.'

'Wondering what I'm saying about him. Why does he have to be so bloody determined to get this quarry started up again?'

'He's a businessman – he wants to see more customers in his shop. It makes sense.'

'But surely he should respect my right to my own opinions? And even if it does start operating again – God forbid – the quarry'll be worked on a small scale. It won't make a noticeable difference to the store, or any other local trade. You're not hungering for it, are you?' Marcy appealed to Ingrid, who raised an elegant shoulder in a half shrug.

'What quarrymen would want to buy paintings or ornaments or cards or hand-made dolls? Or even have a cup of tea or coffee? The Gift Horse is more of a hobby for me and Jenny than our livelihoods. I doubt if the quarry's going to make any difference to us.'

'It will if the place turns into a noisy dust bowl.'

Ingrid took a sip from her glass and then considered the thought, her head to one side. Finally, she said, 'I'm not sure that would happen. As the man said, things have changed. We might not even notice it.'

'That's what Sam says. How can you not notice

189

a quarry not much more than a mile away?' Marcy was saying when a middle-aged man stopped by their table.

'Forgive me for butting in, but I'm looking for Helen Campbell.'

'That's me.'

'Helen, hello.' He held out his hand. 'Bob Green, from the *Dumfries News*. I just wanted to thank you for sending in those reports on the protest meetings. I'm impressed – I never have to alter them before they go to the sub-editors.'

Helen flushed with pleasure. 'Oh, hello.' She shook hands, then introduced Ingrid and Marcy. 'Won't you sit down?'

'For a minute, if you don't mind. Marcy Copleton – you're on the protest committee too, aren't you? Care to give me a few comments?'

'I'd be delighted to.'

'Great.' Green fished a notebook from his pocket. 'But first, can I get anyone a drink?'

'We were just thinking of going,' Helen said doubtfully remembering that Duncan was looking after the children, but Marcy cut in with, 'A gin and tonic for me, please.'

'And a half pint of shandy for me,' Ingrid said firmly, and Helen gave in and asked for a shandy as well.

'Great – I've been hoping to get a chance to have my say,' Marcy crowed as Bob made his way to the bar. She flashed a glance across the crowded room to where Sam sat, then leaned across the table and lowered her voice. 'If you ask me, Sam's all for this quarry just because he knows I'm against it.'

'Now you're being paranoid,' Helen scoffed.

'Maybe I am.' Marcy drained her glass. 'I love living here,' she said. 'For the first time in my entire life I feel at home and at peace. It might be selfish of me, but I don't want anything to rock my boat, and Sam knows it – so why is he so set on wanting the very thing I don't want?'

'The landlord's bringing the drinks over,' Bob Green said, pulling out an empty chair. 'Now then, Miss – Mrs...?'

'Ms,' said Marcy, and launched into her feelings about the quarry controversy. Bob's pen flew across the paper and every now and again he halted to flick a page over and start afresh. He was still writing, and Marcy still talking, when Glen Mason arrived at the table.

'Good evening, ladies – and how's my favourite coven tonight?' He put down the fresh drinks and swept up the empty glasses. 'Ah – we're playing a substitute witch tonight, are we? Where's the lovely Jenny gone?'

'Home with a headache. That meeting was more than she could take,' Marcy told him. 'You've met our local reporter?'

'We had a word in the hall before the meeting. I think it went quite well, don't you? I look forward to reading Friday's *Dumfries News*.' Glen winked at the reporter.

'I have to give both points of view, you do realise that?'

'Of course, but I'm sure your readers will see for themselves that ours carries quite a bit of weight.'

'I'd be happy to do an interview with you – give you space in the paper to express your own opinions on the matter.'

'Sorry, mate' – Glen indicated the packed bar – 'I don't have any time to chat tonight.'

'Tomorrow, then? I could come over mid-morning.'

'Got a delivery due tomorrow. I'm quite happy to leave the talking to Marcy and Helen – there's nothing I can say that they couldn't say better. I never was good with words,' Glen said, and hurried back to the bar.

'Not good with words? That's the first time I've ever seen our Glen lost for them,' Ingrid remarked. 'He's usually brimming over.'

'How long's he been here?' Bob wanted to know.

'About six or seven years?' Helen asked Ingrid, who shrugged. 'He and Libby came here from Birmingham when he retired.'

'I thought they lived in Leicester,' Marcy said.

'What's his name again?' the reporter asked, and when Helen told him, he shook his head. 'Doesn't ring any bells, though his face seems vaguely familiar.' He took a long drink, then asked, 'What was he talking about – covens and witches?'

'It's just a daft joke he's thought up. Ingrid and I are usually with our friend Jenny, and Glen keeps referring to us as a coven,' Helen explained. 'You know, the three witches in *Macbeth*. He's like one of those annoying kids who keep repeating a joke because it was funny the first time.'

'He'll get tired of it,' Ingrid soothed.

'Sure to,' Bob agreed, and then turned to Marcy. 'So, to continue...'

21

On the morning after the meeting Clarissa woke from a deep and restful sleep with her mind filled, for the first time since Keith's death, with a sense of pleasant anticipation. For a few minutes she lay still, her eyes closed, awaiting the sense of apprehension she had become accustomed to, but it didn't come.

When she opened her eyes it was to see the bedroom curtains flutter in the breeze from the open window, and to hear cheerful, busy sounds from outside – birds chattering in the trees in her garden, the voices of children in the street, a dog barking in the distance, cars passing, a man shouting greetings to someone and being answered, a bicycle bell ringing.

Luxuriously, she gave herself time to stretch every muscle, beginning with her toes and working up slowly to her neck and then her mouth and eyelids, following an exercise routine that she had once seen in a newspaper but had rarely been able to follow before because Keith bounced out of bed the moment his eyes opened and expected her to do the same.

Then, finally, she got up and drew back the curtains.

Sunlight flooded the room, and for several minutes she basked in its warmth and absorbed its strength. It was April. Buds were thick on the two small trees in her front garden, and the hedge was now well clothed in fresh green leaves. From where she stood she could see across the width of the green as well as over towards Main Street where Mr Gordon, the butcher, was laying out his window display for the day.

To one side of the butcher's shop stood a row of neat two-storey houses built in soft grey stone, their brightly painted doors opening straight onto the pavement, and to the other side stood the church. From her upper-floor vantage point Clarissa could see a little of River Lane, leading down one side of the church. At the end of the lane, she knew, the river was narrow and quite domesticated, as though trying to be on its best behaviour while running through the village. Once free of the houses and shops it cast off all inhibitions and spread itself out comfortably, like a plump woman unfastening her corsets and giving a sigh of pleasure.

A group of older village children waited outside the church for the bus that would take them to Kirkcudbright Academy. Freya MacKenzie stood out among them, partly because of her height and partly because her long silky hair looked in the sunlight as though it had been spun from pale gold. As Clarissa watched, Naomi Hennessey's foster child erupted from River Lane, his school bag bouncing on his back, and took his place in the middle of the group. He was the perfect foil to Freya with his skin like smooth chocolate and his black hair tightly curled over a neat skull.

He had Naomi's personality – just looking at him and sensing his boundless energy and enthusiasm made Clarissa feel good. It also made her hunger for her days as a teacher, surrounded by young people who embraced life, albeit noisily and at times in a way that made things difficult for the adults in charge of them. But that was part of growing up, and it was sad, she thought as the bus came trundling along the road, that one day those carefree children would have to grow up and tackle adulthood with all its problems.

The bus finished mopping up the jiggling, chattering, laughing crowd and moved away, leaving the pavement empty. A woman carrying a basket over one arm appeared from River Lane, rounded the corner and went into the butcher's. Mr Gordon left the window display and vanished into the depths of the shop to serve her, and Clarissa went to run her bath.

It was the village itself, she realised as she lay in the warm water, that was responsible for her sense of confidence. The meeting on the previous evening had been filled with resentment, even anger, and there had been several sharp exchanges between friends and neighbours who found them-selves in opposite camps. But the thing that had impressed her was that they all cared deeply, not just about their own interests, but also about what they considered best for Prior's Ford. They were proud of their community, and the strength of feeling seemed to have triggered off emotions that had lain dormant in Clarissa since Keith's death.

Perhaps they had been dormant since her mar-riage – a marriage that, viewed in hindsight, had been safe and comfortable, but had only worked because she, rather than Keith, had made the necessary sacrifices that made it work.

'Mum!' Calum roared from the living room, 'this porridge doesn't have any taste in it.'

'Oh no!' Jenny who had just finished ladling porridge into bowls for herself and Andrew, ran a finger over the wooden spoon, and then licked it. 'I've forgotten to put the salt in.'

'You haven't, Jen!' Andrew was polishing his shoes. 'Porridge without salt's as interesting as sucking a rag.'

'Sshhh! Don't let Calum hear you say things like that.'

'I meant a clean rag.'

'Put sugar on it, Calum,' Jenny called.

'Eugghhh!'

'My son, the true Scot.' Andrew grinned.

'You and I are going to eat our porridge in front of him, salt or no salt. And no screwing up your nose at it.' Jenny scooped a jar of raisins and currants from its shelf. 'I'll mix some of these into his to make it more palatable. Yours too, if you want.'

'Jen.' He stopped her with a hand on her arm as she was about to hurry into the living room. 'Are you sure you're all right? You looked drained when you came home from the meeting last night, and you didn't sleep well. You did a lot of tossing and turning.'

'I'm fine – it was such a noisy meeting that I couldn't get it out of my head until the small hours. Sorry, love,' she told Calum as she went into the living room, where the family ate at a table in a dining recess, 'your dozy mum forgot the salt this morning. Let's sprinkle this fruit over

196

your porridge to make it tastier.'

When she went to the door to see Calum off to school, she looked anxiously to left and right, but everything seemed normal. The few people on the pavement were neighbours and there wasn't a stranger in sight.

Andrew had already gone off to work, having manfully eaten his unsalted porridge without a word of complaint. Jenny cleared the table and washed the dishes, stacking them on the draining board to dry. Then she hurried upstairs to make the beds. When they were done, she went to her wardrobe and brought out a shoebox that had been pushed to the back, where it could lie unnoticed and undisturbed.

The first item to be lifted out was a marriage licence from 1990 naming Janet Alice McGrath, spinster, aged seventeen, and Neil Cameron, widower, aged twenty-eight. Then came a few photographs of the bride and groom: she, with long fair hair curtaining either side of a smiling face; he, broad-shouldered, handsome, more than a head taller than the slender girl clinging to his arm.

Jenny glanced up at the wall mirror. She was thirty years old now, with her fair hair cut short, and she had matured a great deal since the day she had trustingly given her future into Neil Cameron's care. She put the photograph beside the licence and picked up the remaining three photographs from the box.

The first was of a toddler, snapped as she staggered towards the photographer across a sunny lawn, her arms outstretched and a huge grin on her face. Jenny smiled back tremulously, her own arms aching to catch and hold the baby.

The second picture showed the man from the wedding portrait sitting on a wall with the little girl on his knee, both laughing into the camera, dark heads tousled by a breeze. In the third photograph, Jenny was holding the child, now some eighteen months older than before, and they were leaning towards each other on the verge of a kiss.

Jenny ran the tip of a finger across the little girl's bonny face, kissed the photograph, and then jumped guiltily as the phone rang. She ran downstairs, then hesitated, staring at the telephone. It continued to ring, the noise drilling through her head until, finally, she could bear it no longer.

'Jenny?' Ingrid's clear confident voice fell into her ear like soothing balm. 'Are you all right?'

'I'm fine – I was upstairs, making the beds,' Jenny lied, her voice almost singing her relief.

'I wondered if you were coming to the shop this morning. Helen's here and she's got good news so we're going to celebrate by finishing off the wine left over from the opening. You don't want to miss that, do you?'

'I'll be there in ten minutes,' Jenny assured her. As soon as the call was ended she hurried upstairs again to put the shoebox and its contents away.

As she walked to the Gift Horse she kept a lookout for strangers, just in case, and gave a small sigh of relief as she entered the shop.

'So – what's your news, Helen?'

Helen was glowing. 'Two things really – I met the reporter from the *Dumfries News* in the

Neurotic Cuckoo last night. He interviewed some people, including Marcy, and he said he liked the news items I've sent in,' she said proudly.

'He said that he was *impressed* with your work,' Ingrid corrected her, handing glasses round. 'At last Helen's getting some praise instead of being taken for granted.'

'And this morning I got the tutor's report on that short story I had to do for my writing course. Gold stars all round – she thinks I'm good at characters, and plotting as well. Isn't that wonderful?'

'It is!' Jenny hugged her friend. 'You'll be starting on that novel soon, then?'

'I've got an exercise book full of ideas and notes – it's a case of finding out how and where to start. And trying to find the time,' Helen added wryly.

'Did the quarry people go to the Neurotic Cuckoo after the meeting?' Jenny enquired casually after she and Ingrid had toasted Helen's successes.

'Apparently they left the village right afterwards but everyone else went for a drink. The place was packed. Have some shortbread with your wine,' Ingrid offered the plate round. 'I met Naomi in the village store earlier; she said they were very tight-lipped as to their thoughts on the meeting. Sam and Marcy were tight-lipped too – with each other. I don't like the way this business is dividing them.' She took a sip of wine. 'So, Jenny, when are you going to tell us what's wrong?'

'Nothing's wrong.'

'You almost ran from the meeting last night – it was as if a ghost was following you,' Ingrid said gently, while Helen added, 'And that man who was staring at you asked us about you, afterwards.'

Jenny felt the colour drain from her face. 'What did he say? What did *you* say?'

'He asked your name, and when we told him, he said he thought you might have known each other as school children, but he was mistaken. Was he?' Helen asked, and then, when Jenny said nothing, 'Friends are there to help each other. Sometimes it helps to share.'

Jenny looked from one to the other of her two best friends, then said, 'His name is Malcolm Cameron and he's my brother-in-law. My husband is a man called Neil Cameron, and we married thirteen years ago, when I was seventeen. It was a mistake. I was too young and he was ... well, it wasn't happy. He worked on an oil rig, and one day when he was at sea I plucked up the courage to walk out, and ended up in Edinburgh. I changed my name from Janet to Jenny, and got a job – in the office Andrew worked in, so that's how we met. I didn't think I would ever trust a man again, but Andrew was so different from Neil. When he asked me to marry him, I had to tell him the truth; instead of walking away, he got a new job in Kirkcudbright. And we moved here and set up house together and had Calum. I've been happy ever since – until last night when I recognised Malcolm.'

She drained her glass and held it out. As Ingrid refilled it, Helen asked, 'You didn't divorce your husband?'

'I couldn't; it would have meant him finding out where I lived. He's the sort of man who looks on a wife as a possession,' Jenny said. 'Andrew was terrific. It was his idea for us to go abroad on holi-

200

day and then pretend we'd had a romantic wedding while we were away. You really believe Malcolm thinks he was wrong about me last night?'

'He seemed to. Lots of women fall into bad marriages, Jenny,' Ingrid said earnestly. 'Your husband was at fault, not you. You did the right thing, to leave him.'

'It wasn't as easy as that, though.' This time Jenny took a gulp of wine. 'Neil's quite a bit older than I am, and he'd been married before. His first wife died in childbirth, and his daughter Maggie was just over a year old when we got married. She was the sweetest little thing – I think she was the real reason I married Neil,' she said with a shaky laugh. 'I loved her as though she were my own little girl, and she loved and trusted me, but when I left Neil, I had to leave her as well. I couldn't take her with me because she wasn't – she wasn't mine to take.' She looked at the other two, tears welling in her eyes. 'I've never forgiven myself for leaving her. I never will.'

Helen's arms went round her. 'You wouldn't have helped her by staying in an unhappy marriage,' she said quickly, and Ingrid nodded, reaching out to stroke Jenny's back. 'Who would look after her when you'd – gone?'

'Neil's parents were caring for her before I married him. They loved her and after I came along they still insisted on taking her for one day every week. That was how I managed to leave,' Jenny explained. 'It was Maggie's day with her grandparents. They're lovely people.'

'Then she's being looked after well – you must

always remember that. And perhaps,' Ingrid said, 'you'll meet Maggie again, one day.'

'I can always hope,' Jenny said, mopping her eyes as the shop bell rang.

22

It was a day of confidences in Prior's Ford. As Jenny told her friends about her secret past, Libby Mason was announcing, 'Mr Ralston-Kerr to see you, Glen.'

Glen Mason was hunched over his computer in the parlour, a small, cosy room he and Libby used most of the time. He jumped to his feet. 'Come in, Mr Ralston-Kerr, it's a pleasure to see you. You'll have a drink?'

'It's too early in the morning for me.' Hector gestured at the computer. 'Am I interrupting something important?'

'Only the accounts – I hate 'em. I can't get the hang of computers, can you?'

'We don't have one. I got a calculator for my last birthday, and I can just about manage that. I wondered if I could have a word?' Hector asked.

'Sure you won't have a drink?'

'He'll have a cup of tea and a scone – they're cooling on the rack,' Libby said firmly, and Hector's face lit up.

'That sounds very nice – thank you.'

'I'll bring a tray through.'

'I understand from my son that feelings were

running high at the meeting last night,' Hector said.

'Sit there; it's a good comfortable seat and I'll sit here. Aye, they were, but that's what the meeting was all about – letting folk have their say.'

'Fliss and I felt it best to stay away and leave it to Lewis. I gather that everyone knows now about us owning the land. The thing is, Mr Mason,' Hector went on as Glen nodded, 'there's been a further develop–' he stopped speaking as Libby brought in a tray of tea and scones. She set it down on a small table between their two armchairs, ordered them to eat up, and left.

'You were saying?' Glen prompted, pushing the milk jug and sugar bowl towards his guest. 'A development, is it?'

'Yes. Last week we received a lawyer's letter, offering us a payment of two hundred thousand pounds if we refused to lease the land to the quarry company.'

Glen let out a long slow whistle. 'That's a lot of money. Who from?'

'That's the thing – we have no idea. We took the letter to our own lawyer at once, and he has verified its legality but the firm who wrote the letter refuse to divulge their client's name.'

'Where's this firm based?'

'Somewhere in England.'

'So it's not come from anyone living in the village. D'you know of anyone who would want to give you that sort of money? Relatives or friends, or perhaps someone who used to live here and still has an interest in the place? Have a scone.'

Hector accepted one of Libby's melt in the

mouth scones. 'We don't have any rich friends or relatives, and we can't think of any former village residents who might have suddenly come into money. All we know is that someone out there is very keen on stopping the reopening.'

'There's more than a few of us right here who feel the same way,' Glen said.

Hector had taken a bite from the scone. He chewed, swallowed, then said, 'This is delicious.'

'My Libby's the best cook and baker I know,' Glen agreed proudly, 'and she loves to feed folk. I've no doubt she'll be setting up a bag of scones for you to take back to Linn Hall with you.'

'Very kind,' Hector said, and then, reverting to the problem uppermost in his mind, 'The thing is, this person, whoever it is, is using me as his or her pawn. I'm being asked to represent their wishes and that's something I cannot do.'

'Is there some way I can help you?'

'I doubt it, but after hearing what Lewis had to say about the mood of last night's meeting, my wife and I felt we should confide our own dilemma in someone, rather than keep it to ourselves.'

'What about the vicar?'

'Fliss did suggest her, but I thought – man to man,' Hector said vaguely.

'I see what you mean.'

'You appreciate that I wouldn't want this to become common knowledge.'

'Of course not. So what are you going to do about it? It's a powerful lot of money – you must feel tempted.'

'It would be nice to have such an amount in the bank, but on the other hand, it wouldn't be our money.' Hector's brow furrowed. 'I love this village, Mr Mason, and I'm not a Judas – I would never betray it. It seems as though Fliss and I have no option but to wait and see what happens.'

'Is there a time limit on this offer you've got?'

'No, there isn't.' Hector finished his tea and folded his napkin neatly before laying it on the tray. Then he struggled out of the comfortable armchair with a cracking of knee joints. 'I appreciate you listening, Mr Mason; even though I knew you couldn't possibly suggest a solution to our dilemma it has helped me to talk it over with you. It's reassuring to know it isn't just our secret now, and that we can trust you.'

He held out his hand and Glen shook it.

'Indeed you can, Mr Ralston-Kerr. I love this village too, and I want what's best for it,' he said.

As Clarissa set out with her shopping basket she met Alastair Marshall coming along Main Street, a large and bulky canvas bag over one shoulder.

'Good morning,' he called, 'lovely day, isn't it?'

'Beautiful!'

'What did you think of the meeting?'

'It was very interesting and I was impressed by the number of people who care passionately about this village. But at the same time, there was such strength of feeling that I don't know if this business can be settled amicably.'

'We shall just have to wait and see. By the way, I've got something for you.' He lowered the bag to the ground, then dug into his pocket and produced a booklet. *The Highway Code.*

'Thank you, that's kind of you.' She put it into

the basket while he hoisted the strap of his bag back over his shoulder. 'That looks very heavy.'

'The final batch of paintings for the Gift Horse.'

'And you carried them all the way from your cottage?'

'I didn't think it a good idea to try loading them on my old bike. They're not too heavy – I can manage. I always have.'

'Will there be more?'

'If I'm very lucky and these sell.'

'You should borrow my car next time.' It felt good to be able to say, 'my car'.

'I couldn't do that!'

'Of course you can. It's just sitting there in the garage doing nothing at the moment. You're welcome to use it any time.'

'Well, thanks – if you're sure,' he said, adding, when she nodded, 'And talking about your new car, isn't it time we set a date for your first lesson?'

'It probably is.'

'The first thing to do is to get your provisional licence, and your L-plates. Have you got a computer? You can do it online,' he said when she nodded.

'It's – it was – Keith's computer. I'm not an expert. I suppose that's something else I should come to terms with.'

'I know my way around the little devils. I can do it for you this afternoon, if you're free.'

'All right. Two o'clock? Or better still, make it one and we'll have lunch.'

'Okay, thanks.' He went off along the road while she crossed over to go into the village store.

'So what are you painting now?' Clarissa asked during lunch.

'Would you believe? A garden shed. Someone living on the Mill Walk estate has just bought a new shed and wants it painted blue to match her plant pot.'

'Isn't that a mundane job for an artist?'

'A brush is a brush, and we artists can't afford to pass up on anything that pays. Actually, I'm enjoying it – honestly, I am,' he added as Clarissa eyed him doubtfully. 'I'm getting lots of fresh air and it's nice to be able to do something completely different for a change. You should try it some time.'

'Painting sheds?'

'Doing something entirely different.'

'You know, you could be right,' Clarissa said thoughtfully. 'Perhaps I should.'

'Which,' Alastair pushed his chair back, 'brings us to the business in hand. Thank you for a lovely lunch, but now it's time to get this provisional licence sorted out. Lead me to the word processor!'

'If you ask me,' Glen said at the next committee meeting, 'we managed to get our message across to the platform party last week.'

'But so did the opposition,' Lachie pointed out. 'We need to keep the protest going.'

'You're right. Any bright ideas?'

'I think we should have had the bright ideas a good while ago,' Marcy sounded glum. 'The local kids like to play at the quarry – if we'd only thought of setting up a proper play area there for them, the quarry people might not have come up with the idea of reopening it.'

'A play area!' Glen thumped his big fist on the table and Helen, about to pick up her glass of lager shandy got some of it over the back of her hand. 'Why didn't anyone think of that? We could still go for it, surely?'

'A bit late, isn't it?' Robert said, while Pete added, 'It would take money. Where do we get it?'

'The lottery people?'

'That would take ages,' Marcy pointed out. 'We should be thinking of raising money for legal fees rather than a play area in a quarry that might be starting up again. You need money to fight a big company.'

'You're right – how do we do that?' Glen looked round the table, rallying his troops. 'Collecting boxes in the village shops?'

'I doubt if that would raise much. Something sponsored,' Robert suggested. 'A run, or a hill climb?'

'Don't be daft,' Pete scoffed. 'The way the village's split over this quarry business a sponsored event wouldn't work. Those against the quarry would be up for it but those for it wouldn't. It's got to be something general, something everyone would enjoy, no matter how they feel about the quarry. Something to bring us all together.'

'A village event,' Pete chimed in, and Robert nodded. 'Exactly.'

'A summer fayre,' Marcy said.

'There's the garden party up at Linn Hall every August – no point in having two events,' Glen argued.

'Not a garden party – an old-fashioned summer f-a-y-r-e.' Marcy spelled it out. 'With stalls and a coconut shy, and a maypole...'

'And a tug of war – and what about a pillow fight on a greasy pole?' Helen chimed in. 'And toffee apples and a lucky dip...'

Suddenly everyone was beginning to sit up and take notice. Helen scribbled ideas down as they were fired at her, her hand moving swiftly down the page.

'Reckon we could do it?' Lachie asked, and, when he was assured by his fellow committee members that they could certainly do it, 'But where? The Ralston-Kerrs already do the garden party and if the old fellow up there's unhappy about backing either side, he won't want to let us use his land.'

'The church hall?' Pete offered.

'With a greasy pole and a maypole? I don't think so.' Glen threw cold water on the idea straight away.

'What about one of Bert McNair's fields? The one nearest the road down by the river. Bert's neither one way nor the other about the quarry – he'd probably be willing to help us out for a small share of the proceeds,' Marcy suggested, and it was decided.

With renewed energy and interest, the committee members each took a deep draught of their drinks, and got down to the business of planning the new village event.

23

'I don't see the sense in having a summer fayre when the Hall already does a very nice garden party for the village,' Sam pointed out.

'The summer's long enough for both events,' Marcy argued from the counter where she was setting up a display of Easter eggs.

Sam was behind a stack of shelves, out of sight. 'Not as far as I'm concerned,' she heard him say. 'For one thing, I suppose this new idea of Glen's means that you're going to have to go to more meetings and get involved with setting up this "fayre". Haven't we got enough to do, running this place?'

'I don't mind working on both things at the same time.' Marcy wished he would lighten up and stop being such a wet blanket. When she had first met him Sam had been fun, but now he seemed to be settling too quickly into middle age. Worse than that, he was already showing signs of becoming a grumpy old man; he was beginning to make Victor Meldrew look quite tolerant. 'Women can multi-task, you know. And in any case' – she raised her voice to drown the exasperated snort from behind the shelves – 'I'd enjoy having something different to do.'

'What are you talking about, woman? There's always something different needing doing here or in the house.'

'Not different enough.' Marcy hoisted a large, brightly wrapped chocolate egg in one hand, glanced over at the shelves and imagined for a moment that she could pull a pin from it with her teeth, lob it over the top of the shelving and watch it explode, showering Glen with a lethal burst of wrapped toffees. The thought was enough to bring a broad smile to her face and put her into a happier frame of mind.

'You'll never get this fund-raising thing off the ground in time,' he narked on, returning to the counter. 'It takes months to set up fairs – perhaps even longer to set up *fayres!*'

'You are *so* funny. And you never know – we might do it. Many hands make light work, and this is something for the whole village to enjoy.'

'It's a sneaky way of raising money for the fight against the quarry.'

'It's also a bonding exercise. The village needs to come together and this is the perfect opportunity. What better than a fun day?'

'I can guarantee,' Sam sneered, 'that this shop'll be making a nice profit from the quarry workers before you're halfway through setting up your fun day.'

'Perhaps, but at least we'll have tried to keep the village quiet and dust-free. Failing isn't a matter of trying and not succeeding, Sam, it's not even trying at all.'

He gave a heavy, martyred sigh. 'Does that mean you're going to stay with this committee of Glen's?'

'I am. And it's not just Glen's, it's mine and Helen's and Pete's and Robert's and Lachie's. I'm

211

enjoying it,' Marcy said, thinking to herself that at least the committee had some life about it, which was more than she could say for Sam these days.

The bell gave its usual double-note signal as the door opened and shut. 'Good morning,' Ingrid MacKenzie greeted the two of them.

'Ingrid, you'd support a summer fayre, wouldn't you?'

'You mean, as well as the garden party at the Hall? Of course, it would be fun.' Ingrid moved swiftly round the shelves as she spoke, picking up a loaf here, a packet of biscuits there. 'When and where will it be?'

'Probably nowhere and no time,' Sam said. 'It's a daft idea from this protest committee Glen set up. I've just been pointing out to Marcy that by the time they get it organised, summer'll be over and the quarry might well be in operation.'

'It would take some time,' Ingrid agreed, arriving at the counter with her basket half filled. Then, as she saw the Easter egg display, 'I had better take two of those for the girls before they're all sold.'

'Which ones do you want? You wouldn't be willing to come on board the committee, would you, Ingrid? You're good at organising.'

'This one, I think – and another the same. If I give them different eggs, Ella will only want Freya's. I would have loved to help, Marcy, but with the Gift Horse open now, I won't have the time – nor will Jenny.'

'That'll be six pounds thirty-seven pence.'

'But Sam's right,' Ingrid said as she rummaged through her purse, 'you have left it a bit late for a summer fayre. Why not have an Easter egg hunt instead? You could get everyone to boil some eggs and hide them about a field for the children to find. And if you set up a trestle table and supplied paints and brushes, they could paint their eggs once they found them. If the weather's bad, you could use the village hall.'

'And we could still have a tug of war, and games,' Marcy said, 'and some stalls selling home baking and second-hand books to raise funds.'

'Exactly. That wouldn't take much organising.'

'Ingrid, you're a marvel!'

'Not really – just a mother,' Ingrid said as she gathered up her basket.

Molly was about to leave the kitchen garden, her arms filled with rhubarb, when she spotted Lewis coming out of the kitchen. She turned away hastily and stooped to pick another stalk, making sure that she was in his line of vision, then moved slowly towards the gate.

When he stepped into her path with a triumphant, 'We meet again,' she squeaked like a startled kitten and took a step back, clutching the stalks to her chest.

'I-I didn't see you there!'

'And every time you do see me, you pretend that you don't.'

'I do not!' lied Molly, who had always found that 'treat 'em mean and keep 'em keen' worked very well.

'You do so!' he teased, using the childish phrase spoken in every primary-school playground argument, startling a faint smile out of her before she managed to control her features.

'I have *not* been pretending that I didn't see you. That would be childish.'

'Yes, it would. So what've I done to upset you?'

'Nothing.'

'That's what I thought. We've only spoken to each other once, and it seemed to me we got on well that day.' Then, as she stared past him, biting her lip, he said, 'I did upset you, didn't I?'

'You didn't upset me, you just made a fool of me and I don't like that.'

'Made a fool of you?'

Molly pouted up at him. 'You knew that I thought you were working here the same as me, and you let me go on thinking this. Why didn't you tell me your name was Ralston-Kerr?'

'Oh, that. I don't know – you obviously thought I was employed here and I felt that if I put you right, you'd be embarrassed at making a mistake. So I left it. I was going to tell you the next time we met – in the pub, or around here. Only you kept avoiding me, so I didn't get the chance.'

'Yes, I would have been embarrassed, but not as embarrassed as I was when I mentioned you to the others and they laughed at me because I didn't realise you're the owner's son.'

'Okay, I'm sorry. I really didn't mean to upset you. Do you think you could possibly forgive me, perhaps in a few years' time? I'm willing to wait.'

Her mouth trembled, then relaxed into a smile. 'I suppose I might, if you play your cards right, Mr Ralston-Kerr.'

'Mr Ralston-Kerr is my father. I haven't grown into the name yet. I'm just plain Lewis.'

214

'And I,' she said, holding her hand out, 'am plain Molly. Pleased to meet you again, Lewis. Don't you agree we plain folk should stick together?'

'I do indeed. We could start by meeting for a drink in the Neurotic Cuckoo this evening.'

'A drink would be very nice – but not in the local pub because the others will probably be there and I don't want them to start teasing me again.'

'There are other villages with other pubs. I'll come to the gatehouse at eight.'

'Not in front of the others,' she insisted. 'I'll meet you at the old stables; that's where you keep your car, isn't it?' Then, when he nodded, 'See you there at eight o'clock tonight.'

When he arrived at exactly eight o'clock Lewis found the stable area deserted. He opened the double doors of what had been the coach house and drove his small car out into the weedy court-yard where once the family horses had been saddled and bridled by grooms. He got out to close the doors again and jumped as Molly sud-denly appeared round the side of the building.

'Boo!'

'Where did you come from?'

'I've been waiting round there for the past five minutes.' She stuck her fists in the pockets of her knitted jacket and grinned at him. 'I was begin-ning to think you were going to stand me up.'

'As if!' He opened the passenger door for her, but she shook her head and settled into the rear seat instead.

'What are you doing back there?'

'Drive on, Jeeves, and I'll tell you.' She snuggled

215

into the seat, resting her head on the back. Glancing in the rearview mirror as he set off down the drive, Lewis saw her eyes were shut tightly.

'What are you up to now?'

'I'm imagining I'm Lady Molly, and you're Jeeves, my faithful chauffeur, taking me off to Lord Someone's house for cocktails and dinner,' she said dreamily. 'Oh, it must have been marvellous to live like that.'

'I wouldn't know.'

'But you were brought up in that lovely big house. It must have been wonderful,' she insisted.

'You haven't seen much of the house, have you?'

'Only the kitchen so far. Will you show me round some time?'

'Yes, if you want. But I have to warn you, most of the rooms have been shut off – they're never used. And growing up in Linn Hall was a very chilly experience because my parents couldn't afford to heat the place. You'd have hated it.'

'Are you an only child?' she asked, and when he nodded, 'Then one day Linn Hall will be yours?'

'Yes, if it's still standing by then.' Much as he loved the place, the thought of inheriting it nagged constantly at the back of his mind. Lewis wanted his future to hold more than just continuing the grinding struggle that was gradually wearing his parents down. And, glancing in the rear-view mirror at Molly, he thought, wistfully, that he would really like his future to have someone like her in it.

24

On the day of her first driving lesson Clarissa suffered all morning from butterflies in the stomach. On more than one occasion she picked up the phone to tell Alastair that she wasn't feeling well, or that something important had come up that could not be put off until another day, but each time she made herself hang up before she had finished dialling.

As a school teacher she had been good at convincing pupils – and, on occasion, parents and colleagues – that they could and would achieve anything they aimed for; but it wasn't nearly as easy to try to convince herself. A small voice tended to snap back that it may be possible to fool most of the people most of the time, but not possible to fool oneself.

She bustled about the house, trying to find work to keep her mind off the forthcoming ordeal. It helped to soothe the butterflies a little, but when the phone rang they woke and lifted in a rainbow cloud, battering against the walls of her stomach.

She jumped, almost dropping the crystal vase she was washing. Hurriedly lowering it into the safety of the kitchen sink she picked up a tea-towel as she went to the hall.

It was Alexandra – lucky Alexandra, who had sensibly passed her driving test before her twentieth birthday. Capable Alexandra, who, in the unlikely event of suffering an attack of butterflies in the stomach, would have used them to start up a butterfly farm.

'Clarissa, how are you?' she enquired in the brisk tone of one who did not wish to be told the truth unless it were both brief and pleasant.

Clarissa obliged, as always. 'Very well, Alexandra. And you?'

'The same. I had lunch with Steven yesterday and we were wondering if you had done any more about selling the house. Steven brought along brochures for two small flats that would suit you, not far from where you and Pops used to live. I'll tell him to post them to you, will I? Or email if you'd rather.'

'No, don't do that.'

'You don't do email? Then he can post–'

'I mean, I haven't decided what to do yet.'

There was a brief, exasperated pause before Alexandra said, in the tone of someone speaking to a very old grandmother in her dotage, 'But it's been quite a while, Clarissa, and we really thought you would have moved back to England by now – where we can see more of you.'

Clarissa translated that as 'where we can keep an eye on you'.

'I read somewhere that bereaved people should wait for a year before making major decisions such as moving house.'

'I think that that applies only if one has been living in the same house for a long time,' Alexandra informed her. 'You and Pops had only just moved to Scotland – you hadn't even settled in properly.

We assumed you would be anxious to come back to familiar surroundings, and to your friends.'

A mental picture of Stella – best friend, sister-substitute, and betrayer – swept into Clarissa's mind.

'Hello? Are you still there?' Alexandra asked, and Clarissa realised that she was staring at the wall, gritting her teeth so tightly that it took a few seconds to unlock her jaw.

'Yes, I'm here. I thought I saw someone coming to the door, but I was mistaken.'

'You're not really planning to wait for a whole year before you decide on your move? Steven pointed out that with house prices rising as they are, it's a case of the sooner the better. Look, I'm in the office so I can't stay on the phone for too long. Would you like me to come up so we can talk about things properly? I'm quite busy but I could probably fit in an overnight visit in about two weeks' time.'

'No, don't do that,' Clarissa said swiftly. 'I promise I'll give the matter some thought, but I don't have much time myself at the moment. My driving instructor's due at any moment.'

'Your what?' Her stepdaughter's voice soared into a yelp and Clarissa wondered if heads were turning in the office.

'My driving instructor. I'm going to learn to drive.'

'In Dad's *Jaguar?*' Heads in the next office were probably beginning to turn as well, Clarissa thought.

'Oh no, that's not a car for a learner. I've traded it in for a very nice Vauxhall Astra.'

'Clar–' Alexandra's voice seemed to catch in her throat and she had to try again. 'Clarissa, are you sure you're doing the right thing?'

'Absolutely, dear.'

'But learning to drive at your age – is it wise?'

If challenged on a quiz programme like *Mastermind* to tell where one's hackles were, Clarissa had always assumed she would have been hard put to find the right answer; but now she felt hers beginning to stir. 'Perhaps I can be classed as elderly, Alexandra, but I'm not yet senile.'

'I didn't say you were, but what's wrong with taxis? You can afford them, can't you?'

'I can afford a lot of things that I have no intention of getting. Ah,' Clarissa said with relief, as a shadow darkened the glass panel in the front door, 'here's my instructor. I must go, Alexandra. Thank you for phoning; give my love to Steven the next time you talk to him. Goodbye, dear.'

'Ready?' Alastair asked when she opened the door.

'As ready as I'll ever be.' Realising she was still holding the teatowel, she thrust it into his hands, took her coat off the hook and put it on, and then took the teatowel back and hung it over the banister before picking up her bag.

'Oh – car keys and garage opener.' She took them from the drawer in the hall table and then smiled up at him. 'Let's go.'

Thanks to Alexandra the butterflies had disappeared, swept away by the realisation that Clarissa wasn't just learning to drive for her own sake – she was doing it to prove to herself, her stepchildren and the entire world, including Stella (aka Deceitful Friend) Bartholomew that she was quite capable of taking control of her own life.

Alastair tied the L-plates to the rear and front bumpers and ushered Clarissa into the passenger seat before taking his place behind the steering wheel.

'Watch, listen and learn,' he instructed as he started up the engine, then began a running commentary on every move he made. Clarissa tried hard to follow everything, but all too soon he brought the car to a standstill on a quiet country road, saying, 'And this is where we change places.'

An overlooked butterfly somewhere behind Clarissa's midriff gave a weak flutter of its wings. 'Wait,' she said and Alastair paused, one long leg already out of the car.

'What?'

'Do you seriously think I can do this?'

'Of course you can do it, woman. You've got a perfectly good brain and functioning arms and legs, not to mention eyes and ears. Some of the drivers on our roads are total idiots who don't even know what indicators are for. If they can drive, you can drive.'

'My stepdaughter phoned just before you arrived. She questions the sense of me learning at my age.'

'She sounds like one of those idiots who don't know what an indicator's for.'

'Actually, she's a very clever person. She can drive with an empty cigarette packet balanced on the dashboard and never let it topple over.'

'I'll bring an empty cigarette packet next time and teach you how to drive while balancing it on your head if you want. Anything she can do, you can do better. Repeat that, if you please,' he requested and then, when she had done so, 'And now, let's get on with the business of turning you into a first-class driver.'

When the lesson ended Alastair, with regret, turned down Clarissa's invitation to stay for dinner. 'Glen Mason and his committee have come up with the idea of an Easter egg hunt at Tarbethill Farm on the day after Good Friday and they want me to design a poster for it.'

'That sounds like fun.'

'I think it will be. But there's not much time, and I said I would go along to the pub to discuss it this evening, so I have to go home to finish off the ideas I've come up with. Once they approve a design I'll have to get cracking so the posters can go up as soon as possible. Same time next Wednesday suit you for your second lesson?'

'That would be fine. Thank you, Alastair, you're a very good instructor.'

'No problem, I enjoyed it. You're an apt pupil,' he said before loping off with a wave of the hand. Clarissa, feeling rather pleased with herself, went indoors to change into her gardening clothes.

She was kneeling by a border in the back garden, gently trowelling round clumps of spring flowers, when Naomi Hennessey came round the side of the house an hour later.

'Hello there – don't let me interrupt you at your work,' the minister said as Clarissa began to scramble to her feet. 'I'll sit here for a moment, if I may.'

She was wearing a long black skirt and a brightly coloured blouse that looked marvellous against her smooth brown skin. She settled down on the bench with a contented sigh.

'I really am going to have to start making more time for the garden,' Clarissa said. 'It was always my husband's area, but I like gardening, though I'm not sure that I'll manage all of it on my own.'

'There's a lad in the village who has a good natural touch where gardens are concerned. I think he would suit you very well – let me know if you need his help. So how are you, Mrs Ramsay? Or may I call you Clarissa? Such a lovely name.'

'Of course.' Clarissa had always thought her name old-fashioned and stuffy, but the way Naomi Hennessey's voice spread itself over each syllable like golden syrup gave it a richness it had never held before.

'You look well.'

'I am well, thank you. I had my first driving lesson today.'

'Good for you; you're beginning to forge your path into the future.'

'I suppose I am,' Clarissa said slowly. 'I hadn't thought of it like that.'

'Life is an adventure. We never know what lies just around the corner.'

'Sometimes there be dragons.' Clarissa stabbed at the ground with the point of her trowel. 'It was hard enough losing my husband, without losing my best friend as well.'

'I'm so sorry; when did your friend die?'

Clarissa gave a short, mirthless laugh. 'Oh, she's still very much alive. What I meant was that she – well, she let me down badly, just when I most needed her support.'

'My dear,' Naomi said gently, 'you didn't lose her. We can never ever lose a friend. You only lost someone you had *assumed* to be a friend.'

Clarissa sat back on her heels and stared at the minister. 'Do you know, I believe that you're right.'

'I know I am, in this case at least. You should consider the possibility that your dragon is in fact a blessing – you are now free of someone who didn't deserve your friendship, and they will never be able to hurt you again. We must always conquer the dragons and rejoice in the blessings. Did you find the protest meeting interesting?'

'Very. I had no idea people cared so much about this place.'

'That's what I like about the villagers – they *do* care, very much, even when they can't agree,' Naomi said, then closed her eyes and lifted her face to the sun for a long moment before letting her breath out in a sigh. 'We really are nearer to God's heart in a garden. I just wish that He and I could find the time to do a bit more work in mine.'

Again she lapsed into silence while Clarissa returned to her work. She had been content enough on her own, but somehow Naomi's silent presence brought an added air of serenity and peace to the garden.

A small bird fluttered down from a tree to land nearby. It cocked its head to one side and surveyed Clarissa for a moment before starting to peck at the newly disturbed earth. She worked on, turning the rich brown soil carefully, while the bird foraged and Naomi mused – or possibly dozed – in the sunshine.

When the bird finally flew off the soft flutter of its feathery wings disturbed the minister. She sat upright, opened her eyes and said reluctantly, 'Well, I suppose I had better be going.'

'Can I offer you some tea or coffee before you go? I'm so sorry, I should have offered refreshments when you arrived.'

Naomi smiled her wide, warm smile. 'My dear Clarissa, I'm a minister, and as part of my ministry I'm expected to drink gallons of tea and pints of coffee every single day. It's a pleasure to have spent time with you – dry time!' She gave a laugh that came from the very depths of her body, and got up, reaching down to help Clarissa to her feet. Then she enfolded both of Clarissa's hands in her warm, strong clasp, looking deep into her eyes.

'It's good to see you looking so refreshed,' she said as she stepped back.

'I feel refreshed, but I thought ministers liked to end their visits with a prayer,' Clarissa said teasingly. 'Don't you want us to pray together?'

Naomi, on her way towards the path that ran round to the front of the house, turned back. 'Oh, we did that,' she said. 'Didn't you notice?'

And she winked before disappearing round the side of the house.

25

Clarissa was not entirely surprised when Steven phoned that evening.

'Clarissa, how are you?'

'I'm well, Steven, and how are you and Chris?'

'Fine. I was talking to Alexandra earlier and she tells me that you're taking driving lessons.'

'My first was this afternoon, as it happens.'

'How did it go?'

'I hit a sheep grazing in the middle of a field but fortunately I managed to miss the toddler on the bike.'

'In other words,' her stepson said, amusement in his voice, 'you did well and you think Alex and I should stop fussing.'

'I think you should stop worrying. I appreciate your interest, but I *can* look after myself.'

'I know you can, Clarissa. But I wondered when Alex said that you'd traded in the Jaguar – did you get a decent price for it? It was almost new and Pops always looked after his cars.'

Nobody knew that better than she did; Keith used to spend hours washing, waxing and polishing the car, as well as examining the gleaming bodywork inch by inch after every drive to make sure that not the smallest scratch or slightest dent went unnoticed. Clarissa had never fully learned how to shut a car door to his satisfaction.

'Don't worry,' she said now. 'I got the local

garage owner to have a look at it and he advised me as to how much I should accept.'

'And you got it?'

'Actually, I pushed them up by a thousand pounds. I can haggle when I have to and I knew they wanted the Jaguar more than I wanted the Astra they were offering me. Alastair was quite impressed.'

'Alastair?'

'A young man who lives in the village. He's teaching me to drive. You'd like him – I'll invite him to dinner the next time you come north.'

'So you aren't planning on putting the house on the market at the moment?'

'I don't think I've reached that stage yet, Steven. There's so much going on – the people here really *care* about the place. You don't get that sense of determination in many communities,' Clarissa said thoughtfully. 'I suppose it's something to do with being a village. And I just heard today that there's to be an Easter egg hunt.'

'Really?' Keith's son couldn't keep the surprise from his voice. 'You want to be involved in that?'

'I think I'd enjoy it.'

'Did Alexandra tell you that we have a couple of flats for sale that might suit you?'

'Yes she did, and it's kind of you to think of me, Steven, but I'll let you know when I'm ready to move back south. *If* I decide to move. What's meant for me won't go past me,' Clarissa said, quoting a phrase she had heard an old woman use in the village store a few days earlier.

Once the call was ended she poured herself a glass of sherry and then settled down for an

227

evening with *The Highway Code*.

That night she dreamed she was a child again, skipping along a hilltop, one hand clutching the string of a large yellow balloon. When she paused and looked up at the balloon, she saw it was imprinted with a picture of Stella Bartholomew's face.

She opened her fingers and let the string slip through them, then watched, laughing, as the wind lifted the balloon and carried it over the trees, and into the sky. It grew smaller and smaller until finally it was gone for ever – and Stella with it.

On Good Friday pans of eggs were boiled on almost every stove in Prior's Ford, and almost every oven was filled with trays of buns or cakes. Pancake batter bubbled on griddles and Marcy, to Sam's annoyance, took delivery of extra boxes of soft drinks from their wholesaler.

'I hope you're not expecting me to take these to the field for you,' he grumped. 'I don't see why I should donate time or petrol to help your precious protest committee.'

'It's not for them, it's for the children and the village. And I don't expect you to do anything,' she snapped back at him. 'Glen's coming to collect them tomorrow.'

'Why couldn't he order them? He's the one with the pub.'

'He's seeing to the crisps and the refreshments for the adults. I wanted to contribute something, since I haven't got time to bake. And by the way, I won't be in the store tomorrow – I'll be enjoying myself at the Easter egg hunt.'

He turned away and she watched him as he fussed around one of the shelves, unnecessarily rearranging packets of cereals. She had fully expected that by now they would have come to some sort of compromise over this wretched quarry business, but instead it seemed to be driving a wedge between them. They were both stubborn people but perhaps it was time for one of them to give a little.

'Sam, come to the field with me tomorrow. It'll be fun and we need some fun in our lives at the moment.'

He didn't turn to look at her. 'And leave the shop to run itself?'

'Close it for once. Nobody's going to come in anyway – they'll all be at the Easter egg hunt.'

'Not all. I'm surely not the only person sticking to his principles. In any case, I can't close down the post office.'

'The hunt doesn't start until twelve, and that's when the post office shuts.' Again, she waited for a reply, and when she got none she shrugged and said, 'Oh, please yourself! You always do.'

They had to get up early every working day to take in the newspapers. When the alarm rang on Saturday morning Sam rose at once and went into the bathroom without a word. Yawning, Marcy, got out of bed and drew back the curtains to see a pearl-grey sky flushed to the east with the first signs of the morning sun. It was going to be a glorious day.

Because she and Sam had little spare time to

look after a garden, the front of their house had been paved, with big tubs of flowers placed here and there. Looking down into Clarissa Ramsay's garden next door, Marcy saw that the trees there, now covered in new green leaves, were motionless.

The need to get to the shop early every morning had created a routine consisting of Marcy setting out the dishes, milk and cereals, boiling the kettle, and starting on the cooked breakfast they both enjoyed while Sam washed, shaved and dressed. When Sam came downstairs they ate together and then he cleared the table and washed the dishes while Marcy had a quick shower and got dressed. Once, they had laughed over the way they could work everything out so perfectly that usually, as Sam reached the front door, Marcy was on her way downstairs, ensuring they left the house together.

But this morning they ate in silence, and although Marcy was on her way downstairs as Sam made for the front door, she was dressed in the brightest clothes she had – a full floral-printed skirt, sandals and a vivid blue blouse – instead of her usual overall.

'I take it from the outfit that you're not coming to the store?'

'I have to help hide eggs for the children. Did you notice,' she couldn't help asking, 'how many boxes of eggs we sold this week? Nice for Bert McNair – and for us. Lachie's coming by to collect me in five minutes' time.'

'Right,' he said, and went out, ignoring her when she called after him, 'See you this afternoon?'

By mid-afternoon almost everyone in the village was in the field. Children rushed around like flocks of colourful birds, combing every grassy hillock, every tree root and every hollow for eggs, squealing with excitement each time they discovered treasure. Once found, the eggs were carried off to trestle tables where they were piled into bowls ready for the next part of the fun – the egg-painting competition, divided into age groups.

Hector Ralston-Kerr and Naomi Hennessey, wearing one of her rainbow-like outfits for the occasion, had been roped in as judges, and Fliss was going to present the prizes. Then, once the children had been given time to eat their hard-boiled eggs, young and old alike would compete in the Easter bonnet competition, judged by Ingrid and Clarissa.

'Can't one of your friends do it?' Clarissa had begged when Ingrid asked her to be a judge. 'I don't know anything about fashion!'

'Jenny and Helen both want to enter, and it has nothing to do with fashion,' Ingrid assured her. 'It's just a bit of fun, Mrs Ramsay! Think of us,' she swept on, flapping her hands about her own head, 'as mad March hares.' And then, with the dazzling smile that had made Peter MacKenzie fall madly in love with her, '*Please* won't you be my fellow judge?'

Clarissa had agreed, though she woke that morning with a sense of trepidation rather than anticipation.

But Ingrid was right – it was a day for fun and nothing, including the Easter bonnet competition, was being taken seriously. To the children's delight, Glenn Mason wore a huge eggshell on his head, while Libby had made herself a proper Victorian bonnet trimmed with lace and bedecked with flowers. There were top hats, rabbit-ear hats, hats made of real flowers and artificial flowers, floppy scarecrow hats, Australian outback hats strung with corks and, in one case, little Easter eggs. There were crowns, tiaras, a bonnet that looked like a cake and a Thomas the Tank Engine hat.

The problem lay in deciding on the winners, but finally Glen was awarded the adult prize – a bottle of sherry from his own pub, which he immediately offered up as a raffle prize, thus making more money for the quarry protest fund. The children's prize went to a little boy, so small that he was almost hidden beneath the elaborate cardboard cake balancing on his head. He accepted his prize, a box of sweets, from Fliss Ralston-Kerr and immediately scurried off to the safety of his mother's skirt lest someone should make him follow Glen's example.

'Well done,' Alastair said as he and Clarissa met up after the prize-giving. 'You're getting into the village spirit. Fancy joining me in the three-legged race?'

'The last time I tried that the girl with me fell and I ended up with a twisted ankle. I think I've done my bit.'

'True. I'll find someone else, but in the mean-time, let me treat you to a well-deserved glass of lemonade.'

In the end he and Marcy entered the three-legged race together, though the couple most eyes were on during the race were Lewis Ralston-Kerr and a pretty red-haired girl.

'Who's that with young Lewis, then?' Clarissa heard a woman mutter behind her.

'One of the lasses working up at the big house this summer. My Tommy says they've been seen together quite a lot this past week or two.'

'Think there's anything in it?'

'Hard to tell, though they do look happy with each other. It'd be nice if he got himself a proper girlfriend – he's a pleasant lad and a good son. Better than some.' The words were uttered in the tones of someone with experience of not such perfect sons.

'That's all very well, but they need to be careful, don't they? The Ralston-Kerrs, I mean. She could be a gold-digger.'

'Not much gold there, surely. They've scarce got two pennies to rub together. Haven't you seen the state of the big house? Needs all sorts doing to it!'

'I know that, but there's money in land, isn't there? A developer would pay well for that estate. Pull the big house down, build all over the place and make millions.'

'Young Lewis'd never do that, would he?' The voice was shocked. 'He loves that place as much as his mother and father do. He'd never let it be knocked down!'

'His wife might have different ideas. See what I mean when I say that he needs to be careful about who he marries?'

Then the voices were drowned in cheers as Alastair and Marcy breasted the tape inches ahead of Ingrid and Peter MacKenzie.

Several collection buckets had been placed on the trestle tables so that those who wanted to contribute to the quarry protest fund could do so, while those in favour of the quarry could refrain. But when the committee counted the takings in the living room behind the pub that evening they were pleasantly surprised at the result.

'I think that even folk who're for the quarry put something in to show their appreciation for a good afternoon.'

Marcy said. 'And it *was* good – just about everyone was there.'

Everyone but Sam. She had watched for him until her eyes ached, but he had not come. And when she went home to find him seemingly immersed in watching a football match on television, he didn't ask how the day had gone.

26

Sam and Marcy said little to each other for the rest of that weekend, and on Monday morning they walked across to go about their usual routine in silence: Sam bringing in the bundles of newspapers, Marcy arranging them on the shelves and setting aside those earmarked for delivery.

The paper boy was fourteen-year-old Jimmy McDonald, a member of the large family belonging to Jinty McDonald. Jimmy, a gangly, good-natured lad with a mop of red hair, came into the shop yawning and knuckling sleep from his blue eyes.

'Mornin', Marcy.'

'Good morning, Jimmy, how are you today?'

'Okay,' he said, and then stretched long thin arms above his head and yawned so widely that Marcy feared that his jaw might dislocate. Eventually, to her relief, he closed his mouth and gave her one of his broad grins. 'Papers ready?'

'Won't be a minute.'

'Okey-dokey,' Jimmy said amiably, and propped himself against the counter, watching idly as she noted names on the front pages of the newspapers and packed them into the delivery bag. One of the magazines slipped to the ground and Jimmy picked it up. He was handing it back to Marcy when he paused and took another look at the cover.

'I've seen that bird.' He stabbed a bony finger at the picture.

Marcy, who had once gone out with a keen bird watcher, glanced at the picture. 'I don't think so, Jimmy. They're quite rare.'

'No, I have,' the boy insisted. 'It's a big bu– a big bird, and it flies just like in the picture, with that sort of tail spread out like a fan. It can move fast, too.'

She eyed him sceptically. 'Where was this?'

'At the old quarry. They were there last year as well,' he went on casually, while Marcy's heart skipped a beat. 'We think they've got a nest. Me and some of the others tried to find it last year but the rock face is too steep. My brother Grant took a tumble and twisted his ankle. He had to miss out on some football tournaments so we won't be trying that again.'

'And you're sure,' Marcy tried to keep the excitement out of her voice, 'that it was a bird like this one?'

Jimmy nodded. 'Almost finished, are you?'

'Oh – yes.' Marcy hurriedly packed the rest of the papers and handed the bag over. As the boy cycled off on his round the first customer arrived and the day's routine began to fall into place.

Marcy found it hard to concentrate or to hide her excitement, but she had no choice. Jimmy, a pupil at Kirkcudbright Academy, returned the empty bag and went off to join the other students gathering at the bus stop. Marcy had to wait for a further half hour before the store quietened, then told Sam she had to return to the house to collect something.

'Fine – on you go while we're quiet,' he said without lifting his head. She ran across the green and into the house, where she riffled through the telephone directory until she found the number she needed.

When a voice told her that she had got through to Scottish Natural Heritage she said swiftly, 'I want to speak to someone who knows about rare birds. I live in Prior's Ford, and we have an abandoned quarry that might be opening up again. The thing is, I believe that there may be a pair of peregrine falcons nesting there...'

Jenny was in the middle of stitching a floral apron onto a knitted rabbit when the doorbell rang.

'Oh, bother!' She pushed the needle neatly into

236

the paw of the rabbit she was making to ensure it didn't get lost, and hurried to open the door. Then she stood gaping up at the man on the step.

'Hello, Janet. I thought it had to be you when I saw you at that meeting. Long time no see, eh?'

'Malcolm!'

'That's me. You don't look very pleased to see me – it's all right,' he added, putting a foot forward to block the door as she took a swift step back, 'I'm not here to cause trouble.'

'You're not? You know what could happen if Neil finds out that I'm living here...'

'He won't, I can promise you that. Can I come in for a minute?' When she began to shake her head he held out the clipboard he carried. 'It's an official visit. I'm canvassing local people to talk to them about the quarry, so nobody's going to wonder why I came to your door.'

'I'm busy. I have to go out...'

'Half an hour, Jan. You surely owe me that,' he said, and after a pause she nodded and stepped back to let him in.

'Through there.' She followed him into the living room, where he surveyed the table, covered with knitted toys and scraps of material.

'You're busy.'

'I make things for a friend's craft shop. That's where I have to go, soon. She's expecting me,' Jenny added, anxious to get rid of him as soon as possible.

'You always were good at making toys. You made something like this for Maggie.' He reached out to pick up the rabbit.

'Don't touch it,' she said swiftly, but it was too

237

late; the threaded needle had already found its victim.

'Ouch!' Malcolm Cameron dropped the rabbit back onto the table and sucked at his finger.

'I tried to warn you. D'you want a plaster?'

'No, it'll be all right,' he mumbled. 'I could murder a cup of coffee, though – if you're making one.'

'I wasn't planning to, but I will.' At least it gave her an excuse to escape to the kitchen, where she leaned against the sink for several minutes after switching on the kettle, staring through the window at the back garden and breathing slowly and deeply in and then out, silently chanting 'Peace in' with each breath she took, then 'Stress out' each time she exhaled.

The magazine where she had found this tip was wrong – deep breathing didn't help much though, to be fair, the writer might not have been referring to the shock of finding one's past catching up with one.

'It's only instant,' she said five minutes later as she carried the tray to the living room.

'Instant's fine.' Cautiously, watching for lurking needles, Malcolm cleared a space on the table for the tray.

'Sugar?'

'Two, please.'

'How did you know that I live in Prior's Ford?'

He picked up his coffee. 'I didn't. I got quite a shock when I saw you in the audience on the night of that meeting in the village hall. When I couldn't find you afterwards I spoke to the people you were sitting with.'

'I know.'

'You'll also know that I said we might have gone to school together in Dundee. When they said you were called Jenny Forsyth I pretended I was mistaken. But I knew I wasn't.' He indicated the clipboard lying on a chair. 'We have names and addresses of all the local folk – so it was elementary, my dear Jenny. Only you were called Janet when I knew you. Thanks.' He took the mug of coffee from her. 'You've changed since then. You've had your hair cut and the colour's different. You look great – and happy.'

'That's because anything's better than life with your brother.'

'I'd be the first to admit he was a difficult man.'

'Difficult? He made my life a misery almost from the day we married. I don't know how I would have survived if I hadn't walked out on him – and met Andrew.'

'You're still with him?' Malcolm asked, and then, as she nodded, 'And there's a child – a boy.'

'How did you know that?'

'I could pretend to be as clever as Hercule Poirot but in actual fact I saw the bike in the hall.'

'Calum. He's nine. You won't tell Neil you've found me, will you? Please don't tell Neil!'

'Even if I wanted to, which I don't, I couldn't tell him.' He drank some more coffee, and then said, 'There was an accident on the oil rig. Neil was killed.'

'Dead? Neil's dead?' She found it hard to believe that the domineering bully she had been married to was no longer part of the world. Disease and death happened to other people, but

Neil had seemed fated to go on for ever. She had thought that even the grim reaper would be afraid to lay a chill finger on him. 'When?'

'A good while ago – almost two years after you disappeared. I thought you might have read it in the papers.'

She began to shake her head, then said sharply, 'Maggie – where's Maggie?'

'With my parents. She's all right.'

'She'll be fourteen now – a month ago. I never forget her birthday. I always wish I could send her a card, but I've never dared to.'

'Best not. She's well settled now.' Malcolm finished his coffee, and shook his head when she offered him a refill. 'She missed you badly when you left, though. She cried for you for weeks. You were the only mother she knew.'

The very thought of wee Maggie sobbing her heart out brought tears to Jenny's eyes. She scrubbed them away with the back of a hand. 'I wanted to take her with me, but I couldn't. Neil would have set the police on me. He would have accused me of kidnapping her.'

'I'm sure he would. But it's all water under the bridge now, so best forget it.'

'That's what I was doing, until you came to the village.'

'I just wanted to make sure you were all right. Liz and I still talk about you, and wonder if you're happy. Now I know you are, I'd best be going.'

'How is Lizbeth? Have you any children of your own now?' Malcolm had married not long before Jenny escaped from her own unhappy marriage. She had liked her cheerful, efficient sister-in-law

'We didn't get time to start a family.' His voice was bleak. 'Liz developed multiple sclerosis, not much more than a year after the wedding.'

'Oh Malcolm, I'm so sorry!'

'So are we. But she's got guts and she copes very well. Better than me.' He picked up his clipboard. 'Since this is supposed to be an official visit, do I list you as opposed to the quarry, or for it?'

'Opposed. If it goes ahead, does that mean that you'll be working here?' The thought of seeing him about the place, reminding her of a past she had struggled so hard to forget, was disturbing.

He made a note and then, to her relief, shook his head. 'I'm not likely to be back here, whether the quarry goes ahead or not.'

In the hall, he glanced at Calum's bike, then asked, 'Will you tell your partner about my visit?'

'Yes, I will. Did you tell Lizbeth that you'd seen me?'

'No. It's difficult – with her health. I'm never sure about what she can cope with. And she's fond of my parents, and Maggie. I'll wait and see.' He gave her a wry smile. 'Lucky I know how to hold my tongue, isn't it?'

He opened the front door, then turned to glance down at her. 'I'm glad you're happy, Janet. Liz and I always thought you deserved better than Neil. It looks as though you have it, now.'

'I have. Give her my love, if you can.'

'We'll see,' he said, and stepped out on to the garden path.

'I was going to phone you,' Ingrid said when Jenny arrived in the shop. 'That quarry man's back in the village, talking to people.'

'I know – he came to the house. And it's all right,' Jenny said swiftly as her friend's blue eyes clouded over. 'He had news – Neil, my husband, died in an accident not long after I left.'

'And the little girl?'

'She's fine. Living with Neil's parents.'

'So – is it over?'

'Yes, it is.'

Ingrid hugged her tightly. 'I'm glad. You'll tell Andrew, of course.'

'Oh yes,' Jenny was saying when Helen burst in to the shop, her eyes shining.

'You'll never guess – I got my cheque from the newspaper this morning, and they've paid me double the usual amount because of the report I wrote on the Easter egg hunt!'

'I should think so,' Ingrid told her firmly. 'It was an excellent article and you deserve every penny of your payment.' The *Dumfries News* had run a double-page centre spread on the egg hunt, with half a dozen colour photographs of the children collecting and painting eggs, the Easter bonnet competition and the three-legged race. After hours of agonising over her computer, Helen had provided the story as the newspaper had been unable to send a reporter along on the day.

She produced the cheque from her bag and showed it off proudly. 'I think I'll frame it.'

'You will not frame it, you will take it to the bank and cash it.'

'Sometimes, Ingrid, you're too practical.'

'And sometimes, my dear Helen, you are too much of a dreamer. You earned that money and you should spend it on yourself.'

'Perhaps I will.' Helen put the cheque away and then suddenly remembered something else. 'Oh – Jenny, I met that quarry man this morning, the one you know. He said he's here to find out more about local thoughts on the quarry.'

'Yes, he came to the door.'

'What did you say?'

The door opened and a group of people came in.

'I'll tell you all about it,' Jenny said, 'later.'

27

Andrew Forsyth was a home-lover who preferred spending his spare time with his family rather than taking part in sports or spending every evening in the local pub.

Jenny and Calum were his reason for living, and he knew as soon as he got home that evening that Jenny had something on her mind. He waited until Calum had gone upstairs to finish his homework and he and Jenny were washing and drying the dinner dishes as they did together every evening, before saying, 'Come on then, spit it out.'

'Spit what out?' She scrubbed fiercely at a saucepan.

'Whatever's bothering you. That pan's supposed to be non-stick,' Andrew pointed out mildly. 'You're going to rub the coating off if you don't leave it alone.'

'Are you sure Calum's out of the way?'

Andrew, still polishing a glass, went to the foot of the stairs and listened. 'Kylie's belting out some song on his music centre,' he said when he returned to the kitchen. 'I think he's settled up there for a while.' And then as she turned from the sink to face him, wiping her hands on a teatowel, 'What is it, Jen? Tell me – you know that whatever it is, we can deal with it together. You're not–' His breath caught in his throat, making him choke slightly. 'You're not ill, are you?'

'No, of course not. I'm fine, but – Neil's brother came to see me this morning.'

'What?' Andrew put the glass down very carefully. 'How did he know where to find you?'

'He didn't. He works for the company that wants to reopen the quarry. He was at the protest meeting. That's why I came home as soon as it was over. I was trying to avoid him.'

'Why didn't you tell me at the time? I knew something was wrong that night!'

'I didn't want to start the whole thing up again by talking about it. And the next morning I heard that the quarry people had left the village right after the meeting. So I thought I was safe – until he arrived on the doorstep today.'

'Did he threaten you?' His voice was quiet, but his eyes were suddenly cold and hard beneath lowered brows. 'Because if he did I'll–'

'Of course not, Malcolm's a lovely man – not the least bit like Neil. But he had some unexpected news about Neil. He – he died in an accident, a while ago.'

She told the whole story, and Andrew heard her out without making any further comment.

244

'At least I know Maggie's all right,' she finished, 'and I don't need to worry about Neil any more. I can't believe he's gone, Andrew. He's – was – the type of man you'd think would go on for ever.'

'Is this brother likely to be working here if the quarry reopens?'

'Apparently not. He was only here today to get some local opinions. He spoke to Jenny and to Ingrid and lots of other people apparently, not just me.'

Andrew let his breath out in a long, slow sigh, then said, 'You know what this means? It means we can get married. I can make an honest woman of you at last.'

It was something he had wanted from the time Jenny got a job as secretary in the firm where he worked. At his first sight of her, with her fair hair wisping about a small, worried face, Andrew had been filled with a desire to look after her – to make her happy.

It had taken some time before she would agree to go out with him, and it wasn't until he proposed to her that she told him she was already married and why she couldn't sue for divorce.

Andrew had always been a firm believer in marriage, but when he realised how scared Jenny was of letting her husband know of her where-abouts, and how much she missed the little stepdaughter she had had to leave behind, he guessed that if Neil Cameron were to find her he could use small Maggie as bait to entice Jenny back. If that happened, Andrew would lose her. He decided that if the only way he could share his life with her was by living outside wedlock, then he would be happy to do so.

'I've been thinking about being free to marry all day,' Jenny said now, 'and I wondered – why bother? Everyone here thinks we're married, and under Scots common law we are.'

'Wouldn't a proper legal marriage ceremony make you feel safer?'

She put her arms around him and laid her cheek against his chest. 'I've been your wife for over ten years and a bit of paper wouldn't make any difference,' she said, and Andrew took her into a bear hug and kissed her soft hair, no longer wispy, but shaped by a good hairdresser into the nape of her neck.

'Same here – aren't we lucky?' he said.

At least she was free of her brute of a husband, and for the moment, she should be left to enjoy her freedom. But one day – and Andrew hoped it might be one day soon – he was determined to make their relationship legal.

After a great deal of thought Marcy called on Robert Kavanagh, who lived with his wife Cissie in a smart little two-storey house on Main Street.

She was welcomed in by Cissie, and offered tea. 'Not for me, thanks, I have to get back to the store. Actually, I wondered if I might have a word with you, Robert,' she said awkwardly. 'Committee business.'

'Aye, of course.' Robert glanced at his wife, who said at once, 'If it's business, I'll leave the two of you alone.'

'I'd not want to keep you out of your own living room...'

'Don't you worry about that, m'dear, I get quite enough committee talk from Robert after your meetings, and I'd as soon get on with my ironing in the kitchen and listen to the radio.'

Cissie bustled off and Robert ushered his visitor into the living room, where she faced him nervously.

'The fact is, Robert, I'm here about a matter that needs to be kept secret – perhaps even from the rest of the committee. I thought you were the one I should talk to first.'

'Oh?' He waved her to a chair and then listened in silence while she told him about Jimmy McDonald recognising the picture of a peregrine falcon, about her call to the local headquarters of Scottish Natural Heritage, and about the phone call she had received, confirming that there was indeed a nest at the quarry.

'The man I spoke to said that the birds have been known to nest close to working quarries, but he agreed that to reopen the Linn after the falcons had already established themselves there could well drive them away.'

'Well, it certainly strengthens our case. In fact, this is very exciting information.'

'That's what I thought. The quarry company might push ahead yet, but apparently this is the birds' breeding season. They'll have eggs in the nest and it's not a good time to disturb them.'

'It'll never be a good time,' Robert pointed out. 'They'll come back next year and, if the quarry's being worked, they won't settle. We'd miss a good tourist attraction. And that alone means we must talk the quarry company out of this idea.'

'Exactly. But I'm hesitant about telling the entire committee,' Marcy said. 'Apparently quite a lot of people who find rare birds keep quiet about them because sightseers can cause more harm than good. If we want to make this a tourist attraction then we need to go about it carefully with the full support and cooperation of the SNH. The fewer people who know about it at the moment, the better. That's why I thought it best to come to you before telling Glen. To be honest, I don't think he could resist spreading the news.'

'You could be right. He means well, but maybe he's not the best person to handle information as delicate as this. Though we do have to get word to the quarry people as soon as possible. Maybe get the SNH to give us a report that we can pass on?'

'I was hoping you might take charge of that side of things. You probably know that Sam and I don't see eye to eye on this matter, and since we're together most of the time it would be difficult for me to contact people without him noticing that something was going on. You have more freedom than I do.'

'Of course I will. Give me any contact names you have and I'll take it from here,' Robert said at once. 'I'll keep you informed. It's wonderful news, Marcy. It looks as if we might win our fight after all – and do the village a bit of good into the bargain. Well done!'

Spring, always an easy-going season, gave way to summer without protest. The fields around Prior's Ford became lush with soft, thick green grass and the trees and bushes clothed themselves in leaves and blossom. The spring lambs grew out of their need to play, concentrating instead on grazing beside their mothers who were beginning to find their growing babies more of a hindrance than a joy. Soon, though neither mothers nor offspring knew it, the farmers would separate them, some ewe lambs being kept to replenish the flock, others to be sold the following spring as breeding ewes. The lambs would be fattened on good grass during the winter before being sold for their meat.

The tourists and holidaymakers arrived in increasing numbers and the Gift Horse was kept busy. Robert Kavanagh and Marcy Copleton both knew how to keep secrets and although Robert was in almost constant contact with the quarry company and the SNH nothing was getting back to the villagers.

Gardens burgeoned with weeds as well as flowers, and Clarissa was glad to take Naomi Hennessey up on her offer to provide the name of someone who might be willing to do some gardening for her.

'You want Jimmy McDonald,' the minister said. 'They're a local family. His mother Jinty helps out at Linn Hall during the summer. Her father was the head gardener there. He moved in with Jinty and Tom when his wife died. Jinty's a jewel of a woman – always there to lend a hand when anyone's in need. Tom's a joiner by trade, but he hurt his back in a fall years ago and apparently it still troubles him so he's not always working. Nobody's quite sure whether or not that's true, but Jinty believes him.' She took a sip from the mug of tea that Clarissa had made for her. 'From all reports, Tom was a handsome devil when Jinty fell for him – a head of blazing red hair and sparkling blue eyes. He's still good-looking in spite of the bad back. Their two oldest are Stephanie and Grant, twins aged sixteen. Both good-looking like their father and both talented. Steph's the star of all her school shows, and I'm told that Grant's a fine footballer. Then comes Jimmy – he loves gardening, and he learned well at his grandfather's knee before the old man died. I remember when I first came here seeing the two of them working out in the garden together. Jimmy's fourteen, Merle's twelve, Heather's ten – I believe that she's a clever wee thing – Norrie's eight and then there's another set of twins, Faith and Frankie. They're six.'

'Goodness. How many does that make?' Clarissa had lost count.

'Eight, and every one of them nice, well-mannered kids. All church members too, like their mother. They live on Slaemuir council estate, and I suspect that their house walls are made of some sort of elastic material. I'll tell Jimmy you'd like a word with him, will I?'

'Jimmy McDonald,' the boy said when Clarissa opened the door. 'The minister – Ethan's mum, like' – he added in case she didn't know who the minister was – 'said to come and see ye about doin' yer garden.'

'Oh, good.' Personally, she doubted if this lad had the strength to lift a spade, let alone a spade laden with soil. He was tall, and so thin that with his white skin and the blazing red curls tumbling over his head and into his pale blue eyes he looked like a walking safety match.

Even though there was scarcely a pick of flesh on his bones, his T-shirt was too small for him, so tight that it outlined every one of his ribs, and too short to cover his midriff. As if to compensate, his jeans were at least a size too large; beneath the narrow leather belt cinched tightly round his waist the denim material gathered into folds, and the bottom of each leg was folded back several times. Clarissa was reminded of the time she had borrowed dry clothes from Alastair.

'Ye've got a nice garden,' he said, nodding at it.

'I'll show you the back garden.'

He glanced down at his feet, clad in dirty trainers, then said, 'I'll walk round and meet you there.'

When they met up again his red hair bounced as he nodded like a solemn mandarin, his pointed chin dipping and rising with each suggestion she made about weeding, pruning and mowing. When she led him to the green-painted hut in one corner of the garden and opened the door to reveal Keith's gardening tools, the carefully cleaned hoe, rake, spades and forks all hung on their allotted hooks and the smaller items sitting where he had last placed them on the shelves, the boy's face lit up with sudden enthusiasm.

'It's like – perfect, isn't it? It's – cool!'

'My husband liked to look after his tools.'

'You look after them and they'll look after you,' Jimmy McDonald said. 'That's what my grand-dad always said. He worked up at the big house,' he went on proudly, 'and in his own garden, like. He did other folks' gardens too, and I helped him. That's how I learned. I like gard'nin'. When d'ye want me to start?'

'We haven't talked about money yet.'

'The minister said ye'd see me right,' he said confidently. 'I can work Sat'day mornings. I do football in the afternoons.'

'Playing?'

'Watchin'. It's my brother that plays. He's good. See ye tomorrow, then?'

While he worked in the garden the next morning – dressed in the same floppy jeans, but this time with a T-shirt a size too large for his skinny body – Clarissa made sandwiches, cutting thick slices of bread and cheese. When she took them out to him, Jimmy folded his body onto the bench beneath the apple tree and started eating with relish, washing the food down with a soft drink. Five minutes after she had carried it out to him, he tapped on the door and handed in the empty plate.

'Ta,' he said, and went back to work.

28

'I see you've got young Jimmy McDonald helping in your garden,' Marcy Copleton said when Clarissa deposited her loaded wire basket on the counter by the till.

'I wouldn't say that he's helping me, exactly – he works so fast that there's little for me to do. The minister recommended him, and I'm grateful to her.'

252

'He's a good lad. He delivers papers for us, and we've had him working in our garden from time to time, and as you say, he's a miracle worker. Takes after his grandfather on his mother's side, I've been told. Folk still sing the old man's praises.'

'Jimmy doesn't look as if he's got the strength to do heavy work – but he can.' Clarissa pointed to the tin of meat Marcy had just taken from the basket. 'I never eat that stuff myself, but he enjoys it and every time I look at him I want to keep his strength up.'

'You and everyone else he's worked for. That boy can eat like a horse and never put on a pound,' Marcy said enviously. 'They're a remarkable family, the McDonalds.'

'So I've heard.'

The only thing Keith had disliked about living in a small community was the interest everyone showed in each other's business. That was why he and Clarissa hadn't joined anything, or even gone to church. But as Clarissa carried her purchases home across the village green, she felt a warm glow as she remembered how easily Marcy had chatted to her. It made her feel accepted and less alone.

She had started attending church, and now she looked forward to her Sunday mornings, letting Naomi Hennessey's rich, sunshine-filled voice envelop her like a golden blanket, chatting to the other worshippers after the service before making her way back home.

She was also progressing well with her driving lessons and had discovered, much to her surprise, that she enjoyed being behind the wheel instead of in the passenger seat. Each lesson showed a marked improvement but when Alastair suggested that it was time to apply for her driving test Clarissa was aware of a faint, panicky flutter in her stomach.

'Are you sure? I feel as though I need more lessons before I can even think about that.'

'Better to apply now, because when they do give you a date it'll be quite far ahead. If you leave it until you feel you're absolutely ready you'll find the wait frustrating.'

Clarissa changed gear, took the car smoothly round a corner, and changed gear again. 'All right, I'll do it. I'm glad you agreed to teach me, Alastair, you've got such a relaxed way of going about things. You don't make me feel inadequate.'

'Why would I? You're not in the least inadequate – and don't let anyone tell you that you are.'

'I won't,' Clarissa said. 'Not any more.'

July arrived, and suddenly the village was filled with children celebrating the summer holidays. They played down by the river and out at the quarry, and on sunny days they lounged on the village green.

Jimmy McDonald, Clarissa discovered, helped in the gardens at Linn Hall during his summer holidays, but he stayed true to his promise to spend Saturday mornings in her garden, which had never looked better. Keith had been meticulous, but if it were possible for anyone to have green thumbs, then that person, Clarissa realised, was Jimmy McDonald.

Even when it started to rain one Friday night

and was still raining heavily on Saturday morning, the lad turned up at Willow Cottage and spent a happy hour or so in the shed, cleaning, oiling and rearranging Keith's tools. When Clarissa took a plate of corned beef sandwiches out to him he was perched on an upturned bucket, working industriously. Today he wore jeans that fitted and a striped shirt with the long sleeves folded back to leave his hands free. An enormous anorak dripped from a nail on the door.

'Nice here, in the rain,' he said contentedly, picking up the first of the sandwiches. 'Workin' and thinkin' and listenin' to the rain on the roof. More peaceful than it is at home. There's such a lot of us there.'

She wondered, as she made her way back to the house, skirting the puddles, if being part of a large family meant that in the mornings, he just put on whatever came to hand rather than wear clothes that were strictly his own.

It would certainly explain the irregular sizes.

The rain, as so often happened in Scotland, behaved like an inconsiderate visitor who lingers on, oblivious to every sign that his hosts have become tired of his company.

It was particularly unwelcome at Linn Hall, where the Ralston-Kerrs and their motley staff were beginning to prepare for the annual garden party. The gardens were in danger of becoming waterlogged, and indoors, every pail, basin and reasonably-sized bowl available was pressed into use on the top floor to catch drips from the ceilings in almost every room.

'Look on the bright side,' Hector tried to console his wife as they tracked down each drip and put a bowl beneath it, 'we've finally managed to find a use for all those chamber pots my grandparents used when they held their house parties. Thank goodness we kept them.'

He found another damp spot on the floor and carefully placed a fat china chamber pot decorated with circlets of blue flowers and wreaths of ivy on top of it. 'I rather like the musical sound the drips make when they first fall into the pot, don't you?'

'No, I don't,' Fliss snapped. She was tired, and she was worried. 'To tell the truth, Hector, I would much prefer the sound of rain hitting a solid waterproofed roof and then running down into gutters and drainpipes.'

'The good thing is,' her husband went on doggedly, 'that we don't need this floor. The two below it are dry and snug.'

'But for how long? How long have we got before the roof gives way entirely? Once that happens we'll have to move into one of the gatehouses.' Fliss put down the last of the containers, a large and very handsome crystal vase, narrow at the base but wide at the top, which made it ideal as a drip-catcher, and then went over to one of the windows, wiping a patch clear of dust so she could look down at the weedy garden two storeys below. 'I wish I could have seen this place in its heyday.'

'And I wish I could find a way to bring those days back.' He went to join her, putting an arm about her shoulders. 'I wish you could be the lady of the house, instead of having to work so hard all year round just to keep things going.'

'I know you do, my dear.' She leaned back against him, enjoying the rare opportunity to relish a quiet moment together. They were silent, looking down on the garden, watching fat raindrops running down the window, listening to equally fat drops of water splash into the containers behind them, then Fliss said tentatively, 'There's still that letter, offering you all that money.'

'I know.' She felt his body tense against her back. 'I think about it and about the offer to lease the quarry land every night before I go to sleep and every morning when I wake. I don't know what to do for the best, Fliss.'

'Two hundred thousand pounds.' She rolled the words around her tongue, relishing the taste and the sound of them. 'Think what we could do with two hundred thousand pounds!'

'Yes, but where does it come from? If I agree to the quarry and take the rent, or if I refuse to lease it and get the other money I'll feel like a Judas.' He glanced up at the ceiling, with its plaster cracked and discoloured, and its beautiful cornices thick with dust. 'But you're right, the roof can't take this punishment for ever.'

Although Fliss wished at such times that her husband could be a little less honourable and a little more mercenary, she was well aware of his inner struggle between integrity and need, and she couldn't bear to see him suffering.

'It'll probably hold together for a few years yet,' she said gently, 'and who knows what could happen by then? We might win the lottery, you never know.'

'Fliss, we don't *do* the lottery. We can't afford it and in any case, we agreed from the start that we weren't going to contribute to a scheme that gives far too much money to its winners instead of putting charities first.'

'I forgot,' she said guiltily. They had never kept secrets from each other, and it was hard to keep remembering that he knew nothing of the two pounds she gave Jinty McDonald every week from the housekeeping to buy lottery tickets. Two pounds that they couldn't afford – but desperation sometimes turned people into gamblers. And deceivers.

She glanced up at her husband, hoping he wasn't looking down at her, recognising guilt in her face and guessing at the reason. But he was still gazing down at the garden, where two anoraked and hooded figures walked hand in hand across the lawn.

'Isn't that Lewis?'

'Yes, I think it is,' Fliss agreed just as the people below reached the slope that led down to the lower lawn. One of them let go of the other and ran down, arms spread wide and face lifted to the rain so that the hood tumbled back to reveal a splash of red hair.

'And that's Molly, the nice girl who works in the kitchen.'

'Oh yes. They look very – friendly, don't they?'

'Yes, they do,' Fliss agreed. Lewis had run down the slope after Molly, who turned to face him, her arms still held wide. He caught her up and whirled her round before setting her back on her feet.

'Isn't that lovely?' Fliss said as the couple ran

258

across the lower lawn towards the shrubbery, Lewis's arm about the girl's waist. 'It's good to see Lewis so happy.'

And she and Hector smiled at each other, remembering similar moments from years ago, though it seemed like only yesterday to both of them.

'Isn't this wonderful? Isn't it great?' Molly hadn't bothered to pull the hood of her anorak back over her head, and now, as she and Lewis crossed the lawn, oblivious to the watchers in the window high above, she lifted her face to the lowering grey sky, opening her mouth to let the raindrops fall on her tongue.

'Actually, it's not great at all, not with this bloody rain holding up the outdoor work. Put your hood up, your hair's getting wet.'

'It's all right.' Molly shook her head and her long plaits swung around, showering rain into Lewis's face. 'I'm drip-dry. And the garden likes the rain too.'

'Not as much rain as this. The annual garden party's only three weeks away, and this rain looks as if it's settling in for the summer.'

'Your parents are holding a garden party? How – posh!'

'We don't do posh – it's for the village, and we run it every year.' They had crossed the lawn now and were entering the copse; rain hissed through the trees, bouncing from one leaf to another on its way to the ground, like a child jumping from step to step down a staircase.

'You mean they all dress up and have cucumber

sandwiches and tea on the lawn? Can I come?'

Lewis laughed, and tightened his grip about her shoulders, heedless of the wet undergrowth soaking his trousers. 'It's like the egg hunt – we all wear whatever we want to wear, and there are stalls on the lawns and games, and people can have tea and scones in the kitchen – or out on the terrace if this dratted rain lets up.'

'Do your parents run tours of the house that day?'

'No, because there's nothing to see. Most of the rooms on the upper floors are empty because the roof leaks. Some of the middle floor rooms are used as stores.'

Molly snuggled against him. 'Will you show me round one day? Give me a private tour?'

'Of course, if you want. But, honestly, there's nothing of interest to see.'

'Not as far as you're concerned, because you've lived here all your life and you're used to it. If you came from a council house like I do, you'd think differently. Your house, and all this ground' – Molly flapped a hand at the trees around them – 'for me, it's like walking into a fairy story with its own castle. It's exciting!'

Everything was exciting as far as Molly was concerned, Lewis thought fondly. That was one of the things that made her so fascinating – her boundless enthusiasm for life. Being with her had given him the opportunity to see the things he had always taken for granted – the village, Linn Hall and its untidy grounds, the surrounding countryside – with new eyes. It was as though until she came along, he had spent his life looking but not seeing.

'Listen...' She stopped and drew him over to the sturdy trunk of a tree, leaning her back against it and taking both his hands in hers.

'What?'

'The rain – listen to it. Did you ever see that film – *Bambi?*'

'Once, when I was little.'

'I've seen it lots of times. D'you remember that bit when it was raining, and the drops were splashing and children's voices were singing?'

He tried hard, but couldn't recall it. 'Sorry, no.'

'It was wonderful. Let's go and see the film together if we ever get the chance.' Molly's eyes sparkled up at him, lighting up the green-tinged gloom they stood in. 'I always cry when I watch it, 'specially the bit where his mother dies. We'll take a big box of tissues and cry together, you and me.'

'You're absolutely mad, do you know that?' Lewis asked, and when she nodded, laughing up at him, he kissed her.

Her mouth was soft and welcoming, and her kiss tasted of rain.

29

The rain finally took pity on the Ralston-Kerrs and ceased in time for the annual garden party. Once the weather improved, Duncan Campbell and Lewis, with the help of the summer staff, worked from dawn to dusk to make the gardens look as they had in their heyday when an army of gardeners had cared for them. The broad, paved terrace at one side of the house was weeded and cleaned, and tables and chairs brought out from the stables, where they were stored, so that people could sit and enjoy a cup of tea or coffee and home baking.

For the past three years at least, it had seemed as though the old oil-driven lawnmower was serving its final year, but each spring, Duncan and Lewis managed to coax it back to life for one more season. It obliged yet again, and the lawns looked almost as neat as they were meant to look. The borders around the lawns were weeded and planted to provide a riot of colour.

On the day before the garden party stalls were set up on the lawn and the kitchen invaded by a small army of local women bearing plastic boxes filled with cakes, biscuits and scones. Chattering like a flock of starlings, they joined Fliss, Jinty and Molly, filling the big kitchen and giving a glimpse into the way it must have been when a host of servants prepared for house parties.

While the women worked and gossiped and laughed, Hector, in the pantry as usual, wrote out cards for the stalls, and signs leading to places of interest. There was a sign for the old tennis court, where members of a local archery club had offered to tutor prospective Robin Hoods, one for the little wooden gazebo in the middle of the shrubbery, where a fortune teller was to ply her trade, and a third for the paddock, where children could enjoy pony rides on animals loaned by a nearby riding school.

On the day itself, every family in the village

headed for Linn Hall early in order to claim their territory on the lawns. By noon, when Fliss, wearing her only decent frock and with a wide-brimmed straw hat confining her untidy hair, used the sound system borrowed from the village hall to officially declare the garden party open, the grass was already covered with a patchwork of brightly coloured rugs and even a good number of deckchairs, tucked between the stalls.

Mothers unpacked picnics while bare-footed toddlers staggered around close by, squealing with pleasure at the feel of cool grass beneath their fat little feet. Older children were already exploring the shrubbery or racing down to the paddock and tennis court.

'That's that over for another year, thank goodness,' Fliss said as she joined Jinty and the volunteers in the kitchen. She hung her hat on a hook, patted her flattened hair, and put on a big wraparound pinny to protect her dress. 'I hate opening the garden party. Nobody listens – they're all too busy enjoying themselves.'

'It's tradition,' Jinty said comfortably, the knife in her hand swooping back and forth between a large tub of margarine and a mountain of halved scones, 'they expect it and they like it, even if they don't listen. It's part of the garden party – part of the village year.'

Lewis handed over the responsibility for the plant stall to Duncan and was on his way to the kitchen to find something to eat when he met Molly, her red hair loose today and curling about her shoulders.

'Hullo, I was looking for you. I'm on duty in the kitchen in an hour's time, and I was hoping you might show me round the house first. You did promise – remember?'

A flared blue skirt swung around her legs and a flowered blouse made of some soft material slipped off one rounded shoulder. As Lewis looked down at her his hunger evaporated – or, rather, took off in a different direction. 'So I did. Come on, then.'

She slipped a hand into his as he led her round to the front of the house. Most of the villagers were on the lawn and nobody saw the two of them go up the semicircular sweep of steps to the front door. Molly gave a little gasp of delight as he ushered her into the big entrance hall and closed the door behind them.

'It's – wonderful!' She ran to the middle of the hall, her feet silent in their summer sandals, and Lewis watched as she turned slowly, taking in the massive fireplace, now dark and empty, the paintings on the panelled walls and the wide doors leading to the dining room, the drawing room, the study, the library and the family parlour. She gazed up the great sweeping staircase to the middle landing with its stained-glass windows where the stairs divided into two flights, one going up to the left and the other up to the right, each flight leading to the hallway of the first floor.

'Imagine coming down that staircase, dressed for a ball,' she said, clasping her hands together beneath her chin. 'I can just see myself!'

'So can I.'

'Can you, Lewis? How do I look?'

'Fabulous,' he said, and she blew him a kiss before twirling again, this time kinking her head back to look up at the ornate ceiling.

'Such a beautiful house! Can I look in there?' She pointed to one of the doors.

'Of course, but it's all very dusty. We don't use any of those rooms now.' He followed her as she went through the rooms one by one, exclaiming at their size, at the furnishings, now shabby and sorely in need of attention, and at the great windows overlooking the grounds. She marvelled at the marble fireplace in the formal drawing room, and at the length of the table in the dining room, which could easily sit twenty people.

'We're more comfortable in the butler's pantry,' Lewis told her. 'For one thing, it's warm. Imagine me and my parents eating at that huge table – we'd scarcely even see each other.'

'I'd eat here if this were my house,' Molly told him. 'I'd love to be the lady of the manor, even if nobody else saw me and I was only eating fish and chips. So where do you and your parents sleep, then?'

'Upstairs, in the two smallest rooms. The others are all locked up and the top floor's uninhabitable because the roof leaks.'

'Why don't your parents get it repaired?'

'They don't have the money.'

'But they must have pots of money! How else could they afford to live in a place like this?'

'They haven't got a bean. We live here because we can't afford to live anywhere else. My father inherited Linn Hall's debts as well as the Hall itself, and we have to work hard just to keep it going. It needs all sorts of things done to it. That's why most of the house is closed up,' Lewis explained. 'Your father probably has more money than mine.'

'I doubt that. I heard someone say that your family own the ground where the quarry is.'

'That's right, it's part of the estate. The quarry people have offered to rent it, but my parents want to find out what the villagers think about the idea before they make a decision.'

'I expect,' Molly said, 'they're hoping most of the villagers will want the quarry.'

'Even if they do, the rent wouldn't be enough to repair the roof, though it would certainly help us to keep going for a while longer. A funny thing happened, though,' he went on without thinking as they returned to the hall, 'someone – we don't know who it is – has offered my father two hundred thousand pounds to help towards getting work done on the house on condition that he refuses to rent out the quarry ground.'

'Two hundred thousand pounds!' Molly breathed the words out reverently. 'That's a fortune! Is he going to take it?'

'He doesn't know what to do.'

'If someone offered me that much money, I'd take it! Wouldn't you?'

'Maybe – I don't know.'

'You don't know?' She looked up at him, incredulous.

'I can see his point of view. If I were offered money to vote against something the villagers might want, or need, then I don't think I could take it. We used to be the lairds here – we still have a duty towards the people who live in Prior's Ford,' he explained, adding swiftly, 'Listen, I shouldn't have told you about that offer. It's my parents' business, not mine. Please don't breathe a word to anyone.'

Molly widened her eyes and drew a finger swiftly over her soft bosom. 'Cross my heart and hope to die – honest! Now can I see upstairs?'

'Come on.' He took her by the hand and led her up the staircase, noting with tender amusement that she mounted each tread slowly and formally, her hand in his, back straight and head held high.

She spent some time on the broad middle landing, peering through the small panes of coloured glass. 'It must look wonderful when the sun's shining through!'

'It does, in the mornings – when we have sun, that is.' They went up the short flight of stairs to the right and he led her down a corridor. 'That's my parents' room,' he gestured to one side of the corridor, 'and this' – he opened the door and stood aside to let her in – 'is mine.'

'Oh, *Lewis!* You've got a four-poster bed!'

'It used to be in one of the guest bedrooms. I pestered my parents to let me have it when I was a boy. I can't even remember now why I wanted it so much. It's not very comfortable, or very large.'

'What do you mean, not very large? It's a *four-poster bed!* It's *fantastic!*' She ran forward, caught one of the carved posts at the bottom of the bed, and twirled past it, her other hand reaching out for the next post. A twirl round that one brought her almost to the window; she danced over to it and looked out. 'And you're overlooking a bit of the rose garden – look! You're so *lucky!*'

'Yes, I am,' Lewis said, watching her as she danced, light as a ballerina, around the room, looking at his books and his school photographs, still on show. When she returned to the bed she stopped with her back to it and raised her slim bare arms slowly and gracefully from her sides. Then, with a squeak of excitement, she allowed herself to fall back onto the patchwork quilt.

'Look at me, I'm lying on a four-poster bed!' She patted the space by her side. 'Come here.'

'We ought to be getting back.'

'I know we ought to be getting back, but nobody's ever made love to me on a four-poster bed.' Molly smiled at him – a slow, sultry smile – and wriggled luxuriously. The movement slipped the soft material of her blouse aside so that both creamy shoulders were now uncovered.

'What's the matter, Lewis – too shy?'

'No.' Rosalind came into his mind, a fellow university student. He had thought himself to be in love with her, and had been devastated when she accepted a job that took her off to America. But she hadn't been nearly as tempting as Molly.

'Come here, Lewis, come to me,' she said, holding her hands out to him, fingers outstretched.

And Lewis, unable to help himself, went to her.

When the garden party was over and everyone had gone, Fliss and Hector found time to take a leisurely stroll as dusk fell. The rose garden had been weeded and dug thoroughly before the party, and now the smell of freshly turned soil mingled with the scent of the old-fashioned blooms. In the last of the daylight the flowers were a patchwork of colours ranging from deep crimson through pink, salmon, yellow, cream to snowy-white blossoms that seemed, in the twilight, to be floating in mid-air. The beds were slightly raised and walled in soft grey stone, and the same stone had been used to flag the winding paths between the beds.

When they reached the ornamental pool in the middle of the rose garden Fliss sank down on to the broad stone seat with a sigh of pleasure. 'This is my favourite place. Just think of the people who've walked among those very bushes over the years, Hector – you can almost believe they're still here. It's where I would want my spirit to be, if we're allowed to visit once we're gone for good.'

'Mmm.' Hector was standing on the edge of the pool, which had been drained long ago. Normally it was left empty to collect dead leaves, twigs and anything else the winds brought to it, but during the week Duncan Campbell had had it cleared of assorted debris before filling it with large pots of double begonias. Once, the young nymph balanced gracefully on her pedestal in the centre of the pool had poured a constant fountain of clear water from the urn between her slender hands; now she peered down in mild surprise at the flowers clustering about her bare feet.

'It went well, didn't it? I think they all enjoyed themselves.'

'Mmm,' Hector said absently.

'I won a live elephant in the tombola,' Fliss went on conversationally, 'so I put it into the old greenhouse until we can find a proper enclosure for it. You don't mind, do you?'

'Mmm,' her husband said again, and then suddenly turned, hands clasped behind his back. 'I'm going to write to that lawyer first thing tomorrow morning to tell him we're not taking the money.'

'Oh.'

'It would be wrong, Fliss. I was watching everyone today, having such a good time, being happy together. They like us and they trust us. Taking the money – I would be deceiving them.'

'Not entirely. Some want the quarry, some don't. Whatever we decide – to speak for it, or against it – we'll please some members of the community and disappoint others. The only difference is that if you speak out against it, we'll be two hundred thousand pounds better off, and nobody ever need know.'

'I'll know and you'll know. And Lewis and the lawyer and whoever's offered us the money. And – I told Glen Mason about it.'

'Why did you do that?'

'I just wanted someone in the village to know, and he was the only one I could think of. Fliss, the villagers aren't stupid – if we suddenly start to spend money on the estate they'll wonder where it came from. How could we possibly keep such a thing secret for long?'

Fliss looked at her husband. He had told Glen Mason about the money because he hated keeping secrets. He hated deceit, in himself as much as in others. That was one of the many things she loved about him. How could she ever have allowed herself to hope that he might accept that windfall offered them?

'You're right,' she said. 'We can't take the

money when we don't know who's giving it to us. Or why.'

'I'm so glad you understand.' Hector straightened his shoulders and went on firmly, 'The village will have to accept whatever's decided about the quarry and so will we. To be honest, I doubt if we matter much in any case. I have a feeling that the real official thinking behind the meeting in the village hall was to make the village believe that we have input when we don't.'

'You think the decision has already been made?'

'Yes, I do. I don't know whether I want to see the quarry working again or not, Fliss, and so I'd rather keep out of it altogether. You really don't mind?'

'Of course I don't mind. You're a very honest man, Hector Ralston-Kerr, and I'll go along with whatever you want. I'm as confused as you are over the whole business.' Fliss held out a hand to him, saying as he took it, 'Haul me up; I'm beginning to stiffen. Old bones!'

She studied the house as they walked back across the lawn, wondering how many more years of rain and winter snow the roof could take. The money they had been offered would have come in very useful, but nothing that made Hector unhappy was worthwhile. They had no option but to stand shoulder to shoulder, as they had done since their wedding day and always would do, and say 'Thank you, but no thank you,' to their mysterious would-be benefactor.

'What did you say about the tombola?' Hector asked.

'Just that it seemed to be very popular.' She

took his hand, twining her fingers around his. 'I fancy a nice mug of hot tea and some bread and honey. What about you?'

30

It was early afternoon on the first day of the new school term, and Ingrid, Jenny and Helen were celebrating their newfound back to school freedom by having lunch at the Neurotic Cuckoo.

The lounge bar was quiet, and Glen Mason, with nothing else to do, was wiping down the counter as they went in. 'Well now, if it isn't the coven!' he greeted them cheerfully. 'What can I do for you? Eye of toad and tail of newt, is it?'

'I think we'll settle today for three white wine spritzers and some of Libby's delicious sandwiches,' Ingrid told him sweetly. 'What's the soup of the day?'

'Apple and parsnip, nice and light for a warm day.'

Ingrid raised her eyebrows at her friends, then said, 'Three soups and a ham and tomato sandwich for me, please.'

'Don't you find,' Jenny muttered when they had given their orders and retired to a table with their drinks, 'that some men never grow out of that stage where three-year-olds think that just because something raises a smile the first time, it's worth repeating ad nauseum?'

'Perhaps it's like an attack of the hiccups,'

Ingrid said thoughtfully. 'Perhaps he needs to be scared out of the habit.'

'If you think that leaping over the bar and sinking a set of teeth into his wrist would work, I'm willing to have a shot at it,' Helen offered. 'I've been seeing altogether too much of Glen lately because of this dratted quarry committee. I could do with a bit of light relief.'

'I was thinking of something much more subtle than–' Ingrid stopped short as Glen arrived with the soup.

'Libby's making up your sandwiches. How are the letters coming along, Helen?'

'I've not done them yet; I've been busy with a thesis for a college student.'

'Be a love and see to them as soon as possible. I'm not happy about the silence from the quarry people – and the council. We need to find out what's going on behind our backs.'

Helen sighed, then said, 'I'll do them at the weekend.'

'Fine. I'll come round on Sunday afternoon to sign them, shall I?' Glen beamed at his customers.

'Just think, Helen,' Jenny said sweetly when he had left them on their own, 'if you were the witch he keeps saying you are, you could just wiggle your nose and the letters would all be done in a trice.'

'I wish!' Helen took a spoonful of soup. 'This is gorgeous. I wish I could cook like Libby. Now *there's* a magic touch if ever I saw one.'

'How is the newspaper work coming along?' Ingrid asked, and Helen beamed.

'It's great – people are beginning to come to me with information and Bob Green says that the editor likes the news items I've sent in so far. They don't even change anything – they just print them the way I've written them!'

'That's because you're a born writer and they're very fortunate to have you working for them,' Ingrid told her. 'Now think about this, Helen – you're getting paid to do that work for the newspaper, but you are not paid to do the work for this quarry protest committee. You must get your priorities right.'

'The committee work's for the village, though.'

'Even so, the paid work must come first. You don't think Glen would give up this place to concentrate on the committee, do you? He makes sure that the money keeps coming into his till. Talking of tills...' although they were the only people in the bar and Glen had disappeared through the door leading to his living quarters, Ingrid lowered her voice and the others leaned forward '...have either of you sensed an atmosphere in the village store?'

'You're not talking about drains, are you?'

'No, Jenny, I'm talking about this worrying coolness between Marcy and Sam. They're both taking this silly quarry business too seriously.'

'They're strong-minded people.' Helen shrugged. 'And they quite like to disagree now and again. You've surely heard them arguing over all sorts of things – they don't make a secret of it.'

'This is different. You must have noticed Sam didn't turn up at the Easter egg hunt, and Marcy was definitely put out about that.'

'They were at the garden party together,' Helen said swiftly.

'There's together – and there's together.' Ingrid's intensely blue eyes stared into Jenny's, then Helen's. 'I was watching them and they didn't speak much to each other or smile at each other. They had supper with us last Friday, and even Peter remarked after they had gone that they were surprisingly quiet with each other.' She took a spoonful of soup and then said, 'And as you both know, my Peter is usually so busy thinking about his next lecture or his students that he would scarcely notice if the house went on fire.'

'They'll be all right once the matter's settled,' Helen insisted. 'Whichever way it goes, one of them is going to be pleased and the other disappointed, but they've been together for too long to let it damage their private lives – or the business. You wait and see.'

'I hope you're right, because I like both of them,' Ingrid said as Glen appeared with a tray of sandwiches.

Ingrid insisted on paying for the meal as a thank you to Jenny for helping in the shop all summer and to celebrate Helen's success with her newspaper work. Ignoring their protests, she shooed them on their way before marching over to the counter.

'How much do I owe you, Glen?'

'Thirteen pounds and eighty-four pence, love.'

Ingrid burrowed in her bag, then held out her hand. 'There you are: she said cheerfully, but when Glen put his own hand out, all she emptied into it was air.

'Oy, where's the money?'

'There.' Ingrid pointed to his palm. 'I gave you the exact amount – plus the correct tip.'

'But – there's nothing there!'

'Can't you see it?' Ingrid's blue eyes widened in surprise then, when he shook his head, she blinked at him as though confused, 'Oh, I am so sorry, Glen. I thought that you were one of us.'

'One of you? Do I look like a woman?'

'No, I meant – you know,' Ingrid cast a hurried look around the empty room, then leaned across the bar and whispered, 'a *vikja*.'

'A what?'

'It is the word in my country for a witch. I thought you must be – what do you call it? – a warlock.'

Glen swallowed hard. 'I'm a pub landlord and nothing else!'

'Then how did you know that *I* am a *vikja?* It takes one to know one.'

'I didn't know anything of the sort!' It was Glen's turn to glance at the door leading to the private rooms, as though wishing that Libby would come bustling in to save him.

'But you keep referring to us as a coven.' Again, Ingrid leaned across the counter, and this time Glen took a step back.

'It's just a joke! You know, like the three witches in *Macbe–*'

'*Ssshhh!*' Ingrid almost spat the word out and Glen flinched. 'You must never ever mention those women to me, it could be dangerous for both of us! Here you are' – she drew a note from her wallet and put it on the counter – 'take this to pay for our food. I thought you would have recognised the *vikja* gold but now I know that I'm wrong. Please, you must say nothing of this to anyone, even to my friends who were with me. They're not *vikja*, like me.'

Glen scrabbled in the till for change, fumbling with the coins. 'I like a joke as much as the next man, Ingrid, but enough's enough, eh?'

He counted out the change on the counter and pushed it towards her. Now it was her turn to step back, staring at the coins as though they menaced her.

'No, you must keep it – all of it.'

'There's too much there. Look...' Glen separated some coins and swept them into the bowl put aside for tips. 'There – the rest's yours.'

'No, you must take all of it. It would be very bad luck,' Ingrid said urgently, 'for me to touch any of it or for you to give back any part of it, after we have been talking about' – she glanced at the door leading to the street, then at the door to the living quarters, before whispering – 'forbidden things.'

'Well, I don't want it either!' Glen's alarm was beginning to mount.

'No no, it's all right. It's safe for you to touch it, since you're not *vikja* like me.'

She turned to go, then spun back to face him. 'By the way...'

Glen, demoralised, gripped the edge of the bar with both hands. 'What?'

'Jenny and Helen – you *do* believe me when I say that they are not witches?'

'I never thought they were. I never thought any of you were. It was a *joke!*' Glen pleaded.

'Never play jokes on a *vikja*, my friend. It can

cause great worries for you in the future if you do. As soon as I get home I will search through my books for an incantation to protect you. If you feel a sudden shiver as though a cold wind is passing over you, or even right through you, don't worry – it will be telling you that I am weaving the spell over you to make you safe. We will let this conversation be our secret, yes?' Ingrid said, putting not one, but two fingers to her lips. Then she bathed the landlord in a sudden, sunny smile, said, 'Tell Libby the sandwiches were delicious,' and left.

'You took your time,' Jenny said when Ingrid emerged from the lounge bar. 'Was Glen still pulling your leg about us being a coven?'

'No, this time *I* was pulling *his* leg.' Ingrid linked arms with both her friends. 'I told him that I am a *vikja* – it is what they call a witch in my country.'

'You didn't!' Helen gasped, while Jenny wanted to know, 'And he believed you?'

'Of course. I keep telling you that Glen is a very simple man who likes to appear wise to others. Easy to tease. Don't worry, I told him you two are not witches – but I believe from now on he will treat the three of us with more respect. And no more silly jokes. Isn't that a relief?'

'That Ingrid's a funny woman,' Glen was saying to Libby in the kitchen at that moment.

'Oh? Telling a joke, was she?'

'I didn't mean funny ha ha, I mean funny peculiar.'

'I've never noticed it. I think she's very nice.'

'You can't judge a book by its cover.'

'What on earth are you on about?'

'Nothing.' Glen gave a sudden shiver and moved closer to the fire. 'Did you feel a draught just then?'

'Not me,' Libby said placidly, and went on trimming the pastry on her apple pie.

When the phone rang in Rowan Cottage, Marcy was busy in the kitchen.

'Can you get that, Sam?' she called, and heard him hurtling down the stairs to the hall. A few minutes later he came into the kitchen. 'It's for you,' he said. 'Committee business – as usual.'

'Keep stirring this for me, will you? It'll go lumpy if you don't.'

He took over the task with a resigned sigh as she escaped to the hall.

'Hello?'

'I,' Robert Kavanagh said in a tone of quiet triumph, 'have had a very busy day, but a very productive one.'

'Oh yes?' Aware that Sam could probably hear her, Marcy kept her voice casual. She had been right to take her discovery about the falcons to Robert; he had taken on the task of dealing with the SNH and the quarry company with enthusiasm, yet at the same time he had given nothing away during committee meetings. She herself had kept well out of it, for fear Sam might become suspicious.

'How did you get on?' she enquired.

'Very well. In fact, we've won.'

'That's fine,' she said, while her heart leapt.

'Isn't it just? Watch out for tomorrow's issue of the *Dumfries News*. They're delighted with their scoop. They don't know about the falcons, though, so keep that one under your hat. It's been decided that nothing will be said about them until arrangements can be made to protect them. The company will simply say that the quarry isn't really viable. As a matter of fact, they didn't put up much of an argument once they heard about our feathered friends. I suspect they were already wondering if it was worth going ahead with their plans.'

'Fine. Thanks for letting me know. See you at the next meeting.' Marcy hung up and allowed herself a wide, triumphant grin before smoothing all traces of it away.

'So what was that about?' Sam asked, relinquishing the pot, sauce and wooden spoon with relief.

'Oh, just another fund-raising idea.'

'What is it this time?'

'A bring and buy.'

'Good grief. Fancy a drink in the pub after dinner?'

'Yes, I think I do,' Marcy said.

31

'I'd be careful if I were you, Lewis.'

Lewis, sitting at a corner table in the Neurotic Cuckoo, looked up from his half-empty glass. 'Hello, Cam – careful about what?'

'Molly Ewing, what else?' Campbell Gordon swung the chair that Molly had just vacated round so he could straddle it, leaning his forearms along the back. 'They tell me the two of you are walking out together.'

'What's that got to do with you?' Years ago, when they attended the local primary school together, Lewis and Cam had been close friends. The friendship had endured through their time at Kirkcudbright Academy, but had swiftly soured once they reached the permitted school-leaving age.

Cam's father, who worked for a building contractor and believed in earning a living rather than in higher education, had taken Cam from school as soon as he could and put the boy to work with his company, while Lewis stayed at the Academy until he was eighteen.

Cam, who had loved his school years and burned with a hunger for knowledge, had harboured resentment against his former friend ever since.

'Oh, Molly's got a lot to do with me,' he said, his gaze holding Lewis's. 'Last year, when I went with some mates to Canada, Molly was working in the hotel we stayed at. We got to know each other – quite well. And here *is* the lovely little lady,' he went on, as Molly emerged from the Ladies.

'Campbell? What are you doing here?' Her eyes flickered from Cam to Lewis, then back to Cam.

'I live here, pet, don't you remember?' Cam had risen to his feet when she arrived and now he turned the chair round and held the back of it, as though inviting her to sit. 'I was just telling Lewis how we met last year, in Canada. I'm the one who told you all about Prior's Ford, don't you remember? You know what I'm like when I've had a few, don't you, Lewis? I tend to get quite nostalgic. Now that I look back on our time together, Moll, I must have been quite boring, the way I rambled on about this village and the folk who live in it – and the folk in the big house.'

'I don't remember you telling me anything about Prior's Ford.'

'You're just being polite. Can I buy you a drink – for old times' sake? You too, Lewis.' Cam glanced from one to the other, clearly enjoying Molly's discomfiture and Lewis's growing anger. A group of young people from the estate glanced over from where they sat at one of the larger tables, watching and listening with interest.

'I have a drink, thank you. I don't need another one!' Molly snapped.

'Nor do I. Why don't you go back to your own table, Cam, and leave us alone?'

Cam spread his hands out in mock surprise. 'No need to be like that, Lewis. We used to be great pals, Molly – oh, but I told you that last year, didn't I? Me and the boy from the big house. That was before I started work as a brickie, of course, and he went on to college.'

'For pity's sake, Cam, that's all in the past,' Lewis groaned. 'It wasn't my fault, or yours – it was down to our parents. And I only went to college to do horticulture so I could work on the estate. When are you going to get over it?'

'I am over it. That's why I wanted to speak to you about pretty little Molly here – because you

282

and I used to be such good mates. We looked out for each other, remember?'

'Campbell, shut up and go away!'

'You heard her.' Lewis pushed his chair back and rose to his feet, noticing from the corner of his eye that Glen and Libby were watching from behind the bar. 'Just leave it!'

'Okay, okay – but be careful, Lewis, old mate. This lovely lass might seem to be all sugar and spice and everything nice, but underneath, she's different. She'll give you a good time, I can vouch for that, but deep down, the girl's a tease – know what I mean? Only out for one–'

As Molly's hand cracked across his face he lurched back and then steadied himself. Her hands flew up to protect her face and she cringed away as Cam's arm began to rise. Lewis threw himself at the other man.

A glass went spinning off a table, showering its contents and then smashing on the floor as the two grappled with each other. A girl screamed, chairs were scraped back, and then Glen Mason, moving surprisingly quickly for a large man, was separating Cam and Lewis.

'That's enough!' he snapped. 'I'll have no fighting in my pub! What's got into you, Lewis? Cam, outside with you!'

'I'm the one who was attacked – isn't that right?' Cam appealed to the friends he had been sitting with. He tugged his jacket into place and smoothed his hair, well pleased with the way he had rattled Lewis's cage. 'Why am I the one who's being thrown out? Just because he comes from the big house – just because he's a Ralston-

Kerr he thinks he's better than us villagers!' He glanced around the bar. 'Him and his family have never cared a jot about the likes of us!'

'That's not true!' Molly shouted at him, her face almost as red as her hair. 'Lewis's father's just turned down a huge amount of money, all because he doesn't want to upset anyone who lives in the village!'

'Molly!' Lewis warned, but it was too late. Suddenly, the whole bar was listening.

'What was that?' someone called out, and Molly shook off the hand Lewis laid on her arm.

'It's time they knew how wrong they are,' she told him, and then, to the others, 'Lewis told me that someone offered Mr Ralston-Kerr two hundred thousand pounds if he would refuse to let the quarry people work on his land, but he wouldn't take it because he said it would upset some of you people.' She glared around the hushed, crowded room. 'That's how much he cares about you. I bet none of *you* would say no to two hundred thousand pounds just because it might upset your neighbours!'

'Lewis,' Sam Brennan said from the table where he sat with Marcy, 'is this true?'

'Come on,' Lewis grabbed Molly's wrist and almost yanked her from the pub.

As they hurried up the road leading to Linn Hall, he said in despair, 'Why on earth did you blurt that out? I told you in confidence!'

'I'm sorry, Lewis, but I was just so angry with Campbell. He was saying horrible things about you and your parents and it wasn't fair. I wanted them all to know what an honourable man your father is. They *ought* to know that.'

'They already know it. God knows what my parents'll say when I tell them.'

'Do you have to?'

'Of course. They'll hear about it soon enough and I have to warn them.' They had reached a quiet part of the road now, flanked by trees, and Lewis stopped and turned, looking down at her. 'Molly, why didn't you tell me you knew Cam Gordon?'

'I didn't – well, only for two weeks. I was working in this hotel in Canada last year when I was backpacking round the country, and he and his friends were guests. If he told me he came from this village, I certainly don't remember it.'

'What happened between you?' Lewis was suddenly consumed by jealousy. Something about the way Cam had looked at and talked about her niggled at him.

'Nothing happened.'

'That's not what it sounded like to me.'

'Oh, for goodness' sake! We went out a couple of times, that's all. He's good company – at least, I thought he was until tonight. I'm not a nun, Lewis, I have gone out with other men in the past, just as you must have been out with other girls.'

But it was Cam's comments about the village that bothered Lewis. 'Did you come to Prior's Ford this year because Cam told you about us – the village and me and my parents and Linn Hall?'

'Of course not,' she said angrily. 'Why on earth would I do that? It was only two weeks last summer – I just told you I'd forgotten all about him until I saw him tonight. Can't you see he was trying to upset you? He doesn't like you, does he? Why's that?'

'Oh – it's nothing. We used to be mates as school. Cam was the brainy one but his father made him leave as soon as he was old enough. Cam hated me because I was allowed to stay on at school when he couldn't.'

'There you are, then – he's jealous of you and he wanted to use me to hurt you. Don't be angry, Lewis,' Molly said softly, sliding her arms about his waist. 'Forget about him, he doesn't matter. I'll tell your parents I opened my big mouth in the pub tonight and let slip about the money they were offered.'

'No, leave it to me. It was my fault for telling you.' Lewis held her tight, smelling her perfume, and the fresh apple scent of the shampoo she used. 'I should have taken you out of the place as soon as he started bothering us. I shouldn't have lost my temper like that.'

'To tell you the truth,' Molly said softly, 'I thought it was very romantic. I felt like a lady being protected by her knight.'

'Knights who protected their ladies usually asked for favours in return,' Lewis told her, and she laughed.

'Ask away, Sir Knight,' she said, 'and it shall be granted.'

So he did. And it was.

As soon as the door closed behind Lewis and Molly someone bellowed, 'Did I hear right? Did that girl say that the Ralston-Kerrs were offered two hundred thousand pounds to stop the quarry

286

being opened up again?'

'Damned cheek if it's true,' Sam Brennan said, and was immediately countered by Marcy's, 'She said they turned it down!'

'Did you know anything about this, Glen?' a voice called.

'Not until a minute ago, like the rest of you,' Glen lied, and then, to a man who was mopping his trousers and complaining bitterly about losing his pint, 'I'll fetch a cloth and another pint for you.'

'On the house?'

'Aye, go on then. Settle down, everyone,' Glen ordered his customers as he headed for the bar. 'Give me a chance to clean up this mess and don't go tramping glass and beer all over the floor.'

'Can I stay now that Lewis has gone?' Cam Gordon asked hopefully. 'It was him that started it.'

'Aye, sit down.' Glen thrust out an arm and pushed Cam into an empty chair. 'And don't you be so lippy in future. I won't have brawling in my pub.'

'I can't believe it,' Sam muttered as the bar began to calm down. 'Why would anyone want to pay that much money to stop the quarry?'

'It'll be something of nothing,' Marcy told him. 'That girl was talking nonsense – or she's heard something and got hold of the wrong end of the stick.'

'Whatever it is, I'm going to find out the truth of the story. There's no smoke without fire. I've got a feeling Glen knows more than he's letting on.'

'For goodness' sake, Sam,' Marcy said, 'you're becoming paranoid! I'm sick of this nonsense.'

'Not as sick of it as I am. I'm going to see the Ralston-Kerrs tomorrow morning.'

'Let it be! You're only going to embarrass them, and me.'

'Look who's talking! You didn't mind embarrassing me, joining this protest committee when you know that bringing more industry to the area could be good for the shop.'

'Don't start on that again!'

He drained his glass and got to his feet. 'I'll fetch more drinks.'

'I'm tired. I'm going to finish this and then go home – and so should you. You've had your quota for the evening.'

'Perhaps,' Sam said levelly, 'I feel like going over my quota, just this once.'

Marcy watched him make his way to the bar, taking the long route to avoid falling over Glen, who was busy sweeping up the broken glass. Then she drained her own glass and left the pub without a backward glance.

When Sam finally returned home Marcy was already in bed and asleep – or pretending to be asleep. He sat down on a chair to take his shoes off, letting them thump on the carpet, and when she didn't move he knew sleep was only pretence. He hauled his clothes off, letting them, too, fall to the floor – something she hated – and then got into bed, punching his pillow and deliberately taking time to settle. Marcy, bounced about on the mattress, kept her eyes tight shut and her bottom lip nipped between her teeth, determined not to let him rile her.

When he said 'Goodnight, then,' she didn't reply, and the two of them lay awake for a long time, unhappy and lonely, but both feeling that there seemed to be no way of resolving their differences without being seen to give in.

In the morning, Marcy rose first. Sam was still asleep, lying on his back, one arm above his head. He looked vulnerable, and normally she would not have been able to resist the temptation to kiss him awake; but today she went off to the bathroom, leaving him to his sleep and stepping on, rather than over, his scattered clothing.

When she returned to the bedroom he was up and waiting his turn in the bathroom. They bade each other a formal good morning and while he showered and shaved Marcy went downstairs to eat her breakfast alone.

It was early when they walked across the green to the store, and there was nobody else about. Marcy looked up at the sky, scrubbed clean in readiness for the day apart from a few wisps of white cloud. Until recently, she had loved this time of day, and loved the way she and Sam had the place to themselves before the hustle and bustle began.

Now, the mornings only signalled the start of another long and difficult day. But today, she recalled with a sudden lift of the spirits, the *Dumfries News* would be among the newspapers piled outside the shop. Today was going to be different.

As it happened, the *News* bundle was the first to hand. Sam hoisted it up as Marcy unlocked the door and keyed in the alarm code. He swung the bundle on to the counter and went back for another while she fetched a knife from the drawer behind the counter and cut the twine binding the papers tightly together.

She ran her eyes over the front page and breathed a long sigh of relief.

'You can read it in your tea break,' Sam said as he dumped another bundle on the counter. 'Folk'll be in any minute.'

'Are you still determined to go to Linn Hall and pester poor Hector Ralston-Kerr?'

'Of course. If he's selling us out, we have a right to know.'

'I think you ought to read this first,' Marcy said, turning the top newspaper round so that he could see the headline.

32

'Oh dear,' Fliss said.

'That's the cat let out of the bag,' her husband agreed. The three Ralston-Kerrs were having breakfast in the pantry, as usual.

'I'm really sorry, Mum – Dad. Molly didn't mean to tell anyone, it just slipped out.'

'But how did she know?' Hector looked at his son's reddening face. 'You told her?'

'In passing. I was showing her round the house on the day of the garden party and I explained that there was no sense in going up to the top floor because the roof leaked. She asked why we didn't just get it mended and – well, that's how the subject of money came up. But she did promise not to tell a soul.'

'It's a pity you didn't get her to promise not to tell an entire pub full of people,' Fliss said wryly, and then, as her son flinched, 'I'm sorry, dear, that was unfair.'

Hector was still trying to puzzle things out. 'What I can't understand is, why did the subject come up in the first place?'

Lewis had anticipated that question, and in the still dark of the night he had managed to come up with a somewhat feeble answer. 'Oh, someone said something about the quarry not really affecting us here in Linn Hall as much as in the village itself. Molly likes you both, and she likes working here. She was just trying to defend you.'

'Nice of her, but I have to say that I wish–' Fliss had started to say when Jinty McDonald, still in her coat, burst in with such energy that the door flew back on its hinges and banged against the wall. Lewis, his nerves already ragged, was pouring himself a cup of tea; he jumped at the sudden noise, splashing tea across the wooden table.

'Lewis, pour me a cup, there's a good lad.' Jinty collapsed into a chair, fanning herself with the newspaper. 'I stopped off at the store to get my paper and when I saw it I bought one for you and ran all the way across the green and up the hill – I'm puffed out! Look...' She spread the paper on the table so they could see the headline splashed across the front page.

'NO NEW QUARRY FOR PRIOR'S FORD' it proclaimed, and then, in smaller letters, 'Too Costly After All, Says Company'.

'They're not going to reopen the quarry?'

'They're not, Mr Ralston-Kerr – and isn't it a relief that the thing's finally decided, though it might have been of help to some of my kids. But there we are – that's life!' Jinty spooned three lots of sugar into her tea, stirred, then drank deeply while Hector snatched up the paper and started to devour the lead story.

'So that's that.' His voice sang with relief. 'No more fretting!'

No more faint chance of mending the leaky roof, Fliss thought wistfully, or of finding the money to heat the bedrooms during the winter. But seeing the naked relief on Hector's face and the way his shoulders were straightening as though a weight had been lifted from them, she told herself to stop being so selfish.

She reached across the table and covered his freckled hand with her own work-roughened fingers. 'Isn't that good news all round?' she said.

The four round the table beamed at each other, then a hefty hiccup shattered the moment.

'Oh no, look what I've d–done,' Jinty moaned, clapping a hand to her mouth. 'That's what c–comes of drinking hot tea t-too quickly!'

Hector and Fliss weren't the only ones to feel as though the news about the quarry had lifted a weight from their shoulders. Jenny Forsyth had been surprised, when she went to the village store to do her shopping, to find a number of people chattering outside the door; when she got inside, she found more customers than were usual at that time of day, and an air of excitement about the place.

'What's going on?' she asked Sam when she reached the counter.

In answer, he took her copy of the *Dumfries News* from the shelf where the orders were kept and laid it on the counter.

'They're leaving the quarry as it is?'

'Apparently.'

'But that's wonderful!' Then looking up at his grim face, 'Sorry, Sam, you were in favour, weren't you?'

'It doesn't really matter one way or the other any more, does it?'

Jenny hurried outside, leaving the rest of her shopping until later, and turned down River Lane, her heart singing. Now that the quarry had been reprieved there was definitely no risk of Malcolm Cameron returning to the village. No need to see him again, or to be reminded of the past she and Andrew had worked so hard to keep secret. Her life was back on an even keel, and she was safe again.

Over the next few days there was an air of celebration in Prior's Ford. Those who had opposed the quarry reopening went about with huge grins on their faces; those in favour, while disappointed, were relieved to know that the uncertainty and the arguing were over and done with. Friends and neighbours who had fallen out began to talk to each other again.

'The best thing that's come out of this decision,' Duncan Campbell said to his wife, 'is the end of this dratted protest committee.'

Helen was draining a pot of boiled potatoes while Duncan, who had just returned from work, hauled off his boots in the back porch, which was large enough to be turned into a utility room.

'Actually, Glen's already been in touch,' she said through a cloud of steam, 'and it looks as if the committee's taken another turn.'

'What sort of turn?' Duncan asked suspiciously, coming into the kitchen to wash his hands.

'A while ago Marcy happened to mention that if we'd only thought to set up a children's playground in the old quarry we might have had a stronger argument against it being reopened. Now Glen thinks that we should go ahead with the playground. He's already spoken to the Ralston-Kerrs about it and they've given the idea their blessing.'

'Oh no! You didn't agree, did you?'

'It's a good idea, Duncan.'

'And I suppose you'd go on being the secretary?'

'Just for a little while – I hope. I mean, I'm sure it *would* be just for a little while. And I'd rather work on a playground scheme than a protest.'

'Here we go again – me having to stay at home in the evenings to look out for the kids while you swan off to the pub for one of your boozy committee meetings.'

'It's not boozy! One half pint of shandy – maybe two at the most. And they're on the house, which is more than I can say for your nights at the pub,' Helen said heatedly. 'You should be interested in something that benefits our children and helps to keep them safe.' And then, as

Duncan groaned and wrenched the tap on, 'Turn it down, the water's going everywhere!'

Gregor, detailed to set the table that evening, had come into the kitchen to collect the cutlery during his parents' conversation. Now he asked, 'What were you saying about keeping us safe, Mum. Are we in danger?'

'No, of course not. I was just telling Dad that some of us are thinking of raising money to turn part of the quarry into a playground. That'd be nice, wouldn't it?'

'But the quarry's fine as it is. We like it that way – it's our place!'

'It still will be, only better than before, with swings and – things.'

'I don't want the quarry to change!'

'You tell her, son.' Duncan turned from the sink, sprinkling soapy water over the floor. 'I played there when I was a youngster, and we liked it the way it is, too. *Au naturelle* or whatever you call it.'

'I don't think that *is* what you call it, and stop encouraging him. Gregor, go and set the table, I'm just about to put the soup out and the potatoes are going soft. They'll be turned to mush by the time we're ready for them.'

'It's not fair,' Gregor grumped as he wandered from the kitchen, clutching a handful of cutlery. 'I'm going to have to talk to the other kids about this.'

The prospect of her approaching driving theory test filled Clarissa with fear.

'When I was teaching I managed to soothe

hundreds of nervous pupils before their exams, and convince them they could do it, but it's not so easy trying to convince myself.'

'How many of them passed their exams?' Alastair wanted to know. 'Most? Half? A small percentage?'

They were driving through Kirkcudbright, and now Clarissa drew the car smoothly to a halt at an amber light. 'More than half, I'd say.'

'And did you really have the confidence in them you pretended to have?'

'Not every time, but it's amazing how people react when they think that someone else has total belief in their ability. But it's one thing convincing my students and quite another convincing myself.' The lights changed to green and she put the car into gear and moved off.

'You'll sail through the written test – and the practical one as well. You're a good driver and we've been over the theory stuff again and again. You can do it, no bother,' Alastair said, and then, as she shot him a doubtful sidelong glance, 'If it's any help, I believe in you.'

'Really?'

'One hundred per cent,' he said stoutly. It was true – he was impressed by the way Clarissa had gradually changed from the broken, weeping woman he had first encountered on a stile to the person who, at that moment, was driving calmly and confidently through Kirkcudbright's busiest street.

Whether it was her own determination to succeed, or his faith in her, or, perhaps, a mixture of both, she didn't know, but she did pass the written test, and when she was offered a cancellation date for her driving test she accepted. The sooner she got it over with, the better, she told herself, trying to suppress the inner voice when it asked her what on earth she thought she was doing.

'At least I can find out what the driving test's like, even if I don't pass it first time,' she told Alastair.

'You'll pass it. But I think you should go to a driving school for your final lessons. They know how to get people through their tests,' he explained as she began to object. 'You've been a good pupil but I'd rather not take on the full responsibility. There's a good school in Kirkcudbright – I wrote down their phone number for you. Give them a ring.'

Word of the plan to create a playground area spread round the local children like wildfire, and on the following Saturday afternoon a crowd of them gathered at the quarry.

'We have to have a proper meeting,' Freya MacKenzie said when she and Ella arrived. 'We need a spokesman. I'll do it.'

Everyone within earshot nodded enthusiastically; Freya, who had inherited her mother's ability to organise as well as her looks, was well known to them as a leader rather than a follower.

Now she scrambled on to a large rock near the workmen's hut. 'Over here, everyone,' she shouted, and individual clusters of children immediately broke up and re-formed about the rock.

'Okay, you all know why we're here.' Freya set her long denim-clad legs astride and put her hands on her hips. 'Now that the quarry protest committee isn't needed any more, they've decided to turn themselves into a committee to give us a proper playground, right here.'

'We don't want a playground,' someone shouted, while another voice chimed in with, 'We like it the way it is!' A roar of agreement followed the second remark, and Freya gave it time to grow before holding up a hand to calm it.

'Right – hands up those who want the playground to go ahead. And hands up those who don't want it,' she went on when all hands remained by their owners' sides. This time, a forest of arms waved frantically in the air.

'It looks as though we want this place to stay the way it is.'

'But who's going to listen to us?' someone yelled.

'They have a committee, so we'll have a committee. We'll demand a meeting and we'll tell them what we want.'

'They won't listen!' the same voice insisted, and heads nodded all over the quarry.

Ethan, who had a very secret crush on Freya, had been drinking in the sight of her standing above everyone else, balancing with ease on the rock with the sun forming a halo about her head. She looked like a warrior queen, he thought, enraptured; then, realising he should be taking part in the discussion rather than leaving it all to her, he suggested, 'We could compromise. That means we could come to an arrangement – meet them halfway. We could tell them that we'll agree to a playground, but it needs to have what *we* want in it, not what *they* want.'

'Good for you!' Freya smiled down at him and his heart sang. 'Ethan's right – we could tell them that we'll agree to their idea as long as we get to choose what should go in the playground. That way they're more likely to listen to us, and we'd at least get things the way we want them. What do you think?'

There was a moment's silence, and then as the children clustered round the rock realised that the compromise could bring them benefits, suggestions began to come from all over the place. 'A climbing frame – a see-saw – stuff to play Tarzan on – a trampoline – tyre swings – rope climbing!'

Again, Freya had to hold her hand up for silence. 'Right, we've got started. The next thing we have to do is to form our own committee, and then go home and think about what you would like to see in our playground. Write it down, and we'll have another meeting here in a week's time. The committee will make a list of your demands and pass them to the adults' committee. Okay?' Then, when heads nodded vigorously. 'Now we have to nominate our committee.'

'Freya as the leader,' Ethan shouted, and the others cheered.

'Ella, write that down,' ordered Freya, who had equipped her younger sister with an exercise book and a pencil before they left the house.

'I don't want to. I hate writing and I want a football pitch!'

'Just do the writing for now and we'll get a secretary later,' Freya snapped, and Ella reluctantly started to write.

'Me as the chairperson, and then we need a

secretary and some committee members – three should do it. Anyone good at writing and willing to be our secretary?'

'*Please!*' Ella added.

Heather McDonald put up her hand, and Ella began to forge her way through the crowd towards her, anxious to be relieved of her duties as quickly as possible. Freya voted Gregor in as a committee member since he had been the one to alert the others to the plan to turn their beloved quarry into an official playground. Ethan volunteered and was voted in, and Calum Forsyth became the third committee member.

'So over the next week you have to write down the things you want to see in our new playground, and pass it on to one of the committee members,' Freya instructed. 'We'll get together on Friday afternoon to have a look at your lists, and on Saturday we'll have another meeting here before we talk to the adults. We'll have to be quick and we'll have to be firm. You know what adults are like; if they discover we're fighting back they'll probably fill the place with baby swings and a tiny see-saw before we can stop them!'

33

'Are you sure about this? My kids haven't said a thing about setting up a committee!'

'I only know about it because Freya was working on Peter's computer last night, going into the

Internet to find out all about playground equipment. Why shouldn't the children have a committee, Helen? You and Glen and Marcy and the others did it.'

'But they're children!'

'Never demean children. My Freya is a very intelligent girl. She's organised the others into writing down their ideas of what they want in this playground,' Ingrid said proudly.

The short tourist season was drawing to a close; there were fewer visitors from outside the village now, and the Gift Horse was empty apart from Ingrid, Jenny, Helen and Marcy, all sitting round one of the small tables.

'Calum told us about it – he's never been good at keeping quiet about things,' Jenny put in. 'They're determined, Helen, so you and Marcy ought to warn Glen and the others that the kids will soon be looking for a meeting with them. Personally, I think it's a good idea. Why should our children settle for a playground designed by adults? Far better to give them what they want, then everyone will be happy.'

'That depends on *what* they want. There's some money in the quarry protest account, thanks to the Easter egg hunt, but not much. We'll have to raise quite a lot before we can even think of a playground – and we'd probably have to get planning permission.'

'I imagine you would get that all right, and the children will probably save you money. Children are good at making the most of few materials. How do you plan to raise funds?' Ingrid wanted to know.

'We haven't really started to think about that, have we, Marcy?'

'A Hallowe'en dance, perhaps, in the village hall, and a special bonfire night for Guy Fawkes,' Jenny suggested. 'And you could ask the drama club to let you have a collection for the playground when they do their pantomime. The pantomimes always get great audiences.'

'Good idea.' Helen dug into her bag, produced a notebook and pen, and began to scribble busily. 'You should join the committee.'

'No thanks!'

Marcy had been silent, but now she said abruptly, 'Actually, there's something I ought to tell you. I'm leaving Prior's Ford.'

'When?'

'Soon.'

'When are you coming back?'

'I don't know.'

'You and Sam are giving up the village store?' Jenny asked in dismay. 'But why?'

'I'm not talking about the two of us, I'm talking about me.' Marcy took a deep breath, and said, 'Sam doesn't know it yet, so please don't say anything.'

'You're leaving him?' Looking at Ingrid and Jenny, Helen saw by their faces that they were as stunned by the news as she was. 'But I always thought you were so strong together!'

'That's the important word – together.' Marcy's voice was bleak. 'I don't feel we're together any more.'

'It's this quarry business, isn't it?' Ingrid guessed, and when Marcy nodded, she said, 'I couldn't understand why people allowed it to split the village the way it did, but it's over and done with now – people are putting it out of their minds and getting back to the way they were before it happened. You and Sam can do the same, surely?'

'I don't think so. You're right, Jenny, we *were* good together, and I was daft enough to let myself think that nothing could change what we had. But the first problem to come along – whether or not a quarry would be reopened, of all things...' Marcy attempted a laugh, and then, as it caught in her throat, she swallowed it down and stumbled on hurriedly. 'The first problem proved me wrong. We weren't just opposed – we became enemies. The quarry's staying as it is, but for us the damage has been done and I can't see us ever getting back to the way we were before.'

'Give it time,' Helen begged, but Marcy shook her head.

'I'm not exactly a spring chicken; I don't *have* time to waste on a relationship that's never going to get back to where it used to be. Neither of us seems to know how to mend the rift, and perhaps that's because it's too wide and too deep and just not worth the bother. In fact–' She stopped abruptly and looked at her friends, one by one, then went on, 'In fact, now that you three know about it, I think I should just bite the bullet and go today.'

'Today?' Helen yelped. 'You can't do that! This isn't a television soap opera!'

'What does that have to do with anything?' Ingrid's eyebrows rose.

'You know what I mean – in soap operas the

303

characters decide to go away and then they just go – no planning, no packing, no booking flights – they just vanish and it's as if they'd never been there. But this is real life, Marcy!'

'Why stay when it will only prolong the misery for both of us?'

'Talk to him!'

'That's the problem, Jenny – we've stopped talking. We just argue.'

'But if you tell him you're thinking of leaving–'

'Then he'll ask me to wait so we can talk. And we'll end up arguing. That's my point – the time for talking's over. I have no option!'

'Where will you go?'

'I've a friend in Stirling – she's already said I can go there at any time and stay with her for as long as I want.'

'That sounds as though you've been making plans in advance,' Jenny said, and Marcy nodded.

'I've seen this coming for some time. I've given Sam – and myself – time to get back to the way we were, but it's just not happening. I don't want to go on being miserable and I'm sure he must feel the same. Please don't say anything because I don't want Sam to hear about this from anyone else. I'll tell him when the store shuts.'

'You're really going today?'

'Yes, I am, Helen. It's for the best, believe–' Marcy broke off and got to her feet. They had been drinking coffee, and now she put her half-empty mug down on the table. 'Sorry – I'll write,' she said, and almost ran from the shop, ignoring Ingrid's cry of, 'Marcy, wait!'

She followed Marcy to the door, and then

turned back to the others. 'She's running off across the green as if the fiends of hell are after her. Poor Marcy!'

'Poor Sam. What will he do without her?' Jenny asked the other two.

'He's going to have to cope, the same as the rest of us,' Ingrid said firmly. 'The same as Marcy will have to cope, in Stirling, trying to start a new life – again.'

'Why do they both have to be so obstinate? Surely, once Sam knows how strongly Marcy feels about the way things are between them, he'll work to mend fences.'

'Let's hope so, Helen, let's hope so. It's up to them now. We can only wait to see what happens.' Ingrid picked up her mug and held it out. 'To Marcy, and Sam – and a better future, for both of them – hopefully together,' she said solemnly, and the three of them touched mugs and then drank.

Marcy had intended to return to the store where, no doubt, Sam was trying to cope with the post-office counter and a growing queue of housewives with wire baskets full of shopping. He must be wondering how long his partner's idea of 'just a quick coffee with the others' was. But once she had run from the gift shop she hesitated before turning towards Rowan Cottage instead, her mind in too much of a turmoil to cope with the store.

It had seemed to her, when news came that the quarry had been reprieved, that if she and Sam had had any chance of rebuilding their relationship, it would start then, but instead they had remained distant from each other, at work and at home.

Why, she didn't know. She must take her share of the blame; she had allowed herself to become too involved in fighting the quarry company, and the more Sam was in favour of the project the more she had argued against it. But once the quarry was no longer an issue she could see it had only been a small part of the problem. Now she had told her three closest friends she was leaving there could be no going back. The die was cast, and there was no point in pretending her life in Prior's Ford could ever be the same again.

She let herself in to the house, and went upstairs to pack her things.

When Jenny and Helen had gone home Ingrid locked the shop and then walked across the green to Rowan Cottage.

'So you really are going?' She nodded at the two suitcases standing at the bottom of the stairs.

'Yes, I am.' Marcy's voice was defiant.

'Then we should drink to your future. I would enjoy a gin and tonic,' Ingrid said sweetly, and after a slight pause, the other woman stepped back to let her in.

'I presume you've come over with some idea of talking me into staying,' she said as she poured the drinks.

'I wouldn't dream of it, but I just wondered' – Ingrid relaxed into a chair and crossed one slender denim-clad leg over the other – 'if you're leaving for the right reason.'

'I'm not doing this lightly, Ingrid.'

'Of course not. But I would like to know – do

you really feel you and Sam have no future together, or are you angry with him because he refused to see things your way?'

'Oh dear, it's going to be one of those discussions, is it?' As Marcy handed a glass to Ingrid the phone rang in the hall, but she ignored it.

'Just a talk between friends. Aren't you going to answer that?'

'No.'

'You know what I'm getting at, don't you?'

'You think that because of my background – uncaring parents and a bad marriage – I can't cope with controversy. You're saying I need Sam to see things my way every time, no matter what.'

'It's possible,' Ingrid said calmly, and Marcy eyed her in silence for about half a minute – during which time the phone fell silent – before taking a long drink.

'That is damned cheek. I wouldn't let many people get away with saying that to me.'

'I agree. It's the sort of thing only close and caring friends can say to each other. So – what do you think?'

'Since we heard the quarry stays as it is I've tried to look at things from every angle, including the one you just brought up. And I don't agree. I think I'm strong enough to accept that the man I live with doesn't share my opinions, but there's something more than that – deep down; it's as if something's broken and I don't know how to fix it. Perhaps going away will give me the chance to find out what it is and whether or not it can be repaired.' Marcy took another drink and then added, 'Perhaps Sam and I have been living in a fools' paradise, waiting without realising it for something to come along and destroy what we thought we had.'

'I don't think so.'

'I have to find out, and I can't find out here. Everything's too close. It's like trying to read a book that's jammed up against my face.'

The phone started ringing again, and this time both of them ignored it.

'If you find out what's broken and you think that it can be fixed, you'll come back?'

'Yes... I don't know. People change, Ingrid. Perhaps Sam and I will have changed by then and we won't fit together the way we did before.'

Ingrid sighed, finished her drink, and got to her feet. 'Well, I tried,' she said.

'And it was appreciated. Friends are valuable – perhaps more valuable than partners,' Marcy said. 'I'll miss you and Helen and Jenny. And Prior's Ford.'

Ingrid's arms went about her in a close, but brief, embrace.

'Take care, and keep in touch.'

'As long as you don't let Sam know where I am.'

'We're your friends, of course we won't let anyone know where you are unless it's what you want,' Ingrid said, and walked past the clamouring telephone on her way out.

Marcy was in the sitting room when Sam came across from the store. From where she sat she saw him open the gate and start up the path, then heard his key in the lock. He came in and then stopped short, no doubt looking at the suitcases in the hall, then he called her name.

'I'm in here.'

He walked in, half truculent, half bewildered. 'Where the hell have you been? You said you were only going to be away for a few minutes. Have you got any idea how busy I was? I tried to phone but your mobile was switched off. Then I tried here but there was no reply. What's going on?'

'Isn't it obvious? I'm leaving, Sam, and don't ask why – you know why as well as I do.'

He stared at her in silence, then went to the sideboard and poured out a whisky, asking, with his back turned to her, 'When did you decide this?'

'Today. I went over to have a coffee at the Gift Horse because I had to get out of the shop. I meant to go back, but while I was with the others I realised the time had come to call it a day. So I said goodbye to them, and then came back here to pack.' She looked at her watch. 'I ordered a taxi, it'll be here in ten minutes.'

He turned to face her, his face shuttered. 'And you're not going to give me the chance to discuss it?'

'Sam, we've had all the chances we needed, and neither of us took them. We work together, we live together, we sleep in the same bed, and yet we never spoke about what was happening to us. Why start now? It's not your fault,' she went on when he said nothing, 'and perhaps not mine either. It's just that we're both so damned stubborn. Sometimes that works and sometimes it doesn't. Right now, it doesn't.'

'It's all to do with this damned quarry, isn't it? Are you really going to let it split us up?'

'How could something like the quarry do that?'

'If you hadn't joined that committee–'

'I did that because you were determined I should agree with your views on the quarry. I wanted to show you that I'm my own person, not one of those pathetic women who vote for the party her man votes for. And – I'll admit it – I wanted to annoy you, to see how far I could push you. I wish now,' Marcy said, 'that I hadn't, because I found out whatever brought us together wasn't strong enough to hold us together. All it took to finish us was someone wanting to reopen a quarry!'

'What about the store? I can't manage it and the post office on my own, you know that.'

'I'm not going to work my notice if that's what you're after. I couldn't do it. Now I've made my mind up I can't delay any longer. You'll find someone in the village willing to help you out with the store. You don't need me.' She hadn't meant the last sentence to sound the way it did; she felt the pain of the words lance through her heart, and saw the same pain twist Sam's face before he managed to wipe it away.

'Is this a sabbatical? Are you planning to come back?'

'I don't know – right now, I don't really know anything, Sam, except that I need to have time to myself. Perhaps we both do. I think we just need to be apart for a while, at least.'

A horn tooted outside and, as Sam glanced out of the window, Marcy got to her feet.

'That's my taxi.'

'You could send it away and let me drive you to the railway station.'

310

'Thanks, but no thanks.' She brushed past him and he followed her as she went into the hall and bent to pick up the cases.

'I'll do that.' He put her aside firmly. 'You open the door. What do I tell people?' he asked as he followed her down the path. 'You know how folk gossip in a place like this.'

'Whatever you want. Tell them I've got a sick grandmother to look after – tell them it's all my fault, if it makes things easier for you. I don't care any more.'

He put the cases in the boot of the taxi while she got into the back seat. Then he came round to the window, motioning her to roll it down. When she did so, he said, 'Marcy, don't do this to us. Don't go.'

'I must,' she said, and then sat back, staring straight ahead as the taxi carried her out of Prior's Ford.

34

Helen, landed with the task of telling Glen Mason about the children's playground committee, persuaded Jenny and Ingrid to back her up.

'I know he's going to look on it as a joke and refuse to have anything to do with them. I need support – you have to come with me,' she insisted.

'Why not?' Ingrid said cheerfully 'Let's go there tomorrow for lunch, then we can break the news afterwards.'

When they met in River Lane the next day Helen carried a large envelope.

'We'll need to stop off at the store to post this. It's the short story my tutor liked; I've decided to bite the bullet and submit it to a magazine.' She was pink with excitement and when they reached the store, she put out a hand to halt the other two. 'This,' she said solemnly, 'is my first ever submission, so we must wish it luck.' She kissed the envelope, whispered, 'Good luck,' then handed it to Jenny. 'Now you.'

'You're expecting me to stand in the street and kiss an envelope?'

'It's what friends do for each other.'

'When have I ever asked you to kiss my letters?'

'Don't be so picky, Jenny.' Ingrid took the envelope from Jenny's hands and bestowed a smacking kiss on it, to a passer-by's surprise. 'Good luck, brilliant little story,' she said, and handed it back to Jenny who glanced around before dropping a swift kiss on it.

'I wish it all the luck in the world, Helen,' she said, returning it to its rightful owner, 'but I hope I don't have to do that again – at least, not in the street.'

After they had had lunch Glen and Libby joined them for coffee.

'That was a bit of a shock about Marcy and Sam, wasn't it?' Glen said, avoiding Libby's stern gaze as he stirred several spoonfuls of sugar into his cup. 'She was friendly with you three – did you know that she was planning to walk out on him?'

'Not until the day she went.'

'Poor Sam looks downright ill,' Libby said. 'He's

312

missing her. Do you think she might come back?'

'She might,' Ingrid said. 'But that's up to her, isn't it?'

'Aye, I suppose so. We'll miss her on the committee, won't we, Helen? We have a lot to do, planning the new playground and thinking up ways to raise funding.'

'Jenny suggested we could ask the drama group if we can have a collection after each of their pantomime performances.'

'That's a good idea. Note it down for the next meeting, will you?'

'I already have,' Helen said. 'And a special bonfire night, and a Hallowe'en dance in the village hall?

'Well done! I knew you would be an asset to the committee!'

'There's something else to discuss, isn't there, Helen?' Ingrid said sweetly.

'The more the merrier – we need to raise as much money as we can before the spring.'

'This isn't about funding; it's about the children themselves. As soon as they got wind of this playground idea, they decided they want to be involved in planning it.'

Glen's eyebrows shot up. 'The kids want to sit in on the committee?'

'No, they've formed their own committee and now they're putting together ideas on the sort of playground they would like.'

'You're kidding me!'

'She isn't, Glen,' Jenny said. 'My Calum's on the committee, and they're all taking it very seriously. They want a meeting with your committee before anything's decided.'

'Oh, bless!' Libby beamed.

'Now just a minute. The kids'll be looking for all sorts of fancy things like water slides and so on. We've got to work on a sensible layout first, and then start costing it – and we have to apply for planning permission. Tell them they can come in on the discussions then when all that's done – perhaps.'

'I think we need to hear their views earlier than that, Glen. They say if we go ahead without talking to them, they'll have nothing to do with the new playground.'

'Who are these kids, anyway?'

'Most of the children in the village between the ages of five and fifteen,' Jenny said. 'They don't all want to meet with you, of course, just the committee.'

'Who else is on this so-called committee?'

'Young Ethan, and Helen's son Gregor, and one of the McDonald children – and my Freya's the chairperson.' Ingrid gave the publican her sweetest smile as Libby refilled her coffee cup. 'And, as Jenny says, they're taking it seriously.' She sipped at her coffee, her clear blue gaze meeting and holding Glen's eyes. 'I think you should take it seriously, too,' she said as she placed the cup back into its saucer. 'We all do, Glen. It could be more – *important* – than you think.'

'Please do, Glen,' Libby urged. 'I think it's a lovely idea, the little ones wanting to plan their own playground.'

Her husband wrenched his somewhat uneasy gaze away from Ingrid and glanced at Helen and

Jenny who, trying not to laugh out loud, nodded solemnly back at him. 'I suppose we could meet them if they're that keen on the idea,' he said reluctantly, adding, 'but they'll have to be businesslike about it.'

'I think you'll find they are,' Ingrid told him as Helen produced notebook and pen from her bag.

'Can we make it a Friday evening?' she asked as she scribbled. 'They have to go to bed early Monday to Thursday because of school the next day.'

'All right, though I don't know what the rest of our committee will say about this.'

'That can be your job, Glen.' Ingrid beamed at him. 'You can tell them all about it before the next meeting.'

'I just hope the children put forward a good case when the time comes,' Jenny said as they left the Neurotic Cuckoo together.

'I have a feeling they will. Freya is working very hard on the project, and she's turning out to be quite a perfectionist. She takes after her father that way,' Ingrid said proudly. 'He's talking of giving her a computer of her own for Christmas.'

Glen paid another visit to the manse, this time in an attempt to persuade Naomi to take Marcy's place.

'She didn't even write a letter, just asked Helen to hand in her resignation, and I can't get a word out of Sam. I don't suppose you know why she suddenly left the village?'

'Glen, you know as well as I do that if Marcy *had* told me anything I couldn't repeat it to you or anyone else without her agreement. Though as it happens, she said nothing, so I am as much in the dark as anyone else.'

Naomi did not add that, being a woman, she had her own ideas as to what had happened. She had watched Marcy and Sam become estranged over the quarry issue, and had wished one or other of them would confide in her, but knowing what they were like, she had not been entirely surprised when they kept their own counsel.

Glen nodded. 'No point in crying over spilt milk – we've got to look ahead. I know you've got enough on your plate, but we'd appreciate it if you would agree to become a committee member. We would normally have disbanded once the quarry company changed their minds, but now this business of a playground has come up we want to try to see it through.'

'A laudable scheme, but don't you have enough members to deal with it?'

'The thing is, we only had two women on the committee, and now Marcy's gone it leaves Helen on her own. You've probably heard that the kids want to meet us to put forward their views on this playground, and it would be good to have more than one woman in our group.' Glen gave the minister what he hoped was a 'please help a helpless male' look.

'Ah yes – the children. You know, I'm impressed by their approach to this idea of a new playground.'

'You are?'

'Since it's for their benefit, it makes sense to work with them, doesn't it? Ethan has become really involved in choosing the right equipment.

From what he tells me, Freya MacKenzie seems to be a very efficient young lady. She's very like her mother in many ways.'

'Yes,' Glen said uneasily. 'So – you'll agree to come on the committee, then?'

Naomi gave him one of her wide, warm smiles. 'Yes, Glen, I will. In fact, I'm rather looking forward to it.'

Freya had her committee members well briefed. They filed in, all of them smartly dressed and with hair well brushed, and solemnly shook hands with the adults.

Freya and Heather, the secretary, both carried borrowed briefcases, which they opened as soon as they were settled round the table in the Masons' living room. Heather brought out a brand new exercise book and two biros, and proceeded to record the date carefully on the first line of the first page, the tip of her tongue protruding from one corner of her neat little mouth. Helen, sitting beside her with her own reporter's notebook at the ready, sneaked a sidelong glance as Heather moved to the next line, and saw that she was writing, in large rounded letters, 'First Meeting Between Playground Organisation Group and Fund-raising Committee'.

When Glen asked if they would like anything to drink, the children each opted for a fruit juice. Naomi did the same, and so did the other adults with some reluctance. Glen sighed, and went through to the bar, where Alastair Marshall was assisting Libby.

She raised her eyebrows when her husband

started pouring out the drinks. 'Taken the pledge? A group decision, is it?'

'There's something about that MacKenzie girl – she's got her mother's eyes. I couldn't bring myself to drink whisky in front of her.'

'Good for her,' Libby said. 'She could do wonders for your waistline.'

'She's not going to get the chance,' Glen told her curtly.

Once he returned with the drinks and the meeting was underway, Freya spread the papers she had brought with her over the table. They were all pictures of playground equipment printed from the Internet, each one priced in a neat, clear hand.

'May I start?' she asked, and when Glen nodded, went on briskly, 'We've collected ideas from all the village children who are interested in this play area, and we've also had a meeting with them to find out what they want us to tell you tonight. Now, on the whole we like the quarry as it is. We like the old hut and we use it as our headquarters. It's very useful when the weather's wet. So we want it to stay, though it could do with a bit of improvement.'

'The roof leaks in one of the corners,' Heather put in, 'and when the winds are bad there can be a terrible draught.'

Freya nodded. 'So it would be nice if it could be patched up a bit.'

'That sounds sensible, and it shouldn't cost much,' Naomi agreed.

'That's what we thought. As I said, we like the area the way it is, so we've decided, since you're willing to raise the money for some playground

318

equipment, it should all be wooden, not coloured plastic. That way, it will blend in.'

'You do need to think of the little brothers and sisters,' Naomi suggested.

'We realise that, so we thought we could have, say, four swings for them, and perhaps a little see-saw, and a fenced-off area where they can play safely.'

'And a climbing frame for us older ones,' Gregor butted in.

'Yes, and one of those things' – Freya tapped a clean, neatly trimmed fingernail against a page – 'where children can swing from bar to bar.'

'And some of us would like some sort of frame with rope ladders for climbing,' Calum spoke up.

'Yes. And that's all, really.' Freya nodded at her young committee, and they nodded back. 'We've priced them and they won't cost as much as some of the other things on the Internet. Our wants,' she added, fixing Glen with clear blue eyes so like her mother's, 'are few. Heather?'

'What? Oh – yes,' Heather said as her chairman mouthed some words at her. She dug into her briefcase again and handed a sheet of paper to Glen. 'That's the list of things we'd like, and where they can be found on the Internet, and the cost of each one. And a total.'

'There is, of course, the instil– the putting up bit,' Ethan said. 'But we don't know how much money that will take.'

'Not yet, but we're going to try to find out from local firms,' Heather added.

There was a stunned pause before Lachie cleared his throat and said, 'You seem to have put in quite a lot of work on this.'

'Haven't they just!' Naomi agreed proudly, beaming at the children, who beamed back at her.

Freya took a sip of juice and then put her glass down. 'We felt we owed it to you to be workman-like about the project. We didn't want to waste your time and have you thinking we're just a bunch of silly children. And we do realise that even a small playground will cost money, so we're willing to help out as much as we can with the financial side, too.'

'We've held a survey, and quite a few of the mothers are willing to make toffee and fudge and things like that,' Gregor explained. 'We're going to sell it at school and from house to house to help with the fund-raising.'

'And we thought,' Heather put in, her grey eyes huge behind the lenses of her spectacles, 'that it might be nice for both committees to organise a special fancy dress Hallowe'en party for everyone in the village hall this year. We could charge an entrance fee and have a raffle.'

'We'd already thought of that ourselves, so that's definitely going to happen,' Helen said.

'I think it's ideal – fun for the whole village,' Naomi added.

'We will, of course, be keeping you fully informed, and we hope you'll do the same,' Freya said. 'I'll leave these pictures with you – I've got copies. There's one request...'

'What's that?' Glen's voice was apprehensive.

'Can we meet at the quarry, soon? We would like to show you where we think the pieces of

320

equipment should go. A week tomorrow at two o'clock?'

When it was agreed, she finished her drink and closed her briefcase with a decisive click.

'We'll go now and leave you to the rest of your meeting. Thank you for your time.' She held her hand out to Glen, who took it gingerly in his large paw.

'Tell me, lass,' he said as the young committee members began to slide off their chairs. 'What do you hope to be when you grow up?'

'Possibly a model,' Freya told him. 'But probably an accountant.'

'No doubt you'll manage one or the other,' Glen said, 'or both.'

When the children had gone he glanced around the table. Robert Kavanagh, Lachie Wilkins and Pete McDermott all looked slightly stunned, while Naomi was wreathed in smiles. Helen kept her head bent over her notebook in an attempt to hide her amusement. She couldn't wait to tell Ingrid and Jenny about the meeting.

'Well, I thought that was most interesting – and informative,' Naomi said. 'I believe we are going to end up with a very good playground.'

'Yes. I don't know about the rest of you,' Glen said, 'but I could do with a drink – a proper drink.' Then, remembering their new member, he added hurriedly, 'If you don't mind, that is, Naomi.'

'Not at all. A whisky and lemonade please,' Naomi said easily.

35

'It's not been a bad season,' Ingrid said as she and Jenny started clearing shelves in the Gift Horse.

'Not bad, but it'll be nice to get time to ourselves over the winter,' Jenny was replying when the door flew open and Helen arrived, waving a letter.

'They bought it! I've sold my first story! Look!' She handed the letter to Jenny, and Ingrid moved in to read it over her shoulder.

'Imagine wanting to know if I'll agree to their payment!' Helen was jumping round the shop like an excited child. 'Of course I agree! Oh, it's going to be wonderful to see my name in print. I'm a real writer at last – I can't wait to start on that novel!'

'Leave the packing for now, Jenny, we're going back to my house,' Ingrid announced when she had hugged her friend. 'This calls for champagne and we always keep a bottle in the fridge for special occasions.'

'Champagne at this time in the morning?'

'Absolutely, Helen. This is the first day of the rest of your life.' Ingrid was putting on her coat as she spoke. 'And celebrations should always be impetuous and spur of the moment. Aren't you glad now we all wished the story good luck, Jenny?'

She was so fortunate, Helen thought half an hour later, to have such good friends – and how wonderful to know someone who could afford to keep champagne in the house for special occasions. She took a sip from her glass and decided that when she was a famous author she, too, would always have a bottle of champagne in her fridge.

'I wish Marcy were here to celebrate with us,' she said.

'Never mind,' Ingrid topped up her glass, 'you can tell her your news in a letter.'

A woman from the village was now working in the store, and Sam Brennan's curt response to questions about Marcy's whereabouts was, 'She's gone to visit a friend.' His expressionless face and the chill in his voice deterred customers from asking further questions, but at the same time, it meant that the village gossips sensed a story. Whispers began to flow from mouth to ear as swiftly as the river in spate.

The core of the story was, naturally, that Marcy had left Sam, but the reasons guessed at were wild and wonderful. She had fallen in love with someone else, possibly a summer tourist who had visited the store and swept her off her feet. Sam had thrown her out for some shocking misdemeanour, or had simply tired of her. Marcy was already married, had left her husband for Sam, but had now returned to the marital home for some unknown reason.

'It makes my blood boil to hear what people are saying about Marcy,' Helen said. 'They all know her and like her, and yet they're willing to believe any daft thing they hear. They're like vultures picking over the bones of a corpse.' She was racked by a sudden shiver. 'I can even see the curiosity in the other committee members' eyes, and they're men. I thought it was only women who gossiped and wondered about folk.'

'Oh, men can be old sweethearts – no,' said Ingrid, 'what is it? Some sort of old wives?'

'Sweetie wives?' Jenny suggested, and Ingrid's forehead, which had been wrinkled in thought, smoothed again.

'Yes, that's it. Some men can be old sweetie wives and enjoy gossip as much as women. But fortunately, not our men. We three chose well.'

'Did you see the notice Sam's put up in the store, asking for someone to work there on a permanent basis? I wish he had at least said it would be a temporary appointment. It's only made them gossip even harder. It's certainly difficult to listen to people talking, and not be able to defend Marcy.'

'Remember, Helen, that if we told the truth, we would be accusing Sam of driving Marcy away And every cloud has a silver lining – now that the gossips are busy talking about Sam and Marcy, they're giving poor Lewis Ralston-Kerr a rest. Why do they have to make such a meal of him making sheep's eyes at that pretty red-haired girl?' Ingrid wanted to know.

'They've certainly been spending a lot of time in each other's company,' Helen mused. 'I've heard they're in the pub together most evenings, and Duncan says she spends more time out in the gardens with Lewis than she does in the kitchen where she's supposed to be working.'

'Now don't you start,' Ingrid admonished, wagging a finger at her. 'We must hold our tongues and not make things worse for any of them. The talking about Marcy and Sam will die down, and in any case, she might come back soon.'

'I hope so!' Helen said, and then, sadly, 'But somehow, I don't think so.'

'One thing's for sure, we don't want to make things worse for Sam.' Jenny shook her head as Ingrid picked up the bottle. 'He's missing her so much – he looks downright ill.'

'And so he should. He was a fool to turn this quarry business into a personal matter between himself and Marcy,' Helen said. 'I'll never forget the way she kept watching for him during the Easter egg hunt – but he never arrived. He let her down.'

'I know, but – he must be very lonely. The shop was quiet when I went in yesterday, so I invited him to supper last night.'

'Did he come?' Ingrid's voice, and her expression, showed that she already knew the answer.

'He said he had a shop full of food, and he didn't need sympathy, or charity.' The memory of the curt rejection burned Jenny's face.

'You see? How can we help a man like that? Only by respecting his and Marcy's privacy and by not gossiping about them.'

'I wish Marcy had been at the committee meeting when the children came along to discuss the new playground.' Helen tried to change the subject. 'Glen's face was a picture, and the children were all so grown-up about it.'

'Freya had them well schooled beforehand. She got Peter to go over all their ideas with her, and teach her how to present them.'

'She did very well – Marcy would have loved it. They even persuaded the committee to meet them at the quarry on Saturday afternoon so they could show them how the playground should be laid out – and they're offering to help raise funds too. We should be proud of our children,' Helen said. 'In fact, we should be proud of all the village children.'

'You should tell your friend at the newspaper, Helen,' Ingrid suggested. 'Or write the story yourself and send it in. I'm sure they would like it.'

'Yes,' Helen said, 'I think I will.'

Clarissa was tempted to cancel her appointment for a driving test and give up all thought of getting her licence. But Alastair insisted that she go ahead.

'You're going to pass, believe me.'

'You don't think it's too soon?'

'I would have told you if I thought it was too soon. Have faith in yourself, woman!'

'I'm not terribly happy about using the driving school car, and having the driving school instructor there instead of you.'

'Driving school cars are safer.' There had been a slight problem with the Astra's clutch, and though it was now working, Alastair was nervous in case it let Clarissa down during her test. 'And I'll go to the test centre in your car, if having me around makes you feel less uptight. Then you can drive us both home once you've passed.'

On the day, she swallowed down two homeopathic tablets that would calm her, if the label on the bottle kept its promise; then, looking in the bathroom mirror, she gave herself the sort of talk she used to give students who were bright but nervous about exams. All too soon her driving instructor arrived and she went out to the car, feeling like a doomed prisoner taking the final walk.

At her insistence, Alastair had gone ahead, and when they arrived he was waiting outside the test centre. The very sight of him helped to calm Clarissa's nerves. He sat with her until the examiner arrived, and went outside with them.

Clarissa obliged the examiner by reading the registration plate on a car parked further along the road, and then they both got into the driving school's car. Trying to ignore the butterflies now congregating, strangely enough, in the region of her heart, she put the key into the ignition, made sure the mirror was in the correct position and the gear in neutral, and then switched on.

Nothing happened.

She switched off, and then on again, and still nothing happened.

'Nothing's happening,' she said, somewhat unnecessarily.

'Are you sure you turned the key properly, Mrs Ramsay?'

'Of course I'm sure!' She did it again, but the car remained mute. The instructor rushed forward to open the bonnet, and Alastair joined him.

'Wait here,' the examiner said, and got out to have a word with the two of them.

After a moment, the instructor tapped on the window. 'I'm terribly sorry, Mrs Ramsay, the engine appears to have jammed. It's never happened to this car before.'

'I'll get out, shall I?' she offered eagerly.

'No – oh no, you stay there. We'll get it going in a jiffy,' the man said, and disappeared behind the bonnet again. The examiner appeared from the other side of the bonnet and went to stand against the test centre wall, checking his watch every few minutes.

All at once an almost mystic calm fell over Clarissa. It was as though someone had dropped a soft black shawl on her from on high. It was meant to be, she told herself. It was kismet – fate. She was not meant to be a driver.

Through a gap at the bottom of the raised bonnet she could see two pairs of hands fluttering about the engine. Every now and then the instructor appeared at the window, asked her to try the ignition again, and repeated, as the car remained silent, 'I can't understand it!' before rushing back to join Alastair.

Clarissa, now in a state of beatific inner peace, drummed her fingertips lightly on the steering wheel and hummed 'Where Have All the Flowers Gone?' under her breath. It had been decided by an order higher than anything she had ever known – no more driving lessons, no more worry. She would get rid of the car, which was unfortunate in a way as she had come to like it. It had been part of the New Clarissa. Perhaps she would replace it with sturdy boots and become a walker.

She glanced at the examiner and saw him frowning at his watch again. Perhaps she should give the car to Alastair, on condition she could call on him if she were in need of transport. He could certainly do with a car.

The examiner took one last look at his watch and stepped forward, mouth open to speak. It was almost over; soon, she would be free.

Then the bonnet suddenly slammed down and Alastair leapt to the pavement, giving her the thumbs up as the instructor appeared at the window for the final time.

'Switch on,' he rasped, and Clarissa, startled from her contented reverie, did as she was told. The engine burst into life, the examiner jumped into the car, Clarissa checked the mirror, put the gear into first, made sure that the way was clear, and was off along the street before she knew what was happening.

She was so convinced she was not meant to become a qualified driver that she didn't feel nervous at all as she covered the test course, pausing only to reverse round a corner, do a three-point turn and a hill start, and slam the brakes on for an emergency stop. So it came as a surprise when they arrived back at the test centre and the examiner congratulated her on passing the test.

'And I would like to thank you,' he added, smiling at her for the first time since they had met that morning, 'for going round the course so efficiently that you've brought me back to the centre in plenty of time for my next client in spite of the delay.'

Then she was on the pavement and Alastair was hugging her, and it was all over.

The instructor, grinning from ear to ear, drove off in the driving school car while Alastair led

Clarissa round the corner to where her own car was parked. 'I brought these,' he produced a pair of scissors from his anorak pocket, 'so you can cut the L-plates off before you drive me back to Prior's Ford. And there's a bunch of flowers and a bottle of champagne in the boot.'

'You shouldn't have!'

'Yes, I should. I wish I'd had a video recorder with me, Clarissa. Once we got that car started you took off like the getaway driver in a bank raid.'

'But you can't afford to buy champagne! How much did it cost?'

'It's not the most expensive kind and actually, I can afford it, for once. Ingrid and Jenny managed to sell almost all my paintings this summer.'

'That's wonderful!'

'Isn't it? So we've both got something to celebrate,' he said, opening the driver's door and ushering her in with a courtly bow.

'I wonder,' Clarissa said as they headed for Prior's Ford, 'if you would be willing to hold on to that champagne for a week or two? I'd like to invite my stepson and stepdaughter up. I've got something to tell them, and I would like you to be there when I do. It would be nice to include them in our celebrations.'

'Are you sure that you want me to be there – won't it be a family occasion?'

'I definitely want you there,' Clarissa told him. 'So if you're willing to put your champagne on hold, I'll take you to the Neurotic Cuckoo for dinner this evening.'

36

When Glen arrived at the quarry on Saturday afternoon the place was full of people. As well as his own committee members and the children's committee, most of the other village children were there, together with a number of parents. The photographer from the *Dumfries News* was taking photographs of Freya and her committee.

'How come he's here?' Glen muttered to Helen. 'Is this your doing, or theirs?'

'Mine, I suppose. I sent in a story about the children forming their own committee to help design the playground, and they've decided to use it in next week's paper.'

'This is all we need – bringing the press down on top of us!'

'For goodness' sake!' Helen exploded, surprising herself as much as Glen. 'You were the one who wanted maximum publicity when we were trying to stop the quarry from being reopened – surely the fact we're now going to make good use of the area and that the children care enough to want to get involved in our plans can bring us even more publicity?' As he stared at her, open-mouthed, she went on, 'In fact, when I mentioned it to Bob Green he said it was a great human-interest story and he's going to arrange for a double-page spread – and they'll pay me for it, too!'

'Good for you, Helen. Personally, I think it will

make a great story, and it can only benefit the village,' Naomi said, while Lachie Wilkins added, 'Adults and children working together instead of slagging each other off – that's the sort of publicity we need, and the sort of story the papers like. Don't forget we're going to have to raise money for this venture, and the newspaper might be willing to help us with that if we give them material to fill their pages.'

'Yes – well – I suppose so,' Glen said uncomfortably. 'Well done, Helen.'

'Thank you,' she said sweetly. 'It's nice to be appreciated instead of taken for granted.' And it was nice, too, to realise that she could stand up for herself– and that she could cut Glen down to size.

Freya and her committee came bustling over just then, bearing a carefully drawn plan of the quarry, marked with proposed sites for the various pieces of equipment the children had chosen. The photographer followed both committees around, staying in the background and snapping away busily, and when they were finished he came forward to ask for a posed group picture.

'Haven't you got enough?' Glen asked.

'Plenty, but it would be nice to have one of the two committees, d'you not think so?'

'Absolutely,' Naomi agreed, and everyone but Glen nodded enthusiastically.

'Well, if you insist – but I've got to go,' he said. 'There's a delivery coming in and I promised Libby I'd get back as soon as I could, to deal with it.'

'Come on, Glen, it won't take a moment and we can't have a group photograph taken without our chairman – the man who fought so hard to make this playground possible.' Naomi linked her arm through his and towed him, protesting, to where everyone was being organised by the photographer.

'Tell you what – why don't the two chairpersons stand here, in the middle, holding the plans between you, and the others can group round?' he suggested.

'Why not take the kids together, with the rest of us in the background?' Glen countered, but Freya, elegant in black jeans and a deep blue anorak, and with her corn-coloured hair in a single plait looped over one shoulder, caught hold of his arm.

'We'll stand here, Mr Mason, and hold the plan between us.' She fixed him with a gaze so like her mother's that Glen's protests died on his lips, and he merely mumbled, 'Well – let's just get it over with!'

As soon as the photographs were taken he stumped off towards the village with Robert, Lachie and Pete. The photographer packed up his equipment, said, 'You're going to send in the story, aren't you, love?' to Helen, nodded cheerfully to the others, wished the children good luck with their new playground, and climbed into his shabby little car.

'What's wrong with Glen?' Naomi asked as the children went off to their hut. 'I thought that as chairman, he would be courting publicity instead of shunning it.'

'I think the children have stolen his thunder,' Jenny suggested, grinning.

'If so, they deserve it. They've done really well

and I'm impressed by their planning,' Ingrid said warmly.

'I'm impressed by Helen, too.' Naomi winked at her. 'You certainly stood up to your chairman a while ago.'

'I even surprised myself – but I thought he was being unfair. The newspapers are so quick to criticise young people these days, and our children deserve to be praised. By the way, I got a letter from Marcy this morning,' Helen said. 'Not much – just saying she's with her friend in Stirling, and job hunting. And she doesn't want anyone in the village to know her business, including Sam.'

'Of course, though I feel sorry for poor Sam.' Naomi shook her head. 'It's a sad business. Well, I'd better get back; I've got a sermon to write.'

'Oh, come on,' Jenny teased, 'it's Saturday. I always understood that ministers only work on Sundays.'

'So did I – that's why I decided to be one,' Naomi told her. 'But I discovered too late that the actual rule is "on Sundays as well", and not, as I thought, "only on Sundays".'

'What's the matter with your face?' Libby Mason wanted to know when her husband stumped into the Neurotic Cuckoo. 'Don't tell me you're having problems with the new playground already?'

'Helen's only gone and told the local newspaper about the meeting!'

'She writes the village news for them now, doesn't she? So of course she had to tell them what's going on in Prior's Ford. She did a very nice piece about the Women's Guild bring and buy

334

sale the other week,' Libby said placidly. 'Gave my chocolate sponge cakes a special mention.'

'They sent a photographer. I had to have my photograph taken beside that MacKenzie girl.'

'That would be Freya, the oldest one. A lovely girl – very like her mother. The younger lass, Ella, she takes more after her dad, poor wee soul.'

'Never mind who looks like who. I'm telling you that I had to have my photograph taken, Libby – for the newspaper!'

'I knew that this would happen – didn't I try to warn you when you insisted on being part of the quarry protest committee? Don't fret, it's a local paper. You've got nothing to worry about.'

'I don't know about that,' Glen muttered. 'There was something about the way that girl insisted on me being photographed with her. Something knowing in her eyes. She *is* like her mother, isn't she? Maybe *too* like her mother.'

'Now what are you on about?' his wife wanted to know. 'Ingrid and Peter are a very nice couple and their girls are well brought up – and that's more than you can say for some families nowadays.'

'They make me feel – strange – that woman and her daughter.'

'Don't be daft!'

'If you knew what I know.'

'Tell me, then I'll know – and I'll be able to tell you again to stop being daft,' Libby began to sound irritable.

Glen opened his mouth to speak, and then closed it, remembering how Ingrid's narrow-eyed gaze had held him rooted to the spot that time she had tried to pay for her lunch with invisible money. He could still hear her say quietly, 'Never play jokes on a *vikja*, my friend.'

And today, the girl had given him exactly the same look. A look too old and knowing for a chit of a girl. He felt a shiver run down his back.

'Well?' Libby asked.

'Oh, never mind!'

'That's fine by me. We could do with getting more bottles of beer up from the cellar. That'll take your mind off whatever's bothering it,' Libby said.

Autumn had always been Fliss Ralston-Kerr's favourite season and even though it now meant that chilly winter, spent in a largely unheated Hall, was on its way, she still loved the clear, clean scents of autumn in the air and the sight of thick clusters of scarlet rowan berries glowing on the trees. She delighted in watching the leaves on the larger trees turning to gold and orange and flame-red before drifting down to cover the ground briefly with richly coloured carpets. It was in autumn that Fliss always wished she were artistic enough to capture those colours on canvas.

For Duncan, Lewis and the young people working the last few weeks of their time at Linn Hall, autumn was the final rush before everything came to a standstill. The fallen leaves that Fliss delighted in had to be raked up and wheeled to the kitchen garden, where they were shovelled into a large netting enclosure and left to settle into leaf mould. A mixture of rotted manure and straw from Bert McNair's farm was dug into the flower-beds, tubs that had held summer flowers were emptied and planted with spring bulbs and the lawns were raked. Fliss, Jinty and Molly Ewing worked in the herb garden, potting some of the plants for use indoors over the winter, and gathering herbs to dry.

The young people who had lived in the two gatehouses all summer were beginning to feel as restless as migratory birds. The time had come to move on to pastures and adventures new. To Lewis's alarm, Molly was among them.

'You're not going to leave like the others, are you?'

'We were hired for the summer, and it's been lovely, but it's time to head back home and find work in an office or a shop until the spring. I need to get some savings together for next year.'

'You could stay here.'

'Live in that cold gatehouse on my own all through the winter? I don't think so,' she said, and then, with a sideways glance, 'or were you going to suggest that I move into the Hall, and share your lovely four-poster bed?'

'Why not?' It was what he wanted most in the world. 'I've got plans for next year – I'm going to try to persuade my parents to let me clear out part of the stable block and turn it into a shop where we can sell plants.'

'Who would buy them?'

'That's the next idea – I want to open up the grounds to visitors; have a picnic area and walks. But to do that we'd have to put in a lot of work during the winter. I've already spoken to Duncan and he's up for it: Lewis said, 'and if you stay, you can help us.'

They were sitting in his car near the old priory. Below the road the ground dropped away in a series of small rock-strewn terraces to the river below. The windows were open to the cool air and Molly was cuddled close to Lewis, his arm about her.

'The picnic area and all the other things you would need before you open up the gardens would cost money, wouldn't they?' she said now, and he admitted that she was right. 'But your folks don't have any, do they?'

'I know. I'll have to try to find ways of raising it.'

'It's such a pity they didn't get that two hundred thousand, isn't it?'

'My father would never have accepted it. There are other ways – I'm going to try to get some sort of grant. Please stay, Molly.'

'Babes, what would your mother and father say about me moving into their home?'

'I'd – they'd be all right about it.'

Molly tipped her face up to his. 'Have you ever had a girl staying with you before?'

'Of course not – there's never been anyone like you!'

'But there must have been girls before.'

'One or two, just never anyone I wanted as much as I want you.'

She kissed him, her lips cold but soft on his cheek. 'That's lovely, Lewis, but I don't think your parents would be very happy. They're sweet, kind people and I wouldn't want to upset or embarrass them.'

'I could come with you, then.'

'If you did that, who would help Duncan get

the place ready for those visitors you're hoping for? In any case, my parents have a tiny house and there's just not room. I've never had a bedroom to myself, or even a bed to myself, in my life. I have to go, and that's all there is to it.'

'Will you come back in the spring?' he asked, and then, as she didn't reply,. 'Promise me you'll come back in the spring!'

'Does it really matter so much to you?'

'You know it does.'

'If it matters, then I promise,' Molly said, and kissed him again, properly this time.

'There you are, Bob.' The *Dumfries News* photographer dropped an envelope on Bob Green's desk. 'Got some nice pictures of the adults and kids at that old quarry in Prior's Ford for you. Something a bit different, eh?'

'Thanks, Walter.' It had been a slow news week and Green was busy trying to expand a fairly ordinary story into a front-page lead. Glad of the distraction, he spilled the photographs across his desk and riffled through them – a golden wedding party, an award presentation, some shots from a flower show – and picked out the Prior's Ford photographs.

There were several of the two committees studying the plans and the area available that would look good in the double-page spread he wanted to do, but the best picture was of both committees posing with the plan of the proposed playground held up between a smiling Freya and a disgruntled-looking Glen Mason. He stared long and hard at the picture for a while before passing it over to the reporter sitting at the desk facing his.

'D'you recognise that big fellow in the middle? I keep thinking that I've seen him before but I can't think where.'

'I've seen him too,' the other man said. 'A while back, it was.' He thought hard for a minute, his brow furrowed. 'Cliff – Clifford?'

Green shook his head. 'No, it's Mason. Glen Mason, and he's the landlord of the pub in Prior's Ford.'

'Mason – that's it! Clifford Mason, the lottery winner. Right?'

'By God,' Bob Green breathed, visions of the best lead story he had ever written beginning to dance through his brain. 'Thanks!' he said, and turned to his computer. Glen Mason, landlord, was about to be well and truly Googled.

Five minutes later he knew that he had found a story that couldn't wait until the Friday, the day when the *Dumfries News* hit the streets.

This was one for the national newspapers.

37

For several days an idea for a short story had been growing in Helen's mind, and now she was crouched over her computer, fingers flying across the keys. It was evening, and she had persuaded Duncan to supervise the children's homework so she could have half an hour or so to herself. She knew from experience that she had reached the stage where, if she didn't note down the characters dancing through her head and the scenes her inner eye could see as though on a cinema screen, they would vanish, never to be recalled.

There was a phone in the bedroom as well as down in the hall. When it rang, Helen decided to leave it for Duncan to answer. It could be her mother, or Duncan's mother, or, more likely, some pest wanting to fill her life with joy by modernising her kitchen for more money than she and Duncan could afford.

It stopped ringing, and then she heard Duncan yell from the bottom of the stairs. 'That fellow from the *Dumfries News* wants a word. Says it's important.'

Sighing, Helen picked up the receiver. 'Hello, Bob.'

'Just phoned to tell you, love, to check out the national newspapers tomorrow. I've just sold them a story about your village.' Bob sounded pleased with himself.

'You've sold the playground story to the national press? That's great!'

'No, that one's going to have a double-page spread in our next edition, like I promised, with a load of photographs. We're going to do you proud, Helen. But this is about something else. It's a cracker!'

Pleading for more information and promising to keep secrets did no good. And when he ended the call, Helen realised he had managed to knock the fantastic ending she had thought of for her story right out of her mind.

She sighed, saved what she had already written

and hoped that somehow, she would think of an even better ending. Then she phoned Jenny and Ingrid.

'What next?' Jenny groaned. 'I don't think I can take much more. We used to have such a quiet little village, but this year it's gone mad.'

'Are you sure it isn't about the playground?' Ingrid asked. 'He'd get money for anything he sold to the nationals.'

Duncan tended to agree with Ingrid. 'He's pulling your leg. If I were you I wouldn't tell anyone else because you'll only feel like a fool if it turns out to be a few lines about nothing.'

'I suppose you'll be going to the pub for your usual pint tonight?'

'We're practising for a darts match on Monday I promised I'd be there. In fact' – he picked up his jacket – 'I'd better be on my way.'

'Keep your eyes and ears open then,' Jenny said. 'Someone might say something.'

But according to Duncan when he got back, the Neurotic Cuckoo was its usual self that evening. Apart from Lewis Ralston-Smith. and that little redheaded girl he'd fallen for murmuring at each other over a corner table, there was nothing to report.

So Helen had to go to bed with her curiosity unsatisfied.

The primary school was only five minutes' walk from the Campbells' house, but as her youngest, Irene, had only just started school, Helen still took the little girl there in the mornings and collected her in the afternoons. Gregor, Gemma and Lachlan ran ahead, terrified in case their friends thought they were being taken to school by their mother.

Once she had seen Irene trot inside, turning at the last moment to wave, Helen made for the village store, only to find people milling about outside, clutching newspapers and talking to each other. A few were straggling across the village green, and a little knot of people had gathered outside the Neurotic Cuckoo's closed door. Someone was knocking on the door.

'I knew it,' she heard Sam Brennan bellow as she went into the store, pushing her way through the crowd. 'I knew there was something fishy going on and by God, I was right! No wonder he didn't want work to come to the village – he didn't need the money it would have brought with it!'

One of the national papers lay on the counter. The front page featured the photograph of the two playground committees grouped about Glen Mason and Freya MacKenzie, each holding one side of the plans for the new playground.

Beneath the photograph, the caption read, 'MULTI-MILLION POUND LOTTERY WINNER APPEALS FOR MONEY TO GIVE VILLAGE KIDS A PLAYGROUND'.

Glen and Libby were in their bedroom, packing while at the same time trying to ignore the incessant banging on the door and the phone's ringing. The newspaper that someone had pushed through, their letterbox early that morning lay discarded on the floor.

'It's that Ingrid MacKenzie!' Glen snarled, grabbing an armful of clothes from the wardrobe and tossing them onto the bed.

'No, it's you, with your need to play the big man when we'd both agreed to keep a low profile,' Libby snapped back at him. 'In any case, how could Ingrid have found out about us?'

'That's not what I mean. She cast a spell on me and look how things have turned out!'

'She what?' Libby abandoned the blouse she had been folding and eyed her husband, fists on hips. 'Don't be such a pillock!'

'I'm telling you, she's a witch – a vicky!'

'A what?'

'It's what they call witches where she comes from. She admitted it to me herself. She thought I was one, too.' Glen winced as an extra loud bang landed on the sturdy front door and the telephone, having been silent for all of five seconds, began to ring again.

'One what – an idiot? If you don't stop raving about spells and wishes and – vickys, whatever they are, I'll have to have you certified. If it's anyone's fault we've been found out,' Libby snapped, returning to her packing, 'it's yours. I told you when you insisted on being chairman of that protest meeting that someone might recognise you and put two and two together. Using your middle name instead of your given name wasn't much of a disguise. Oh, don't let's argue, Cliff – is there not some way of staying on here? I like this place.'

'You know what it'll be like – folk spinning hard luck stories, and us never knowing whether or not they're genuine. And everyone expecting free drinks. We'll *have* to move out. Anyway, I've already phoned the brewery and they're sending someone to keep the place going. We've got no other option, Liz.'

'I'm sticking with Libby, I like it. How about a nice little bed and breakfast business?' Libby suggested, brightening. 'I like cooking for folk.' Then, holding up a hand, 'Listen – that's your mobile ringing.'

'Ignore it.'

'But not many folk know that number, do they? Here, give it to me.'

They both made a dive for the mobile and Libby won. She put the phone to her ear, slapping her husband's hands away.

'Hello? Oh, hello, love. Yes, he's here.' She gave the phone to Glen. 'It's Helen and it's urgent.'

'Look, Helen, I can explain everything,' Glen started, then stopped as Helen almost shouted down the line, 'Never mind that, just listen! Bob Green from the *Dumfries News* is here in my house and he wants to talk to you.'

'That little...' Glen began, his face reddening. 'Put him on now I want to talk to him!'

'I am on,' Bob said, 'and I want you to give me your side of the story.'

'Why the hell should I? You've ruined me!'

'I'm a journalist, it's my job to dig up stories. But I'm offering you the chance to explain yourself to the good people of Prior's Ford, and in return I'll try to help you get out of the village. Do you have a delivery due today?'

'Yes, right after lunch.'

'Okay, give me the name and phone number of the company and I'll talk to them. When they arrive, I'll arrange for certain people to be at your door, and I can fix it so that you and your good lady just have to get out of the pub as quickly as you can when the lorry stops. The driver will be waiting to get the two of you and your luggage into his cab and away before anyone realises what's going on. How does that sound?'

'It would be a help,' Glen said cautiously

'Consider it done. And now,' Bob winked at Helen and settled himself comfortably at her table, notebook and pencil at the ready, 'give me a follow-up story and I'll make sure nobody finds out where you're going.'

Green's plan worked, and Glen and Libby were spirited out of the village before anyone realised what was happening. And when the *Dumfries News* came out at the end of the week its front page lead, written by Bob Green, told the story of Clifford Glen Mason and his wife Liz, an ordinary couple who ran a small corner shop in Birmingham. Overwhelmed by the shock of becoming wealthy and famous lottery winners overnight, they decided to change their names and run away to fulfil their long-held dream of running a pub in a small, sleepy village. The piece ended with Glen expressing an abject apology to the people of Prior's Ford for the deception that had been practised on them.

'And they lived happily ever after – until the quarry business started up,' Jenny said when she and Helen went to Ingrid's house for morning coffee, each clutching a newspaper. 'Now we know why Glen didn't need the extra business it would have brought in.'

'Duncan says that everyone's muttering about having to pay for their drinks at the Neurotic Cuckoo, when Glen and Libby could have afforded to let them have them for free.' Helen raised her eyebrows at her friends. 'I pointed out that that would have given the game away, but he just sat there trying to work out how much of his hard-earned money had gone into their till.'

'And people are moaning about him fund-raising for the quarry protest and the play-ground, when they could have used their own money,' she added. 'It does seem a bit of a cheek, Glen persuading us to dig into our pockets to fight this quarry business just because he wanted the village to stay as it is. Mind you, Bob said that when he went into the pub after they were whisked away, he found a great pile of begging letters that had been stuffed through the door. It didn't take long for folk to start scrounging!'

Ingrid poured freshly percolated coffee into their cups. 'I can't feel sorry for Glen, because he and Libby could have gone on living here if he hadn't made such a fuss about the quarry and set himself up as chairman of the protest committee. He just couldn't resist feeling important.'

They sipped in silence for a moment before Jenny said dreamily, 'It would be lovely to win a lot of money like that.'

Helen nodded. 'Yes, it would, but nine million pounds is too much. Wouldn't it make more sense for nine winners to get a million each?'

'I wouldn't say no to a million,' Jenny sighed.

'I would rather see more of it going to deserving charities,' Ingrid said firmly. 'After all, the bulk of the money comes from poor people who can't really afford to lose it, but who see it as their only chance of achieving a decent life. That's why I'll have nothing to do with it.' She smiled at her friends. 'In fact, I can truthfully say that not one pound of Glen and Libby's wealth has come from my purse.'

'I put in a pound a week,' Jenny admitted.

'And so do I, but Duncan doesn't know. He's like you, Ingrid, he doesn't approve of the lottery, but the way I see it, my pound's less than he spends on a pint of lager at the pub.' There was another short silence before Helen went on, 'It's Libby I feel sorry for. Glen was always a bit of a loudmouth, but she's such a nice person.'

'No need to feel sorry,' Ingrid advised. 'They are still very rich, and they'll find somewhere else to live. Perhaps Glen should have been – what do they say – lower key? I feel,' she added, narrowing her blue eyes at her friends and looking, for an eerie moment, like a different person, 'that perhaps he brought his misfortune on himself.'

38

A week later, the scandal and gossip had almost died down. The Neurotic Cuckoo had been closed for only one evening, causing great hardship and distress to its most devoted customers, but now a standby barman and barmaid were installed and life returned to normal.

During that week the summer workers had gone from Linn Hall, taking with them their youthful exuberance, ringing voices and their laughter and sense of fun.

'Good riddance,' Duncan Campbell said, as he always said at this time of year. 'Now we'll get some peace and quiet.'

'Sometimes I worry about us having four children,' Helen told him, 'because sometimes I wonder if you like young people. It wasn't all that long since *you* were young, you know.'

'You should try spending a summer with a collection of youngsters just out to enjoy themselves instead of getting on with the work.'

'They're teenagers,' Helen protested. 'Teenage is the time to have fun and enjoy yourself.' And secretly, remembering the cheerful young man she had so happily married, she worried that Duncan was growing old before his time.

Molly went with the others, vanishing from Lewis's life without a proper farewell, leaving nothing of herself for him to remember other than a swiftly written note that Jinty handed to him one morning.

'What's this?'

'Molly asked me to give it to you.'

He glanced around the kitchen. 'Where is she?'

'Gone last night with some of the others. Did she not tell you?' Jinty added as he looked at her, stricken.

'I thought...' He gulped, then said, 'I thought she was staying on for another week at least.'

'You know these backpackers, Lewis – they put me in mind of flocks of birds,' Jinty said. 'One day they're settled and the next, they seem to sense that it's time to go, and they're off.' Then, kindly, 'But like birds, they can come back again in the spring.'

Lewis took the note to the herb garden, where he and Molly had spoken on the first day they met, and there, leaning against the old stone wall and hidden from prying eyes, he opened it.

'Dearest Lewis,' Molly had written in a school-girl hand, 'one of the boys is heading towards Inverness so he's agreed to take me on his motor-cycle. I couldn't miss the chance of a lift. Sorry I didn't get time to say goodbye properly. I wanted to say things to you, but I didn't know how to when you were with me, so here goes. I do like you a lot, Lewis, more than any man I've met, but I've still got such a lot of things to do with my life, and I think you're a more serious person than me. I have some growing up to do, I know that. So I don't think I will be back in Prior's Ford next year, but never say never – perhaps the year after? Sorry. Thank you for a lovely summer, I won't forget it. Love from Molly.'

Then followed a neat little row of kisses.

He read the note three times. But she had *promised* to come back next year, he thought, dazed. Then he replayed the memory of their last, and final, meeting in his mind. 'Does it really matter so much to you?' she had said when he asked her to return next year. And when he replied, 'You know it does,' she had said, 'If it matters, then I promise.'

There were two ways of reading her words. He, in his eagerness, had taken it as a promise to return but now he realised that she could have promised simply because it meant so much to him, even though it meant nothing to her.

He recalled the scene in the Neurotic Cuckoo, when he and Cam Gordon had come to blows. Perhaps Cam had indeed been trying to warn him. Could Molly have gone away because she realised that, with the quarry no longer under threat, the mysterious offer to pay his father a vast sum of money if he refused to lease the land was no longer a possibility?

What a fool he had been, he thought, crushing the note in his hand. Then he smoothed it out again, folding it and putting it into his shirt pocket.

Perhaps he was wrong to doubt her. Perhaps she would come back to him next year.

Perhaps.

Alexandra and Steven arrived together on a crisp sunny autumn day towards the end of September. Clarissa had included Steven's partner, Chris, in her invitation, but he'd had to cancel at the last moment.

'Something involving a prize bull that's eaten something it shouldn't have,' Steven said. 'Vets lead more interesting lives than estate agents, I can tell you.' He stretched muscles that had stiffened during the car journey and filled his lungs with country air. 'This is a lovely place on a day like today.'

'It's a lovely place at any time of year,' Clarissa

said as she led the two of them up the path to the house.

'And your garden's looking good, too,' Steven commented.

'I've found the perfect gardener – he's still a schoolboy, but he loves gardening.'

'You sound very settled,' Alexandra said suspiciously

'Oh, I wouldn't say that,' Clarissa told her, and watched her stepchildren glance at each other.

When they had freshened up and joined her in the living room she said, 'I've invited a friend to dinner; someone who has been very kind and helpful. His name's Alastair Marshall.'

'Oh?' Alexandra's eyebrows shot up.

'Don't worry, Alexandra, I'm not planning on taking another husband, and even if I were, Alastair's far too young for me. He befriended me when I was in great need of a friend, that's all. And it's thanks to him I got through my driving test. We'll tell you about that over dinner.'

'What does he do, this Alastair?' Alexandra wanted to know

'He's an artist, and he lives in a rented farm cottage on the outskirts of the village.'

'What sort of things does he paint?' he asked.

'I'll show you. In fact, I want some help from the two of you, before he arrives,' Clarissa said.

In his cottage, Alastair had dragged the ironing board out and heated the seldom-used flat iron on the gas cooker. When he judged it hot enough he carefully ironed his best T-shirt, black, with 'I'm for Monet' across the chest in fiery orange

352

letters, and his best jeans. Then he hung them up on the back of the door while he had a bath and shampooed his hair.

When he was dressed and his towel-dried hair had been combed he studied himself in the full-length, fly-spotted mirror leaning against his bedroom wall. He reckoned he might just about be respectable enough for Clarissa's dinner party. He would far rather have stayed at home, but she had insisted on introducing him to her family.

He looked at his watch, sighed, pulled on his anorak, and set off for the village with all the enthusiasm of a doomed man going to inspect the gallows being built on his behalf.

'You look smart,' Clarissa said admiringly when he arrived at Willow Cottage.

'I didn't want to let you down.'

'As if you ever could! Would you like a glass of sherry?'

'Thank you.' He followed her into the empty living room. 'Where are your guests?'

'They'll be down in a minute. They're probably summoning up the courage to meet you,' she told him briskly. 'Young folk can be surprisingly shy at times. Pour your own sherry – and one for me too, please.'

He was handing Clarissa her glass when Steven came in, wearing, to Alastair's relief, a striped, open-necked polo shirt and jeans.

'Hi, Alastair.' He held out his hand. 'Steven Ramsay – good to meet you. Thanks for looking after Clarissa.'

'Believe me, she doesn't need looking after. Sherry?'

'I can look out for myself,' Clarissa said as her stepson nodded. 'But Alastair has been very helpful and I appreciate that.'

As Alastair turned to hand Steven his sherry the door opened and the most beautiful woman he had ever seen walked into the room. He blinked, realised he was staring, and hurriedly turned his attention to Steven's drink, which was in danger of being spilled on its way from one hand to the other.

'Alexandra, this is Alastair; Alastair, this is my stepdaughter, Alexandra.' Clarissa had noticed Alastair's reaction, and there was a faint hint of amusement in her voice as she went on, 'You'll have a sherry, won't you, Alexandra?'

'Thank you.' Alexandra removed her hand from Alastair's and went over to look out of the window. Her shining, nut–brown hair was swept into an intricate cluster of curls at the back of her head, and she wore a black square-necked dress under a floral jacket with elbow-length sleeves. When Alastair took the glass to her she studied him thoughtfully as she accepted it. Her eyes were dark blue and long-lashed beneath perfect brows, and her gaze was direct and cool. She was flawless, and although he had always been more interested in landscapes than in portraits, Alastair suddenly longed to capture her on canvas.

'We're eating in the dining room tonight,' Clarissa was saying. 'If you'll excuse me, I'll just go and get the first course ready.'

'I'll help,' Alastair said eagerly, but she held up one hand.

'Tonight, Alastair, you're one of my guests. I

won't be a moment,' she said, and left the three of them alone.

Steven filled what might have been an awkward silence, talking about the drive north and asking Alastair about life in Prior's Ford, while Alexandra stayed by the window, sipping her drink and saying little.

Brother and sister, Alastair realised almost at once, were very different. Steven was ruggedly good-looking and possessed of a friendly nature, while his sister was reserved to the point of being wary. He found himself wondering what it would take to get her to smile, and what that smile would be like.

When Clarissa summoned them to the dining room she put a hand on Alastair's arm, delaying him so that the other two went in ahead of them.

'I have a surprise for you,' she murmured. 'You go in first.'

The dining room was small, with just enough room for a sideboard and a table with seating for six. The table was beautifully set, with Clarissa's best tablecloth, china and cutlery, and the room was lit by candles burning in a low candelabra on the table, candlesticks on the sideboard, and, on the wall opposite the door, two lights positioned to illuminate paintings.

The lighting had been installed by Keith to show off his favourite paintings, but with Steven's help that afternoon, Clarissa had removed the original artworks and replaced them with a painting of the old stone bridge over the river that ran through Prior's Ford, and another showing a road shaded on a sunny summer day by an archway of trees.

Alastair stopped short, staring, aware of colour surging up from beneath the T-shirt to flood his neck and face. 'They're mine!'

Clarissa was beaming. 'My two favourites – remember the day I saw them in your cottage? I bought them from the Gift Horse.'

'Two of them? You shouldn't have!'

'Of course I should have. I wanted them, so I got them.' There were two more of his paintings upstairs, to be given to Steven and Alexandra as Christmas gifts.

'They're very good,' Steven said as Clarissa seated them all. 'I'm impressed – the only paint-brush I can handle is the large one needed to paint walls and ceilings. And I'm not very good at that, either.'

'It's such a pity you two have to leave tomorrow – if you had more time I would take you to the cottage and show you the rest of Alastair's work,' Clarissa said proudly.

When she had served the main course she brought in an ice bucket containing a bottle of champagne. 'This is from Alastair – he bought it to celebrate me passing my driving test, but I asked him if I could keep it until you two came to the village so we could celebrate together. And once he's opened it, we must tell you all about my driving test.'

Even Alexandra mellowed slightly under the influence of the driving-test story, and thanks to the champagne the mood round the table became quite merry as Alastair went on to tell Steven and Alexandra about the efficient way in which their stepmother had bested the car salesman.

356

When the champagne was finished Clarissa produced a bottle of wine that Steven had brought.

'I was going to suggest we go to your nice little pub for a drink after dinner,' Steven said as he opened the bottle and filled the glasses, 'but we seem to have more than enough right here.'

'Oh, it's cosier here,' Clarissa said. 'And in any case, things aren't quite the same in the Neurotic Cuckoo at the moment. We're about to get a new landlord,' she explained when Alexandra's eyebrows floated up in a silent question, 'and although the temporary man's nice, he's not what you could call a real mine host.'

'What happened to the last chap?' Steven asked, and choked when Clarissa replied casually, 'The local people went off him, rather, when they found out that he was a multi-millionaire in disguise.'

'I thought village life was notoriously quiet and uneventful,' Alexandra said when the story was told.

'Oh, it is, dear, most of the time. But now' – Clarissa tapped on her glass with a spoon – 'I have an announcement to make. I've decided to settle permanently in Prior's Ford.'

'But why? You have friends back home – and us.'

'I have friends here too, Alexandra. Good friends.' Clarissa smiled at Alastair. 'And as you've discovered tonight, it's such an interesting place to be. People from all over live here; many of them incomers like me, and yet they really care about the village. And so do I, now. We're still close enough for you to visit me – and me to visit you now that I have my licence. But when I said that I was staying, I didn't mean right away.' She looked round the table. 'Before I settle down, I'm going away for a while. I've always wanted to see a bit of the world, but so far I haven't got any further than school trips to Europe. So I'm going to take a year out before I settle down.'

'A year?' Alastair was dismayed.

'First of all, I fly to San Francisco and join a cruise ship. We're going to Honolulu and then West Samoa – I'm going to be able to visit the house where Robert Louis Stevenson lived, isn't that exciting? Then we're heading for New Zealand. And by the time I get there I'll have worked out where to go next.'

'Who are you going with?' Steven asked.

'I'm going on my own – but there will be other people there. Lots of new friends to make,' Clarissa said enthusiastically. 'It's all arranged – I drove into Kirkcudbright the day after I passed my test, and the travel agent helped me to work it out.'

'When are you going?' Alastair wanted to know.

'The thirtieth of October – quite soon. I'd arranged everything before I heard about the Hallowe'en party – there's going to be a big party in the village hall,' Clarissa explained to her dumbfounded stepchildren, 'and it sounds as though it's going to be such fun. But I'll be gone by then. Never mind, I'll probably be back for next Hallowe'en, and if they're having another party you two must come to it. Chris as well, of course.'

'What about this place?'

'It will be let out for a year.'

'Have you put the letting in the hands of a reputable company?'

'Yes, Steven, I have, and I have every faith in

them. I thought I should allow myself a year, since I want to see a lot of places and I want to stay in each of them long enough to make it worthwhile. I'd hate one of those ghastly whistle-stop tours where I'd have to look at the photographs afterwards to find out where I'd been. Now then,' she smiled at the three of them as she got to her feet, 'coffee in the living room, I think. And liqueurs.'

39

'I can't believe you're going away for a whole year,' Alastair said accusingly when Clarissa opened the door to him on the following afternoon.

She gave him a mischievous grin. 'Did you see Alexandra's face? She got the shock of her life. She's like her father – never does anything on impulse. She doesn't know what she's missing.'

'Are you sure that you're doing the right thing?'

'Oh tosh, don't you start on me. I've already had to put up with Steven and Alexandra fussing before they left this morning. They think I'm moving into my dotage – if Alexandra had her way I would be tucked up in a nice home somewhere, drinking Horlicks and staring at the opposite wall. And dribbling, probably. In any case, it was your idea. Don't you remember? That day when I was at my lowest ebb ever and you rescued me in the rain; we came back here and you made spaghetti Bolognese and we talked. You said that I could do anything I wanted to and gradually, I've come to realise you were right.' She opened the door wide. 'Come in and have a glass of wine, there's some left.'

In the kitchen, she raised her glass to him. 'If it hadn't been for you I would be back in England by now, being organised by my stepchildren. Steven's a nice boy, and you'll like his partner when you meet him, but Alexandra's like her parents – clever, ambitious, but not good with people. I don't want to be like that.'

'You could never be like that. I'm the one who watched you trading in your husband's car for the Astra, remember?'

'That was the school teacher in me. And it was you who helped me to rescue her. We work well together, don't we?'

They smiled at each other, then the smile suddenly left Alastair's face. 'I'm going to miss you.'

'And I'll miss you – a lot. Perhaps,' Clarissa said, 'it's just as well that I'm going away for a while.'

'I don't agree. Clarissa–'

'I'll send postcards,' she said briskly, moving away from the hand that reached out to touch hers, 'and if it all gets too much for me I'll sneak back to the UK and hide in a comfortable hotel until the year's up, then return to Prior's Ford bragging about my world tour. I have all my options covered. There's enough left in the bottle for another glass each, and I've got some home-made shortbread fingers. Shall we?'

'You're going to be the talk of the place, with your gallivanting.'

'Am I?' Clarissa gave him an impish grin. 'Well,

you know what they say – when folk are talking about you, you know you're still alive.'

The Ralston-Kerrs were having breakfast when the postman banged on the back door, opened it, yelled 'Post!' and dropped the envelopes on to a wooden chair sitting just inside the door.

Fliss looked hopefully at Lewis, but he was stirring his porridge and milk into mush, lost in his own world. He had been withdrawn for a week now, ever since Molly Ewing left. Fliss knew from Jinty that the girl had written her son a note, and she suspected from Lewis's silences that as far as Molly had been concerned, their love affair had been no more than a summer romance. As she went to fetch the post she hoped his wounded heart would soon mend. She hated to see him so unhappy.

Gathering up the usual collection of bills, pleas from charities, magazines and catalogues wrapped in plastic, which made them slither about in her grasp like snakes, she carried them back to the pantry, where she set the pleas and the catalogues aside before slitting three business envelopes open and handing them to Hector.

He received them reluctantly, his brow creasing with worry, as it always did when he read his post. The first and second enclosures were greeted with heavy sighs, which meant that they were bills, but he retained the third one, reading it several times.

'What is it?' Fliss had been watching him, and now she could contain herself no longer. 'Hector?'

'Eh?' He looked at her in a dazed way, then handed the letter over to her. She picked up her reading glasses and slipped them on.

'Oh, my goodness! Lewis, listen to this – it's from Glen Mason.'

'Glen? What does he want now?'

'He doesn't want anything – it's quite the opposite. He says he's sorry for the upset he caused by trying to bribe us into voting against the quarry. And he wants us to accept the enclosed cheque,' Fliss said, her voice beginning to rise, 'as a gift from him and his wife, with no strings attached. He hopes that the money will be of use. Where's the cheque?'

Hector peered into the envelope and then withdrew the slip of paper and passed it over to her without looking at it.

'Two hundred thousand pounds. Oh, my God, Hector, he's given us the two hundred thousand pounds – with no strings attached!'

'Are you sure?'

'Lewis?' With a trembling hand Fliss passed the cheque over to her son, who read it carefully.

'That's right, Dad. Two hundred thousand pounds, made out to you and Mum.'

'Is it genuine?' Hector asked doubtfully.

'It's genuine all right. Wow!'

For a long moment the three Ralston-Kerrs sat in silence, looking into the future. Hector dreamed of paying final bills with red writing on them, and Lewis, forgetting Molly for the moment, visualised a plant shop in the stable block and a garden fit to be opened to the public. Fliss's mind was occupied with roof repairs and gas convector heaters in the bedrooms.

Then Hector asked nervously, 'Do you think it would be right to accept it?'

'Oh, for goodness' sake!' The authoritative boom in his wife's voice caused him to flinch. It startled Fliss too – she had never used that tone to him before, but nevertheless she forged on. 'Glen Mason isn't a member of the Mafia laundering stolen money, he's a fabulously rich lottery winner and he wants to help us save Linn Hall.' She plucked the cheque from Lewis's fingers and waved it at her husband. 'We are fully entitled to this money and since it comes from the lottery it will make up for the two pounds I've put in every blessed week since the whole idea started. Every week,' Fliss stormed, 'and not as much as ten pounds back yet. Well, now I'm going to get my revenge!'

'You put two whole pounds into the lottery every week when we'd agreed we wouldn't? How could you, Fliss?'

'For the same reason that most people put their pounds in – because we're broke and we need money desperately. And I know we don't keep secrets from each other but I didn't tell you about it because I knew you would make me stop. But now we've got money, and Hector,' Fliss said, 'we're keeping it.'

She got to her feet, stuffing the cheque back into the envelope. 'In fact, we're going to Kirkcudbright to bank it right now, and then I'm going to buy three rump steaks and a bottle of wine, and tonight over dinner we can start deciding how we're going to spend it.'

'But...' Hector began, then as he looked at her, the protest died on his lips, unspoken. In her excitement and determination she reminded him strongly of the girl he had courted all those years ago; the girl who had married him and given him a son and struggled uncomplainingly over the years to keep his cold, uncomfortable family home going.

He gave her the smile that had captured her heart all those years ago. 'Yes, Fliss,' he said, his voice deepening and strengthening. 'Yes, my dear, you're right.'

At exactly the same moment Ingrid was opening her door to a breathless Helen, waving an envelope at her.

'Another story sold?'

'No, this is from Glen and Libby,' Helen gasped. 'It's an apology, and a cheque to cover the cost of the playground!'

She whipped the cheque out of the envelope and thrust it into Ingrid's hand. 'A hundred thousand pounds for the playground! Isn't that wonderful?'

'Wow!' Ella's brown head appeared by her mother's elbow. 'That means we can get a football pitch too!'

Ingrid, as sleek and neat as ever despite the early hour, studied the cheque carefully.

'Well done, Glen,' she said. 'You seem to have redeemed yourself.'

'I believe I can trust the agent,' Clarissa said as Alastair drove her to Dumfries on the first leg of her world trip, 'but I would be grateful if you kept an eye on the house for me.'

'Of course I will.'

'Thank you, you're a good friend. And I want you to have my nice little car while I'm away.' She patted the dashboard affectionately.

'I couldn't!'

'Of course you could. It wouldn't be good for it to just sit there. The tenants will probably have their own transport, and in any case I don't want strangers to drive my car. I've put an envelope in the glove compartment with some money to cover at least part of the petrol. And I would appreciate it if you could see to repairs and so on. Steven's address is in there too – you've to send any accounts to him and he'll reimburse you.' She smiled at him. 'I'm so excited! I need time to get to know myself and have one big adventure before I settle down to enjoy the rest of my life.'

Their goodbyes, at Clarissa's insistence, were swift and businesslike, and as Alastair drove back to the village he felt as though he had left a part of himself behind. It was ridiculous, he told himself, for a man of his age to feel so emotional about a woman who was probably the same age as his mother, but sometimes life paid no heed to what was considered acceptable.

He drove into Prior's Ford behind the bus bringing the older children home from school in Kirkcudbright, drawing up behind it when it stopped outside the butcher's. Like water spilled on the ground the village teenagers hit the pavement and seemed to vanish almost immediately, darting off in twos and threes.

Tomorrow, they would rush home to change into their Hallowe'en costumes, and in the evening the village would be taken over by ghosts and witches, fairies and Supermen, Batmen and Frankensteins, each with his or her carrier bag bulging with fruit and sweets.

As the bus started to move and he put the Astra into gear Alastair glanced over at Willow Cottage. He had fitted timers for Clarissa and now lights glowed in the hall, the living room and one of the upstairs bedrooms. But it was a façade – despite the warm welcoming lights, the house was empty and as far as he was concerned it would remain empty, no matter who rented it, until Clarissa returned to it. With luck, the year might pass quite quickly.

Later tomorrow, villagers old and young would gather at the village hall for the Hallowe'en party. The party had been born out of a need for funds to buy playground equipment, but thanks to Glen and Libby Mason the playground was already paid for; now the party was a thanksgiving, and another chance for the people of Prior's Ford to have a good time together.

Next week they would gather again, for bonfire night. Then there was Christmas and the local drama group's pantomime, then New Year.

And after that, Prior's Ford would settle down for the winter, and wait for whatever the new year brought.

The publishers hope that this book has given you enjoyable reading. Large Print Books are especially designed to be as easy to see and hold as possible. If you wish a complete list of our books please ask at your local library or write directly to:

Magna Large Print Books
Magna House, Long Preston,
Skipton, North Yorkshire.
BD23 4ND

This Large Print Book for the partially sighted, who cannot read normal print, is published under the auspices of

THE ULVERSCROFT FOUNDATION